Indian
Summer

A Mirabelle Bevan Mystery

Sara Sheridan

CONSTABLE

CONSTABLE

First published in Great Britain in 2019 by Constable

3 5 7 9 10 8 6 4 2

A CIP catalogue record for this book
is available from the British Library.

ISBN: 978-1-47212-711-2

Typeset in Dante by SX Composing DTP, Rayleigh, Essex
Printed and bound in Great Britain by Clays Ltd, Elcograf S.p.A.

Constable
An imprint of
Little, Brown Book Group
Carmelite House
50 Victoria Embankment
London EC4Y 0DZ

An Hachette UK Company
www.hachette.co.uk

www.littlebrown.co.uk

'All things are only transitory'

Goethe

Indian
Summer

Prologue

All things are only transitory

Brighton, 10.15 p.m., 7 May 1957

He hated the sound of a woman crying. Always had. In this situation it seemed unprofessional for the girl to do so. They had wrapped the body in a green sheet that would do as a shroud but he'd have to wait to remove it until the residents of the street had gone to sleep. That was the problem with the light nights – civilians stayed up later. He pulled a lighter out of his pocket to spark up a cigarette but the nurse, still comforting her friend, scowled at him so violently that he reluctantly replaced the gasper in the silver case he'd bought the year before from a stall on Portobello Road market and fumbled it into his jacket. He checked his wristwatch and crossed his arms. Another half an hour would do.

At length, the nurse bundled the other, younger woman away with a handkerchief on loan and the assurance that she should go home now. He listened to the sound of their goodbyes, the front door clicking behind the snivelling woman. When the nurse came back into the room she sank heavily into the chair at the desk and sighed.

'It was bad luck,' he said, breaking the silence. 'That's all.'

The nurse nodded. 'It goes that way sometimes,' she replied. 'Did she have any family?'

How was he supposed to know? 'We'll see to it,' he said vaguely, and momentarily the nurse looked alarmed. A grin spread across his face. 'You think we're real bad guys.'

'You are bad guys,' she said. 'In different circumstances this poor girl mightn't have died.'

'Don't bother with the sob story. You get paid.' He hated it when people blamed him.

The nurse's eyes flashed. 'You see to it she has a proper burial.'

'Sure I will,' he snarled, thinking that he might risk leaving now just to get out of here. Early or not. This nurse had some lip on her. 'I know what I'm doing. What kind of a monster do you think I am?'

The nurse didn't reply. Instead, she opened a leather-bound logbook and examined its contents. 'I'm going to do my rounds,' she said. 'Don't let me keep you.'

Chapter One

*How paramount the future is when
one is surrounded by children*

Brighton, noon, Saturday 21 September 1957

The summer had been so warm that people had come to rely on the weather, and for months had hardly had to think twice about organising a picnic on the beach. The crowds started early even on weekdays, flocking to the front in a flurry of polka-dot cotton. Music from the wireless floated over the hot air, cut by the sound of motorbike engines zipping along the seashore. Children ate ice cream, lapping like thirsty puppies. The long windows of Mirabelle Bevan's flat had been open since the heatwave started so she could catch the slightest breath of cool air coming off the sea.

For a month now the staff of McGuigan & McGuigan Debt Recovery had been anticipating a break in the weather. Every Monday since the end of August, Vesta had announced that soon it would be too chilly to walk into work with the pram and that she would have to make other arrangements with Mrs Treadwell, the woman who looked after nine-month-old Noel H. Lewis while Vesta was at work. Noel had arrived on Christmas Day the year before and was, Mirabelle felt, a regal sort of baby. There was something serious about him that she liked. His grave eyes had appraised the world unflinchingly when she had visited Vesta in hospital on Boxing Day.

Vesta loved her son with a ferocity that scared her. She

believed herself to be an easy-going sort of person but in matters of Noel's welfare she was uncompromising. Mrs Treadwell, a mother of seven and grandmother of eight, was a doughty woman whose services were bought by a fee paid weekly in cash augmented by rock buns and sponge cake baked by Vesta's husband, Charlie. Familiarity with all matters pertaining to the upbringing of children had not lessened the seriousness with which Mrs Treadwell took the task. She called the baby 'Mister Noel'. Once, when she had been questioned about minding a coloured child by a shop assistant, she had insisted on making an official complaint to the manager. She came to the office to pick up Noel at 9.30 sharp every morning.

But today was the weekend. Mirabelle gathered her thoughts. She stretched underneath the covers and smiled. She had slept in. Slipping over the edge of the bed, she drew back the long curtains and noted several people were ensconced on the pebble beach on the other side of the road – a man who had taken a dip was drying himself with a thin blue towel and a group of children were squabbling over something in a small zinc bucket. One woman sat in a deckchair knitting, with a green Thermos flask at her side, while several more ladies basked on colourful towels, enjoying the sun, the ripples of gossip around them practically visible from Mirabelle's vantage point on the first floor. Normally, she would have sat and watched, but today Mirabelle turned away from the window and glanced at the clock. She needed to hurry. Vesta and Charlie were having a party – a barbecue in the American style to celebrate Charlie's birthday. 'A taste of home, baby,' Vesta had promised him, indulging her husband, who only occasionally missed his hometown Detroit.

Mirabelle was running late. She swept up her hair, pinned it in place and opened her wardrobe. She'd bought a few new frocks as it became apparent that the good weather would last the whole summer, and now she perused the clothes on the rail, choosing an elegant red cotton dress with a cinched waist which, she decided, she would team with a wide-brimmed straw hat. She had turned to lay the dress on the bed when her attention was drawn back to the people outside. There was a rhythm to a crowd, she always thought, and it changed when the child fell. The other kids scattered along the beach, boys in shorts, their tanned legs a blur as they ran away.

The man drying himself didn't take any notice as the little girl on the pebbles slowly picked herself up and smoothed down the skirt of her sea-green summer dress. She clutched something in her hand. Mirabelle peered. The child's skin wasn't as dark as Vesta's – more a nut brown. Her hair had been braided in pigtails with navy ribbons tied at the end. Mirabelle could just make out the tears running down her cheeks and a splay of gold sweetie wrappers that showed between her fingers. A woman offered sympathy, but the little girl waved her off. Grasping the bucket, she limped up to the grassy verge where she climbed on to one of the benches, carefully unwrapped a sweet and popped it into her mouth.

Mirabelle scrambled into her dress and appraised herself in the mirror before emerging into the sunshine. She slipped on her aviator sunglasses and turned along the main road before hurrying away from the sea. Her best chance of buying flowers for Vesta and picking up a taxi were both in the vicinity of the rank on Church Street. It would be fine, she told herself. She was set to be fashionably late.

She'd forgotten about the little girl when six hours later a taxi dropped her back at her door. It had been a hectic afternoon. Charlie's friends had brought guitars and a saxophone and one of the neighbours had turned up with a fiddle, so everyone ended up dancing in Vesta's garden to a strange but palatable mixture of Irish folk music and jazz. Mirabelle had enjoyed catching up with Vesta's mother, Mrs Churchill, and Vesta's friend Marlene, the nurse who had delivered Noel. 'Best promise I ever made good on,' she said, rocking the baby when she finally managed to extract him from Mrs Churchill's ample bosom. 'Yanks. Everywhere,' Marlene rolled her eyes. The party had been fuelled by iced bottles of beer, and by sausages and mustard. 'You darkies have got it good,' Mirabelle heard one of the neighbours say cheerily. Vesta had just smiled. Several locals still wouldn't speak to her in the street. At least the man was friendly. By the end, Noel lay fast asleep, a plump little bundle smelling of sour milk and sunshine as Mirabelle kissed him goodbye. 'See you on Monday,' she said.

Mirabelle had lived on the Lawns for years, but she never tired of watching the wide, ever-changing expanse of sea and sky. Now the late afternoon light was buttery and the air rich. As she got out of the taxi, she noticed the little black girl was still there, sitting on the bench. The beach was almost clear. The picnickers had gone home for the night. Two dog walkers exchanged pleasantries as their pets sniffed each other close to the surf and, further along, a teenage couple held hands, staring out to sea. The boy put his arm around the girl's shoulder. There was no denying that though the air was still warm, you could feel autumn coming once the sun began to sink.

Mirabelle's heels sounded on the tarmac. She hesitated beside the bench. The little girl had twisted the empty gold sweet wrappers into rings, which decorated her plump fingers. She couldn't be more than ten years of age, probably less, and, Mirabelle suppressed a smile, her feet didn't reach the ground. Close up, the girl was very pretty. The child stared straight ahead as Mirabelle watched her. Considering the attention a young black child was bound to get, Mirabelle couldn't blame her.

'Are you staying to watch the sun go down?' she enquired kindly. 'The sky looks lovely when it does.'

The girl nodded gravely but didn't reply.

'Have you spent all day on the beach?'

She nodded again.

'I saw your friends run off earlier. Have you been here all that time on your own?'

The girl looked up. 'They're not my friends,' she said. Her accent sounded almost cockney, but not quite. There was a hint of something longer on the vowels. 'They're sick like me, that's all.'

'Goodness me, you don't look poorly. I'm sorry if you're not well.'

The girl turned her head and Mirabelle watched as a fresh tear ran down the child's cheek. She looked round but there was nobody else to help. 'Here you are,' Mirabelle said, reaching into her handbag for a cotton handkerchief.

The girl wiped her nose. 'I didn't expect it to be like this,' she said.

'Haven't you been to the beach before?'

'Not the beach, silly. England.' The child's tone was insistent.

'Right,' said Mirabelle. It seemed there was nothing for it. 'Well, where did you come from?'

'Jamaica.'

'Jamaica looks exotic in photographs. Paradise.' Mirabelle checked the slim gold watch on her wrist. It felt as if the conversation had somehow taken too serious a turn. 'Do you think your mother will be concerned that you haven't gone home? It must be tea time.'

The girl sighed as if Mirabelle was a fool. 'Mum's not here. She's in London, see.'

Mirabelle considered. 'You can't be in Brighton on your own.'

'They sent me for my chest.' The girl coughed, as if demonstrating the efficacy of her respiratory system, or lack of it. 'I'm supposed to get the sea air.'

'I like your rings,' Mirabelle tried.

'Mum sent me sweets,' the girl replied, her jaw tightening.

'I see. And did those boys try to take them?'

The girl swung round. 'Yes,' she said, her tone imbued with wonder that someone might have noticed.

'Well, I'm glad you didn't let them bully you.'

The girl's head dropped. 'I'd have shared if they hadn't been so nasty,' she said. 'I only managed to hold on to a few.'

Mirabelle reached inside her handbag. Charlie had pressed a slice of cake on her, wrapped in a thin napkin. 'Here,' she offered the little package. 'You must be hungry. You've been here all afternoon and it isn't fair. They got away with your sweeties. Some of them, anyway.'

The child glanced at Mirabelle as if this small kindness was incomprehensible and she had to check this lady in the glamorous red dress was real. 'Go on,' Mirabelle gestured as she sat down. 'It's Victoria sponge.'

The girl broke the end of the slice and slipped it into her mouth. She ate slowly, Mirabelle thought, for someone who must be hungry. At the end she carefully picked every crumb off the napkin before folding it neatly and handing it back.

'Good,' Mirabelle sounded satisfied. She looked past the child at the zinc bucket. 'What's in there?'

The girl gave half a shrug. 'Nothing.'

Mirabelle peered over the lip. There was a tiny slip of sand and some water, four white pebbles and a scatter of crab shell. 'They killed it,' the girl's voice broke as she started to cry again. 'That's worse than the sweets. I'm not playing with them any more. They smashed it to pieces. Poor little thing.'

'Well, that's horrible, but I think we should return the body to the water, don't you?'

The girl looked unenthusiastic.

'You can't carry around a dead crab,' Mirabelle pointed out. This garnered no response. Mirabelle sighed. 'Come on – we'll give the little thing a decent burial.'

The girl nodded.

The two of them got to their feet and made their way on to the pebbles. It was tricky for Mirabelle in heels but she picked across the uneven surface down to the shore. She wasn't quite sure why she was doing this. She really wasn't interested in children.

'I don't have any candles,' the girl said. 'I don't have flowers or anything.'

'It will be all right. I promise.'

Mirabelle looked around and found a discarded piece of cardboard, part of a packet of biscuits. She folded it to make a makeshift platform that could pass as a grave of sorts. 'Here,' she said. The girl reached into her bucket and brought out the crab. 'You have to say prayers.' She sounded nervous.

'Right.' Mirabelle solemnly cleared her throat and tried to conjure the kind of words you might hear at a funeral. 'Back to the sea, oh lord, we commend this precious creature to your care. Amen.' She gestured vaguely and the little girl pushed the crab on to the gently rolling water. The tide took the offering out a little way, then the cardboard disappeared under the surface. Mirabelle wondered if this might worry the girl, but the child had already emptied the bucket and rinsed it out in the salty water. She seemed far better, though her sandals were scuffed and the left one had got wet.

'Well, that's that,' Mirabelle said.

'I don't like it at the home,' the girl's tone was confidential. 'I don't want to go back.'

Mirabelle wasn't sure what to say. 'Well, we can't stay out

9

here. Come on,' she tried. Behind them, as they turned back up the beach, a plump man dressed in black was staring from the pavement on Kingsway. He jumped on to the pebbles and made a beeline to meet them. There was something familiar about him, Mirabelle thought. He seemed like a cannonball, moving without deviation as if he had been fired. The girl's shoulders rose almost imperceptibly.

'There you are, you little rascal,' he said as he got close enough, his voice as rich as Kerry soil.

'Ah,' the sound escaped Mirabelle's lips as the memory hit her. 'Father Grogan.'

The man squinted. He peered underneath the brim of her hat as if he had lifted a rock to examine the insects beneath. 'You. Ah yes, you were Father Sandor's friend. God rest his soul.'

Mirabelle nodded. 'I was,' she said. Sandor had been dead for years now. He'd been murdered right in front of Mirabelle. Her gaze lifted to the long windows of her drawing room where the old priest had been beaten, keeled over and died before she could even call an ambulance. The assailant had got away.

'Sandor was a good man,' Father Grogan said, cutting in on her recollection.

It was what people always said when men died, Mirabelle thought, though she had known some bastards go down in her time. She felt a slick of sweat on her neck, nothing to do with the heat.

'And you've been diverting our little Lali here?'

'What a lovely name,' Mirabelle said, as Lali solidly fixed her gaze on her sandals. Mirabelle wondered if the child had only just realised that her feet were wet. She continued. 'I noticed Lali had been at the beach all day – we got talking.'

'Well, that's the first thing. You shouldn't be out this late, young lady. You know the rules. Back by five. You're over an

hour after your curfew. You need to count the church bells.'
The priest held up his hand, the fingers splayed. 'Five,' he
said.

She'd be easy to find, Mirabelle realised – a little black
girl. All Father Grogan would have to do is ask in the street.
Mirabelle knew from Vesta's experience, having dark skin
was to live your life in the spotlight. Lali seemed oblivious to
the injustice of what had probably occurred.

'Sorry, Father,' she said without looking up. 'This lady
helped me give the last rites to a crab.'

'Last rites to a crab!' Father Grogan hooted. 'Bless me!
We'll make a proper Christian of you yet, girl. A real little
nun.'

Mirabelle held out her hand. 'It was lovely to meet you,
Lali,' she said. 'I'm Mirabelle Bevan.'

'Miss Bevan. Yes. That's the name. Well, you must visit us,'
Father Grogan insisted.

Lali's dark eyes looked sad. Her gaze hardened.

'Visit?' Mirabelle repeated.

'At the Convalescent Home for Children. On Eaton Road,'
Father Grogan spelled it out. 'You'd like that, Lali, wouldn't
you? We can always use an extra pair of hands, Miss Bevan.
We have twenty-seven children at the moment – we're
bursting at the seams.'

Mirabelle made a noncommittal sound. Convalescing
children were not her stock in trade. 'Perhaps I could make
a donation,' she said. 'The thing is, Father, I think little Lali
here is having a spot of trouble with some of the boys. They
aren't being very nice to her.'

'Oh boys,' the priest said dismissively. 'These things find
their own level.'

'Bullying, you mean?' Mirabelle persisted. 'From what I
could see, Lali is younger than them. Smaller too. I would
hope you might look into it.'

Father Grogan turned up the beach. 'I'll have a word with the nurses,' he said. 'Of course I will. Come along, Lali.' He grabbed the girl's arm and proceeded at some pace. Mirabelle raised her hand and watched as the priest climbed the steps to the promenade, with Lali in his wake, and they disappeared along the front and round the corner. The air was still warm. Mirabelle picked her way up the pebbles and drew her key from her purse. It was none of her business, she told herself – an unhappy little girl, like that. The father would look after it. She'd told him about the bullying, after all. He'd have to.

And there it would probably have ended, had Lali not been sitting on the bench opposite Mirabelle's flat the following morning when she opened the curtains. The church bells were ringing but the fact it was Sunday had not diverted the crowds from the beach. Today a line of little boys paddled in the sea with knotted handkerchiefs on their heads. A tall fourteen year old in shorts had set up a bicycle fitted with a Wall's icebox on the promenade and a small queue had formed for his wares – ice-cream briquettes that fitted snugly into rectangular wafers. Beneath him, three women sat in the shade of two huge black umbrellas that, in the history of English weather, had seldom been used for the purpose of giving shade.

Father Grogan would not allow his charges to skip Sunday service, Mirabelle thought as she picked up the Sunday newspaper from her doormat and laid it unread on the long sofa. She wondered if Lali had been spanked yesterday for not going back to the home on time, and if Father Grogan had done anything about the poor kid being bullied. Coming back to the bench like this smacked of some kind of protest. It was not, she noted, a great attempt at running away – returning to the same place she'd been found only the evening before. Mirabelle glanced in the direction of the kitchen door. It was none of her business, she told herself. She couldn't take on every waif and stray. Lali's legs swung over the edge of the bench as if she was keeping time. Mirabelle continued to watch her for a second or two. Then she decided it would do no harm to walk the kid up to Eaton Road and have a word with someone at the convalescent home – she'd see to it herself.

Chapter Two

Nature does nothing in vain

The houses were arranged in terraces built of pale, stone-coloured bricks. Steps led to each front door directly from the pavement, and the basement levels peered over the edge of the paving stones like nosy neighbours. The children's home comprised two whole houses that had been knocked together. At the back of the properties, the gardens opened on to the County Cricket Ground and, as Mirabelle approached, she could hear the satisfying sound of the ball being struck as the teams warmed up at the nets.

Lali had taken her hand as they turned on to the street and walked up the sunny side, away from the sea, across Church Street and up the hill. The child's hot, soft palm made Mirabelle feel uncomfortable. Although she found herself fond of Noel H. Lewis and had agreed to be the baby's godmother, she wasn't sure what one actually did with children if one had them for a protracted period. She had not admitted this to Vesta when she had taken on what was, after all, a lifelong responsibility. Casting her mind back to her own childhood had not helped. Her memories were solitary, of reading books in the old drawing room at her parents' house, or playing alone in the garden on a swing under the trees.

Her grandmother, she recalled, had taken her on outings to museums and art galleries, but not for very long at a time.

'Children must learn to love paintings,' the old lady had explained. 'They must feel satisfied not bored. They need a focus for their attention.' Yes – a focus. Grandmère had had a dog, Mirabelle remembered, as they climbed the steps and rang the bell. Lali twisted round, dropping Mirabelle's hand and hiding behind her frame. 'Don't worry,' Mirabelle reassured her, 'I know you don't like it here, but I'm going to sort things out.'

After a short wait, a middle-aged woman in a nurse's uniform opened the door. She cast her green eyes up and down Mirabelle in some kind of assessment.

'There's no refunds, you know,' she said, looking over her shoulder. 'Didn't we tell you not to come back?'

'I think there's been some kind of misunderstanding,' Mirabelle faltered, pulling Lali out from behind her. 'Is this one of your charges?' Lali's hand clamped itself around one of Mirabelle's fingers as the smell of boiled vegetables and bleach wafted across the threshold. Behind the nurse, the shady hallway was furnished with a huge, dark wooden coat stand along one wall and a line of mismatched chairs along the other.

'Gosh. Sorry. I thought . . . my mistake,' the nurse floundered, turning her attention to the little girl. 'Well, you're a little monster,' she said fondly. 'Sister Taylor nearly had a conniption. You are supposed to be at Sunday School at the Sacred Heart, right now, as you know full well.'

'My name is Mirabelle Bevan,' Mirabelle introduced herself. Unable to divest herself of Lali's solid grip, she smiled rather than offering a handshake.

'I'm Nurse Frida.'

'The thing is, I think Lali is having difficulty with some of the boys. I spoke to Father Grogan about it yesterday. I wouldn't fling around the accusation of bullying lightly, but she's clearly not happy.'

Lali's eyes were glued to the doorstep.

'We can't have that,' the nurse's voice was comforting. She stepped backwards to usher the child into the house, but Lali lingered, unwilling to move. Mirabelle smiled. She tried a different tack. 'Father Grogan suggested I volunteer here, you know, but I haven't the least idea what I might do.'

The nurse laughed. 'Well today there's nothing. We have quite a routine on Sundays. During the week, perhaps?'

'Could I have a look around?'

'There's hardly anybody in,' Nurse Frida retorted. 'If you come back next week, as I say, the father will be able to help you.'

'Is the home run by the church?'

Nurse Frida shook her head. 'The father takes an interest, that's all. He pops in almost every day, though not today – he has services to see to.'

'But it's not a church home. You're not a nun?'

The nurse laughed. 'Heavens, no.' She smoothed down her uniform as she regained her composure and raised her palm to her white nurse's cap, from which a lock of glossy grey hair had escaped. Her skin seemed fragile somehow – it reminded Mirabelle of airmail paper. 'There isn't a convent for miles – way out at Rottingdean. It's a mistake easily made, I suppose. With the cap. I was widowed, as a matter of fact. Harry died in Burma.'

Mirabelle paused. She had been widowed too. After a fashion. Jack had died only a few streets away, the war had been over and the circumstances meant she could never admit their connection. This child seemed to trail all Mirabelle's most painful memories in her wake – Father Sandor yesterday and Jack Duggan today. 'I'm sorry,' she said.

The nurse relented. 'Listen, why don't you have a look around the garden? There are three beds out there. Two boys and a girl taking the sea air. It's a nice dry heat on a day like this. Lali can show you.'

Lali obediently crossed the threshold and pulled Mirabelle through the hallway, which felt several degrees cooler than the air outside and a good deal darker. 'Take the shortcut through the back ward,' Nurse Frida instructed as she headed smartly through a door that took her in the other direction. Lali trailed Mirabelle into an almost empty room painted a cheery bright yellow, through a set of open French windows, and on to a paved terrace at the rear, which was bathed in bright sunshine. Over the back wall, the sound of a cricket match under way wafted on the hot air towards the terrace.

Running along the back of the house, under large green canvas umbrellas, the three beds Frida had described were placed at even intervals, with wicker garden chairs in between. Beyond them, the wall between the gardens of the two houses had been removed and the resulting plot was the size of a small park. On one side there was an open stretch of lawn, peppered with balls of various sizes that had been left outside by the children, and a single tree which boasted a tin swing hoisted on two thin ropes. On the other side there was an attractive orchard with apple and plum trees and a wide vegetable patch planted in neat rows with winter vegetables and potatoes. At the brick perimeter wall, the garden fell into something of a waste-ground. There were several heaps of compost, a couple of broken children's bicycles and a patch of rough mud. The sun was unrelenting. It was like walking into an oven. Away from the front, without the breeze off the sea, the back of the house was sheltered.

'This is Pete,' Lali said shyly as she approached the first bed. 'He comes from Whitechapel too.'

The boy was stick thin and so white his skin almost glowed in the shade. 'Wotcha, Lali,' he said and then wheezed. The trouble he was having breathing didn't seem to discourage him from sitting up, which he managed with determination. The beds were made up like drums, Mirabelle noticed; not, perhaps, as comfortable as a patient might like. It took a moment or two for Pete to work the sheet loose enough for him to move. He wore pale blue pyjamas that seemed to hinder him further as the sleeves were too long.

'I'm Miss Bevan,' Mirabelle said.

'Doctor are you?'

'I'm Lali's friend.'

Pete snorted.

Mirabelle pulled up a chair and sat down. She didn't want to be rude, but she felt she had to ask. 'What's wrong with you?'

The child looked at her as if she was a fool. 'I got tuberculosis, miss. We all got TB. The sea air is good for it. The air up in London isn't.'

Mirabelle's eyes fell back to Lali. The girl looked hale and hearty, if a little thin.

'Oh she's all right now.' Pete raised his eyes and coughed again. 'Lali will be home in no time. When she came here she was as bad as me. Worse!'

Lali shrugged.

'She's not even coughing any more. Some get better, some don't.'

As if to confirm this, there was a chorus of coughing from the other two beds. The girl next to Pete started to wheeze. Her cheeks turned yellowish pink and she gasped for breath, her hair falling over her eyes in a mousey-brown sheet. Like him, she seemed too small for her thin white nightgown.

'Take it easy,' Pete said. 'You'll have Nurse Frida out here and then we'll be for it.'

The girl nodded. 'OK,' she gasped, and flung herself back on to the pillows.

The boy in the end bed put his hand over his mouth.

'Would you like me to read to you?' Mirabelle asked. 'Is there a book somewhere?'

'You could just tell us a story,' Pete instructed, as if it was the most natural request in the world.

Lali seemed happy with this. She hopped on to the end of Pete's bed and sat with her hands folded in her lap, waiting. Mirabelle took a breath. She had no idea about children's stories – she certainly couldn't make anything up and it seemed to her that stories from her own experience would be wholly unsuitable. Anything noteworthy she had ever got involved with included at least one murder. These children had some experience of death, she realised. But still. She tried to remember the books she had read in her parents' drawing room all those years ago.

'Peter Pan,' she said slowly. She had seen the play at the theatre as well. She cast her mind back – it had been a Christmas treat. They had worn thick winter coats and she had carried a muffler. The book had been her present that year. She must have been around the same age as these children. Nine perhaps. She couldn't for the life of her remember how the story started. Something about a children's nursery and a dog. 'Do you know it?' she asked.

Pete shook his head but Lali sat up eagerly. 'Yes. Neverland,' she said. 'My mother got it out of the library last year when I first got sick.'

'Does it start in the nursery?'

'Nanny the dog putting the children to bed,' Lali giggled. 'There's Wendy and little Michael and Tinkerbell. She's a fairy. And Peter – like you, Pete. I'd never thought of that.'

Mirabelle was about to make an attempt on J. M. Barrie's classic, when further along in the second house a back door opened and a woman emerged with a bucket. She wore a nurse's uniform like Frida, but she was younger. Her skin was dark, but not as brown as Lali's, and her glossy black hair was plaited and pinned tidily in a bun under her nurse's cap. An Indian nurse was not unusual these days, Mirabelle supposed. The woman hauled the bucket to the end of the garden and poured the contents on to the compost heap, digging the mulch over them. Mirabelle strained to see what she was doing – it was only kitchen peelings, probably, but she couldn't make it out. It struck her that a nurse shouldn't be working in the kitchen. Surely a place like this had a proper cook, though perhaps not on a Sunday. 'Come on,' Pete insisted. 'What about this story?'

Mirabelle got to her feet and moved her chair, but really she was trying to get a better view. The woman wiped her hands on her uniform, picked up the bucket and was about to trudge back up the garden when two cats appeared on the back wall, jumped down and sniffed the compost. Seemingly infuriated, the nurse shook her bucket at them and they fled. That's odd, Mirabelle thought. Then Nurse Frida emerged from the ward, gave a cursory glance in the other woman's direction and strode with purpose towards the beds.

'It's time for the children to have their medication,' she said. 'I will have to ask you to leave, Miss Bevan. The others will be back from church any moment. We're almost ready for lunch.'

'Aww,' Pete whined. 'She was going to tell us a story.'

'Miss Bevan will have to come back another day.'

'She hadn't even started,' he objected.

From the second bed the girl started to cough again and Nurse Frida folded her arms. 'Miss Bevan.' Her tone was not to be argued with.

'I'll see her out.' Lali jumped to her feet.

'Thank you, Lali, dear.' Nurse Frida nodded curtly.

As Mirabelle walked back into the house, there was the sound of polite clapping from the cricket ground beyond the wall. Nurse Frida tucked in Pete, smoothing down his bed sheet firmly. Lali had taken Mirabelle's hand again and was leading the way. Through the empty ward, the shady hall was a relief. She wondered if it was helpful to bake the children in such strong sunlight, even though the umbrellas afforded a little shade. Lali's eyes became serious suddenly.

'You will come back, won't you?' the little girl checked.

Mirabelle crouched. 'Lali, dear,' she said, 'I've mentioned what happened to you to Father Grogan and to Nurse Frida and I hope they will address it. But I'll check on you again to make sure. I promise.'

'Thank you,' the girl said quietly.

'You sound as if you're from London, you know.' Mirabelle smiled. She didn't want to go.

'The kids give you a hard time if you aren't English.' Lali shrugged, matter of fact.

'You hadn't been here long when you got sick, had you?'

'It was so cold. My mother thought that's what it was – just a cold. The room we rented at first was bad. One of the walls was crumbling with damp and it smelled funny. The doctor said we were too slow in coming to him, but we didn't know. I just kept coughing.'

'You'll be going home soon, I'm sure. Just as your friend said.' And there were those serious eyes again. 'I'll pop in next week. I promise,' said Mirabelle. She tried to frame the feeling of suspicion that was hovering on the fringes of her mind, but the words tingled and then disappeared, like a mirage. The clock by the door said five to one and, Mirabelle noticed, the smell of cooking was seeping through the hall – a meaty scent of long-simmered stew. 'Could I use the lavatory?' She was hedging. Lali pointed towards a door at the rear of the hall.

Inside, the room was baking hot. The bevelled window magnified the sun and there wasn't a curtain or blind to shield it. Mirabelle stared at herself in the mirror. She ran cold water over her wrists. This place made her uneasy somehow. Mirabelle lifted her handbag from beside the sink and as she turned to go back into the hallway she noticed a thick slick of dark blood down the enamel of the lavatory. It pooled where the pan was bolted into the linoleum floor. She tutted. The blood, she noted, must be fresh. It would dry in here in a matter of minutes.

As she stepped back into the hallway, the front door opened ahead of her and a long stream of children flooded back from church. Lali was swept away on the tide. Then, when Mirabelle's eyes lit on her, she was laughing with another girl. She looked over, as if she was asking for permission to play with her friend. Mirabelle nodded. Lali gave a little wave and the two girls disappeared through the ward and into the garden hand in hand.

The boys from the beach the day before clattered in the other direction, upstairs, and what had at first seemed an endless tide of bodies magically dispersed through various doors. In the children's wake, three nurses stood at the row of pegs hanging up their navy capes. One of them wore a darker uniform and Mirabelle surmised she was Sister Taylor, whom Nurse Frida had mentioned.

'Excuse me. I'm afraid there is some cleaning required.' Mirabelle pointed in the direction of the partly open lavatory door.

'The children's toilet?' the sister enquired. Her tone was authoritative.

'Children's? That one there?' Mirabelle pointed again.

'Guests shouldn't use that. We're very careful of cross-infection.'

'Do the nurses have separate facilities?'

'If you're visiting we'd normally ask you to use the staff lavatory. It's upstairs.'

'I'm sorry. I didn't know. Sister? It is sister, isn't it?'

The woman nodded. 'Sister Taylor,' she confirmed. 'No harm done. Can I see you out?'

'Yes. Of course. The thing is, I mentioned to Nurse Frida that Lali has been having trouble with the older boys.'

'Trouble?'

'They have been bullying her. She had some sweets, I think, and they took some of them.'

'I'll look into it.'

Mirabelle was about to ask something else, though she hadn't quite formed the question, when the younger Indian nurse she'd seen in the garden emerged into the hallway and rang a brass bell.

'Thank you, Nurse Uma. Time for lunch,' Sister announced. 'Nurse Berenice,' she said, indicating a strawberry-blonde, younger woman with a pudgy face, who sprang into action. The nurse turned the front door's ebony handle and swept it open to direct Mirabelle through. 'I'll see the mess is cleared up,' Sister Taylor said. 'Thanks for letting us know about the boys. It happens from time to time, you know. I'll have a word.'

From the house the sound of chattering children wafted down the steps as they rushed back through the hallway towards lunch. Then the door closed. As Mirabelle walked down the stairs, she felt a welcome breath of air from the sea. Two girls whizzed past on bicycles, heading for the front. One of them rang her bell and the other squealed. For a second it seemed too quiet. Mirabelle felt her skin prickle as if somebody was talking about her behind her back. She wondered what Nurse Frida had meant about a refund when she first opened the door. She wondered which of the children had bled in the toilet, when she was outside. She wondered why it was Father Grogan who came to find little Lali the day before, and how often the nurses helped out in the kitchen. She wondered if either the priest or the nurse or the sister really would have a word with the little gang of bullies and, if so, what they might say. It was the details that made the difference, Mirabelle always thought, and something simply wasn't right. Lali wasn't happy. She decided to take a walk and try to make sense of it.

Chapter Three

Memory is the art of attention

Mirabelle turned along the promenade above the beach. Today, the air smelled of orange squash with a tang of sherbet and the heavy scent of frying chips. The sound of laughter floated up from the shore. Parents cheered on their children, swimming in the sea and, as they emerged, shuddering into the comfort of thin, scratchy towels, the mothers handed out homemade sandwiches freckled with the tiny amount of sand – or rather, grit – the pebble beach afforded.

Along the front, Mirabelle stopped at a café with a candy-striped canopy. She sat inside, out of the sunshine, and sipped a pot of tea while she considered. In fairness, Lali had seemed contented enough when she had left. The children's home wasn't some dreadful, Dickensian hellhole. But still. Over the last year Mirabelle realised she hadn't taken a single case on the side at McGuigan & McGuigan – not one. And yet here she was, with her suspicions aroused and, as a result, her heart beating a little faster. She made the decision not to go back to her flat and read the *Sunday Times* as she would normally. It would do no harm to keep an eye on things, she told herself. Something was amiss, she was sure of it. It might be minor, of course. It might be nothing, but best to be sure.

She paid, leaving a tip, and stalked into the sunshine, retracing her steps until she turned off Kingsway and towards Church Street. All summer it had seemed dusty up here, like a holiday town somewhere on the continent. She crossed, continuing up the incline towards Norton Road. There was only one place to start, she realised. Mirabelle hadn't visited the Church of the Sacred Heart for years. The last time had been Sandor's funeral. He was buried, like Jack, in the little graveyard next to the church. Despite the baking heat, the skin on her arms raised goosebumps as she glanced over the wall in the direction of Jack's grave, which, she noticed, was devoid of flowers. Jack's wife must have stopped laying them at the base of his gravestone. In weather like this, they'd hardly last.

Mirabelle cut off the pavement and along the shaded stone porch of the church. She pushed open the heavy wooden door and the sound of creaking hinges reverberated around the high ceiling. The church was empty. The air smelled of dusty prayer books, cedar-wood pews and a stale hint of perfume. The congregation was not long gone. After the bright sunshine on the street, the darkness felt intimate and the huge space amplified every sound. Mirabelle took off her sunglasses.

She had only ever come here *in extremis*. The church had been important in her very first case – she'd sought out Sandor for help. Mirabelle sighed. The breath echoed like some kind of ghost, only covered by the sound of her steps as she walked down the aisle and knocked on the door of the vestry. It creaked open to reveal a tidy-looking young woman in a pink summer dress, and a hat that was made out of brown feathers. In her hand, an iron was steaming over an embroidered surplice on a board. Behind, on the shallow windowsill, framed against pale green, leaded glass, a line of pots held straggling plants for which Mirabelle felt sure there must be inadequate natural light.

'Can I help you?'

'I'm looking for Father Grogan.'

'The father won't be back until later. For Vespers. You could try at the house,' the young woman offered. 'It's across the road.'

'Thank you. I wanted to ask him about the convalescent home on Eaton Road. The one for children?'

'The TB kids? We took the choir there to sing carols at Christmas.'

'How nice.'

'Poor things. Most of the parents can't visit. They come from deprived areas. London mostly. Slums, you see.'

'It seems such a wonderful cause. I met one of the children – a little girl. She was from Jamaica.'

The woman's lips pursed. 'Really?' she said, as if she wouldn't expect the home to admit foreign children. 'I didn't know they had tuberculosis in Jamaica.'

There was no measure in offering an explanation. Mirabelle changed tack. 'Father Grogan seems very involved there.'

'Well, it's close to the church. He has such marvellous energy, I always think, for a man of his age. He's very inspirational.'

Mirabelle wouldn't have used that word about the gruff-faced priest. 'Well, you're doing him proud.'

'We can't have the father in disarray, can we? That would never do,' the woman said cheerily as she stroked the surplice and laid on the iron.

Mirabelle's heels echoed back up the aisle. Outside, she walked across Norton Road to the priests' house and peered through the front window. Nobody was inside. The room was a study lined with books and furnished with a leather-topped desk and three comfortable chairs. A large black telephone sat in pride of place on the desk. She tried to imagine what

Jack would do in this situation and realised that he'd just watch. It's Sunday, she thought, what am I going to see but a whole lot of Bible bashing? Then she cursed herself for her impatience. The church was important to people, even if she had lost her faith a long time ago. Perhaps Lali had as well – skipping the service like that. As a child, Mirabelle would never have been allowed to skip a Sunday on the pews. She wouldn't have dared. The kid had spirit, Mirabelle had to give her that. It took nerve to ask for help too. She didn't want to let her down.

She wandered over to the corner and loitered in the doorway of a closed hardware shop, which afforded an unobstructed view of both the church and the house, and, as she did so, her mind wandered. She considered walking down to the beach, but even casting her eyes in the direction of Norton Road brought her back to the feeling in the pit of her stomach – a mixture of concern and excitement. Lali trusting her. Father Grogan searching for the lost child – not the police. Not the nurses. There was something odd about it. She was getting too old for this.

Vespers was at five o'clock. From her vantage point Mirabelle could see the painted sign outside the church. She had been brought up in the Church of England and the evening service to her mind was Evensong. She remembered at school, when she was in infants, she had overheard two Catholic girls in the class talking about Vespers. 'Sounds German. Vespers. Does it mean whisper or something,' one of the other girls had snapped, putting on a German accent. 'Visper. Visper.' Mirabelle had been four years of age when the Great War had ended. There were several girls in her class who had lost their fathers. One or two had lost older brothers. 'I hate those Fritzes,' one of the girls said in the playground, next to the swing. 'I'll never forgive them.' It occurred to Mirabelle that German still meant something bad, though it was over ten years now since the latest peace – hopefully the last one.

At length, Mirabelle watched the woman in the pink dress pick her way along the pavement, back in the direction of town. Across the road, a young couple knocked on the door of the priests' house and were admitted. The parish at Hove was full of young families, and there must be a steady stream of weddings and baptisms with all the attendant arrangements. Mirabelle rarely passed the Sacred Heart on a Saturday when there wasn't a wedding car outside or a photograph being taken at the door. She had found confetti in the mud on Jack's grave more than once. The stuff got everywhere. Across the road, the couple left half an hour later and two old women turned up, one clutching a Tupperware container, which she pressed upon the tall young man who opened the door – a trainee priest, Mirabelle guessed.

At half past four, Father Grogan walked the women down the pathway. He shook their hands before waving them off. Then he continued over the road to get ready for the service. Mirabelle decided to wait until the celebrants had arrived before taking her place to the rear of the congregation. She didn't want to be too conspicuous. At least the church was cool inside – that would be a relief. She checked her watch, then she squinted as she saw Sister Taylor appear at the top of Eaton Road. That's strange, she thought. The sister had attended the morning service with the children. It seemed uncommonly devout to come back for Vespers, besides which she surely ought to be working. Mirabelle hid herself, turning as if she was peering through the shop window as the sister disappeared through the doorway of the Sacred Heart. Then she followed, doing her best to enter the empty church quietly, slipping into a pew at the back just in time to see Sister Taylor hammer on the door of the vestry. It creaked open. Sandor had always said he would oil it but he had never got round to doing so. It sounded as if nobody ever had.

Father Grogan clearly wasn't expecting this visitor.

'I have to speak to you,' the sister insisted. The urgency of her tone filtered to the back of the empty church.

The priest's voice was lower and more difficult to make out, but Mirabelle thought she heard him say something about 'after the service'.

Sister Taylor hissed. 'No,' she insisted. 'It's important, Father. Now. Please.' He relented and she disappeared inside, the door closing with a loud click. Mirabelle crept up to the altar beside the door and knelt on the stone floor. I'm getting too old for this, she thought again as she prepared to peer through the keyhole just as two young women burst into the church. They were wearing cotton dresses, pumps and straw summer hats decorated with thick ribbons. Mirabelle jumped up and stepped back, crossing herself as the women slid into a pew and whispered to each other. A twist of annoyance turned in Mirabelle's stomach at being interrupted, but at least the women didn't appear to have noticed what she'd been up to. Then a man arrived and made his way to a seat at the front.

Mirabelle sighed. The opportunity had passed, clearly. She decided to walk back up the aisle, slip into the sunshine and loiter by the gate. A couple of dozen more people disappeared through the church door – families, women with children, and one or two old men on their own. The congregation nodded their hellos as they made their way along the porch. Mirabelle smiled back. She'd go in at the last minute, she thought, if the sister didn't come out. She was about to do so when the bells sounded five o'clock and Sister Taylor emerged and, with some grace, so you might consider it genuinely an accident, Mirabelle deliberately swung into her, as if she was in a rush. 'Oh hello,' she said, sounding surprised. 'I'm so sorry, Sister.'

'It's you.' The woman was tight lipped. Mirabelle noticed her hands were balled, the knuckles white.

'I'm on my way to Vespers,' Mirabelle proclaimed. 'It must have started by now. Aren't you coming?'

'I have to get back to the home. One of the children left something this morning. That's all.'

Mirabelle let her gaze settle. It was an odd response and, besides, Sister Taylor was empty handed. In the normal run of things, she was sure, a sister might send a nurse on that kind of errand.

'Did you find it?' she asked.

'I'm sure somebody will hand it in. It's fine.'

'What did they lose? I'll keep an eye out.'

'A cardigan.'

'On a day like today?'

The sister gave a half-shrug. 'I have to get back,' she said.

Mirabelle watched as the woman crossed the street. Her shadow was hazy on the hot tarmac – the sun was beginning to sink. More people arrived at the church and disappeared inside – a last-minute rush. After a minute or two the sound of organ music mingled with the noise of a bus chugging along the main road, the dusty tang of lead on the hot air. Mirabelle stared in the direction of Jack's grave. She slipped around the side of the church where the gravestones cast shadows in regular rows, as if the ground was patterned. 'What do you think?' she asked the bare space where Jack's body was buried. She knew what he'd say. *Trust your instincts.* That's what he'd always said. She stepped backwards. 'And you?' Sandor was silent. His gravestone had been carved in Hungarian, his native tongue, apart from one line, in Latin. *Caelitus mihi vires. My strength is from heaven.* She wondered what the Hungarian inscription said as she remembered Sandor's laugh and imagined the advice he'd inevitably have given. *Do the right thing.* He had been a priest, after all, and had never shirked his duty.

The dead didn't understand, she thought as she checked her watch. How could they? Vespers couldn't last more than an hour and what would transpire next would be, at least, a good indication of the urgency of the problem the sister had brought to Father Grogan, she thought. Now there was no rush. As she turned to go she suddenly wondered what Jack would think of her these days – all that youthful promise and the piebald glory of wartime romance long over. The world had changed, she realised. She didn't like to dwell on it.

Quickly she walked up Norton Road and turned on to Eaton Road. The trouble with residential streets, she always found, was that it was tricky to loiter without being conspicuous. There were all kinds of reasons a woman might be waiting near a church, but far fewer outside a house that wasn't her own. During the war, the department had used all kinds of covers, but these days she was on her own.

She took up a position three doors down from the children's home on the other side of the street. Mirabelle thanked her lucky stars she hadn't worn her red dress. The brown, glazed cotton she'd chosen in a hurry that morning blended into the grey brickwork and the summer foliage that dripped over the wall. Inside the convalescent home there was little movement at the windows. The children would be having tea and then perhaps it might be bath time for some of them at least. From the direction of the beach, snatches of women's voices having a singsong floated towards her, and then, after a few moments of silence, shouts on the air from the cricket ground as a player was bowled out late in the match, followed by a scatter of applause. Noise travelled differently in the summer. Everything seemed easier in the warm weather.

It had been a year since she'd taken on something extra like this. A curiosity. A case. She pondered how she could possibly have missed an occupation as dull as surveillance but, she concluded, she had. It was as if she had been sucked into Vesta's domestic bliss but without the domestic bliss. There was no harm in waiting here and watching. She knew she wouldn't be satisfied if she didn't at least try to figure out what it was that didn't sit quite right. In the past, Mirabelle had been branded a busybody – on those occasions the people who had called her that had been wrong. She wondered if that was what she had become now. A nosy poke. A troublemaker. Or someone who just wanted a little girl to feel safe. She'd been bored for months, she realised. Debt collection, baby Noel, the balmy summer weather and nothing of her own – no knots to unravel and nothing to stand up for.

People were beginning to make their way home from the beach. Families carried picnic baskets between them. Their clothes crumpled and their hair in disarray. Rosy-cheeked children with buckets and spades trudged along the pavement and now and then a car slid past crammed with the detritus of the afternoon – windbreaks and tartan rugs packed snugly between the passengers. This, Mirabelle noted, made for better cover. Not that Father Grogan was in an observant state of mind when he finally appeared.

It was just after half past six. The old priest looked neither to his right nor his left as he barrelled up the stairs of the home, even more set than usual on his destination. He looked as if he'd have stepped over a dead body to get where he was going. Is he angry, Mirabelle wondered. She'd see. Nurse Frida had said he didn't visit the home on a Sunday, so whatever news had arrived just before Vespers must have been important. He fumbled in his pocket for a key and let himself in – that was unusual, she thought, surely. The hallway was a black hole in contrast with the dusty street, still bright in the fading light as the priest's frame disappeared inside.

Mirabelle listened carefully but the old houses had thick walls and the windows to the street were closed. Further along, the cricket ground began to empty. Upstairs in the home, a little boy's face appeared at the window. He smiled, betraying a large gap in his teeth, and then disappeared. Around her, a few electric lights snapped on as the sun began to fade. She wondered where Lali was. In the garden behind her, a rose bush released its scent onto the evening air.

Father Grogan emerged shortly after eight o'clock. He seemed, Mirabelle thought, unsteady on his feet, and he grasped the wrought-iron railing as he came down the steps before turning in the direction of Norton Road. He stumbled but recovered his balance, and she wondered if he had indulged in the communion wine. If Father Grogan drank she sensed he'd do so to get drunk. He was a man for the destination rather than the journey. She fell into step on the other side of the street at a safe distance. As he rounded the corner, she noticed he held on to his hat. Then he paused in front of the priests' house. A light burned upstairs but the lower floor was in darkness. The priest's hands moved to his torso. She wondered if he was catching his breath before he continued through the front door which, a few seconds later, closed behind him with a decisive click.

Mirabelle took up her old position outside the hardware shop on the corner. Only one electric light was lit upstairs in the priests' house – an overhead bulb in the bedroom of the younger man, she guessed. Then a lamp flickered momentarily in the front room – the study. It clicked off again. After a few minutes, she crossed the road and peered down the side of the house, but all the windows on that elevation were in darkness. It appeared Father Grogan had gone upstairs to bed, climbing the stairs without any illumination. It was early still. She'd wait. Of course she would. Behind her Jack and Sandor loomed, but she decided not to pay them any mind. The street was quiet now. On Sundays the bus service finished early and most people stayed at home, or close.

Around her, along the main road above the closed shops, lights snapped on in the flats, and windows were left open like squares of yellow butter icing on a dark cake. The sound of big band music on the wireless rolled like a blanket over the rooftops. After the heat of the day, the silky darkness was fresh on her skin. At half past nine the single light clicked off upstairs in the priests' house.

She left only a minute before she sneaked across the road and peered through the letterbox. The hallway was silent. The door to the study closed. What had he done in there, in and out with such haste? Mirabelle's stomach jumped as a clock in the hallway ticked loudly, like a heartbeat. She regained her composure and stepped cautiously on to the flowerbed in front of the study window but she couldn't make out anything different in the room. Nothing had changed since that afternoon – no telltale papers on the desk or an address book left open. Still, she'd like to have a look. The window was painted shut.

Quietly, Mirabelle sneaked down the side of the house. Far off, a cat squealed and two dogs were barking. Upon inspection, the back door was bolted on the inside, so her lock picks would do her no good and the windows on the lower floor had benefited from the attentions of the same painter all the way along. It wasn't until she got to the frosted bathroom window at the rear that she found a way in. Of course, she thought, everyone wanted bathroom windows that opened. If she wanted to find out what Father Grogan had been up to in the study, this was her best chance.

She hesitated. There was, she thought, still time to go home and read the newspaper. Was she going too far? She imagined arriving at the office the following morning and embarking on another week. What would it be like not knowing, not being sure what had piqued her interest? What would it be like not knowing she'd done everything she could?

This decided her, and she pulled up the frame. It was an old sash and case and the wood creaked. She waited but nothing stirred in the house. Then, gingerly, she pulled herself over the sill and dropped on to the floor. Beneath her feet, it was uneven – not tile or carpet but some kind of bundle. Mirabelle wondered if she had landed on a pile of laundry and tried to step off it, but she tripped and only just managed to right herself by grasping the side of the bath. In temper she kicked the laundry, more to get it out of the way than anything, but her foot hit an obstruction and her heel got caught. She bent down, peering through the darkness, trying to release it. And that was when she made him out.

A thin slick of yellow vomit ran down the old priest's cheek. His face was the wrong colour – it was difficult to tell in the darkness but his skin looked livid. His dog collar had become detached. A stone dropping in her stomach, Mirabelle checked for a pulse and quickly realised he was gone. The smell of sweat and vomit rose towards her and, before she could stifle it, a scream had escaped her lips. It was the shock, she realised as she gasped for breath. She glanced at the open window, regretting her decision, but it was too late for that now.

Slowly, she tried to get up, but her knees were shaking. Then there was a hammering sound and the bathroom door crashed open with such force it rebounded off the bath. Out of the darkness, a shout sounded. 'What the hell?' It was a man's voice. Mirabelle made it to her feet. There could be no explanation, she realised, but she took a breath to try, when out of the darkness a cricket bat hit her hard in the face. She reeled and fell what seemed very, very slowly. For a second she was aware that the electric light had been switched on, and then darkness engulfed her.

Chapter Four

Alibi: a form of defence wherein the accused attempts to
prove that he was in another place at the time
an offence was committed

Sound was the first thing to return. Before she could move or speak or open her eyes, Mirabelle could hear. Her nose ached and her head pounded. She wanted to tell them to be quiet, but she couldn't get the words out. Instead she tried to focus on the voices – a man giving instructions and another man talking about injuries sustained. Slowly, she realised the second man was talking about her. With an effort she opened one eye just a sliver. The light was like a paper cut. She snapped her eye shut. 'There,' the voice said, 'she's coming round.' She could smell something acrid but it cleared her head. Then, she steeled herself for the pain and opened her eyelids so slowly, it felt she was prising up the lids. She was still on the bathroom floor in the priests' house, lying between the toilet bowl and the end of the bath. Above her, a man put a cap on a bottle of smelling salts. He had startling blue eyes.

'Miss Bevan,' he said, smiling, as he held up one hand. 'Can you tell me how many fingers I'm showing you, please?'

'Four,' she said.

The man's brow creased.

'And a thumb,' she added.

He smiled. 'She's fine,' he announced, looking over his shoulder.

From the vicinity of the wash hand-basin, Inspector Robinson came into view.

'Good,' Robinson said. 'Well, if you're sure she's all right, Doctor. Mirabelle Bevan, I am arresting you for the murder of Father Sean Grogan.'

Mirabelle tried to lift her head but the room began to swim.

'Don't be ridiculous,' she said. 'Father Grogan was dead on the floor when I came in.'

'Through the window in the middle of the night? Broke in, you mean? Yes, I wondered about that.'

'It wasn't even ten o'clock, Inspector,' Mirabelle objected. 'Hardly the middle of the night.'

'You're saying it was a social call? Visiting a priest by climbing through a bathroom window is perfectly normal, is it? Come on, Miss Bevan, what on earth were you doing?'

Mirabelle thought she might be sick. Her stomach turned as she tried to raise herself on to her elbows. The doctor put out a hand to help her get up. She hadn't eaten all day, she realised – not since Lali and the toast. That seemed a long time ago. Her empty stomach retched as she got to her feet and dropped the doctor's hand. He gave an apologetic smile and picked up his case. 'I'll be off,' he said. 'I have to attend to the body.' He disappeared through the door.

'So?' Robinson pushed her. 'I'm sure you have an explanation.'

'You think he was murdered?' Mirabelle managed to get out. Her voice sounded weaker than usual.

Robinson folded his arms. 'Yes I bloody do. Poisoned. That's what the doc says. You'd better fill me in. It'll be better for everyone.'

Her mind swam. There was no question of not cooperating,

no matter the bad blood between her and Robinson. She'd forgotten how unpleasant he could be – a caricature of a policeman; all the worst traits of the law. She felt hopelessly confused.

'I followed Father Grogan home. I wanted to see if I could find something in the study.'

'Why would you do that?'

Mirabelle sat on the toilet seat. It struck her that there was no dignity in this process of coming to. 'I can't remember exactly,' she said. 'I suppose I was suspicious of something. I must have been right. He's dead, after all.'

From the hallway she heard a voice saying something in Latin. The doctor had left the door partially open and the young priest was kneeling over Father Grogan's body, which lay on a stretcher. The cricket bat that had knocked her out was propped next to the body. Behind that, the doctor was waiting while the young priest said his prayers. At the Amen, the priest made a cross above Father Grogan's head. When he raised his eyes in Mirabelle's direction, they were angry. Robinson crossed to the door, made a gesture as if to say, leave this to me, and closed it.

'I'm taking you to Bartholomew Square station,' he announced.

Mirabelle checked her watch. It was now almost eleven o'clock. She desperately wanted to close her eyes again. 'On suspicion of murder?' she managed to ask.

'Charged with murder.'

'I had no reason to kill Father Grogan. None at all.'

'So what were you doing here?'

'I followed him from the children's home on Eaton Road.' It was coming back to her.

'Why?'

The day was a jumble. Mirabelle remembered Nurse Frida and the blood in the lavatory. Pete on the terrace. The organ music in the church. And something about a missing cardigan. Something wrong. The smell of roses on the evening air. Bath time. Lali and her friend, running hand in hand towards the garden, through a yellow-walled room. The sunshine had been blinding.

'He was up to something. There was something amiss.'

It was all she could get out. Robinson snorted. Then the bathroom door opened and Superintendent McGregor walked into the room. Mirabelle startled. She wobbled on the toilet seat and put a hand on the end of the bath to steady herself. She hadn't seen McGregor since the year before. She hadn't forgiven him either. It had never been the kind of love she'd had for Jack – starry eyed and magical – but they had become close before she'd seen him for what he really was.

'Miss Bevan patently needs medical attention, Robinson,' McGregor said.

'The doc gave her the all clear,' Robinson sounded smug. 'I've arrested her.'

'Well, you can un-arrest her.'

'She's the prime suspect, sir.'

'No, Robinson. She was in the room.'

'It's a woman's weapon,' Robinson objected. 'Poison.'

'Not this woman,' McGregor said sternly. 'If Mirabelle Bevan decided to kill somebody, she wouldn't have a screaming fit over the body and raise the household from their beds. Guaranteed. Go and trace Father Grogan's movements this evening and stop being so bloody lazy.'

Robinson adjusted his collar. 'Just cos she's your bit of stuff doesn't mean—'

'I'm not,' Mirabelle cut in. 'I'm not the superintendent's piece of stuff.'

Robinson grinned. 'Of course not,' he said.

McGregor held open the bathroom door. Robinson hesitated. 'Go on,' McGregor prompted him. 'That's an order.'

Once Robinson had left, McGregor closed the door behind him.

'It wasn't a screaming fit,' Mirabelle said. 'I just got a fright. That's all.'

'I'm sure.' The superintendent looked well – he'd lost a little weight since she'd last seen him and the long, hot summer had left him with a tan. Mirabelle blushed. She had forgotten the sound of his voice – his Edinburgh accent. The manliness of him – the hairs on his wrist and the slight smell of amber when he moved. She tried to avoid her own reflection in the mirror, but didn't quite manage. She had a bruise coming up on her forehead and a mark on her cheek. Her hair was out of place and her skin was unhealthily pale. The collar on her dress had turned in on itself. This wasn't how she'd have liked him to see her. Dishevelled and struggling to stay upright on a toilet.

'I'll take you home,' he offered. 'You probably ought to rest.'

'One of the uniformed officers can do it,' she objected. 'I don't want any help from you.'

'Don't be like that, Mirabelle. I've missed you.'

She felt anger rise in her belly. Momentarily, it overtook the nausea. He wasn't being fair. She'd seen him at his worst – a negligent police officer and a disloyal lover. Did he really think that she'd forgotten?

'I'll go with one of the bobbies, Alan.' She struggled to her feet.

'I'm going to need to question you. Tomorrow, if you like. But you'll have to answer some questions. I can drop by, if you'd prefer.'

She nodded. 'All right,' she said. 'Tomorrow. I'll be in the office.' Then she stumbled past him into the hallway. McGregor put out a hand to steady her but she pushed him off and made her own way through the front door. Outside,

McGregor opened the door of a Black Maria with a constable at the wheel.

'All right, miss?' the man checked once McGregor had given him the address. 'Quite close that, isn't it?'

'I don't think I could walk it,' she admitted.

'Wait till Miss Bevan is inside. Make sure she's all right, Jenkins,' McGregor leaned through the open car window. 'I'll see you tomorrow, Mirabelle.'

The Maria began to move. The cool air through the open window was refreshing. McGregor went back into the house. An ambulance was waiting to take Father Grogan's body to the morgue, but the superintendent would need to release it first. He was the senior officer. She watched him disappear as the car took off smoothly down Eaton Road. The lights in the children's home were out as she passed. They'd all be asleep by now, Mirabelle guessed – the children and the nursing staff. Some of the nurses must live in, she thought, and nobody would have told them what had happened. Not yet. Father Grogan poisoned. Lying in a pool of vomit. She had expected a child was being beaten or a nurse was selling food from the kitchen. Something minor. Small. Not this – the leaden, scarlet-skinned body of a murdered man.

On the Lawns, the officer pulled up and switched off the engine. The sound of the sea on the pebbles washed towards them as he walked her to the door and waited as she fumbled with the key. 'I'll be all right from here. Thank you.'

Upstairs, Mirabelle stood in the long window of her drawing room and watched the car pull away. She stared at the empty beach and then her eyes fell to Lali's bench. After a minute, she stepped back and sank into one of the armchairs by the fireplace. It felt as if Father Grogan's death was somehow her fault. 'I'm a bad penny,' she mumbled. Jack. Father Sandor. Father Grogan. She didn't want to think about all the people who had died.

She contemplated the morning. The children waking to find out Father Grogan wasn't coming back. When had it happened, she wondered. A post-mortem examination would put a clearer timescale on it. She thought of the two women who had arrived with the Tupperware that afternoon and wondered what had been in it. And then there was the possibility that Father Grogan had eaten something after Vespers or when he arrived at the children's home. She'd just thought he was tipsy, that's all. Such a stereotype – a drunken Irish priest. The poor man had been dying. Mirabelle stumbled into the kitchen and scrabbled around for an aspirin, which she gulped down with a glass of lukewarm water from the tap. It wasn't fair. None of it was fair. And she didn't feel one bit closer to finding out what was really going on.

Chapter Five

Excellence is a habit

At a quarter past nine the next morning, Vesta abandoned the frame of the pram at the bottom of the stairs and lifted baby Noel up to the office in a navy canvas basket. Noel was resplendent in a yellow cotton dress and a sunhat. He gurgled as his mother put the basket down on her desk and turned to take off her jacket. Noel's plump little fist bobbed up and down as he stretched, grasping at shadows.

'It's hot out there already,' Vesta said, and went to put on the kettle.

Mirabelle fussed over the baby. She did so every morning, letting him hold her finger and cooing at him. Blowing kisses. Today, it felt particularly restorative. She had fixed her hair so that the bruises didn't show or at least Bill Turpin, the third member of the team at McGuigan & McGuigan, hadn't noticed them.

Bill did not indulge in playing with Noel. He treated the baby as if he were a fully grown man, nodding gruffly in the direction of the baby basket by way of acknowledgement in a 'grab yourself a seat' fashion. The Turpins didn't have children and Mirabelle couldn't help thinking perhaps that was for the best. Bill had declined Vesta's invitation to the barbecue the weekend before. 'We've something on already. Julie's side of the family,' he had explained.

Mirabelle hadn't entirely believed him. She wondered if Bill's marriage was in trouble and hoped it wasn't. He'd seemed tired the last few weeks and, she noticed, he had stopped bringing a lunchbox to work. Though Mirabelle had worked with him for four years now, there was no way she could ask about it. Bill wasn't the kind of man who talked about personal matters – perhaps that was what was wrong at home.

'Bill,' she said without looking at him. Instead she patted her lip and widened her eyes over the cot, as Vesta made a pot of tea and Noel's face broke into a delighted smile, his chocolate-coloured eyes glistening at the thrill of attention. 'Do you know anything about a convalescent home for children on Eaton Road?'

'I do,' Bill replied. He had spent most of his career as a policeman. 'Them kids are trouble. They're turfed out with no connections to the place, no neighbours to keep them right. They go shoplifting something criminal,' he chuckled. 'Down from London most of them and not brought up – dragged up, more like. Pocket-picking little ruffians.'

'Hey,' Vesta objected. She had grown up in Bermondsey.

'But no complaints about the place itself? The running of it? Nurses selling medical supplies? The kids being mistreated?'

'No – nothing apart from them being left to roam free nicking stuff,' Bill confirmed. 'We tried to get them to supervise the little blighters, but they reckon the sea air is good for them and they ain't got the staff.'

Vesta distributed steaming teacups to each desk. At Bill's feet, Panther the office dog raised his head, as if checking each teacup had reached the correct recipient. Then he curled up again.

'What made you ask, Mirabelle?' Vesta lifted the cup to her lips and took a satisfying sip.

'I met a little girl who had been convalescing there. She

was from Jamaica. It was at the weekend, after I got home from your place on Saturday.'

'Convalescing?'

'Yes. The children have respiratory complaints. TB mostly.' Mirabelle was about to repeat what Bill had said about the sea air, but before she could get the words out, Vesta had crossed towards the little crib.

'You've been hanging about with kids who have TB?' Panic rose in her voice. She picked up Noel and interposed herself, as if she might form a barrier to infection.

'Oh goodness. I'm sorry, Vesta,' Mirabelle backed away from the desk. 'I didn't think.'

'What's that on your cheek? Is it a bruise?' Vesta demanded, tight lipped, as she expertly swaddled the plump baby in a thin blanket and squinted at Mirabelle's skin.

'Father Grogan died. Do you remember Father Grogan?' Mirabelle started.

'From the church in Hove? The priest who spoke at Father Sandor's funeral? Did he have TB? Is that what you're saying?'

Vesta had felt close to Sandor. She had been taken prisoner with him for several hours – it had been years ago, when the women had only just met. She had been the one who got away. Sandor had escaped the kidnap later but had only walked into worse.

'No. Nothing like that. Father Grogan was murdered last night. The police reckon it was poison.'

Bill sat back in his chair. 'What would someone want to do that for? Kill a priest?' He made a low, tutting, what-is-the-world-coming-to sound.

'I think Father Grogan's death had something to do with his connection to the children's home.'

Vesta opened the office door and swung the canvas basket outside, depositing Noel briskly on to the linoleum. She

46

wedged the door open with her foot. 'Here's Mrs Treadwell now,' she said.

The sound of the old woman climbing the steep stairs reached the office. At the top she paused to catch her breath.

'Morning everyone,' she chimed, peering around the doorframe. Mrs Treadwell always wore lavender. It was her favourite colour. She had once said to Vesta it meant she never had to put an outfit together – everything in her wardrobe matched. Today she sported a pale purple rayon scarf around her hair and a fitted – if old-fashioned – summer dress in the same colour. In the hallway, Noel gurgled. He loved Mrs Treadwell. Her arrival every morning always seemed an unexpected treat. It had occurred to Mirabelle that Noel would have an affinity for women who wore purple for the rest of his life and never realise why.

'Thank you. I'll see you this evening.' Vesta sounded businesslike. She handed over the cot, and Mrs Treadwell's doughty frame retreated downstairs without asking why Noel had been lying on the floor in the hallway or what the rush was about. Vesta came back in and closed the door. 'We can't work in the same office, Mirabelle, you and I. Not till you're out of quarantine.'

'Quarantine?'

'Forty-eight hours at least. It travels in the atmosphere.' Vesta looked upwards, as if she was inspecting the air for infection.

'I don't think it's as easy as that to catch TB . . .' Mirabelle started.

Vesta's expression brooked no argument, however, and Mirabelle immediately relented. 'Why don't you take a couple of days off?' Mirabelle offered. 'I mean, if you think there's a risk.'

Vesta's foot flexed. 'You should take it. You look as if you

47

need it and it's you who's been exposed. Besides, I have to get on with the Hayward case.'

Bill got up, slurped the last of his tea and picked up some papers. Panther, taking his cue, rushed to the door, tail wagging. The Hayward case had been going on for months. Vesta had made no ground with it. Mr Hayward had money but seemed disinclined to pay his debts. He made promises and reneged on them, repeatedly. Recently he had taken to asking a series of detailed and pointless questions about how the figure he owed had been calculated. 'Educated bloke,' Bill pronounced. 'The worst kind. I'll be off on my rounds, then. Whatever you two decide, I'll see one of you later. And Miss Bevan, leave it to the police this time, eh? If it's the death of a priest, they'll take it seriously. Do they have someone decent on it?'

'McGregor,' she said.

Bill nodded. The superintendent was clearly an acceptable choice. 'Good,' he said, and disappeared out of the door.

Mirabelle looked at the sheet of figures before her. McGuigan & McGuigan continued to prosper. 'There's money in collecting money,' Vesta had pronounced earlier in the year, when they'd completed the annual accounts. But the columns of numbers felt unsatisfying this morning. She glanced at the unread newspaper on her desk and then out of the window, where a slice of startlingly blue sky punctuated the high-walled buildings on every side.

'Go on,' said Vesta.

'What do you mean?'

'Well, you're on to something, aren't you? There's no point in pretending. And I can't help you. Not if there's tubercular children and dead priests. Not now I have responsibilities.'

Mirabelle regarded her cup of tea. A few years ago, Vesta used to beg to be taken on unusual cases. She used to dive in with gusto. It was Mirabelle who used to turn things down

– divorce cases and the like. 'I need to pick up a copy of *Peter Pan*,' she said absentmindedly.

'It'll be good for you. Like the old days – teaming up with McGregor.'

Mirabelle bristled but held her tongue. McGregor was the last person she wanted to spend time with. She hadn't told Vesta what the superintendent had done – the reason for their falling out the year before. Not only had he been complicit in a murder, he'd been unfaithful too. Mirabelle had never met the girl involved, but there had been a girl – young and blonde by all accounts. A prostitute. The betrayal still rankled. She'd trusted him.

'I'll look after things here.' Vesta's tone made it clear the matter was settled.

'Two days,' Mirabelle repeated. 'That should be enough.'

Back out in the sunshine, Mirabelle walked up Brills Lane. She felt disappointed in Vesta. It felt like she had been abandoned, somehow, rushed into the street – thrown out of her own office. Mirabelle understood, of course. If she'd had the chance at a life with Jack and a baby, she'd have taken it in a shot. Still, it was odd Vesta wasn't curious – it seemed such a change in her personality.

Steeling herself, Mirabelle picked up her pace. The smell of baking floated on the morning air and she spotted a half-hearted streak of white cloud, like a tiny frill on the edge of the horizon. Gulls were wheeling above, the sound of the traffic and erratic snatches of distant conversation punctuated by their savage cries. Almost at the top of the street, she caught a familiar flash of a regulation mackintosh against salt-and-pepper hair. The superintendent had just rounded the corner from the direction of Bartholomew Square police station. She didn't want to face him so, on impulse, she dodged into the stationer's and pretended to look at notepaper. Her heart was hammering and she turned away as he strode past the shop window and stepped smartly into the office building on his way to question her. He had no consideration, it seemed, for how much he'd hurt her. Mirabelle tried not to think of it. Vesta would keep him chatting for a couple of minutes at least. She'd give him his interview. Of course, she'd have to – just not now. Quickly, she nipped back outside and made her getaway in the other direction. At the junction, she turned along North Street.

Sexton's bookshop occupied three floors of an old building just off the main road, further west. Wooden racks of second-hand volumes were stacked in order of size beside the door, but Mirabelle wasn't there to browse. Instead she ducked inside. Nobody was behind the counter but an open notepad and a half-eaten apple lay next to the till. Mirabelle peered further into the interior and noted that the door to the storeroom was open. 'Hello,' she called. A boy of no more than sixteen peered out. He wore a heavily starched white shirt, a home-knitted, sleeveless V-neck and a pair of grey shorts. 'Sorry, miss,' he said. 'I just nipped in the back to find J. R. R. Tolkien. There's a gentleman needs it for his lunch break.'

'I'd like a copy of *Peter Pan*,' said Mirabelle, realising there was an urgency in her tone that probably wasn't usually associated with a requirement for children's fiction, though the chap in need of the Tolkien may well have sympathised with her.

'Play or prose?' The boy's face did not betray surprise. Perhaps people often arrived with requests that seemed ill suited to their outward appearance and unexpectedly pressing. Mirabelle didn't imagine she looked the motherly type. Perhaps an aunt. She supposed at some point she might buy a book for Noel. Yes, that much was true. She was a godmother. Definitely.

'Prose,' she said decisively. 'With colour illustrations, if possible.'

'Follow me.'

The boy led her upstairs. The first floor was so crammed that Mirabelle felt almost overwhelmed. She didn't read much these days – only the newspaper. When her flat had been refurbished a couple of years ago, she had replaced whole shelves of smoke-damaged paperbacks with new ones, but the volumes had remained unopened. Now she thought on it, she hadn't been into Sexton's for at least a year. The last time she'd popped in was to buy some George Orwell, back in the days when she used to discuss books over dinner with Superintendent McGregor. The shop, she knew, had recently been bought over and it seemed there was a good deal more stock than she'd seen on that visit.

The boy scaled a ladder and expertly tipped a hardback out of its place. 'Here,' he said cheerily, handing it to her as he climbed capably down. '*Peter Pan* by J. M. Barrie. It's a lovely edition. Good as new. That's three shillings and sixpence, miss.'

Mirabelle did not inspect the book. Instead, she fished inside her handbag and brought out her change purse. 'Thank you,' she said as he put the book into a paper bag and she left the shop, turning smartly down Ship Street towards the sea.

The fact it was a weekday appeared to make little difference to the crowds on the front. People, it seemed, would take holidays as long as the weather held. Mirabelle decided to walk along Kingsway, despite the crush. She was less likely to bump into anyone she knew, Superintendent McGregor in particular. Police vehicles generally stayed away from the seashore unless there was an emergency, though down on the pebbles she spotted three officers dotted along her route – all wearing white pith helmets and police jodhpurs as they helped lost toddlers and gave directions to visitors. If any of the children from the convalescent home were out pickpocketing this morning, the law was ready for them.

As she passed, Mirabelle noted that Lali wasn't sitting on her bench or looking for crabs on the shore. With a shrug she continued along Kingsway and turned up Fourth Avenue, towards Eaton Road.

It took a good three minutes for the doorbell to be answered at the convalescent home – a sign, no doubt, that the news of Father Grogan's death had reached them. Nurse Frida's gaze was hard when she appeared. At first, it seemed the nurse did not recognise Mirabelle. Mirabelle raised the volume in her hand. 'I came to read to Pete,' she said. 'He had never heard of *Peter Pan*.'

Frida looked over her shoulder towards the ward, as if checking it was still there. 'I'm sorry, Miss Bevan. We're in disarray this morning.'

Mirabelle raised a quizzical eyebrow, as if she didn't know that Father Grogan was dead. Nurse Frida didn't explain. 'You'd better come in. The beds are on the terrace as usual. Can you find your own way?'

It was busier today. Several children were playing on the lawn but they avoided the old tin swing, which Mirabelle realised would be scorchingly hot on bare skin in this weather. Pete smiled as Mirabelle approached. Furrows had been combed into his hair, she noticed. Someone was keeping the children spick and span, despite the bereavement. The boy put his fingers to his mouth and let out a piercing whistle, before falling back on to the pillows and gulping in some air. Lali appeared almost immediately at the bottom of the bed.

'Hello.'

'Did Pete just whistle for you?' Mirabelle asked.

'That's how we do it at home. All the kids have got special whistles. Whole families have their own. So you know who's calling.'

'In Jamaica?'

'In Whitechapel. In Jamaica your mama just shouts. You brought a book.'

'*Peter Pan*. Aren't you out and about this morning? Getting the sea air?'

'No one's allowed out. Sister hasn't turned up and the doctor cancelled his rounds. We usually get examined on Monday morning. Nurse Frida said if I got the all clear, I might be discharged by the end of the week. I don't know what will happen now.'

Mirabelle surmised that the children had not been told about what had happened, or that would have surely been the first item of business on Lali's list. She decided it was best not to fill them in. 'Where's the sister?' she asked.

Lali shrugged her shoulders and climbed on to the end of the bed. 'They don't tell us things like that.' She gestured towards the book. 'All children but one grow up,' she said encouragingly.

Mirabelle opened the first page. That was the first line, all right. Lali was a clever little thing. 'Do they send you to school while you're here?'

Lali shook her head. Pete laughed. 'There's a lady who comes to do poetry,' Lali continued. 'The Camel's hump is an ugly lump which you may well see at the zoo, But uglier yet is the hump we get from having too little to do,' she recited.

Pete giggled. 'That's silly,' he said.

'Kipling?' Mirabelle checked. Lali nodded. It struck Mirabelle that it was a curious poem to teach to children who were probably frustrated by how little they could do because of their illness. 'What a good memory you have,' she said, 'Well, once you're discharged, I'm sure you'll catch up at school in no time.' She took a breath and turned the book around so that the children could see the first illustration. From the bed next to Pete, the pale-faced, mousy-haired girl in the large white nightgown strained to see, and Mirabelle held the picture higher so the child had a decent view. 'Well, Lali is right,' Mirabelle said. 'All children but one grow up. That's how it starts.'

She was about to continue when her audience shifted and Mirabelle realised there was somebody behind her. She turned.

'Fancy meeting you here.'

'Inspector Robinson.' Mirabelle kept her voice calm. There was something about Robinson. He always seemed to loom. It was most unpleasant.

'Can't keep away from a crime scene, can you, Miss Bevan? Last night we find you next to Father Grogan's murdered corpse and now I come across you at the children's home.'

'This isn't a crime scene, thank you, Inspector,' Mirabelle said.

Robinson didn't manage to reply before Lali's eyes filled with tears. Pete pulled himself up on his elbows and one or two of the children stopped playing on the grass nearby and gaped. 'Father Grogan's murdered corpse?' Lali sobbed. 'What do you mean?'

Mirabelle reached for the little girl's hand. 'Oh dear,' she said. A younger girl on the grass began to cry and one of the boys threw a red rubber ball at the ground and stepped closer to watch the unfolding drama.

Robinson decided to take control of the situation. He drew his identification card from his inside pocket and held it up. 'I'm Inspector Robinson of Brighton Police Force,' he announced. 'I've come to ask questions because Sister Taylor is missing and she was one of the last people to see Father Grogan alive. Did any of you kids see either the sister or the father last night? It may be important.'

Two of the children crossed themselves and the girl who had started crying let out a strange sound – a mixture between a gasp and a sob. 'Has Sister Taylor been murdered too?' Lali breathed.

Mirabelle put her arm around the girl's shoulder. 'No, dear,' she said. 'I'm sure Sister Taylor's fine.'

'How do you know?' Robinson snapped.

'Oh, for heaven's sake. Can't you see you're upsetting the children?'

He had certainly quietened them. You could have heard a pin drop on the stone terrace. It seemed even the birds had stopped making any noise. Across the garden, the children's eyes turned towards the row of beds. The silence was only broken by the sound of Nurse Frida's steps on the paving stones.

'Inspector Robinson!'

Robinson's spine straightened visibly.

'I thought I had made it plain that the children were going to be told what has happened after lunch.'

Robinson's shoulders rounded as the nurse turned outwards, ready to make her announcement, as if the terrace was some kind of stage. There was no question who was really in charge.

'Children,' Nurse Frida said. 'I'm sorry to have to tell you that Father Grogan passed away last night.'

'Do you mean, he's dead?' one boy shouted.

'Yes, Harry. I do. We'll have special prayers after lunch,' the nurse continued. 'It's a terrible shock and I know you will all be upset. Father Grogan was a wonderful man who gave generously of his time and helped us all when we had difficult days. I know that this may now be one of them because he is no longer with us. Let's be kind to each other this morning, shall we?'

It was as if a blanket of calm had been laid over the assembled youngsters. A boy and girl, who, Mirabelle noted, could not be much more than six years of age, held hands.

'The copper said he was murdered,' one of the older boys said blankly. 'Done for. What about that?'

Mirabelle noticed that the little girl who had been crying now had a lip that was wavering in a most extraordinary fashion.

Nurse Frida's eyes narrowed. She held Robinson and Mirabelle in her gaze. Such was her presence that Mirabelle had to hold herself back from saying that she wasn't the one who had announced the priest's death to the children.

'I think it would be best if you both waited for me in the office,' the nurse said, icily, and stepped back to let Robinson and Mirabelle leave. As they walked through the empty ward, Mirabelle heard her addressing the children. She was leading them in prayer.

Chapter Six

A good marksman may miss

The office was a small room to the rear which appeared to double as a night station. Behind the desk, there was a locked cabinet that Mirabelle assumed contained medication. The room smelled so strongly of bleach that it came into her mind it must be the cleanest place in the home. Next to the window there was a small sink and next to that a kettle and a large, half-empty glass jar of biscuits. On the other side, there was a bed upholstered in green vinyl with a low run of pale tiles on the wall behind. It looked as if it might be used for examinations, but Mirabelle supposed that a nurse might snatch some sleep there if she was working nights.

'It's boiling in here,' Robinson said as he heaved open the window and sat heavily on a chair by the desk, clearly unrepentant. He stuck his hands in his pockets.

'It's been hot all summer.' Mirabelle kept her tone neutral.

'You shouldn't be here. You know that, don't you?' he said.

'I promised the children . . .'

Robinson's eyes widened and she gave up.

'Probably not,' she said. 'You're probably right.'

'McGregor wants a statement from you.'

'Do you want to take it?'

Robinson shook his head, as if this was out of the question. 'The super's got it in for you himself. He's heartsick, I guess.'

'You don't have to be hateful, Robinson. You know we haven't been seeing each other.'

Robinson leaned forward in his seat. 'You don't have to be a busybody, Miss Bevan. It's been quiet without you. Pleasantly quiet.'

They each turned away from the other, just slightly.

'The kids will be upset,' she said quietly after a moment or two. 'We probably could have managed that better.'

Robinson got up and looked out of the window. On this side of the house there was nothing to see but a short stretch of brick wall. 'The father was here directly before he died. Last night, you said you'd followed him.'

'I did. He left after eight p.m. and proceeded back to the priests' house. Do you know what the poison was yet?'

Robinson turned. 'You'd like me to tell you, wouldn't you?'

'Yes,' said Mirabelle. 'And the contents of his stomach.'

The inspector breathed out heavily. 'You can't help yourself.' He raised his eyes. 'Look, the super might go for this whole thing,' he gestured towards her, 'but as far as I can see you're just a sad old spinster who sticks her nose into other people's business 'cos she doesn't have enough business of her own.'

Mirabelle's temper rose. 'Oh for heaven's sake, the super and I no longer go for each other, Inspector Robinson. And it can't have escaped your attention that I'm good at this. Better than you, in fact, on several occasions.'

'A broken clock is right twice a day.' He sounded truculent. Robinson had always resented her hit rate. Her guess was he disliked women more generally, and competent women in particular.

'Why are you here anyway?' she asked.

Robinson's tongue found his cheek. 'You don't know, then?'

'Know what?'

58

'The sister's missing. She didn't go home to her flat last night.'

Mirabelle didn't admit that Lali had told her. 'I assumed the staff must live in,' she said.

'One nurse does. But the sister and three others live locally. She left here last night at nine at the end of her shift. Nobody's seen her since.'

Mirabelle leaned against the desk and thought for a moment. 'Well,' she said, 'that is odd.'

'Not if she poisoned the old buffer, then panicked and bolted.'

'The sister?' Mirabelle couldn't help but remember the woman's balled hands, white at the knuckles, outside Vespers. What had she come to talk to Father Grogan about that was so urgent?

'Is the poison that was used something she had access to?' Mirabelle asked.

'Nice try!' Robinson laughed. 'Trying to get me to tell you.'

This sparring match was interrupted by Nurse Frida's arrival. She sat behind the desk and glared at the two of them.

'Do you think the children will be all right, Nurse Frida?' Mirabelle enquired.

'They are very upset,' Frida said. 'Which, given how they found out the news, is quite understandable.'

Robinson was finding this difficult. He now had to deal with two competent women and, worse, neither of them liked him.

'They had to find out sometime,' he snarled. 'Look, I'm here to get information, that's all.'

Frida was not prepared to back down. 'A sorry would be nice, Inspector Robinson. I'm trusted to look after my charges. They are patients, some of them seriously ill. And for day-to-day purposes, they are parentless. It's my job to protect every one of them and you've made that difficult. I think you ought to apologise.'

Robinson nodded. 'All right,' he said. 'I'm sorry. We're unlikely to get anything useful from them, if I'm honest. A bunch of kids. It's just when I saw *her* here, it got my dander up. I mean what's *she* doing here?'

'She?'

'He means me.'

Nurse Frida waited, but it seemed the inspector had nothing more to say and, moreover, that he was going to hold out for an answer to his question. 'Miss Bevan came to read to Peter Hawkins and Lali Watts. She very kindly brought a book,' the nurse said crisply. '*Peter Pan.*'

'Miss Bevan was the person who found Father Grogan's body.' Robinson's tone was judge and jury.

'Oh.' The word dropped from Nurse Frida's lips like a stone plopping into a pond.

'I have to protect everybody, you see,' he continued smugly. 'Not only the children. That's my job, Nurse Frida. One man's dead and a woman is missing.'

Mirabelle cut in. 'I can explain. I followed the father last night,' she said. 'The inspector is making it sound as if I killed him. I didn't. I found his body, that's all.'

'You followed him?' Frida sounded shocked.

'I had been following him all afternoon. I had a hunch something was wrong – just a few things out of place – and I was right, wasn't I? I just wasn't quick enough to help. Do you have any idea where Sister Taylor might have gone, Nurse Frida?'

Nurse Frida crossed her arms. 'I told the inspector. I don't know. They even sent an officer to check her bedsit on Cromwell Road, but it seems she didn't go home last night. It's most irregular. She had had words with the father, you see. Maybe she went to walk it off and was overcome with guilt.'

'Guilt about what?' Mirabelle asked.

'Whatever they had argued about.'

'And you think that she . . .?'

'Did something foolish? It's a terrible thought. Or maybe she was just embarrassed by it. Maybe she ran away.'

Mirabelle considered this explanation of events. It wasn't impossible but a reason would have been helpful. 'Sister Taylor visited Father Grogan before Vespers last night. She had gone to him, it seemed to me, for help,' she said.

Nurse Frida sniffed. 'I didn't know that.'

'Me neither,' Robinson got out his notepad.

'I was there,' Mirabelle said.

'Of course you were,' Robinson snorted. 'Well, tell me about it.'

'Like I said, I was following him. The two of them spoke for more than five minutes in the vestry before the service. Sister Taylor seemed upset. She was very insistent. Whatever it was about, she considered it urgent.'

'A confession?' Robinson murmured.

'Rita Taylor wasn't Catholic, Inspector.' Frida's voice was matter-of-fact. 'She didn't believe in that kind of thing.'

'It struck me as odd,' Mirabelle said. 'She had been at the service with the children in the morning, so she had seen him only a few hours before and yet she felt the need to go back to the church.'

'You don't think they were . . .' Robinson's voice trailed. He gestured. 'You know.'

'Absolutely not.' Nurse Frida sounded horrified.

Mirabelle raised her eyes. Robinson always took the lazy route in his deductions. Put a man and a woman together in any situation and he would manufacture a love affair out of it.

'You're right, Nurse Frida. I imagine if what Inspector Robinson is thinking was the case,' she said, 'the two of them would have arranged to meet after Sister Taylor's shift to discuss whatever was on her mind. It would have made far more sense than Father Grogan coming down here and confronting her at work, with the other nurses in close proximity.'

Frida got up and closed the window. 'Miss Bevan is right,' she said. 'Sister Taylor was a nurse of the highest probity. Father Grogan was a saint in my opinion. The idea that they were having some kind of liaison,' she wrinkled her nose as if the word itself was sour on her tongue, 'well, they wouldn't have. But if they were, they could have gone to her bedsit. Or the vestry, I imagine. Or Father Grogan's house. Somewhere more discreet.'

'And you didn't catch a single word?' Robinson sounded incredulous.

'I told you before. I don't know what they were arguing about. We left them to it.' She checked the watch pinned to her uniform. 'Well,' she said, 'you can't go on reading to the children, Miss Bevan. Not if you have a connection to this whole business.'

'What connection?' Mirabelle enquired.

'Father Grogan's death. That's what you're implying, isn't it, Inspector?'

Robinson grinned. 'Yes.'

'That's ridiculous,' Mirabelle objected. 'I have no more connection than Inspector Robinson here. I just want to help.'

'I'm a detective,' Robinson said. 'I'm supposed to be here. You're a member of the public.'

Mirabelle ignored him. 'We need to find Sister Taylor. That has to be the priority.'

'That's police business, not yours,' Robinson objected.

Mirabelle glared.

Nurse Frida stood up. 'Well, Miss Bevan, why don't I see you out?'

Mirabelle didn't fight. There was no point. If Nurse Frida wanted her gone, she could hardly stay.

Back in the hallway, at the foot of the stairs, a boy in brown shorts sat holding a moth-eaten teddy bear. 'Frank,' Nurse Frida said, 'you know you aren't allowed to have teddy during the day. Put him away and go back to the garden with the others. Run along now.'

Frank got to his feet and looked aggrieved. Mirabelle stared after the child as he rattled through the empty ward, coughing every second step.

'That was a bit much,' she said. 'Sending him out like that. Poor kid.'

'Miss Bevan, I am going to ask you not to visit again.'

'I didn't do anything, Nurse Frida. I liked Father Grogan.' This, Mirabelle admitted to herself, was stretching the truth. She remembered the first time she'd met him, years ago, when she was looking for Father Sandor. She hadn't liked him, not really. 'He was good with the children, wasn't he?' she checked. That was the company way. Jack always used to say, 'Keep them talking. People will tell you everything.' In Mirabelle's experience, he had been right.

Nurse Frida opened the front door. 'Of course the father was good with them. He loved it here,' she said. 'He never rushed. He always had time to spend. He'd get them colouring or read them Bible stories. These children have been through a lot. By the time they get to us they are over the very worst, but still. They loved him. You saw how upset they were.'

'I'm sorry he's dead,' Mirabelle managed to get out. That much, at least, was true. 'Nurse, can I ask, did he eat or drink anything when he was here?'

'Miss Bevan, the inspector has made it quite clear that this is none of your business.'

'He's not a good detective,' Mirabelle said. 'Please. Tell me.'

Frida considered this. 'Tea was over,' she relented. 'I don't recall him eating or drinking anything. Well,' she said, 'good-bye.' And she held open the door.

Mirabelle walked down the steps and loitered on the pavement. She didn't trust Robinson and his second-class deductions. The puzzle kept on at her. Where might Sister Taylor have gone last night when she left the home, she wondered. If she had turned left she would have passed the Sacred Heart and the priests' house. But if she had left the home at nine sharp, as Frida said, and taken that route, Mirabelle would have seen her. She hadn't broken in and found Father Grogan's body until just after half past the hour and there was no question that Sister Taylor would have had to pass the hardware store. No, Mirabelle decided, the sister must have turned right, in the direction of her bedsit on Cromwell Road. Even if she never got there.

Chapter Seven

The life of the dead is in the memory of the living

The end of Cromwell Road near the railway station was peppered with houses that had been split into bedsits on the upper floors and shops beneath. The shops mostly stocked items one might need on one's way home from the railway station. Newspapers, milk and bread. There was a shoe repair kiosk and a greasy spoon café, which looked as if it had been abandoned. The buildings felt run-down. Shabby curtains with faded, patchy linings half covered the grime-streaked windows, and in a couple of places partitions had been built that split a window in half. On the pavement, a thin terrier basked in the sunshine and ignored Mirabelle as she passed. Mirabelle felt sorry the café was closed. She could have done with a cup of tea.

Nurse Frida had not mentioned a particular number on the street, so Mirabelle simply rapped on one of the doors. Nobody answered so she tried another, and almost immediately an old woman in a floral housecoat appeared. 'Yes, dear?' she said. Her hair was in rollers held in place by a highly patterned cotton square tied in an elaborate knot. Her teeth looked like nails that had been hammered into her jaw. There was a quarter-inch gap between them. Her eyes were dark holes in the snow.

'I wonder if you could help me. I'm looking for a friend's

address. She lives on Cromwell Road in a bedsit. Sister Taylor?' Mirabelle enquired.

The woman squinted into the sunshine. 'You're from that debt collection agency, aren't you? I'm not going to rat on anyone,' she said. She made to close the door. Mirabelle interposed her foot. 'Sister Taylor wasn't in debt,' she said. 'I'm not here in a professional capacity.' She tried to remember where she might have seen this woman before, but she couldn't place her. 'Do you know Sister Taylor?'

'She's a nurse. She works at the TB home – the one for children.'

Mirabelle nodded. 'That's right.'

'What do you want her for?'

'She's gone missing. The police are looking for her. They asked me not to get involved, but I'm worried about her. I saw her yesterday, you see, and she seemed fine.'

The old woman weighed this up. Mirabelle pulled back to give her space to do so. Between a policeman and a debt collector, it was clear the old woman would choose the debt collector. Especially if the debt collector was off duty.

'She's not up this end,' she said after a pause. 'I know who you mean. All hoity-toity. Try number forty-three.'

Before Mirabelle could engage the old lady to ask another question, the door closed. Sister Taylor, Mirabelle realised, must be memorable, but perhaps having a nurse for a neighbour was something people were simply aware of. People who wore uniforms were easily picked out. Debt collectors, too. Bill had got into a fracas in his local pub the year before when a neighbour had objected to Bill collecting a debt. That kind of thing was part of the job, Bill had said, and had taken it in his stride.

Mirabelle glanced further along Cromwell Road and noted that, at the east end of the street, matters improved. It was only this little pocket near the station where the houses were markedly down at heel. As she walked along, she counted the numbers on the gates as the front doors smartened up. Forty-three was on the other side of the road. Things already looked more respectable. As she passed number thirty-nine, a young woman emerged with a basket over her arm. She was pregnant.

'Excuse me,' Mirabelle accosted her. 'I'm looking for Sister Taylor's house. Well, it's a flat, really.'

The woman pointed at forty-three. 'Rita Taylor lives in that one. First floor. What do you want her for?'

'Do you know Sister Taylor?'

'Everyone knows her,' the woman raised her eyes. 'Spends her time leaving notes. *Clean the pathway. Take the bins in. Keep the kids quiet.* Cheeky cow.'

There was clearly no love lost along Cromwell Road.

'That must be annoying.' Mirabelle's face opened in a grin. Occasionally it had occurred to her that she would prefer her neighbours kept their gardens differently, but she would never have dreamed of saying anything. Two doors along from her flat, the front windows could have used a lick of paint, but a critical neighbour was, she reckoned, probably even more unacceptable than a debt collector. In front of her, the woman's eyes had narrowed to slits.

'Annoying's not how I'd put it,' she spat. 'That woman has never had her nose out of other people's business since she moved in. She told Betty Harrison to clean her windows and Betty widowed not two months ago. Someone went over and did them for the poor old soul. But still. A grieving widow – honestly. That woman's just a busybody. And to think she's a nurse. A nurse!'

'You didn't happen to see Sister Taylor yesterday, did you?'

The woman shook her head. 'Sunday? No. We was down on the beach.'

'Well, thank you,' Mirabelle said, and turned away from the tirade and up the garden path of number forty-three.

Interestingly, she noted, the house was about middling for the street. Certainly the brasses could have used a polish. At her feet a wire milk rack with a turned wooden handle lay empty. To the side, there were eight bells drilled into the doorframe. Mirabelle rang one after the other but nobody answered. She checked over her shoulder. The woman's figure receded, her shopping basket swinging on her arm. Apart from that, Cromwell Road was quiet, so Mirabelle slipped inside her bag and brought out her lock picks. The door took only a few seconds to open. Mirabelle had often remarked to Vesta that most people simply didn't buy good enough locks. 'Thank goodness,' she had commented with a grin, and Vesta had laughed.

Inside number forty-three, the hallway smelled of toast and the doors did not run to name plates. Mirabelle passed upstairs, noting the slightly worn, dark carpet. On the first floor, to the rear, a bottle of milk had been placed on a thin coir mat, right in the middle of the doorway. This, she deduced, was probably Sister Rita Taylor's home. The milk would have been delivered as usual that morning – there were eight slots in the wire tray at the front door. The delivery before that would have been Saturday and she could see through the glass that the milk was still fresh – it wouldn't have lasted two days in the heat. No, Mirabelle decided, her hand on the bottle, this milk was delivered only a few hours ago and one of Sister Taylor's neighbours had brought it in. It was kind of them and there were two likely possibilities – either this was the sister's flat and they didn't know she hadn't come home, or whoever lived in here worked the night shift.

To be sure, Mirabelle rapped on the door, but there was no reply. Once more, picking the lock was the work of seconds. The coat rack inside immediately confirmed Mirabelle's suspicion. A nurse's woollen winter cape hung on the wire next to a dark brown coat and a matching felt hat – for the sister's days off. Beside the coat rack three certificates in nursing had been framed and hung on the wall. The flat was tiny and it was furnished sparsely. The thin hallway had only two doors – the first opened on to a cramped bathroom and the second on to a larger room with a small fireplace. A bed was made up with the kind of precision only years of training could endow. To one side there was a hotplate and some neatly laid-out tins and jars – tea, sugar, Campbell's soup and a small butter dish. Though shabby, the place was spotless. The single plate, cup, knife, fork and spoon on the side were arrayed tidily, the handle of the cup at a right angle to the edge of the shelf. It felt austere. Mirabelle could understand how the shabby state of the street outside might annoy somebody who was so exacting. That Inspector Robinson had imagined this place could be some kind of love nest struck her as amusing.

There were, Mirabelle noticed, no personal papers – no letters or postcards, not even a photograph or a passport. Her own flat was more lavish but, like her, it seemed, the sister didn't carry much of her past with her. Not among her things, in any case. People were quick to call an older woman a busybody for speaking her mind. It was easy to dismiss a spinster. Mirabelle wondered if the woman had ever not returned to her bedsit at night before. Somehow she doubted it. It was clear Sister Taylor valued order, and people who liked order, liked routine.

Outside the window, Mirabelle could see the back of the houses on Eaton Road across the cricket ground. She smiled as she realised that Sister Taylor was positioned to keep an eye on her charges at a distance. Mirabelle strained to make out the children, still playing in the garden. Lali was playing patty cake with another girl, while along the terrace a group of boys had chalked lines on to the paving stones for hopscotch. One brave child had even taken to the swing.

Mirabelle sank on to the bed, feeling guilty for loosening the sheet as she did so. She sensed Sister Taylor would not have liked it. The children's home, it seemed, was her life. There was nothing else here but the view from the window. Mirabelle wondered what she had come to see Father Grogan about the day before in the vestry. Inspector Robinson had assumed that if the sister had gone missing, it was because she was guilty of murder, but Mirabelle wasn't so sure. She pondered the sister's personality. Someone who would pull up a recently widowed neighbour about the cleanliness of her windows did not feel guilt easily. That kind of person thought they were right and stood up for what they believed in and, now Mirabelle thought on it, the urgency with which the sister had wanted to speak to the priest was the tone of a woman who was righting a wrong. A woman who had uncovered something. 'Oh dear,' Mirabelle said under her breath. The sister had seemed a nice, practical kind of person, but scratching the surface of her life had revealed her to be inflexible, and abrasive even, but not someone who would run away. If she was missing, Mirabelle feared the worst.

From outside, Mirabelle heard the bell sounding at the children's home for lunch. The children in the garden dropped what they were doing. Abandoned balls of different colours, sizes and shapes peppered the grass as the kids crowded through the French doors. Three nurses wheeled the beds inside. Squinting, she could just make out the book she'd left on top of Pete's sheet. Someone else would have to read it to him.

The empty garden seemed too quiet, suddenly – the swing still swaying. Then she leaned forward and peered as the back door opened and Nurse Uma, the Indian nurse, slipped on to the terrace, leaned against the wall and lit a cigarette. It must be a difficult day for all of them – losing two people in mysterious circumstances. The nurse inhaled deeply – the cigarette a necessary luxury. Then she half turned as if someone had called her name, stubbed out the cigarette hurriedly and made to go back inside. As she did so, she spotted the cats again – three this time – two the same as the day before and a white, smaller one, barely past the kitten stage. The animals slipped smoothly over the wall and into the empty garden, circling the compost heap. Nurse Uma ran through the trees, waving her arms, and the cats scattered. At the compost heap she picked up a spade that was stuck into the earth and turned over the soil. Then she made her way, with some purpose, back up the garden and through the back door.

Mirabelle cocked her head. She was about to turn back into the room when Uma appeared through the back door once more, but this time with a bottle of what looked like bleach in her hand. She made her way back to the compost heap and sprinkled it liberally across the mound. Mirabelle wondered if Indians were superstitious about cats. She must look it up.

Chapter Eight

Reason is not what decides love

As Mirabelle closed the main door of Sister Taylor's building, she put on her sunglasses and decided it was time
for lunch. She considered going into town but dismissed the
notion – it was too far. In fact, she reasoned, the closest place
to get something to eat was to buy it in one of the shops along
Church Street and take it home.

Mirabelle liked to walk. Walking often helped her to
think. She set off, back along Eaton Road, past the church
and down to the main street. A lunchtime queue had formed
outside the bakery and Mirabelle joined it. She chose a small
chicken pie from the selection and decided to treat herself
to a vanilla custard slice. There was something about the
warm weather which lent an almost carnival atmosphere,
even to weekdays. The women in the queue chatted to
each other about the weather and enquired about each
other's families. Afterwards, as she turned down Fourth
Avenue, the breeze off the sea was invigorating. She stuck
to the left-hand pavement where there were more trees. The
intermittent shade was a relief. Down at the front, being
Monday and quite some distance from the pier, the pebbles
were more sparsely populated than the day before. A large
woman wearing a hat decorated with a silk sunflower was
sitting on Lali's bench, her plump knees shining in the sun's

glare. In readiness, Mirabelle scrambled in her handbag for her key, grabbing the gold sovereign that she had had made into a fob.

She only looked up as she actually got to her front door, and then there was no avoiding him. Standing on the doorstep, his shirt sleeves rolled up and a black case in his hand, was the dark-haired police doctor from the night before.

'Hello, Miss Bevan,' he said cheerily, tipping his hat. 'Superintendent McGregor asked if I would make a house call to check you were all right. We weren't properly introduced last night. I'm Doctor Williams.'

Mirabelle removed her sunglasses. It would seem that McGregor had got the message that she didn't want to see him.

'Were you in the air force?' the doctor asked cheerily, making conversation.

'The sunglasses were a present. From a friend,' she explained. The aviators were RAF issue. Just like her lock picks were SOE.

'I wondered if they might have been surplus or if you'd been a flier.'

'Oh no.'

'Lots of women were, you know – fliers, I mean. Wonderful day, isn't it?'

'I feel fine,' Mirabelle hovered on the doorstep. The doctor waited but she didn't move. He smiled.

'The thing is, the superintendent is concerned for you, Miss Bevan, and in fairness you took quite a whack. It wouldn't do any harm to make a quick examination. In my medical opinion.'

'Don't you normally deal with bodies? Dead people, I mean?'

'Yes. Although sometimes I get called in if one of the boys gets hurt. There are more and more girls these days on the force too. I think McGregor thought because I saw to you last night it would be easier . . . and it is only bruising.'

'I'm fine,' she repeated.

'Who is your GP?'

Mirabelle pursed her lips. She didn't have a GP. She hadn't needed medical attention for years, except once or twice when she had been admitted to hospital. There had been the time she was shot but that had been a mistake.

'Someone has to look after you,' the doctor said gently. 'If you prefer, you can drop into the station or I can recommend a GP. It's always a good idea to have one. Even if you are in rude good health. It doesn't cost anything these days. What with the NHS.'

Mirabelle sighed. She felt defeated. 'You'd best come in,' she said.

Upstairs the doctor gave a low whistle. He seemed in an irrepressibly good mood. He stared at the cornice around the high ceiling and then out of the long windows. 'What a lovely place. I've never been in a flat on the front before. It's a jolly view.'

Mirabelle knew she ought to offer him some form of hospitality, but the options were limited. It was early for whisky or gin and she had no milk for tea. She laid the bags from the bakery on the table.

'Would you like a vanilla slice?' she said.

'No thanks. It's early for me.'

She was glad she hadn't offered him whisky.

'How is the superintendent doing? Is the investigation coming along?' she asked.

'Poor man.' The doctor put his bag on the table next to her lunch and drew out a stethoscope.

'He looked well,' she said, 'though I expect he was there till late. It's the young priest I feel most sorry for.'

'Father Turnbull?'

'He had a terrible fright.'

'He certainly gave you a good bashing.'

Mirabelle smiled weakly as the doctor appraised her face. 'The poor man I was referring to was Grogan, by the way,' he said. 'The victim.'

Mirabelle bit her lip. 'Yes, of course.'

'It's a horrible way to go – poison. Painful. Terrifying, really. He probably didn't realise what was happening until it was too late or he'd have gone for help. It doesn't bear thinking about, to die like that. Alone in the dark.'

'And what was it? The poison, I mean?'

'Strychnine. Nothing fancy. The father had a hip flask in his pocket. He hadn't eaten for hours but he'd had a slug or two. Someone had stuck it in there.'

'With his whisky?'

'Well, he was Irish, wasn't he?'

Doctor Williams peered at her bruises. Mirabelle felt sheepish. She wasn't used to being looked at. She certainly wasn't used to being seen. 'These will heal quite quickly. Especially in this weather. I dotted on some arnica cream last night before you came to. I think it's helped.'

He took her wrist between his fingers and counted her pulse against the second hand of his watch. He was very focused, Mirabelle thought. His eyes were a startling blue – the first thing she'd seen the night before when she'd come round – she remembered now. 'How might one get TB?' she asked.

'Do you want me to check your chest?'

'I was at the children's home – the convalescent home on Eaton Place.'

'The slum kids?'

'I just wondered. Is it easy to catch?'

'At the convalescent stage it's not contagious,' he said.

Mirabelle remembered Vesta interposing her body and

she felt relieved. The doctor continued. 'Generally, you need poor conditions – damp and so forth, as well as the exposure. Other factors might be a weakened chest. Poor nutrition. You aren't at risk, Miss Bevan.'

'I wasn't asking for myself.'

'Cough?' He slid his stethoscope on to her skin. She coughed. 'One hundred per cent, I should say. Well done. And again.' She did so. 'Did you sleep well?'

Mirabelle nodded. 'Well enough. I fell asleep in the chair.'

'Headache?'

'Not now. Perhaps a little muggy.'

'It must have been a shock to come across his body. Quite apart from the assault.'

'I've seen a dead man before.'

The doctor put the stethoscope back in his case but he didn't make to leave. His eyes were still on her.

'You aren't wearing a jacket,' she said.

'It's hot today. I tend not to stand on formalities.'

The silence hung between them. Doctor Williams continued to stare at her and she realised she was staring back. Before she could avert her eyes, he leaned inwards and kissed her gently on the lips. Mirabelle felt her heart leap.

'How dare you?' she said. 'I'm your patient.'

'You said you don't have a doctor. But I wouldn't want to do something that you didn't want me to. Do you want me to?' He slid his arm around her waist and pulled her close, kissing her again. He was tall and he smelled of shaving foam and tasted of coffee. When he stroked her hair, he pulled it slightly. Mirabelle let him take her weight for a few seconds before she broke away.

'You're very young,' she said. She guessed he was about thirty. Not much more. A full ten years younger than she was. More than that. Most women would consider him a catch. She could feel herself blushing at the intrusion. She had enjoyed it and there was no point in being coy. It had been a long time. More than a year.

'You're very beautiful,' he said as he reached out and took her hand. She suddenly realised how lonely she had felt. It felt good to let him hold her. Almost like disappearing.

'You're very forward. I don't know you.'

Doctor Williams smiled. He raised her palm to his lips and kissed it. 'I was thinking of ways to remedy that. Why don't we start with a proper introduction? I have the advantage of you. My name is Chris. Christopher Williams.' He bit the fleshy part of her palm, gently, and she pulled her hand away.

'Superintendent McGregor didn't send you.'

'No. Do you mind?'

Mirabelle didn't answer. She didn't know.

'Can I take you out? Dinner maybe? Dancing?'

'Dinner?' she repeated.

'Dinner it is. Tonight?'

'Tomorrow.'

He smiled. 'There, that wasn't so bad, was it?' He kissed her again, lightly on the lips, before picking up his case. 'I'll pick you up at eight.'

As the door shut behind him, she stood, stunned for at least a minute. Then she moved to the window and tentatively peered outside. The doctor was getting into a car further along the front. It was illegally parked. He looked up and she stepped backwards, feeling foolish. She couldn't deny he was attractive. She wondered why she felt so confused.

On his way, his car seemed to glide past the window. Mirabelle sank on to the sofa. She grabbed the chicken pie from the table and opened the bag, breaking off a piece of the crust. It seemed impossible to go into the kitchen to fetch a plate. Instead she ate with her fingers, straight out of the paper. The pie tasted buttery. When she'd finished eating she crumpled the gravy-smeared bag and reached for the bottle of whisky on the drinks tray. She only poured herself a small dram. It was early yet, but it tasted good. Then she stretched out on the sofa. Through the open window, sounds filtered up from the beach – a snatch of laughter, a child squealing and the buzz of a scooter's engine. She kicked off her shoes, yawned, turned over and fell fast asleep.

She woke to the sound of banging on the front door. It must have been going on for a while, she realised as she sat up and scrambled to find her shoes. The clock on the mantle had stopped because she had neglected to wind it. 'I'm coming,' she called.

When she opened the door a crack, McGregor stood on the threshold. He was clearly fuming.

'What the hell is wrong with you, Mirabelle?' he said, pushing past her and into the living room, where he took off his hat. 'I expressly said to you not to get involved and you went back to the home anyway.'

Mirabelle took a moment to focus. 'I did,' she said. 'I saw Robinson. It turns out to be a missing person case as well as a murder.'

'If the two are connected,' McGregor spat. 'That's an assumption, woman.'

Mirabelle suddenly wished she had a cigarette. She wanted to appear nonchalant and she needed a prop. Instead she ran her fingers through her hair. Chris had done the same, she thought, only a little while ago, and a flash of guilt turned in her stomach.

'It's unlikely that they aren't connected, wouldn't you say?' she managed. 'Two people who knew each other and incidents on the same day. It would be a big coincidence. I just hope the sister is all right.'

'You don't think she did it then? Sister Taylor? Killed him?

Of course, you don't.' McGregor raised his eyes to the ceiling. 'You never think it's the most likely thing.'

Mirabelle gave the merest shrug. 'Likely? I don't know. Robinson reckons that she is on the run. But she doesn't seem the type. I looked over her bedsit – she seems an exacting and methodical kind of person. A bit harsh sometimes with her neighbours, but that speaks to me of someone who liked order, not violence. And then there is the complete absence of a motive.'

'I don't want you getting mixed up in this, Mirabelle. I told you not to get involved.'

'I found Father Grogan's body. I'm involved regardless, aren't I?'

'You're a suspect.'

'You know I didn't kill Father Grogan.'

'I repeat, Mirabelle. You're a suspect. People end up charged. All sorts. You know better than this. You need to leave this one alone. Let me handle it, for pity's sake.'

She struggled against the impulse to tell him that what she got up to was none of his business. She wanted to fold her arms, but she held back. McGregor noticed the brown paper bag and the empty glass beside it. 'Have you been drinking?' He checked his watch. It was, she knew, no later than three o'clock.

'I had a small one.'

McGregor snorted. 'On top of a potential concussion?'

'I am not concussed. Doctor Williams examined me. I'm fine.'

'Concussion takes time. You know that. Whatever the doctor said last night . . .'

Mirabelle didn't reply but a guilty shadow must have flickered across her face. McGregor took a moment.

'I'd keep away from Williams,' he said.

She managed to hold her tongue.

79

'I'm warning you as a friend.' He tried again.

'Why? Is the doctor a ladies' man?' She couldn't help it. She hated sounding bitter. She hoped her cheeks hadn't coloured.

'He's not good enough for you, Belle.' McGregor's tone was hardening.

'By which you mean that you are good enough for me?'

'Look, I don't want you getting caught up in this case. That's all.'

'Or with Doctor Williams.'

'If you give me a few days I'm sure I can sort it out. I'll tell you over dinner if you like.'

'Tell me now. What have you found, Superintendent?'

McGregor sighed. 'You can't, Mirabelle.'

'I have a right to know. I was there. What have you turned up? Tell me.'

McGregor relented. 'Very little so far,' he said. 'Though, for what it's worth, I agree with your assessment of Sister Taylor. Robinson said she had been to see the priest before Vespers, but it's impossible to say what she wanted.'

Mirabelle's eyes lit up. 'You see. You do need me. I was the one who followed him, Alan. I saw them.'

'Which is why I went to your office to interview you this morning but you weren't where you said you'd be.'

'Vesta sent me away.'

He reached for her hand but she snatched it back.

'You're all right, aren't you?' He sounded tender.

'I'm fine. And of course I'll give you a statement. Thank you for not making me come to the station to do it.'

McGregor nodded. 'Go on.'

'It strikes me there are a few things that might matter,' she said as she ran through the events of the night before. 'I can't say why Sister Taylor came to see the priest at the Sacred Heart yesterday, but she was upset. Afterwards I saw her and she could have told me, but she didn't – she made up some stupid story. Then Grogan came to the home as quickly as he could and, afterwards, when he got back to the house, after they had fought, he must have felt terrible. He stumbled. I thought he was drunk, but really he was about to die. As soon as he got in, he switched on the study light. It was only for a moment but he must have gone there for a reason. That's what I was trying to do when I broke in. I was going to check over the study and see if I could figure it out.'

McGregor gave this some consideration. 'Do you think he wanted to use the telephone?'

'You'd hope, if that was on his mind, he might have called an ambulance. But he didn't. I don't know why he went in there. Anyway, in the end the poison hit him too quickly. He must have felt ill but perhaps he didn't realise how seriously. He was still in a good enough state to make it up the hall to the bathroom. Perhaps he thought he was just going to be sick.'

'OK. Leave it with me.'

Mirabelle let her gaze fall to her shoes.

'I mean it,' he insisted. 'You'll end up charged, the way you're going. Just lay off the whisky. And keep away from Williams, all right? You're a suspect, Mirabelle. You have to be careful.' McGregor folded his jacket over his arm and put on his hat at an angle. 'I'll let myself out,' he said. 'You'd best get some rest.'

Mirabelle waited. She checked through the window as he walked down the path and turned on to the promenade. She touched her lips for only a second before directing herself to the drinks tray and immediately contravening McGregor's order. He'd made her angry. 'I'm not one of your damn officers,' she said under her breath. 'You can't tell me what to do.' The taste of the whisky opened on her tongue. It seemed to clear her head. He couldn't cut her out like this, she thought as she reached for her handbag and knocked back the last of the dram. She had forgotten the conundrum about the study until she'd said it. And she had nothing else to do this afternoon.

Chapter Nine

Knowledge is true opinion

Norton Road was quiet. Shadows from the trees lengthened on the stones in the afternoon light. A girl was visiting a grave beside the church. She knelt on the ground in front of the large, grey stone and rocked gently. Mirabelle was careful not to stare. Instead she turned into the Sacred Heart. The church was becoming familiar although today there had been some changes. Inside, a wide bank of tiny candles burned next to the altar upon which a black-and-white photograph of Father Grogan had been placed, propped up in a silver frame and surrounded by a small forest of crosses – some made of wood, some of silver and one, even, of gold. In front of the candles, the young priest, Father Turnbull, knelt praying with two women. Behind Mirabelle, a schoolboy pushed open the heavy door and walked purposefully to the font, where he dutifully put a coin into the box and lit two candles, finding a place for them on the edge of the sea of flames, before nodding to the father and stalking back up the aisle. The boy's knees, Mirabelle thought suddenly, seemed too thin to hold his weight. The schoolbag, mounted on his back, was at least twice the width of his body. It seemed extraordinary that he didn't tip over.

As the child passed, she slipped into a pew. After a minute or two, Father Turnbull crossed himself and got to his feet.

The women sat back on the wooden slats as he rose and turned to inspect the interior of the church, checking, she supposed, for members of the congregation. It had clearly been busy today as the news of the tragedy spread. His eyes narrowed when he spotted Mirabelle. Then he put his hands into his pockets and walked up the aisle. Behind him, one of the women drew out a handkerchief and dabbed her eyes. The other put an arm around her friend.

'Oh dear,' Father Turnbull said, examining Mirabelle's face as he stopped in front of her. 'I really hurt you.'

He didn't go as far, she noted, as saying sorry.

'The doctor says it will heal.'

He sniffed. 'But you have been drinking whisky.'

She smiled. 'I have.' She realised she ought to buy peppermints. Father Turnbull slid into the pew. If she smelled of whisky, then he smelled of lavender water. Whoever had laundered his clerical robes had gone overboard with the stuff.

'I keep coming back to you. What on earth were you doing in our bathroom?' he asked.

'I followed Father Grogan home.'

Father Turnbull waited. It was a better technique, Mirabelle thought, than the police employed. Robinson, anyway.

'I knew him. I'm not a member of the congregation but I was a friend of Father Sandor's, you see. And I was concerned something was wrong.'

'Oh. You're that woman.'

'I probably am. The thing is, Father, I am trying to figure out why Father Grogan went into the study.'

Father Turnbull cocked his head.

'When he came home,' Mirabelle elaborated, 'Father Grogan was already suffering. He was unsteady on his feet. But he went into the study, switched on the light, and then left almost immediately. After that, he went to the bathroom. He felt sick, I suppose.'

Father Turnbull looked up. Mirabelle wondered for a moment if he was praying, but then she realised he was trying not to cry.

'I'm sorry,' she said. 'It's only, the detail is important.'

The two women passed them, walking towards the double doors. One cast a sideways glance at Mirabelle, as if she was jealous. 'Goodbye,' the other one called and put her hand on her friend's arm. The priest waved. Once the door had closed, he waited a moment. Just a beat. The church was so silent Mirabelle could have sworn she heard the candles flicker before the priest spoke. 'Why would anyone want to kill him? I don't understand. Sometimes we see evil, of course. A glimpse here and there. But this is truly the devil's work.'

'I'd like to find out.'

He waited again but she didn't rise to the provocation with a theory. 'This is when people need the church most. Times like these,' he said.

Mirabelle nodded towards the candles. 'He was loved, wasn't he?'

'People need something to do in a crisis.'

That was Mirabelle's problem with religion. It had struck her during the war that belief had fed on people's fear. So much of what had passed across her desk had horrified her that she had lost faith in God. After that the ceremonies seemed foolish – hopeless, almost. If there was a god, why wouldn't he stand up against such monumental cruelty, she asked herself. The battlefields. The camps. The executions. Jack had been the same. 'We have ourselves to rely on,' he had said. 'Not all that guff.'

Her affair with Superintendent McGregor had not restored her faith in the church – or in anything, for that matter. Alan McGregor, like her, appeared to have no faith. The matter had never come up, even before Mirabelle had understood the extent of the superintendent's moral corruption. Not that his morality had to make a difference to his religious belief. Some of the world's greatest despots were god-fearing men.

'How long had you known Father Grogan?' she asked.

'Six years. I was Sandor's replacement. Fresh out of the seminary. Father Grogan was a wonderful teacher. He came across gruff at first but he cared very deeply. He was extraordinary once you got to know him. That sounds dramatic, but he helped a lot of people. He was brave in the face of despair. People need that. Somebody who is steady.'

'Will they send someone to help you?'

'I phoned the bishop's palace.'

'Well, I hope they arrive soon. It must be lonely. Father Turnbull, I wonder, would you let me see it?'

'See what?'

'The study. If I could have a look, I might be able to figure out why Father Grogan went in there. There must have been a reason. And that might lead us to the reason he died.'

She wasn't sure what he would reply. 'The police . . .' he started and then stopped.

'I'm sure they've looked. I'm not sure they have seen.' She sounded biblical, she realised. 'I've helped with inquiries before. I've solved a few cases, in fact. I knew Father Grogan – for a little longer than you did. For Sandor's sake, I'd like to help if I can.'

Father Turnbull nodded as he considered this. 'All right,' he said. 'If you think it will help.'

They crossed the road as if they weren't walking together. Father Turnbull drew a key from his pocket and let her in through the front door this time. Mirabelle suppressed the shiver that wavered along her spine. It was, she knew, a visceral reaction to the memory of what had happened. She was glad she didn't have to live in the priests' house. Father Turnbull hovered on the threshold of the study. 'It's in here,' he said.

It felt strange being inside, looking out. The hardware shop on the corner, from where she had watched, was clearly visible from Father Grogan's desk. Today there was a table outside with stacks of pots and pans piled up for sale.

'Do you use this room?' she asked. 'I mean, if you've work to do.'

'We share. That is, I use the desk if I need it. Father Grogan looked after all the paperwork. It's more his room than mine.'

Mirabelle did not correct the priest's use of tense. The bereaved often talked of the dead in a mixture of the present and the past. 'It's very tidy,' she said.

The priest nodded. 'He was good at looking after the old place. People turned away from the church after the war. And there has been so little money. It's not as rich a parish as people expect. But the father was a whizz at making ends meet. A few weeks ago he managed to find funds for the repair.'

'Repair?'

'At the back of the church. The roof and the stonework. It's a terrible mess. The building looks fine from the front but at the rear . . . we joked she was like a duck on the water – fine on top, paddling like crazy underneath. Some debris came off the roof last winter and we were lucky nobody got hurt – do you remember the big storm; the high winds after Christmas? We knew it had to be fixed but we didn't have the money and the diocese couldn't offer any help. Anyway, Father Grogan found a local firm to do the work at a reasonable price. We'd been raising funds ever since – donations and jumble sales and the scouts gave us their bob-a-job money. We were getting there, but slowly. Then he managed to get this donation. It was over half what we needed, all at once. The works start next month. I expect now we will put up a plaque to his memory.' Father Turnbull sank into one of the chairs.

'How much?' Mirabelle prompted.

'Nine hundred pounds. The total, that is. He found someone willing to donate five hundred. These old buildings are expensive.'

'Who was it?'

'They wanted to stay anonymous. But recently, I think, some of our parishioners have been doing well. Financially, I mean. I expect the repair will be a testament to what he achieved.'

Mirabelle slipped behind the desk and sat in the chair. She opened the drawers on a miscellany of paperclips, pencils and elastic bands. In the top right-hand drawer there was a telephone directory and on top of that an address book. She took out the address book and flicked through it. Nothing stood out – most of the addresses and phone numbers were in Brighton and the few that weren't were other parish priests across Sussex and beyond. Then, at the back of the book, on the flyleaf, she noticed faded writing in pencil. Mirabelle squinted. Her eyesight was not what it used to be. She held the book at a distance. It was a phrase, she realised. In German. Mirabelle spoke a little German. Just a touch. *Krumes Holz gibt auch gerades Feuer.* Crooked logs make straight fires. It was an odd thing for a priest to have jotted down.

'Was the father fluent in many languages?' she asked.

Father Turnbull wasn't paying attention. 'Well, Latin,' he said absentmindedly, staring out of the window. 'I think I should go back to church. One or two people have arrived. I ought to welcome them. Will you be all right?'

Mirabelle nodded. 'Of course,' she said, though she didn't feel like being left alone. The priests' house had a strange atmosphere but the places where people died often felt haunted. As the front door clicked behind the young priest, she started to search for a ledger. It didn't take long. Father Turnbull was right, she noted, as she scanned the pages.

The parish finances were strained but there had been a large donation. The bank book clipped to the back of the ledger contained almost a thousand pounds. Next to it, Father Grogan's personal bank statement was more modest. He had ten pounds to his name when he died and had made a donation of £5 of his own money towards the repair. Mirabelle sat back in the chair. Outside, the light seemed rich – the soupy sunshine of late afternoon. He couldn't have been killed for the money, she thought. After all, the money was still here. And yet, something like this had to be taken into account.

A few minutes passed. She was avoiding checking over the bathroom, she realised, but she would need to inspect it. Then the house shifted. There was the sound of movement. She strained to see the front door through the hallway, but, adjusting her seat, she realised the noise came from the other side of the building. Mirabelle's heart beat faster. She got to her feet. She wondered, momentarily, where Father Turnbull kept his cricket bat. Then a wireless turned on and the sound of Nat King Cole struck up, singing faintly in the distance.

As quietly as she could, Mirabelle crept through the hallway and towards the music. It led her to the back of the house. Her hand was on the brass doorknob of the kitchen door when there was a crash, as if someone had dropped some cutlery. She was about to burst in when the young woman with the pink dress swung through the door towards her, carrying a pile of black laundry. Mirabelle jumped back. The woman started, screamed and dropped her bundle.

'It's you,' Mirabelle smiled. She felt like laughing.

'Oh. Yes.' The woman laughed too. 'Yesterday. In church. You were looking for the father.' She smiled apologetically, as if mentioning the dead man was in poor taste. Then she bent down and began to stack the robes. The smell of lavender wafted from the still-warm linen. 'I'm all fingers and thumbs today. I've already made a mess in the kitchen. You gave me a fright,' she babbled. 'It's only natural, I suppose. We're all on edge. I've come with the laundry and I thought I'd make Father Turnbull dinner. I have a potato and a chop.' She nodded in the direction of the kitchen. 'I'll tidy up in there and get them on soon. What are you doing here?'

'Father Turnbull let me check over the study.'

'Ah. Papers. Yes. After a death.'

Mirabelle did not correct the woman's assumption. Instead she helped retrieve the laundry.

The woman held out her hand. 'Teresa.'

'I'm Mirabelle.' Mirabelle noticed the ring on her wedding finger. 'Were you married in the church?'

'Yes. Father Grogan married us when we first came to live here. It must be three or four years ago now. I'm from Hastings, really.'

'It's kind of you to look after Father Turnbull like this. It's hard on him.'

Teresa shrugged. Her eyes slid along the wall, landing on the bathroom door. 'It happened in there, didn't it?'

'He was on the floor.' Mirabelle didn't admit she had found the body. 'He had been at the children's home,' she said.

Teresa nodded but didn't say anything. Her eyes remained pinned to the doorframe of the bathroom as Mirabelle reached out and turned the handle. Inside, there was no sign of what had happened. A yellow hand towel was folded neatly on the chrome rail. The smell of bleach rose on the air. Someone had cleaned up. Mirabelle shook herself. She hadn't really expected Father Grogan's body to be there, nor his ghost, but still.

'Father Turnbull told me about the repair to the church. It seems Father Grogan had been tireless.'

Teresa looked as if she might cry, but seeing the scene of the crime appeared to have calmed her. Imagination was always worse than the reality. 'He said he didn't want the old place falling down. Not on his watch.'

'I'm sorry,' Mirabelle said. 'He seems to have meant a lot to everyone.'

'When my mother died, he was marvellous,' the young woman sniffed. 'He came every day – such a comfort.'

'And he raised all that money. I don't suppose you know who it was? The mystery donor?'

Teresa seemed to relax suddenly – the power of gossip. Her shoulders dropped. 'We all wondered. I mean, it's quite a sum. There are a few people who are doing well. That's obvious. But no one knows who it was. Well, it'd be flash, wouldn't it? To say.'

'Do you mean that it was one of the parishioners?'

'You've never had it so good, isn't that what people say? New cars,' she raised her eyes, as if buying a vehicle was the kind of thing a naughty child might do. 'Houses wallpapered. Swings in the gardens for the kiddies. Holidays down the coast. There are a few people who have been spending their money. But it's a lot, isn't it? I mean, just to give away.'

'It is,' Mirabelle said. 'Yes, that's what I thought too.'

Chapter Ten

The lonely wear a mask

On Church Street Mirabelle stopped at the telephone box and called McGuigan & McGuigan Debt Recovery. Vesta answered promptly and Mirabelle pressed the button to connect. It was hot inside the box – it smelled like the inside of a dusty oven.

'Have you had a good day?' Mirabelle enquired, cheerily, once the coin had dropped.

'It must have been busy at the arcade over the weekend. The Simpsons turned up with a large payment, mostly in sixpences, and I'm just working through what Bill picked up on his rounds,' Vesta reported. 'We had two new clients. I think they might end up being large accounts.'

This wasn't exactly what Mirabelle had hoped for when she asked the question. 'Vesta, I wondered if you might do me a favour?' she ventured.

Vesta's silence was a sign of her dubiety. 'What is it?' she asked after a moment.

'Research. That's all.' Mirabelle realised she felt guilty even asking. 'If you don't mind.'

'Have you figured it out yet? The murder?'

'No. But I did speak to a doctor and he said TB is not contagious at the convalescent stage so there's no risk to you or to Noel, or, well, to any of us.'

'Really?' The relief sounded in Vesta's voice. 'Was he sure?'

'Quite sure,' Mirabelle said. 'He asked me out for dinner.'

Vesta hooted. Suddenly it felt like a flashback to a year ago, when Vesta had liked to gossip and had pushed Mirabelle to take on divorce cases, though she had never succumbed. 'Well, you've got all the fellows falling at your feet.'

'What do you mean?'

'McGregor, of course. He's got it bad. He was all over me this morning trying to find out if you're seeing anybody without actually asking the question.'

Mirabelle dismissed this out of hand. 'He just wanted to ask me about Father Grogan. He was pursuing his inquiries.'

'Sure. Yes. That's what he was after. Inquiries.' Vesta hooted again. 'Look Mirabelle, I think they have you down as a suspect.'

'Oh, honestly, Vesta,' Mirabelle waved off the suggestion. 'McGregor is just being dramatic.'

'I don't know why you two don't make it up. You were happy together,' the girl said.

Mirabelle had never told Vesta about the blonde. Or about the murder McGregor had as good as sanctioned. Vesta had been pregnant at the time and it hadn't seemed right to burden her.

'I don't think we can make up our differences, he and I,' she said vaguely.

'And now there's a doctor on the cards.' Mirabelle could tell Vesta's eyes were gleaming. 'A good-looking one, I hope.'

'He is, actually. And far too young for me.' Mirabelle blushed at her indiscretion.

'He sounds just the tonic,' Vesta said smoothly. 'Well, what is it you need, Mirabelle?'

'I wondered if you could find out how Indians feel about cats.'

Vesta waited. 'Indians? Cats?' she said. 'Big cats? Like tigers?'

'No. Domestic cats. I mean, are Indian people superstitious about them?'

'I can try. I'll ask around.'

Mirabelle waited. She was about to make some kind of arrangement for the next day when Vesta said the word she realised she had been waiting for.

'Why?'

A smile spread across Mirabelle's face. 'So much has happened,' she said. 'The sister at the convalescent home went missing after she had an argument with Father Grogan. I think it must have been less than an hour before he died. And one of the nurses there seems distressed somehow – she keeps chasing off cats in the garden. And the father, it turns out, raised an enormous sum of money to fix the church roof and nobody knows who donated it.' The words tumbled out.

In the background, Mirabelle could hear Vesta's pencil tapping on her notepad.

'How much money?' the girl asked.

'Five hundred pounds.'

She let out a low whistle. 'Leave it with me. You need to be careful, Mirabelle. If you're on the cards for a murder inquiry, it might not be wise to get involved like this – and with money at stake.'

'Well, if you don't want to help . . .' Mirabelle let the words hang. It seemed to her that Vesta took rather too long to reply.

'What's your next line of inquiry?' she said when she did.

Mirabelle felt a surge of relief but she'd need to be careful. Vesta had changed. She wouldn't ask for any more help, she decided, as she checked the slim gold watch on her wrist. 'I expect the children at the convalescent home have tea around five, don't you?'

Down the telephone line, Mirabelle could tell that Vesta was also checking the time. She had her own home to go to. 'Oh lord. I'd better get going. I mustn't be late for Mrs Treadwell,' the girl said hurriedly. 'Bye.'

The telephone line clicked. Mirabelle pushed open the heavy door. It felt cool in the street by comparison. She thought wistfully about all the times she'd called Vesta and Vesta's inquiries had as good as cracked the case. Not any longer.

Feeling heady, Mirabelle turned in the direction of Eaton Road. She noted the cream builder's van was still in place, parked directly opposite the children's home where it provided good cover. She settled in her usual position in front of the rose bush three doors down on the opposite side of the street and tried to look inconspicuous. It was quieter today. A woman returned home and ran up her garden path, further down, rushing to make dinner for her husband. At half past five the first man arrived back. He was wearing a bowler hat, despite the weather. Mirabelle wondered if he worked at the bank on North Street. She was sure she had seen him. Then she heard the muffled sound of the bell ringing inside the convalescent home. Half an hour for tea, she thought, forty minutes at the outside. Then, an hour to clear up and for bath time. The children would be in bed by seven o'clock. Lights out at eight. If the end of Sister Taylor's shift had been nine o'clock, perhaps the nurses had a meeting at the end of the day. It may take a while.

In the end, though, it was just after seven when the door opened. The sun had set but the sky still held some light. There was a full moon and no cloud. Nurse Frida, Nurse Uma and Nurse Berenice trotted down the steps smartly and turned in the direction of the main road, falling into step together. Mirabelle loitered, following at a distance. She didn't want to risk them noticing her. There was something comforting about the three women in their capes and caps, walking together – the camaraderie of it. They must have had a difficult day. As the group turned the corner, they broke into a run, and Mirabelle watched as a bus flew past the junction, heading in the direction of town. She began to run too, but by the time she got to the corner the women had disappeared and the back end of the bus was almost a block away. She caught a flash of cape and cap in the rear window as it moved and the exhaust pipe let out a long puff of smoke. Mirabelle leaned against a shop door and caught her breath. At least she knew the direction they lived in and that none of them lived close enough to walk home, like Sister Taylor could. And it seemed the sister had stayed late the evening before. They all had. Perhaps the argument had upset everyone.

Without thinking, Mirabelle pushed through the door of the pub on Church Street and ordered an orange juice at the bar. It had been a long, hot day and she was thirsty. The pink-cheeked landlord disappeared under the counter and the sound of bottles clanking ensued. He emerged triumphant, levered off the top and poured the juice into a short glass with a red rim, which clashed with the colour of the drink.

'I don't suppose you have any ice?' she asked.

The man sighed. His eyes were rheumy. Heavy-footed, he plodded into the back and returned with two cubes between his thick fingers, which he plopped into the glass. Further along the bar, a man nursing a half-pint of stout grunted.

'Hot day,' Mirabelle explained with a smile. 'Did you hear about the priest? Father Grogan?'

'That's a bad business,' the bartender said. 'The old fellow was poisoned, somebody told me.'

'It was in his whisky.'

The bartender and the stout drinker both raised their eyes to the row of three bottles on the back shelf – gin, brandy and whisky. Mirabelle paddled her juice around the glass to cool it and took a sip. The door of the pub swung open and a beat bobby popped in his head.

'You all right, Constable?' the bartender checked.

'I didn't know you served ladies on their own, Jack,' the bobby said, as if Mirabelle wasn't there.

'It's discretionary,' the bartender replied. 'We was just saying about the father? A priest, I tell you! Poisoned in his whisky, this lady says.'

'Now, now. Careless talk costs lives,' the bobby said, as if it was still wartime.

'Poisoned though,' the bartender persisted.

He pulled a half of bitter and laid it on the bar. The policeman emptied the glass in one, smacked his lips and raised his hand in a parting gesture, leaving as quickly as he had arrived. The door swung closed behind him.

'You got to keep on the right side of the law,' the bartender said sagely as he disposed of the empty glass.

Mirabelle handed over a coin and waited for her change. The stout drinker stirred. 'It's a shame about the priest. I'm not a churchgoing man, but the country's gone to pot if they're killing holy men.'

It popped into Mirabelle's mind that the country hadn't gone to pot, exactly. She'd known it worse than this. But, on the other hand, lots of things had changed for her over the last year – that had become apparent. 'Perhaps I'll just have a Scotch,' she said.

The barman poured a shot and put it on the bar. She handed over another coin.

'You want ice again?' He sounded weary.

Mirabelle shook her head. Ice ruined whisky. Besides, you didn't drink it because you were thirsty. She added a splash of water from the jug and knocked back the glassful. 'Thanks.'

Outside, Mirabelle paused to enjoy the breeze as she wandered towards the seafront. At the front, she stopped at Lali's bench and sat, staring at the ocean. The sound of the surf breaking on the stones set a soothing rhythm. Out here at the beginning of the suburbs it served as a lullaby. Far off, further along the front, the lights of the pier twinkled across the black water. Brighton came alive at night. In town, the smell of frying fish would be hanging on the air. The pubs would be full at this time of the evening and the picture houses would have queues snaking along the pavements even on a Monday. Since she had fallen out with Superintendent McGregor, she hadn't crossed the threshold of a single one of those establishments, sticking solidly to the few shops she frequented routinely. Life had become quiet.

She wondered what she and Christopher Williams might discuss over dinner. Perhaps he'd know something more about the case. Her mind wandered, lighting on the detritus of the day – all the unanswered questions. She wondered where Sister Taylor was. Was Robinson right and the woman had fled? Or had something else happened to her? Something they hadn't accounted for. Worst of all, was the nurse dead, like Father Grogan? Mirabelle shuddered.

Out of the darkness, the figure of the beat bobby from the bar came into view, strolling along Kingsway. His white pith helmet seemed almost luminous in the light of the moon.

'Miss Bevan,' he tipped his hat.

'Officer.'

Mirabelle laughed as the man disappeared into the darkness. Brighton was ludicrously small. You couldn't go unnoticed. With this in mind she scrambled for her house key and stalked back to her flat. The vanilla slice still sat in its brown paper bag on the table. She fetched a plate, a pastry fork and another tumbler of whisky and savoured her dinner alone in the moonlight. Tomorrow she'd eat something proper – a steak perhaps. With the handsome doctor. Yes, she thought, that would be nice, as she sneaked barefoot across the thick carpet and fell into bed.

Chapter Eleven

Justice is moderation regulated by wisdom

Mirabelle tripped down East Street the next morning, just in time to see Mrs Treadwell's lavender figure disappear around the corner, pushing Noel in the pram as she cut into the glorious sunshine along the front. Gulls were wheeling across the slice of sky at the bottom of the street and the breeze had icy fingers. Autumn was on its way after all. She strode smartly down the sunny side and then clattered upstairs to the office where Vesta was sitting alone at her desk.

'Good morning,' Mirabelle smiled. 'Gosh, where's Bill?'

Bill had never arrived late to work in the four years since he'd started.

Vesta shrugged as she laid a cup of tea in front of Mirabelle. 'Your face is getting better – the bruises, I mean. Oh, and Indians aren't superstitious about cats – no more than we are. You know – black cats crossing your path,' she announced.

'You're a marvel. Thank you.'

'I was going to pop into the Taj Mahal and ask, but then I thought how annoyed I'd be. I've never been to eat there. I wouldn't like it if somebody pitched up and just started asking me about Jamaicans – it didn't seem right. So I phoned Mum. There's an Indian family moved along the road from her. They're from Madras. Dad helped them with the plumbing when they first moved in.'

Mirabelle glanced at the pile of papers on her desk. Vesta sat down. She leaned forward. 'Well. A doctor. And a younger man.'

'He said my face would heal.'

'He's right.'

Mirabelle changed the subject. 'How are things going with the Hayward case?'

Vesta pulled her notepad towards her. 'I just can't find a way in. Any time I try to pin him down and make an arrangement, he sidesteps it.'

That had been the problem for months. Mr Hayward, who appeared perfectly solvent, had several outstanding debts that he was not minded to settle. Vesta had made enquiries, but she couldn't find out what he was doing with his money, or why he kept promising to make a payment and then reneging. Repeated calls from Vesta and from Bill had had no effect. It was almost time to call in the bailiffs, in Mirabelle's opinion. But Vesta persisted. 'There's got to be something we can do . . . There's money there,' she started vaguely, only she was interrupted by the sound of Bill's footsteps on the stairs. He pushed open the door, Panther rushing in ahead of him as if the little dog knew that his master was late and was trying to make up for it. He gave a yelp that sounded like an apology and disappeared under Bill's desk.

'Good morning, Bill,' the women chimed together.

'Are you all right?' Mirabelle added.

'I'm fine.'

Vesta set about making more tea. Mirabelle took in Bill's demeanour. He wasn't a man who spoke much, but there was something stiff about him this morning. A small patch of unshaven skin sprouted under his ear. He'd missed it when he had shaved. It wasn't like him.

'Are you still investigating that home?' he asked. 'The children?'

Mirabelle didn't answer but Vesta looked over her shoulder. 'Have you ever known Mirabelle give up?' she said affectionately. 'And she's a murder suspect to boot. Don't help her, Bill. For heaven's sake.'

Bill said nothing but gave a mere nod of his head, which somehow made it clear he accepted what Mirabelle was up to, but didn't approve. He sipped his tea. 'Plenty people end up in prison who shouldn't be there,' he said, flatly. 'You ought to keep your nose clean, Miss Bevan. You're a suspect, is what you are.'

'We were just discussing the Hayward case,' Mirabelle changed the subject.

Vesta picked up her pencil. 'I am running out of lines of inquiry,' she said. 'Mr Hayward is, without question, the most unreliable man I've ever come into contact with.'

Bill shuffled the papers on his desk.

'You missed a bit.' Mirabelle indicated the area beneath her own ear.

Bill put his fingers to his face. 'Blow it,' he said. Then he peered at Mirabelle, tit for tat, looking at her bruises.

'The doctor reckons I'm on the mend,' she said.

'Doctors. Pah!' Bill let out a sharp exhalation and picked up the papers to put them in his pocket. 'You should go to Hannington's,' he said very definitely. 'I was thinking about it, and it might help us to crack Hayward.'

Vesta's eyebrows raised – a silent question.

'When I worked at the nick we sometimes looked at Hannington's accounts to see what people were up to. You get home addresses, delivery instructions – all sorts. When you chase the working class, it's easy to get the measure of them. But with these middle-class types we might need to take a sideways step or two. I thought, it might help – Hannington's, that is. Looking into him, or rather his wife, do you see?'

It was a good idea, though Mirabelle suddenly felt uncomfortable. She had an account at Hannington's. When she had refurbished the flat after the fire, Vesta had charged several items to it – household linen and some electrical goods as well as hats and gloves. Someone would be able to second-guess her apartment's contents using the information, she realised. What you bought could be judged; but Bill was right, in the case of Hayward, they might get an idea of movement of money at the very least.

'It's Mrs Braithwaite you need,' Bill said. 'That's the lady who runs the accounts department. She has Chihuahuas. They're not my kind of dogs but I helped her out a couple of times with training. Tell her I sent you.'

He got to his feet and scooped the untidy pile of papers into his pocket. Panther sprang to heel. 'See you later,' Bill said as he closed the door and the sound of his steps receded down the stairs.

'Do you think there's something wrong with Bill?' Mirabelle asked.

Vesta shrugged. 'He never says much. Do you fancy nipping along to Hannington's now? We could do it together.'

Mirabelle gave one last glance at the papers on her desk and reached for her jacket.

The window displays that ran in both directions along North Street from the main entrance seemed out of place in the bright sunshine. Woollen jerseys, winter coats and hats graced the models on display. A large cardboard cutout of a tree divested of its leaves made a striking centrepiece. Hannington's might have moved on a season and Brighton had icy fingers, in the shade at least, but those fingers still clung to summer. Inside, the cosmetics department smelled vaguely of perfume. The store was quiet on a Tuesday morning and the serving staff were mostly rearranging displays and polishing mirrors with pieces of crumpled newspaper.

A bottle of vinegar stood on the floor beside a display of French eau de Cologne. It released a distinctive tang on to the air.

'Can I help you ladies?' the sales assistant offered.

'We're going upstairs,' Vesta said. 'To accounts.'

Mirabelle and Vesta took the lift to the top floor. Hannington's had grown over the years, adding new buildings here and there. These had been knocked together so that moving from one department to another was a haphazard business, up and down steps. They followed the signs for the Accounts Department, making their way past the hairdressing salon, through the food hall and turning left at a mahogany sign that said 'Foreign Exchange'.

The department itself had an opaque glass door. Mirabelle knocked and entered. Inside, the office was light. The view was far better than the one McGuigan & McGuigan enjoyed, taking in the rooftops and benefiting from far more blue sky.

On the desk stood an open leather-bound ledger and a bell, but otherwise the place was deserted. Vesta rang the bell, which let out a sharp ping that resonated. Almost immediately, a smartly dressed girl of fifteen or so appeared through the door behind the desk. She wore black, kitten-heeled, patent-leather shoes, and a figure-hugging green tweed skirt. A pair of spectacles hung on a chain around her neck. It struck Mirabelle that she was making a great deal of effort to look older. Her skin was like cream.

'Can I help you?' the girl asked.

'We're looking for Mrs Braithwaite,' Vesta said.

The girl pursed her lips, which were carefully painted with thick matte red lipstick.

'Do you have an appointment?'

'I'm afraid not.'

'Can I say what it is regarding?'

'If you just tell her Bill Turpin sent us.'

The girl hovered, as if she felt this wasn't a good enough reason to bother Mrs Braithwaite. Her eyes jumped from Vesta to Mirabelle as she sized them up. One finger rubbed against another.

'I'm sure she'll want to see us,' Vesta said.

'Wait here, please.' The girl gestured towards two plush velvet stools against the wall and then disappeared back through the door.

Vesta leaned on the desk. She squinted at the ledger in an attempt to read the spidery writing upside down. 'It's a different kind of debt collection, I suppose.' Her eyes narrowed as she made out a couple of the payments that had been taken.

Mirabelle sat on one of the stools and elegantly crossed her ankles to one side. 'I have a Hannington's card,' she said.

Since the refurbishment, she had rarely used it. Generally these days she paid cash. Still, it would be interesting to see her file.

A minute or so later the door opened again and an older woman took her place behind the counter. She was tidily dressed but not as smart as the secretary and, Mirabelle noticed, wore sensible brown walking shoes. It was true what they said about dogs and their owners. Mrs Braithwaite was as petite as a Chihuahua with mid-brown hair and bright eyes. Her teeth were small and sharp. Mirabelle wondered if, beneath her sensible bun, the tips of the woman's ears had pricked up. 'Can I help you?' she said.

'Bill Turpin sent us. My name is Mirabelle Bevan and this is my colleague, Vesta Lewis.'

Mrs Braithwaite solemnly shook their hands in turn.

'Bill hoped you might be able to help us. It's a delicate matter. We're trying to track down the details of someone we're looking into.'

'Mr Malcolm Hayward,' Vesta said. 'I have an address.'

'Looking into?'

'We're from McGuigan & McGuigan, Debt Recovery. Bill works in our office now. You know – after that dreadful business with the dog meant he had to leave the police. Mr Hayward owes a substantial sum to our client. We've tried several lines of enquiry. Bill hoped you might be willing to help.'

'Our customers are entitled to privacy, Miss Bevan.' Mrs Braithwaite's eyes narrowed. 'Shopping at Hannington's is a private matter.'

'I know you help the police and, of course, this is different. We'd be so very grateful. Bill hoped you might make an exception. He's a lovely man.'

'Yes.' Mrs Braithwaite tutted involuntarily. Bill had been asked to leave the police force because he had defended his dog against a drunk man who had stubbed out a cigarette on the Alsatian's back. The man had ended up in hospital, which was deemed an overreaction by the police inquiry. Mirabelle had yet to meet anybody who didn't think what Bill had done was right. She let the memory sink in.

'It's only that this is a delicate matter,' she said. 'Bill said you're a marvel, quite apart from your lovely dogs. He said they're just darling, you know.'

Mrs Braithwaite paused. Then she made her decision. 'I cross-reference everything,' she said. 'You never know when details might have a use.' She looked over her shoulder. 'You'd better come in.'

The interior office was larger and darker. The walls were lined with bookcases and filing cabinets. The high desks had black Anglepoise lamps leering over them like nosy ghosts. Here and there tall oak stools peppered the spaces between the desks – most sported tottering piles of papers, although the assistant who had first answered the bell was perched precariously at one of the desks, clearly taking pleasure in typing figures into an adding machine and briskly pulling the handle to get a total. In front of one of the filing cabinets, another girl, as dowdy as the first one was glossy, was on her knees sorting through one of the drawers.

'Amanda,' Mrs Braithwaite said. 'Could you get me the file for a Malcolm Hayward?'

The dowdy girl got up and disappeared behind a row of filing cabinets.

'I wonder, Mrs Braithwaite. Is there a toilet I could use?' Vesta asked.

Mrs Braithwaite nodded. 'Back outside. Along to the end of the hallway and turn left. You'll see the signs for the customer toilets there.'

Vesta looked regretful but there was nothing for it. Mirabelle waited until the door closed behind her. Mrs Braithwaite cocked her head to one side.

'There's something else, isn't there?'

Mirabelle nodded. This woman was certainly perceptive. 'It's a mystery, really, but I do need help. It's three women. I only have their first names. Uma. Berenice. Frida. I'd love to be able to find them. Their addresses, I mean.'

'The names are quite unusual.'

'All three are nurses. They live in Brighton, all to the east of Hove. I don't know any more than that, I'm afraid.'

'We don't carry nursing supplies at Hannington's.'

'It's home addresses I was hoping for. If they shopped here for household items.'

'And the black woman mustn't know?'

Mirabelle didn't like to say it. It felt horribly disloyal. Instead she just tipped her head in agreement.

'Right.'

Amanda had retrieved the Hayward file. She solemnly passed it to Mrs Braithwaite, who passed it to Mirabelle.

'I'll just be a minute or two,' Mrs Braithwaite said.

The glossy junior finished adding up her line of figures. 'See to the post, would you?' the older woman ordered her.

'But it's still early,' the girl objected.

The glance Mrs Braithwaite gave left no doubt who was in charge, and the girl scooped a small pile of envelopes from her desk and disappeared. 'Uma will be easiest,' Mrs Braithwaite pondered. 'Not many names begin with U. Come with me, Amanda. We need the double index.'

Mirabelle hoisted herself on to one of the high stools. The Haywards had bought some lamps and cushions only last week. They were slippery customers – spending money and still refusing to cover their debts. However, they had made several payments to their account, all received only when Hannington's issued a final notice and a further letter. This spoke to what they suspected in the office – Hayward had money, he just didn't like paying his bills. Running her eyes over the file, Mirabelle noticed there were instructions to always deliver on Thursdays in the morning. At least if they wanted to find Mrs Hayward in, that would be a good place to start. Vesta returned and Mirabelle handed her the file. 'Thursdays,' she said. 'We should call in person – especially if we can catch his wife. It might embarrass him into settling.'

Vesta's dark eyes skimmed the pages. 'Yes,' she nodded. 'Maybe.'

Mirabelle peered out of the window. Far below, the faces of passers-by were shielded by their hats, small when viewed from this height. Just across the rooftops she could make out a small band of sea to the south.

'I didn't know you could see the beach from here,' she said.

Vesta peered in the same direction. 'Better than our view. We're in the wrong office. Maybe we should move,' she commented as Mrs Braithwaite appeared from behind the filing cabinets.

'Was that any help?' she asked smoothly.

'Thank you. Yes.' Vesta gave a wide grin. 'It's so appreciated.'

'You can't make a habit of using our files, ladies. Do you understand me?'

She held out her hand and Mirabelle shook it, realising there was paper against her palm. Mrs Braithwaite moved on to Vesta and then led the women to the door. 'Give Bill my very best. He has a spaniel now, doesn't he?'

'It was a big change for him after the Alsatians – when he left the force. Panther's not much of a tracker.' Vesta was in full flow. Mirabelle slipped the paper into her jacket pocket.

'German dogs,' Mrs Braithwaite replied flatly. 'It's not their fault, is it?'

Mirabelle thought of the many Nazis who had fled to South America. Not Mexico, perhaps, where she seemed to recall Chihuahuas were from, but still.

'Many thanks, Mrs Braithwaite,' she said. 'It was very kind of you to help.'

Back at the office, time seemed to drag. Mirabelle didn't manage to read the paper Mrs Braithwaite had given her until the afternoon, when Vesta nipped out for a late lunch.

'Can I get you anything?' she offered.

Mirabelle shook her head. 'I'll be fine with another cup of tea.'

'Well, you have your doctor to look forward to. Where is he taking you?' Vesta asked as she pulled on her summer jacket.

'I have no idea.' Mirabelle realised her cheeks were hot.

Vesta laughed. 'You're like a schoolgirl. That's a good sign,' she teased delightedly before disappearing down the stairs and into the sun.

Mirabelle peered out of the window, catching a flash of Vesta's dress from above as she made for the front. Then Mirabelle unfolded the paper. It contained an address, written in scrawl. Uma Simpson, it said. Seventeen West Drive. Then a note: Husband is Dr Simpson. Deliveries requested: all Tuesdays. Mirabelle crumpled the note into the bin. West Drive ran parallel to the park in the direction of Brighton racecourse. Mostly the houses were brick-built and a nice size for a family, though if Uma Simpson was nursing, it was fair to assume she didn't have any children. Vesta was extremely unusual and, as a nurse, Uma didn't keep office hours.

Mirabelle wrote a note and slapped it on to Vesta's desk. *Changed my mind about lunch*, it said. Then she gathered her bag and her jacket, locked the office door and turned eastwards at the end of the street.

Chapter Twelve

Live your beliefs and you can turn the world around

Mirabelle had kept away from Kemptown for over a year. She felt uncomfortable, even walking along the front in that direction. Superintendent McGregor lived in one of the Georgian streets that ran at right angles to Marine Parade. His housekeeper, Betty Brownlee, had silently made it known that she disapproved of Mirabelle when things had begun to go wrong. Miss Brownlee, a steely sixty-three-year-old, had banged a plate down in front of Mirabelle the last time she had eaten in McGregor's dining room and had not offered butter to go with the bread. It had been a declaration, if not of war, then of strong disapproval that Mirabelle and the superintendent had argued. Miss Brownlee shopped locally and Mirabelle hoped, most heartily, that today she wouldn't run into her. She picked up the pace as she passed the bottom of McGregor's street, casting her eyes unwillingly along the terrace. The sign outside his house declared 'No Vacancies' for bed and breakfast – an indication that business was going well, even now, at the tail end of the season. Mirabelle thought wistfully of Miss Brownlee's delicious pâté, which came with an aromatic dollop of homemade chutney, and then put the matter out of her mind.

At Rock Terrace she cut away from the sea and crossed the main road on to West Drive alongside the park. The sound of children playing floated on the warm air, and she wondered if there were swings across the lawns. It was a lovely area. Today, though, was evidently bin day, and she swerved the rubbish bins out on the street for collection. Number seventeen was a traditional, brick-built semi-detached house. It looked reliable – exactly the kind of place you'd expect a doctor to live. The front door was painted red and the front garden sported a vivid array of red flowers. The last of the summer roses were still on display, as well as a bright scatter of chrysanthemums and a cluster of unusual red nasturtiums. A ginger cat sat on the doorstep enjoying the sunshine. It looked up lazily as Mirabelle opened the gate, only jumping to its feet and stalking off when it became absolutely clear that Mirabelle was not going to deviate from the path.

She rang the bell. It took a minute or two but then she discerned the muffled sound of steps approaching and the door opened. A tall white woman in an elegant green silk dress stood on the doorstep. Her strawberry-blonde hair was tied in a high ponytail. Mirabelle smiled.

'Is this the right house for Mrs Simpson?' she asked.

The woman smiled indulgently, stretching her red lipstick into a long line. 'Yes. I'm she.'

'Oh.' Mirabelle felt quite floored. 'I was expecting a woman who was from India,' she said.

The tall woman shrugged. 'Uma,' she called over her shoulder.

Uma emerged into the hallway. She was wearing an orange sari and gardening gloves. Without her nurse's cap her dark hair fell about her shoulders. 'Oh,' she exclaimed. 'Oh no.'

The tall woman interposed herself. 'Are you a patient? Whatever happened, it isn't Uma's fault, for heaven's sake,' she snapped.

Uma hovered nervously behind her.

'I'm not a patient.' Mirabelle wondered what on earth the woman meant.

'She came to the children's home with the little Jamaican girl,' Uma cut in. 'The one who keeps running off. She was there the day the priest died.'

'Father Grogan was murdered. Poisoned,' Mirabelle corrected her. 'That is why I came to see you.'

'What do you want?'

'Information, I suppose. I'm not a police officer or anything . . .'

'Look, you can't just turn up like this. It isn't Uma's fault. I'm sorry but this really isn't on. Go away.'

The door slammed shut so hard that the small brass handle bounced off the wood. Mirabelle took a step away from the threshold, taken aback as the cat stared nonchalantly from the side of the path and licked its paw with its head cocked to one side, like an embarrassed guest at a cocktail party. Then, with her resolve hardened, she pressed once more on the bell. There was the sound of movement behind the door and the curtains in the window to the left were firmly drawn shut. As quietly as she could, Mirabelle pushed the letterbox open and peered through. An interior door with a glazed panel was closed. Behind it the vague shapes of the two women, one with light hair, dressed in green, one with dark hair, dressed in orange, receded down the hallway.

Mirabelle considered. There wasn't much she could do. They were entitled to not answer the door if they chose not to – she'd turned up unannounced, after all, and she didn't know them. But still, it would seem Uma and her friend were afraid of something. Perhaps disgruntled patients were a regular intrusion. Mirabelle withdrew a business card from her bag and scrambled to find a pencil. Then she wrote *I only want to talk* and popped the card through the letterbox, listening as it fell on to the tiled floor.

There was, it seemed, no point in waiting, but she found herself unwilling to leave. She turned. The street seemed quiet. The park opposite the run of houses was a uniform pale green compared to the peppery, warm tones of Nurse Uma's front garden. Mirabelle hovered for a few moments next to one of the rose bushes. Then she made the decision to cross the road.

A little way down the pavement, she slipped through the wrought-iron gate into the park and found a bench to sit on. Through the fence and the hedges she could still just make out the nurse's house. The red of the front door made it easy to spot through the foliage. She needed a moment or two, she realised, to process what had happened. She kept coming back to the picture in her head of the women's vague figures disappearing down the hallway, and to the blonde woman's strange comment. She clearly had assumed Mirabelle had been a patient or, presumably, given where Uma worked, a patient's mother. It was an odd assumption. Families were usually grateful to the medical staff who cared for them and their families. Nurses made patients comfortable, after all. When she had visited Vesta in hospital after she had given birth, the nurse's station was awash with thank-you cards; one, she had noted, was even from the grandmother of a child who had died.

She was about to get to her feet and go back to the office. After all, perhaps the women would reconsider and telephone. Just as she was turning, her eye was caught by movement through the leaves. The red door was momentarily obscured as a car pulled up in front of number seventeen. Mirabelle peered short-sightedly through the hedge. She got up and pushed her way through the branches so she could see more clearly. The car was a Jaguar – a blue one. A thin, dark-eyed man with a moustache got out and rang the doorbell. There was no reply. He checked his watch and rang again, this time for several seconds. Then he took his finger off the bell and pressed it one more time. Mirabelle had counted to fifteen before he stopped ringing. She would never have done something so churlish. Undeterred, the fellow opened the letterbox and shouted through it. She couldn't quite make out the words but he said something along the lines of 'I haven't got all day.'

A moment later, the door snapped open. The blonde stood on the threshold with her arms crossed. She didn't invite the man in, Mirabelle noted, as she strained to catch the woman's words. Luckily, his bell-ringing had riled her and she raised her voice. 'Jesus! You'll have to wait,' she said. The man's voice was lower and more difficult to make out, but Mirabelle managed a few of the words. 'You bloody dykes,' he snarled. 'You'll do as you're told.' His tone was threatening and he sounded as if he was from London – somewhere rough, she thought, where they didn't normally drive blue Jaguars. From inside the house, Uma appeared. She had changed into her nurse's uniform, and pushed past the blonde and down the path without saying goodbye. The man smirked. He handed over a small parcel to the grimacing woman in the doorway and then followed Uma to his car, where she meekly got into the back seat and waited for him to drive away.

'The women are lovers,' Mirabelle breathed. 'Of course.'

She craned, trying to read the number plate as the car receded, but the hedge was too dense. Instead, she turned her attention to the possible cause of such a visit. Where was Nurse Uma going in uniform, on her day off, she wondered. And in such curious company. As Mirabelle emerged, pushing the branches aside, a couple walking a Labrador glared at her. 'It's just a drunk woman in the shrubbery. Don't look, Cynthia,' the man said under his breath.

Mirabelle smoothed down her skirt and stalked back to the bench, taking her seat as elegantly as she could manage.

Questions were racing through her mind. What was in the parcel the man had handed over? Had the women known this man was on his way? Were the women being blackmailed because of their relationship? The law was murky for women who loved women, with prosecutions reserved for men who loved each other. But still, you wouldn't advertise it or want your family to know.

Mirabelle suddenly wished she had a whisky. She checked her watch. Vesta would be back by now, she thought as she hurriedly got to her feet. She should return to the office before going home to change for dinner. Maybe if she just let it settle, she'd manage to figure out what was going on. She certainly hadn't received the reception she had expected – unannounced or not. As she strode on to the pavement from the park, she cast a glance back at the house. The downstairs curtains were still closed.

Towards town, the streets became busier. The shops on St James's Street were crowded. The buildings were higgledy-piggledy in this part of town, the façades painted different colours. In the sunshine it felt quite continental. Mirabelle enjoyed the feeling of sun on her face. The bustle of Brighton up here, where the locals shopped, was one of the best things about the old place.

She was just striding out when she spotted Miss Brownlee on the other side of the street. She'd been so taken up by the mystery of Uma and her friend's behaviour that she hadn't even been looking. Panicked, Mirabelle ducked into a doorway and watched. Miss Brownlee's shopping basket was threaded solidly over her arm and her hair was covered in a gaudy rayon scarf. Mirabelle had sent her a red silk square two Christmases ago, but Miss Brownlee had never liked it. Almost directly opposite now, she stopped and chatted to a fishmonger in white wellingtons who was sweeping his doorstep – a broom in one hand and a rubber hose in the other. Rivulets of water tipped over the pavement's edge into the gutter. Miss Brownlee stepped back but, Mirabelle noted, did not stop talking.

Suddenly Mirabelle missed the green dining room and Miss Brownlee's warm, yeasty bread so much that she could almost taste it. The easy familiarity of dinner with Alan McGregor, her hand on his thigh beneath the table, felt like a loss. The fishmonger propped his brush against the window and went inside to fetch something. Mirabelle turned, not wanting to be spotted. She waited. Coming out, moments later, Miss Brownlee popped a parcel of fish wrapped in paper into her basket and turned in the direction of home.

Mirabelle stepped out again, pointedly ignoring the pub on the corner. It felt like sadness stalked her the minute she relaxed, but there was no way back. Miss Brownlee didn't know what Mirabelle knew about Alan McGregor. There was no point in becoming nostalgic for past times – she didn't regret leaving McGregor, she assured herself; it was only sentimentality. The truth was that he was entirely the wrong sort of man.

Chapter Thirteen

*Admiration and love are like being
intoxicated with champagne*

D r Williams picked Mirabelle up at eight o'clock sharp.
The sun had gone down and – outside the window –
the navy sky was punctuated by streetlights all the way along
the front. Mirabelle had had time for a steamy hot bath,
perfumed with a peach bubble bath that Vesta had insisted
she buy when they went up to London on their last shopping
trip before the baby had been born. 'It's so glamorous,' Vesta
had enthused, pointing out the gilded cap and the signature
on the bottle.

The last few months, as her stomach had grown larger and
larger, Vesta had craved glamour. She had bought high-heeled
shoes she couldn't wear with swollen ankles, and an array of
lipsticks. 'You should have that, Mirabelle,' she had insisted,
holding up the bubble bath to the light. It certainly smelled
nice, Mirabelle thought, though until now she'd hadn't had
occasion to use it. When she had dried herself, she chose
her outfit carefully – a peacock blue, tailored silk dress and
a pair of very high heels. As a finishing touch, she arranged
her hair in a chignon and then applied a splash of Italian
bergamot scent and a creamy spot of peach Dior on her lips.
She was pleased with what she saw as she checked herself
in the mirror, only just ready when the doorbell sounded.

She grabbed her angora stole as she opened the door, and as the doctor's gaze fell on her he let out a low whistle. When he kissed her cheek, he lingered and she let him. Then he wrapped the stole around her shoulders and she grabbed her clutch bag. 'Let's go,' he said.

The evening air was smooth on her skin. Chris drove along the front and pulled up outside the Old Ship Hotel. Mirabelle passed here almost every day but had never entered. At night, the doorman wore a top hat so shiny that it reflected the streetlights. He bowed as they passed, pulling the door out of their path. 'This way,' the doctor guided her, his hand steady on her back. The restaurant was only half full and they slipped into a table near the window. As she sat down Mirabelle smiled. It felt good to be here. The thick linen cloth and glinting tableware bespoke a treat ahead. The doctor ordered champagne without looking at the wine list.

'What were you thinking of having?' he asked.

'Steak,' she said.

'Not a vanilla slice?'

She shook her head.

He barely looked at the menu. 'The chef here is Swiss,' he said. Then he ordered pâté followed by fillet steak for both of them. 'Medium rare, all right?' She nodded.

When the waiter took away the menu, the doctor offered her a Dunhill cigarette from a smart silver case that was engraved with his initials.

'No, thank you.'

'You don't smoke?'

'Hardly ever.'

He closed the case with a decisive click, without availing himself of a cigarette. Then he raised his glass. 'To dinner with you.'

Mirabelle sipped. This man seemed entirely too smooth, but he was charming and far better dressed than the

118

superintendent had ever been. Miss Brownlee kept McGregor's clothes in good order, but he was no dandy. By comparison, Dr Williams enjoyed the cut of his jacket and the expertly knotted tie at his throat – she could tell. She cursed herself for allowing McGregor into her thoughts – really, it couldn't be helped. She'd better get it over with.

'Doctor Williams—' she started.

'Chris,' he cut in.

She paused. 'Chris. I feel I should tell you. I had a relationship before.'

'With Alan McGregor, you mean? He must be a fool to let you go.'

'He hasn't entirely. It's been over a year. I don't want to make things difficult for you at work.'

'Let me worry about that.'

'You'll come in for some stick. They think I am a kind of harpy at Bartholomew Square.'

'As I understand it, you're very efficient.'

'Compared to Inspector Robinson.'

'You do yourself down.'

She realised that she had and wondered why. She wasn't usually so coy.

The pâté arrived – a thick slab, sealed with butter, served with small rounds of toast. Beyond the window, the bright lights of the pier twinkled against the dark sky. Outlined by the low moon, Mirabelle made out figures promenading along the front – girls in pastel dresses striding out with men in dark jackets; a silent fashion show. Brighton felt exciting every evening of the year this close to the centre. People dressed up. Once she had genuinely worried about being able to breathe on the bus because there was so much hair lacquer on the air. That and the cigarette smoke.

'Where did you read medicine?'

Chris bit into a slice of toast to which he had liberally

applied the pâté. 'Bristol,' he said. 'I come from Bristol. Well, just outside. Then I went up to London and finished at Guy's.'

'You missed the war?'

'Not quite.'

She took this in. 'I'm thirty-eight years old, Mirabelle. Just ask, if you want to know.'

'I'm sorry.' She blushed. It seemed such bad manners.

'It's all right. It's on your mind. I look younger, I know. I shouldn't but I do.'

Mirabelle laughed.

'What?' his tone was insistent.

'You make yourself sound like some kind of hard-living Lothario.'

'Maybe I am hard living. Do you like your men dangerous?'

Her eyes slid across the tableau of the dining room. The sound of cutlery on porcelain accompanied the low hum of conversation. The scene was nothing if not civilised. She felt glad the nearest table wasn't close enough to hear their conversation. The doctor put down his knife.

'Next time, I see I'll have to take you to some dreadful dive. Would you prefer that?'

'I don't know,' she said honestly.

He laughed. Then sipped the champagne and leaned forwards, reaching for her hand. His touch was firm. He appeared quite unabashed by her frankness. She clasped his fingers and focused on his blue, blue eyes.

'I like you a lot already,' he said.

'Is that unusual for you?'

'Yes. Actually. Yes.'

'You go out with women you don't like?'

'Sometimes. I suppose.'

'Because they are beautiful?'

'And then I get bored. I don't suppose I will get bored with you.'

Mirabelle pushed away her plate. 'I'm not sure I can do this. Embark on it, I mean.'

'Really?'

'I'm not sure I want to.'

She blushed at her bluntness, but he brought it out in her. It had taken years before she had had a conversation even approaching this honest with McGregor. Chris filled her glass. 'Tell me, what did you do today?'

Mirabelle sipped. The champagne was refreshing. She wondered how much to tell him.

'You haven't given up on the case,' he surmised. 'The dead priest, that is.'

The waiter cleared away their half-eaten plates of food.

'No, I haven't. I visited one of the nurses from the home this afternoon.'

'Why?'

'The story doesn't make sense. Father Grogan's last hours, I mean. The sister comes to him before Vespers. She's desperately concerned about something. She confides in him. After the service he comes to the children's home. He and Sister Taylor go to the office and they argue for a long time. Nobody knows what they're arguing about. He is poisoned at some stage either before or after this argument. Then Grogan leaves. Sister Taylor is upset. She leaves. He dies. She disappears.'

'So, she poisoned him, right?'

'I don't know. She would have had to do it covertly, but she wasn't a covert kind of person. And there's no motive. What on earth were they arguing about?'

'Lovers' tiff?'

'I doubt it. There's no indication.'

'So did she help you? The nurse?'

'She wouldn't let me in. She wasn't expecting me. I almost felt as if they wanted to have a fight with me. There was something odd about it.'

Mirabelle felt his leg pressing against hers. His eyes flashed. 'I want to have a fight with you, Mirabelle. Then I want to make it up.'

She was about to move her leg, then she realised she didn't want to. She bit her lip and, slowly, she moved her hand underneath the table and laid it on his knee. Time stopped. He smiled. 'God,' he said. 'At this rate we'll never make dessert.'

The steak arrived. The waiter spooned vegetables and potatoes on to the plates – little wedges in different colours that had been fried in butter. Chris ordered mustard. They began to eat. Conversation stopped. People will think we're married, she thought. That I'm a doctor's wife. The idea amused her. She had never been taken for a wife before, not even when she was with Jack. It had always seemed so obviously a lie when they booked into hotels together, or, at least, something bigger than just matrimony.

When the steaks were finished, they drank the rest of the bubbly. Dr Williams's gaze slid across her collar bones and down, into her lap.

'Shall I get us a room?'

Mirabelle stopped breathing momentarily. 'Can't we go home?'

'My place is a real bachelor pad. It's a mess. I live in a mews. We're just round the corner from it, actually. But you're a lady.'

She liked that he knew he couldn't come back to hers.

'How many women have you taken to bed in this hotel?'

He blushed.

'Do you sign them all in as Mrs Williams?'

'I can't help that I've had women before.'

'Let's not do what you normally do.'

This, she reasoned, did not mean that she didn't intend to at least kiss him.

'Would you like something else to eat?'

She waved off the suggestion.

'Coffee?'

'Maybe. That would be nice.'

The waiter was on his way when Mirabelle's dilemma became theoretical. A plain-clothes policeman swung through the restaurant door, his profession obvious to anyone who had an eye for deduction. Mirabelle hadn't seen the man's face before, though she thought he must be a new detective constable. They'd taken on a few new people of late, she'd heard. The man approached the table.

'Doctor,' he said. 'I'm sorry. There's a body. Suspicious circumstances.'

Chris looked crestfallen. 'Really? That's the second time this week. I'm on call, Mirabelle. I didn't think there would be another death so soon. I'm sorry.'

Mirabelle wondered if he would be able to work. He'd drunk the best part of a bottle of champagne, but then, his patient would be dead.

'What happened?' she asked the constable. 'Is it the missing nurse?'

'Yes, fill me in,' the doctor said. It was an order and it made it feel as if discussing a case in public was normal.

The young officer looked round. He lowered his voice and bent towards them. 'The body was washed up on the tide. Two women found it. They screamed the pier down, practically – over by the aquarium.'

'Is the victim female?' Mirabelle couldn't help herself.

'It's not the nurse. A man,' the policeman said. 'Early fifties. Apparently he's in a pretty grim state. The body has been in the water a while.'

'Have you identified him?'

The policeman shrugged. He looked at Mirabelle sideways, clearly uncomfortable with her level of involvement. She cursed herself for pushing him too far.

'They have all the details at the scene,' he said to the doctor. Chris motioned for the bill. He thrust money at the waiter. 'You'll need a taxi,' he proffered a note across the table.

'I'll be all right,' Mirabelle said.

'Please. Take it.' He propped the money next to the salt.

The waiter brought the doctor's coat and Chris leaned in and kissed her cheek. 'I'll ring you,' he whispered. 'I'm sorry.' His hand lingered on her arm. She watched through the window as he made for his car. The scene was so close it was hardly worth driving to it, but then, she thought, he would need to go back to the morgue. The young detective constable slid into the front seat. When the car had disappeared completely, Mirabelle ordered a whisky with her coffee and drank both quickly before asking the waiter to fetch her stole. A woman on one of the other tables eyed her with pity before slipping her arm through her boyfriend's and laughing loudly. It was always the same in a restaurant if you were a woman on her own. As Mirabelle swept out, the waiter held the door for her.

Outside, along the front, Mirabelle pulled the stole around her shoulders and made for the vantage point of Marine Parade. Chris was already on the beach when she got there, his car abandoned outside the aquarium, the young officer nowhere to be seen. Two ambulances had drawn up on the pavement and several police officers in uniform were directing the public on to the other side of the road. A clutch of policemen hung around the railings at the top of the pebbles, smoking and staring down at the scene unfolding on the beach.

As Mirabelle crossed the road and made for the huddle of vehicles, a young officer on the cordon tried to stop her.

'Press,' Mirabelle said with authority. 'Superintendent McGregor said it would be all right. He asked for our help, actually, in appealing for information. I have a deadline to make.'

The boy hesitated and then stepped back. They really didn't train officers properly these days, she thought. At the railings an older policeman peered at her, recognition glimmering. She didn't meet his eyes, instead turning to stroll across to the parked vehicles. 'Hello,' she smiled, offering one of the ambulance drivers a mint from her purse. He took it gratefully.

'It's a man, I heard,' she said, striking up a conversation. 'Been in the water for a while.'

The driver shrugged. 'You from the *Argus*, then?' He sounded petulant.

She shook her head. 'I lied,' she whispered conspiratorially. 'I was only passing. I used to drive one of these old things during the war.' She slapped the side of the vehicle as if it was familiar. It was another lie, but she told herself it was justified. 'It was scary driving in the blackout during the Blitz. We ate all our carrots, I tell you that. You get an instinct for it. When I saw something going on, I couldn't stay away. Poor soul, eh? Him down there on the pebbles.'

'The fish have eaten the soft parts, one of the guys told me, but they know who he is. Jerry Bone. Bad Luck Bone.'

Mirabelle noted the name. She'd never heard of him. 'Drowned, I suppose?'

The man pouted. He didn't know. It occurred to her that nobody but Chris knew. Not yet.

'Two suspicious deaths in Brighton inside a couple of days,' Mirabelle kept the conversation going. 'I don't know what the world's coming to.'

'Two?'

'There was a priest died in Hove. Poison.'

'I heard that. One for heaven and one for hell, eh?'

'What do you mean?'

'Well, the priest – I assume – is in heaven. Bad Luck Bone on the other hand . . .'

'You knew him?'

'Lots of people knew him. Why do you think there are so many coppers about? Bad Luck by nickname, bad luck by nature. He was a bad lot. It won't be natural causes, let me tell you that.'

Mirabelle stood on tiptoes and craned to see what was happening on the stones. In the darkness it was difficult to make out much detail other than the shape of the huddle – Chris and a couple of officers and the body laid out, mostly obscured from view.

'I expect the police doctor is down there,' she said vaguely.

The ambulance driver acquiesced. 'I wish he'd hurry up. It's parky at night. It's September, after all.'

From further along, she noticed the older uniformed officer still watching her. It wouldn't take him long to remember who she was, and she didn't want to cause a fuss, so she said goodbye to the driver and retreated to the other side of the main road, where the public were congregating. Most people had been on a night out, it seemed, and the chat among the crowd was the same you'd hear in a bar. A man passed round a hip flask. A woman sang a snatch of a song, slurring the words – *The party's over, it's time to call it a day, They've burst your pretty balloon, And taken the moon away . . .*

The man beside her put an arm around her shoulder. 'That's it, just like Doris Day,' he said.

A few minutes later, two policemen carried up the body on a stretcher, covered with a grey woollen blanket. People strained to see. It was odd, Mirabelle always thought, the bleak impulse to see mutilation up close. She stood as far back as she could – there was no point in rubbernecking and she didn't want the doctor to spot her. There wouldn't have been much that Chris could do in the dark, she thought.

Inspector Robinson arrived, the siren on his Black Maria sounding, the last pulse of it a long moan as the car drew to a halt. Mirabelle shifted and turned sideways on to the street. It was easy to camouflage herself among the crowd. A man offered her a cigarette and she took it. The ambulance driver was right about the chill, she thought, as she puffed, watching the doctor return to his car, walking with Robinson, gesticulating as he went. He was so very good-looking that she felt a flush of pride. She relished watching him like this, without him knowing.

As he ducked into the driver's seat, she ground out the cigarette under the toe of her shoe and fumbled with her peppermints. The ambulance drove away and the doctor followed in his car. Robinson pointed in the direction of the beach and several of the uniformed men set off to search the pebbles.

Mirabelle pushed her way through the clutch of bodies. It was a straight walk along the front to get home. The crowd thinned as she crossed at the bottom of Old Steine, walking westwards. But then, when she got as far as the Old Ship Hotel, she paused. The doorman recognised her and tipped his top hat.

'Taxi, madam?'

'Yes. All right.'

He drew a whistle from his pocket and sounded it.

'It's a cold night. If you'd like to wait inside?'

'I'm fine.'

The whistle worked quickly and within a minute a cab pulled up. The doorman ushered Mirabelle into the back seat. 'Where to, madam?' he asked.

Mirabelle didn't hesitate as she slipped him sixpence. 'Tell the driver West Drive,' she said. 'Number seventeen. Right beside the park.'

Chapter Fourteen

Grief is the garden of compassion

You wouldn't think there was a murderer on the loose, Mirabelle thought, as the cab glided off silently. A woman in a yellow dress with a ruched underskirt ran across the street ahead of the cab, laughing. Turning left at the pier, a teenager pelted up the road trying to catch a bus, cigarette in his hand, his heavily Brylcreemed quiff static as the rest of him hammered along. In front of the aquarium, the crowd had thinned now the ambulance was gone. In a doorway a couple pressed their bodies together. It was getting late. Beyond St James's Street, the roads were darker. Lights glowed behind the curtained windows. The bins had been collected. Mirabelle noticed a football under one of the lampposts, abandoned by a child earlier in the day. The cab drew up on West Drive. 'Drop me over there. By the gate to the park,' she said.

The wrought-iron gate was locked. Mirabelle paid hurriedly and scrambled on to the pavement. The whisky and the champagne had gone to her head. It was almost as if she had drunk on an empty stomach. The taxi pulled off and left the street silent. Across the road, number seventeen lay in darkness. An owl hooted. Mirabelle's heels echoed as she crossed the road and crept up the path. The cat, she noted, was nowhere to be seen.

Gingerly, she set off down the short alleyway that ran down

the side of the house. The wooden gate at the bottom was bolted. She shook it as quietly as she could and ascertained the bolt was fitted on the other side and halfway down, where it was impossible to reach. The gate fitted snuggly and there was no manipulating it.

Sometimes the old-fashioned methods trumped a modern lock and key. She'd have to climb over. Securing her handbag under one arm, Mirabelle found a foothold in the bricks of the gatepost and pulled herself up. Then she peered over the top into the back garden. It wasn't what she had expected. While dark to the front, one or two lights were lit at the rear of the house – just enough to illuminate the patch of land beyond. The vivid red at the front was unusual, but the planting at the back was extraordinary. Even in the half-dark, it boasted a riot of colour.

Mirabelle squinted. There were plants she recognised – irises, lilies and roses. There were more, however, that were unfamiliar on the stretch of lush green, which was punctuated by purple, yellow, red and orange flowers, banked against the high walls. Closest to her, an overgrown herb patch was surrounded by a carefully trimmed, low bay hedge. Clouds of clary sage and pennyroyal in flower covered almost one side of it. In a small glasshouse, a bright burst of peacock flowers grew up a brick wall. The air was scented – was it lilac, she wondered.

Mirabelle stopped to take it all in. The effect was beautiful – tropical almost. From her vantage point she could see over the boundary fence where the neighbours had planted square stretches of lawn and tidy flowerbeds, carefully weeded. She pulled herself further up to get a better look when, ahead of her, she saw Uma, barefoot, coming out of the open French doors and into the little jungle which, Mirabelle surmised, she had created.

She wore a pink sari, which moved enticingly over her

hips as she walked. Her hair was plaited and tied. The light around Uma's frame brightened as a lamp turned on at the back of the house and the blonde woman followed her into the thick of the garden. The other woman wore dark slacks and a white shirt. Her hair was cut in a bob, shiny in the low light. Surrounded by flowers and leaves and herbs, the women kissed, holding each other. Their arms intertwined like vines, growing together. The scene had an ethereal beauty, almost as if the figures were living statues.

Mirabelle found herself entranced. It was seldom there was another place – something so different. This sense of peace was broken when Uma looked up and Mirabelle couldn't dodge her gaze. There was a moment during which the nurse took in what she had spotted and then her eyes lit with fury.

'What are you doing here?' she shouted.

The blonde woman spun around.

'I'm sorry,' Mirabelle started. 'I . . .' She tried to think why she had come all the way out here in the middle of the night. But there was no explanation except her curiosity and a desire not to go home. The questions that kept niggling. And, she supposed, a mixture of champagne and whisky. As she twisted at the top of the wall, her handbag tumbled into the planting below and disappeared into the lush foliage. She pulled herself up to climb over and retrieve it.

'Don't come down. You'll hurt the plants! Don't touch them!' Uma sounded furious or, maybe, Mirabelle realised, panicked. 'Go back over the other side,' she said, gesticulating. 'I'll open the gate.'

Mirabelle slid back on to the path. There was the sound of the bolt pulling back and then the two women appeared in the frame. They looked like negatives of each other, one dark and colourful, the other blonde and monochrome. The blonde held out Mirabelle's handbag.

'You can't come here, like this,' she spat. 'In the middle of the night. Spying on people. What the hell's wrong with you?'

'I'm sorry,' Mirabelle repeated. 'I didn't know you were in. The house was dark at the front.'

The blonde snorted. 'So you intended to break in? Is that what you're saying? That would be fine, would it?'

'I only want to ask some questions,' Mirabelle objected. 'That's what I wanted all along. I'm sorry if it's an intrusion. I didn't mean it to be. It's just some questions, that's all.'

The blonde took in a sharp breath as if she was about to launch into a tirade, but Uma laid her hand on the woman's arm. 'Ellen,' she said, 'it's all right. I might as well.'

'Are you sure?'

Uma nodded.

The blonde glared at Mirabelle, but she relented. 'Uma has told the police everything, you know. She's cooperated fully.' Her tone remained firm.

'And you are?'

'I'm Ellen Simpson.' The woman held out her hand.

'I'm not the police. But I have some questions. Mirabelle Bevan.'

The women stepped back from the gate to allow her to enter.

'Simpson? I understood you were married to a Dr Simpson, Uma? But . . .'

The white woman laughed. It was the kind of weary laugh that escaped Vesta's lips sometimes when people made assumptions about the colour of her skin. 'I'm Dr Simpson,' she said. 'We both use the surname, that's all.'

Mirabelle felt mortified. 'Oh heavens,' she cut in. 'I'm so sorry. What a stupid mistake. I mean, we need more women doctors. I apologise.'

Uma stood to one side, shielding the plants as she waved Mirabelle through.

'Come in,' she said as Ellen spun on her heel and led the way.

'My, your garden is beautiful,' Mirabelle tried. 'What a display. What did you mean about the plants? Not hurting them?'

'We're medical people, Miss Bevan.'

It flashed through Mirabelle's mind that Father Grogan had been killed using strychnine, though she was sure the poison was difficult to make. It came from tree bark, if she recalled correctly, and would require a larger glasshouse than the one in place here. She would need to check.

As they rounded the side of the house, she smiled. The garden felt exotic – almost like some kind of dream. Dr Simpson hovered at the back door. 'Uma's been very upset,' she said. 'Since Father Grogan died. That's why I didn't let you in this afternoon. And we were busy. She wasn't expecting you.'

'Stop talking about me as if I'm not here, Ellen.'

The doctor relented and Mirabelle moved across the doorstep as if by default. Inside, the carpet – she noticed – was red, woven in an ornate pattern. On a beautifully carved coffee table sat a copy of Narayan Sanyal's *Bakultala P. L. Camp* and an album of black-and-white photographs open at an Indian street scene. The low sofas were scattered with cushions of Indian silk edged with thick strips of brocade.

'This is lovely,' she said. 'So colourful.'

Ellen closed the doors and languidly glided across the room. A large yucca plant in a bronze, hand-beaten pot grew as high as the cornice.

'We brought everything with us when we left,' she said. 'Everything we could. Would you like a drink?'

'Yes, please. Scotch if you have it.'

The doctor tidied her hair, slipping a stray lock behind her ear. She poured a Scotch and topped up the two gins with tonic that already lay on the table. Uma sank on to the cushions and wrapped her fingers around her glass.

'Where did you live?' Mirabelle asked, looking around.

'In India? How many places do you know in India? How many could you point out on a map?' Ellen's tone was facetious.

'Not many, I suppose.'

'Delhi. We were just outside Delhi.'

'In 1948? At the time of the partition?'

'We left a little before. We ran a clinic. It's how we met each other.'

Uma made a tutting sound, as if telling Ellen to be quiet. Mirabelle waited, but neither of them said anything else.

'Well,' she said. 'I have some questions about what happened at the children's home the other day.'

Uma nodded. 'All right.'

'What time do you finish work normally?'

'About seven. When the children go to bed. Most weeks I cover the night shift a couple of times. But I wasn't on shift the night that Father Grogan died.'

'Night shifts must be tiring.'

'Most medics do them,' Ellen said. 'It's normal for us.'

'On the day Father Grogan died were you at the home later than normal, Uma?'

Uma nodded.

'Why?'

'They were arguing. We all stayed. It was an odd situation.'

'So the father came to pick a fight with Sister Taylor? Is that what you're saying?'

Uma nodded again. 'I suppose so,' she said and sipped her drink.

'Do you know what they argued about?'

'No.'

'That's my problem. I can't figure it out. Sister Taylor had come to see the father before Vespers at the church, you see. They had already spoken, yet afterwards he went down to the home to pick a further argument with her. Is that what you're saying?'

'I don't know why he came. I was there but I didn't hear anything other than the shouting.'

'But you stayed.'

'We all stayed.'

'Where?'

'What do you mean?'

'I'm trying to place everyone. Where did you stay? Where did they fight?'

'They were in the office,' Uma said slowly, as if reasoning her answer. 'Nurse Frida, Nurse Berenice and I were in the hallway. We were concerned about the children, you see. The upset.'

'And then Father Grogan left?'

'Yes.'

'And Sister Taylor?'

'Shortly afterwards. She had been crying, I think. She was pink under her eyes.'

'You have a lovely cat.' Mirabelle changed tack. 'I saw him this afternoon.'

'Ginger?' Uma's eyes lit.

'You like animals?'

'Always have.'

'Do many patients visit you at home?'

'What do you mean?'

'When I was at the door this afternoon, Ellen said "it's not Uma's fault", as if she knew why I had come. As if it was common. Do many patients come to see you at home?'

'That's not what I meant!' the doctor interjected. 'Poor Uma has been upset, that's all. She's been blaming herself.'

'Why would it be your fault?'

Uma's finger pawed the glass. 'It isn't.'

'She's too conscientious, that's all.'

'And you like gardening?'

Uma nodded. 'On my day off. It's relaxing. I've always liked plants. And gardens.'

'It doesn't make sense to me. What happened to Father Grogan.'

'Does murder ever make sense?'

Mirabelle sipped the whisky. She felt alert. 'Yes. Almost always,' she said crisply. 'Even if what makes sense is some-body's passion – something that is essentially nonsensical. But I can't see whose passion might have killed Father Grogan. That's my stumbling block. I feel there's more to it.'

'More?'

'Is somebody blackmailing you?'

'What do you mean?'

'I saw you kissing. In the garden.'

Ellen rolled her eyes. Uma averted hers.

'I saw the man who came this afternoon. After I'd left,' Mirabelle kept pressing.

Ellen sprang to her feet. 'That's enough. Look, you can't come in here and ask about that kind of thing.'

'What kind of thing?'

'We have a right to privacy. The law in this country doesn't cover our particular perversion, Miss Bevan. As it is we live together, we share my name – because having a white name is easier – and the postman and the grocer and all the people we deal with assume we're Dr and Mrs Simpson – a man and a woman – and that's just fine. So if you want to go public and tell the neighbours, fire ahead.'

Mirabelle shook her head. 'I'm not threatening you. I merely asked if someone else might be.'

'Uma didn't kill Father Grogan.'

'But, Uma, do you know who did?'

135

Uma put down her glass. 'Ellen is right. I've told you what I know. I'm just a nurse. That's all. I think it's time you left.'

Mirabelle took a moment, putting down her glass slowly and gathering her things. 'And you don't have any idea what happened to Sister Taylor?'

Uma didn't reply.

'Did you know her well?'

'Quite well, I suppose,' the nurse said quietly.

'They're painting her as a murderer at the police station. I didn't know the sister but I don't think she could have killed somebody. That's my sense of her. That she was a moral person.'

Uma shrugged. 'Do we ever know anybody?' she asked. 'I mean, really know them and what they're capable of?' She pointed at the door.

'What do you mean?'

'I mean, we can't tell what somebody will do. What they might be like in difficult circumstances. I can't help you, Miss Bevan. I'm sorry.'

Mirabelle left through the hallway this time. The cat was asleep under a radiator. As the front door closed behind her, she decided to walk back to town. Far off she could hear a church bell chiming. She counted carefully. It was eleven o'clock. As she turned down West Drive she glanced back at the house. Mirabelle hadn't had a home for a long time – not a real one, not since Jack. Places and people didn't mean so much to her these days, but she could still recognise love when she saw it. And the women kissing in the garden would have done anything for each other. Maybe somewhere, just beyond her reach, out there among the jungle plants, there was a motive. She just had to think things through. As she set off southwards she realised she wasn't tired, but both of those women, it came to her, were exhausted. And she didn't know why.

Chapter Fifteen

*Between men and women there is
no friendship possible*

Chris had said his place was just round the corner from the Old Ship Hotel – a mews. Half an hour later, back towards the front, Mirabelle walked past the closed shops circling the area to the rear of the hotel building. This close to town there weren't many flats, and this late at night most upper floors above the shops were in darkness. Her heels echoed on the paving stones. At the top of the road a man stumbled out of a pub, still serving after hours. He was singing some terrible army song she vaguely recognised. She hung back until he had turned the corner at the top of the street and silence descended once more. It must be near here, she thought. She just had to be methodical.

It didn't take long in the end. Brighton boasted a labyrinth of interconnected alleyways where the horses and carriages of the wealthy used to be housed. Now the stables were garages mostly. Some boasted two storeys with an old hayloft over the stable. This one was on a dead end just off Russell Road. As Mirabelle turned off the main street, the cobbles she stepped on to were not as regular as usual. The alley had not been well maintained and individual stones were raised, like teeth in an uneven smile. There was a huge pothole at one end and, at the edges, in the absence of a pavement, moss furred the stones. On a rainy night it would be treacherous in heels but luckily it was dry.

Mirabelle set off. Only two of the garages had been converted into living quarters, she realised. The rest housed cars, by the look of them. A tower of empty oilcans was piled beside one door. Another had glass panes fitted in a vertical line, some of which had been smashed, leaving a chessboard effect of ragged, dark spaces. Of the two houses, side by side, one was currently occupied. The sound of a gramophone playing music emanated from it, along with a thick wash of light where the curtain hadn't been fully drawn. This gap illuminated a slice of the cobblestones and the front door, which was newly painted in British racing green and bordered by three chipped terracotta pots of dry-looking rosemary. The high tone of a woman's laughter cut into the night air over the music. Mirabelle positioned herself so she could see through the crack in the curtains. Inside, the walls of the mews had been plastered and painted pale pink. A man and a woman were playing cards at a table with a half-empty bottle of rum beside them. She felt a buzz of relief and turned her attention to the mews next door.

The house was in darkness but, as she got closer, she could make out that the nameplate said Dr C. Williams in engraved script. She trailed her fingertips over his name. Ahead, there was a parking area, she realised, just the right size for Chris's car. It was bounded by two largish boulders. Double-checking over her shoulder that there was nobody to see, she put up her hand to block out the light from next door and peered through the doctor's window. Inside, it was pitch black, and the most she could make out was the vague shape of furniture. Clearly, he was working late.

She considered using her SOE lock picks to gain entry, but decided against it. Chris wasn't a suspect and, despite her exploits climbing walls and fences only an hour or two before, she knew she should extend the respect she'd demand from him if the tables were turned. If he'd broken into her flat, she'd be furious, so instead she leaned against one of the boulders and waited. She told herself it was because she wanted to know about the dead body, but the truth was far more complicated. She wondered when she'd turned into the kind of woman who would behave so brazenly. She tracked her progress. It had been coming a long time. It was after McGregor. After she'd met Lali. It was probably the moment Chris kissed her the day before. It felt as if she had changed.

It was almost midnight when the car turned the corner, its lights blinding. The engine cut out as it pulled up abruptly in the spot between the boulders. The lights dimmed and Chris opened the door. Then he spotted her.

'Hello,' he said. He sounded weary.

'I'm not here because I want . . .' Mirabelle's voice trailed. 'It's only . . .' she tried again and failed, cursing herself for not planning something to say that would make sense of her presence. She'd had time, after all.

He laughed, keys dangling in his hand. 'Red rag to a bull, I suppose, telling you that my place wasn't up to much. Well, don't say I didn't warn you. I could use a nightcap. How about you, darling?'

Inside, he threw his keys on to a side table and snapped on a lamp. He had not underplayed his housekeeping skills.

'It's clean,' Mirabelle said hopefully as he closed the door and directed her towards a comfortable-looking sofa upholstered in chocolate-brown velvet.

'I have a woman who does. She sorts out my clothes and cleans the place. I'm not tidy, that's the thing.'

Mirabelle cast her eyes over the piles of papers and magazines and decided that was an optimistic understatement. Some of the sheaves of printed paper were comprised of copies of the *Lancet*. Others were piles of salmon-pink racing newspapers. There were several of these and beside them a tottering tower that seemed to be solely made up of issues of the *Financial Times* – a different kind of wager. Chris was a man who liked taking risks, she decided with a frisson. And a man of science, too.

She felt herself relax. The place might be untidy but it felt familiar – it put her in mind of her own flat before fire had engulfed it a couple of years ago and Vesta had redecorated. Her old drawing room had been peppered with several piles of the *Argus*. She had found herself unable to fling them away. Afterwards, one of the firemen had told her off – they'd been a fire risk, he'd said, as if the blaze that had started had been her fault, which it wasn't.

Chris extracted a green bottle of spirits from the sideboard. He moved to what might loosely be termed the kitchen area and put his hand on two cut-crystal glasses, pouring generous measures of honey-coloured liquid.

'Thank you.' She warmed her lips on the whisky.

'So, you like crosswords, I take it?' Chris's tone was familiar. He was teasing her.

'You think it's just any puzzle? I knew Father Grogan. I have a duty. I'm the one who found his body.' She knew she sounded earnest, but she couldn't help herself.

'Fair enough,' he said. 'And you're here because . . .'

'I didn't want to go home,' she admitted. 'I find you confusing. Or maybe intriguing is a better word.'

Chris sat next to her on the sofa. She felt her skin prickle. 'Good,' he said.

He stroked her hair and ran his hand down her cheek. 'It's late,' he whispered as he kissed her neck.

'I don't want to go to bed with you. Not yet,' she replied.

It flashed through Mirabelle's mind that, once, a prostitute had told her that her favourite clients were doctors. They knew what to do, the girl had said. Chris seemed to fall into that category. He removed the whisky from her hand, and pinned her wrist to the sofa. She could feel how strong he was. For a moment, she let herself go and kissed him. Then she pushed him away. He put up his hands in surrender.

'I wouldn't,' he said. 'But I want you to know that you're the most attractive woman I've ever met. I thought it the moment I saw you.'

'On the floor of the lavatory, covered in bruises, unconscious and next to a dead man.'

'Yes. Even then.'

She took his hand. He lay his head on the back of the sofa and let out a sigh.

'Tired?'

'A little. It's not easy.'

'Did you come straight from the post-mortem?'

He laughed. 'Yes.'

'The gangster?'

'How did you know?'

'They were talking about it – along the front. I followed you. I was curious.'

'Followed me?'

'How long do you think he'd been dead?'

Chris's brow furrowed. 'Do dead people turn you on, Mirabelle? Is that what it is?'

'No.' She sounded shocked.

He seemed to accept her answer, though for a second she doubted it herself. Jack Duggan. Alan McGregor. Now Chris Williams. She was certainly fascinated by danger.

The doctor took a sip of whisky. He leaned back, put his arm around her and began to talk about his night. 'It's difficult to tie down the cause of death sometimes, that's the thing. He had a bad heart, poor bastard. It's not surprising. He was overweight and his liver was in a state. Do you mind me talking like that?'

'Not at all. It's interesting. Didn't he drown?'

'There wasn't any seawater in his lungs. Not a drop. And he went into the water days ago. Water corrodes evidence. He looked a little like your friend, come to think of it.'

'Father Grogan?'

'Yes. His skin was livid. It's the water again. I can't tell how he died. Not yet. It feels like a heavy responsibility and they rely on me to figure out as much as I can. But there was nothing obvious. Nobody caved the poor guy's head in, stabbed him or shot him. That much I can rule out. I'll run more tests tomorrow.'

Mirabelle slipped off her shoes. The heels toppled with a dull clunk on to the carpet. She put down her drink. 'Tomorrow's hours away. The morning, I mean.'

'Well, if we're not going to bed.' He loosened his tie. 'Let's not talk about all this Jerry Bone stuff – it's grim. Let's just lie here.' He reached to turn out the light. In the dark she curled around the length of his body and he kissed her forehead. The moon cast a slice of light across the room. A window open somewhere let in a thin shaft of fresh air. She breathed in the smell of him – the faded trace of an expensive cologne, a tinge of metallic sweat and the sting of whisky fumes. It had been a long time since she'd been held like this.

'Your place looks better in the dark,' she said.

She felt him smile. He laid his hand in the small of her back. She put her head on his chest so she could hear his heart. She thought about asking him more about the post-mortem but somehow she couldn't form the words. He kissed her and then he kissed her again. Her confusion dimmed like a lamp running out of oil. It was unaccountably peaceful and it didn't take long before they were both fast asleep.

Though Mirabelle was used to the sound of seagulls, her flat was on the first floor, the road at the front was tarmacked and cars passed, if not silently, then at a low rumble. It was early, she supposed, when she snapped awake as a sports car shot past, the sound like thunder rattling the window frames. Cobblestones, she thought as she shifted and the silence settled once more. Sunlight filtered in from the back of the mews in stripes that reached across the floor and along the furniture. She raised her head and realised there were Venetian blinds. Two gulls were calling to each other somewhere very close. Chris opened his eyes. He wound his arm around her shoulder. 'Sleep all right?'

'Yes.'

He kissed her neck, nuzzling her collarbone. She pulled back, despite herself. The intimacy of the night before felt uncomfortable, as if falling asleep had reset matters on a more formal basis than when they were last conscious.

Chris ran a finger down her forearm and raised her fingers to his lips. He kissed the flat of her hand and then bit the fleshy part between her thumb and forefinger. 'Coffee?' he offered.

She nodded.

He rolled off the sofa and pulled a stovetop espresso pot from the cupboard. His hair was out of place and his shirt crumpled. She felt a strong pull towards him but she resisted.

'What else have you got in there?'

'Everything I need. Whisky. Good coffee. And breakfast. It's a magical cupboard.'

He laid a packet of macaroons on the surface while he busied himself with the coffee. The smell of it brewing quickly overtook her. It was bright outside – the beginning of another sunny day. This place looked, she thought, as if it had been searched by the police. The bedroom must be upstairs. She wondered what it was like. The mews would drive Sister Taylor to madness, she smiled, remembering the tidy, tiny bedsit with everything in exacting order.

'I can see why you prefer the Old Ship Hotel when you're out with a lady.'

'We can get a room there, whenever you're ready. There's no rush. The Royal Suite, if you'd like it. Or another hotel. Anything for you, Miss Bevan. I'm at your service.' He saluted.

She wondered exactly what this man had done in the military, and if he'd seen action, but decided not to ask. Instead she ran a hand through her hair and slid around the side of the sofa. The pot began to bubble as she kissed him. As she broke away he held her gaze, poured two small cups of inky espresso and opened the macaroons.

'Breakfast is served,' he said as a newspaper fell through the letterbox on to the mat.

'Mmm.' Mirabelle sipped and felt the bitter taste spread on her tongue. 'That's good.'

'I lived in Italy for six months. I can't bear watery English instant any more. Or chicory. Jesus. What are you doing today?'

'Work, I suppose.'

'What is your work exactly?'

'I own a debt recovery agency. McGuigan & McGuigan. The office is at the bottom of East Street.'

'That is a very unusual job for a lady.'

'I fell into it.'

'After the war?'

'Which was in no way as interesting as your war, I'm sure. Italy?'

'Only for a few months. I was in charge of a field hospital.'

'And you'll be cutting up Bad Luck Bone today. I hope you can figure out why he died.'

'You know what they say about pathologists?'

'What's that?'

'We have an infinite capacity for suspicion. I'll get there in the end.'

Mirabelle kissed him again. This time he tasted of coffee.

'I suppose I should get going,' she said, lifting a macaroon.

'I could call a taxi for you.'

'It's a nice morning. I'll be fine.'

'Mirabelle, can we try again? I mean, dinner.'

'At the Ship?'

'Anywhere you like.'

'Yes,' she said. 'That would be good.'

'I know an Italian place towards Hastings.'

'Well, that's fitting. Italian it is, then.' She bit into the macaroon and headed for the sunshine outside.

He watched from the doorway with the coffee cup in his hand, as Mirabelle picked her way down the cobbles. She squinted, annoyed that she hadn't brought her sunglasses the night before – not that she could have known. The sun was so bright you'd think it was springtime. The world seemed hopelessly optimistic. She glanced back as she rounded the corner on to the main road and he raised a hand.

At the front, she couldn't decide which way to turn. It was still early, she realised, and she was overdressed for the office, but it seemed a palaver to head home just to change. Instead, she crossed Kingsway and stood enjoying the sunshine. The teashops were opening and the smell of baking bread wafted on the air. Behind her a young lad was winding down a candy-striped canopy over a shop window.

As she reached the bottom of East Street, she saw there were still two bobbies on duty on the other side of the pier, where the ambulances had gathered the night before. It was pleasant, walking, so she continued.

'Good morning, officer,' she said cheerily.

'Miss Bevan,' the man greeted her. 'Can I help you?'

'I just wondered if you'd found anything.'

'If we had, miss, it would be evidence, and you're a member of the public.'

'It seems strange you're still here.'

'Tides,' the policeman said after a short pause. 'What isn't washed up on one might be washed up the next. We didn't want anyone to get a fright this morning.'

'You think there might be more bodies?'

'Oh no, miss. I didn't say that.'

'Was part of him missing? Mr Bone, I mean?'

'There's nothing to concern yourself with, miss. Nothing at all. We're only here as a precaution.'

Mirabelle let out a sigh of frustration. 'But I am concerned,' she said stubbornly.

The policeman, however, would give her nothing more, and she decided there was limited information to be gained simply watching the officers walking along the foreshore with their eyes on the pebbles. Instead, she turned towards East Street.

In the office she stared at the kettle momentarily, before dismissing the idea of putting it on to boil. It seemed almost sacrilegious not to make tea, but these days she realised she was doing several things against the grain. She checked her appearance in the mirror and carefully combed her hair. It made her think of Chris stroking her head on the sofa the night before in the dark, and the taste of strong coffee mingled with sweet macaroon. Suddenly, it felt too shady to be inside. She switched on all the lights and, without considering too carefully, reached for the telephone directory.

Bone was a more common surname than she had suspected, and the directory ran to three pages of them. Still, if the dead man had a telephone, which wasn't a given, he'd be here. Jerry, the man had said. There was a string of J. Bones in the Brighton area. 'Jerry. Jeremy,' she said, and then ran a finger down the listings and checked the addresses. Then she checked them again. 'Or G,' she considered, and checked those.

Now, that was interesting, she thought as she sat back in her chair and rifled her drawer for the map of Brighton. 'It can't be right,' she said under her breath. But she checked the telephone directory one more time and it was. If it was him, it was G. Bone. Gerald, perhaps. Quickly she scribbled a note and left it on Vesta's desk before locking the office door behind her and clattering down the stairs. Her heart was pounding as she tried to piece together what she'd found and make sense of it.

Outside, a van had pulled up at the kerb and a man in a brown apron was reaching into the back.

'Is McGuigan & McGuigan up there?' he asked over his shoulder. 'An office, is it?'

'Yes,' said Mirabelle, scarcely stopping. 'Debt Recovery. There's nobody in. They'll be here any minute, I expect.'

The man closed the van door, a large bouquet of white and yellow roses over his arm. 'For a Miss Bevan,' he announced. 'Would that be right?'

Mirabelle came to a halt. 'Is there a card?'

The man proffered the bouquet so she could see it. Smartly, Mirabelle picked the little envelope out of the flowers. She didn't want to waste time. 'Leave it at the top of the stairs. At the door,' she said. 'They'll look after it when they get in.'

Then she turned up the pavement and made her way towards the main road to catch a bus. The one that ran up Dyke Road, if she remembered correctly. Back in the direction of Hove.

Chapter Sixteen

The gods are too fond of a joke

Tongdean Avenue looked as upmarket as ever it had in the spring of the year before when Mirabelle had first visited. The area, two miles from the front, consisted almost exclusively of detached houses with large gardens that were mostly occupied by families. The children were back at school by now, but Mirabelle spotted the signs of a well-spent summer – roller skates abandoned under a bush, and a tree-house she was sure hadn't been in place the last time she'd been up here. Halfway up the street, a Silver Cross pram sat on one of the lawns with its cover raised and a baby asleep inside. After Uma's garden, nothing would ever seem quite as bright, but the green plots along the avenue made a brave attempt. Several of the houses were painted white, which lent a summertime feel, and the beds were planted with bright yellow and white flowers with dark, glossy leaves. It seemed, she realised, more than a year since she had first set foot on this pavement, in the days she was still connected to McGregor. She'd been told about the house by her friend Fred, who had now been dead for more than sixteen months, she counted carefully. Him and his son.

Outside a brick-built, five-bedroom property on the corner she came to a halt. Last year there had been a scatter of forlorn-looking irises poking through the muddy ground, but now they had been removed and the low privet hedge had grown so that it almost obscured sight of the front door. The house's lead-paned windows remained discreetly shielded by prim white net curtains, and the front gate was closed. Of all the properties on the street, it looked the least welcoming by far. Mirabelle considered the irony of this for moment. Then she pushed open the gate and rang the front doorbell.

In due course, the door was answered by a maid in an ill-fitting dark wig. Last year the old woman had worn a housecoat that Mirabelle had considered too young for her. Today, however, she wore a more mature plain green apron as she peered short-sightedly across the threshold.

'Good morning,' Mirabelle said. 'I don't suppose you remember me?'

The woman made a harrumphing noise that neither denied nor confirmed any recognition.

'I'm looking for Jinty,' Mirabelle said. 'Is she at home?'

'It's twirly,' the woman replied, sucking her false teeth.

'Excuse me?'

'Twirly. She's not up yet.'

'Ah. Too early. The thing is, I wanted to speak to someone about Mr Bone.'

The woman's blue eyes narrowed. They were so watery that Mirabelle almost expected tears to run down her plump, thick-skinned cheeks, squeezed out under the pressure. The maid appeared to be in the process of deciding whether to acknowledge that she knew the name.

'Gerry Bone. Bad Luck Bone, as I think he was known.' Mirabelle left the poor woman nowhere to hide.

'You best not,' the maid said at last. 'There's nobody here.'

'No one at all? Couldn't you wake Jinty? I think she'd want to speak to me about this. Really I do.'

But the maid didn't reply. Instead she stepped away from the door and closed it in Mirabelle's face.

'Well, really,' said Mirabelle.

With a sigh, she cut back down on to the main road, slightly wearily, and made for the nearest phone box where she dialled the number she'd looked up earlier. It rang out for almost a minute before a woman's voice picked it up. It wasn't the maid, that much was clear.

'Yes, darling,' a glamorous voice said. 'What can I get you?'

'Hello. I need to speak to Jinty, please,' Mirabelle replied. 'It's her sister.'

'Hold on, ducks. She's still sleeping, I think. Do you want me to get her to ring you back?'

'If you wouldn't mind fetching her. I'm sorry to trouble you.'

'Mum sick again is she?' the girl sounded sympathetic.

Mirabelle didn't like to implicate Jinty's mother, but she didn't have to because, before she could speak, the voice disappeared; a minute or so later, Jinty picked up the handset.

'Hello. Peggy?'

'God. I'm sorry. It's Mirabelle, Jinty. Do you remember me?'

'Mirabelle?' the voice sounded unsure.

'We went to that party down the coast.' Mirabelle realised that this probably wasn't the best way to describe herself – Jinty went to a myriad of glittering parties. 'You showed me the ropes. I was considering . . . joining the team. Last year.'

Jinty squealed. 'Mirabelle! How nice to hear from you? Changed your mind, have you?'

'I came to the door but your maid turned me away, just now.'

'Oh, she's like that in the mornings.'

'Could I come up and see you?'

'Of course. Come round the back. I'll let you in.'

Mirabelle walked back up the avenue. Down the side of the house, the gate to the back garden was unlocked. She pushed it open, stopping as soon as it creaked, and slipped through the gap that had been afforded. The back garden was well kept. A large willow tree dominated, with most of the rest laid to lawn. Mirabelle surveyed the windows on the first floor. Three were shielded by drawn curtains. She waited for a moment or two, enjoying the sun. Then one of the curtains shifted and a slice of a woman's face appeared between sheaves of cream fabric printed with huge pink roses. As far as Mirabelle could make out, she was wearing pale blue satin pyjamas and her hair was in rollers. It wasn't Jinty. The woman was black. She opened the window and leaned out.

'Are you Mirabelle?' she said.

Mirabelle nodded. The girl called back into the house. 'She's there,' and then disappeared without opening the curtains. A minute later the back door opened and Jinty stood, rubbing her eyes. Her hair was pinned up in seeming disarray.

'Belle!' she shouted delightedly, as if she had run into Mirabelle at a party. 'When the phone went early Tanya thought you were some desperate fella. We get some mad ones, you know. Deranged bastards. So, are you here to reconsider?'

'I don't have the nerve,' Mirabelle admitted. 'But I do want to speak to you. About Mr Bone – if you don't mind.'

Jinty ran a hand over her head, feeling for the rollers that were haphazardly pinned into her hair. She began to pick them out, shoving the hairpins in the corner of her mouth as she removed them into the pocket of her cream cotton dressing gown. 'We heard last night,' she said. 'The rozzers were here. The place cleared quicker than when the wife comes home. Come in then.'

Jinty stepped back, almost tripping over her fluffy white slippers. With the rollers gone, her hair fell in a perfect arc, with just the right amount of curl. She directed Mirabelle through a short lobby and into an old-fashioned kitchen.

'I'm sorry if I woke you,' Mirabelle apologised.

'It's all right. I got to bed earlier than usual. Want a cuppa?'

Inside, the kitchen smelled of stale alcohol, and the maid glowered as she emerged from the pantry.

'Don't be silly, Doris. Don't you remember Belle?'

Doris didn't speak, only passed by with a duster in her hand. Jinty ignored her and made to put on the kettle. She reached for a tin of tea and sorted some cups on the table. The scene was oddly domestic for a brothel.

'How have you been?' Mirabelle asked. It wasn't only out of politeness. Mirabelle realised that she cared about what happened to the girl. Jinty was always cheerful but her chosen profession wasn't easy. Mirabelle should have come back earlier, she realised. She'd been remiss.

The girl scooped tea leaves into a glazed, earthenware teapot and poured on hot water. 'Fun and games. You heard what happened last year?'

Mirabelle nodded. Jinty's boss, Ernie Davidson, had been murdered. Mirabelle didn't tell Jinty that she had been present when it happened. It seemed, she realised, an occupational hazard for the men associated with this house, now she came to think about it.

'And Mr Bone?' she put the question. 'Do you know anything about it?'

Jinty sounded light-hearted. 'Different kettle of. Gerry wasn't our boss. I've been running the place, truth be told, ever since Ernie died. I'm the management. Can you believe it?' She laughed.

'That's odd. This place is down as Bone's address. That's how I made the connection.'

'Oh that? They had to put a bloke's name in the directory, didn't they? I mean, if the punters think it's all women . . . No.

Gerry Bone was single, is all. None of the married fellas wanted their name on it. Can't blame them, if you think about it.'

'So he didn't really live here?'

'That didn't stop the police pitching up, of course. Geniuses. They know. But they have to hit the bases, if you see what I mean.'

'They know?'

'Sure.'

Mirabelle tried to form a question that did not involve Superintendent McGregor's name. Jinty stirred the tea in the pot, which, Mirabelle realised, hadn't been properly warmed. The girl struck the spoon twice on the lip and replaced the lid with a decisive click before pouring immediately. The making of tea was not one of Jinty's greatest accomplishments.

'But you knew Mr Bone?' Mirabelle checked.

'Yes. Of course.'

'Was he a customer?'

'Not mine. But yes and no. He was one of Davidson's cronies. We have to have protection, Belle. It's got to come from somewhere.'

'So, Mr Bone provided protection, did he?'

'Bone and others.'

'You pay for that?'

'Of course we pay for it. What do you think? It's a good job this place is a little gold mine. I've got six girls working out of here. We've got it cosy. No blokes about 'cept the obvious ones. We look after each other. Listen, what's on your mind? He wasn't your fella, was he?'

'Bone? No.'

'Good. He was a tough nut. A bit of a bully, truth be told. And fat.'

Jinty sat down and stirred her cup of weak tea, adding several spoonfuls of sugar. She proffered the bowl in Mirabelle's direction, but it was declined.

'I took your advice, actually,' Mirabelle admitted.

'Really? I can't remember what I said.'

'You said that doctors were . . . you know, good lovers.'

'I can see you with a doctor!' Jinty sounded delighted. 'Nice, is he?'

'I don't know yet. Dr Williams. Chris Williams. He works with the police. Don't tell me he's a customer.'

Jinty shook her head. 'I've never heard of him.'

Mirabelle was surprised at her relief. It was Jinty last year who had told her about McGregor's interest in one of the girls who lived here. The moment remained vivid in her memory. It had been horrifying.

'I'm glad you don't know him,' she said.

Jinty hooted and then sipped her tea with a loud slurp. 'So why are you interested in Bone?'

'I was there last night, out for dinner with the doctor, actually, when his body washed up on the front. Right at the aquarium.'

Jinty turned up her nose. 'Must've put you off your meat and two veg.'

'Well, I wasn't on the beach. Only nearby. But I looked up his address, saw he lived here and thought . . .' Mirabelle's voice trailed. What had she thought? Why had she considered this her business? The kitchen clock ticked past nine.

'You're just curious, that's all,' Jinty said sagely. 'I think you have a bit of the wildcat in you, Belle.'

'Maybe.' Mirabelle smiled. 'It's been something of a week.'

'Really?'

'Mr Bone wasn't the only death. I had a friend who died. Well, not so much a friend as an acquaintance. Father Grogan. I don't suppose you know him?' Mirabelle lifted the tea to her lips, not expecting a reply.

'Course I do.' Jinty's voice was earnest.

Mirabelle felt her heart sink. 'But he wasn't a customer? He wasn't, was he?'

Jinty laughed. 'He wouldn't be the first. What? Do you think they put on the dog collar and just switch it off? Like a light? Them Catholic ones ain't allowed to marry or anything. I don't know how they bear it.' The girl eyed Mirabelle mischievously. 'But, you're right,' she said. 'He wasn't a customer, the poor old fellow. A couple of the girls go to confession, you know. Once,' she leaned in conspiratorially, 'he tried to save one of them.'

'Save?'

'Her soul. I mean, you'd think that she didn't know what she was doing. The devil had led her astray, he said. It quite upset her. She'd only gone to get absolved for not writing to her mother. What we do here isn't moral but it is honest. The devil indeed!'

The kitchen door opened and a slim blonde girl slunk in and sank on to one of the chairs. She was all arms and legs, and didn't seem able to settle until she put up her feet on one of the empty chairs and propped a skinny elbow on the table.

'Tea,' she declared, and reached for a cup.

Jinty poured. 'This is Rene,' she said. 'Rene, this is Belle.'

Mirabelle stiffened. She felt her cheeks colour. Rene was the girl McGregor was involved with.

'I'm exhausted,' Rene said, barely acknowledging Mirabelle's presence. 'I mean, I've got a real menagerie at the moment. Georgie bought me more of that French perfume.' She rolled her eyes though she sounded smug. 'And I can't fit them all in. I can't, Jinty. Tanya said she'd take some of my bookings, but they don't want *her*. You need to do something about it. It's getting difficult.'

'Better busy than quiet,' Jinty said cheerfully, ignoring what Mirabelle took to be Rene showing off. Encouraged, the girl continued.

'It's just that there are limits. Mind you, Georgie is a sweetie. I told him I wanted some of those satin French knickers we saw the other day when we were up in London and he said he'd see what he could do. Meantime, I'm a wreck, I tell you.'

Doris trudged back through the kitchen door.

'Make me some toast, would you Dorrie?' Rene demanded.

The old maid put down the bucket she was carrying and made for a chipped bread bin on the side.

'Is there any jam left?' Rene continued. 'I do like jam. Jinty's mum sends it down but it goes, you know. Even the big pots don't last long.'

Jinty smiled indulgently. Mirabelle realised she was gritting her teeth. She tried to relax her jaw.

'Is it all just about what you can get from them? The men, I mean?' She couldn't help it. She hated the way her tones were clipped. She knew she sounded prissy.

'Name of the game,' Jinty cut in. 'I mean, we give quite a lot too. Is that what put you off, Belle? The contractual nature of the job?'

Mirabelle shrugged. Everything in life was give and take. She knew the argument.

'I don't mean to judge,' she said.

'Oh, but you do,' Rene leaned towards her, malice lighting her eyes. 'It's written all over women like you.'

'What do you mean women like me?'

'Old women. Bet your old fella can't get it up any more, eh? There wouldn't be a queue for you, would there, darling? Bet that stings a bit.'

'Rene,' Jinty cut in. 'Stop it. Belle is almost one of us.'

'Yeah. Not quite, though. What's got into her knickers, anyway? I'll have it away with whoever I like. And they'll pay me.'

Mirabelle felt sick. What on earth had McGregor seen in this horrible girl? How could he have stomached her at the same time they'd been courting? The very same time . . . She pushed away the cup.

'Well, it's been nice catching up,' she said.

Rene smirked. Jinty got to her feet. 'Oh come on, Belle. Finish your tea. Go on.'

'I feel like a drink. A proper one.' Mirabelle heard the words cross her lips. She could be a good-time girl, she told herself. Certainly, she could.

Jinty laughed. 'Well, I could do with one myself, truth be told. More than one to get me going today. That was a helluva shock last night. Tell you what, why don't we nip down to the boozer on Dyke Road?'.

Mirabelle's eyes rose to the clock.

'Oh, don't worry about that. There's no rules for the residents of this house. I'll get dressed. Teddy behind the bar is a doll. He'll let us in.'

'You two are crazy,' Rene declared as Doris laid a green plate with a slice of buttered toast on it in front of the girl. 'Dorrie,' she complained, 'Really. Is there no jam anywhere?'

Chapter Seventeen

It is never too late to give up our prejudices

'You don't need to look after me like this,' Mirabelle insisted. 'I'm not an old lady.'

'Don't be silly.'

Jinty had dressed quickly, just as she had promised. She looked, Mirabelle noted, like a young housewife, very much on the modern side. Extremely pretty. She'd chosen a pair of check trousers with a crisp white blouse and had teamed the outfit with navy shoes and a calfskin handbag with a polished steel catch. At the gilded mirror in the hallway, Jinty stopped and tied a large silk square, emblazoned with a gold and red geometric pattern, over her hair. As the women walked through the front door, the girl drew a pair of sunglasses from the side pocket of the handbag and put them on.

'What do the neighbours say?' Mirabelle asked.

'Very little,' Jinty replied. 'Most of them don't realise. We're discreet. Generally, we work out of the house. Hotel visits make up over half the business. You remember, don't you?'

Mirabelle thought of the lost afternoon she'd spent with Jinty at a grand hotel down the coast. It had been more in the way of a party than anything else, although Mirabelle had left before Jinty had got down to what she had coyly termed, 'the bad business'. The phrase had stuck in her head ever since.

'Do you still do it . . . I mean, now you're in charge?' she wondered out loud.

'I've got to keep my hand in. I'm saving up,' Jinty declared. 'I'm going to buy myself the sweetest little cottage in one of those dinky villages away from the sea. And a car. A Triumph maybe. Something marvellous. I learned to drive last year.'

'That girl . . .' Mirabelle started.

'Rene? She's all right. She's a grafter. She just rubbed you up the wrong way.'

As they turned towards the main road, Jinty slipped her arm through Mirabelle's. 'Look, you can't let little idiots like that annoy you. She's young. She'll learn.'

Jinty, Mirabelle noted, was not much older than twenty-five. 'How much money are you making, Jinty?'

'I can't tell you.'

'Don't you know?'

'Of course I know. Pounds, shillings and pence. But it's none of your business.'

'Well, I'm glad you've got a plan.'

'Course I do. Another five years and I'll be out. I'll join the Women's Institute and it'll be jam and "Jerusalem" and the village choir. I bet you I'll find myself a local worthy to get hitched to. There'll be a sea of Chanel Number Five and an acre of apple pie. You'll see.'

'It must've been difficult last night. Doesn't it worry you? The men involved with your house seem to die at an alarming rate.'

Jinty squeezed Mirabelle's arm. 'Of course it was difficult,' she said.

'Don't you worry you'll get arrested?'

'We've got that covered. The coppers get their share. Don't worry, Belle.'

'You pay the police?'

Jinty raised her eyes as if Mirabelle was a fool. 'Pay them.

Entertain them. We've got to keep everybody onside. Besides, they'd rather we were discreet, working out of a house up here, private cars down to private rooms. Cooperating. Safe and all that. The last thing they want is even more girls hanging out in doorways around the railway station. Respectable Brighton is up in arms as it is. Rapes left, right and centre. Girls beaten up and most times nobody to prosecute. It happens all the time. They know they can't stop us. It's called the oldest profession for a reason. They'd prefer we were up here than down there and that's that.'

Mirabelle suddenly recalled what it had felt like being with Jinty the year before. The girl was easy company, both pragmatic and direct. She recalled experiencing the sensation that anything was possible, though it had yet to assail her on this visit. Still, it was a quality the girl's customers probably appreciated. And Jinty was right – the stories of the women in the doorways by the station were most likely very different.

The Grapes was closed this early in the morning. Jinty stood on tiptoes and rapped on the thick stained glass set into the heavily varnished, dark wooden door. She bent down and peered through the keyhole. Then she banged again. 'Ah, here he is,' she said, peering at the vague shape as she made out the figure of a man approaching through the glass.

The door opened. Teddy was about fifty years of age. He wore a striped blue shirt that was so heavily starched you could have taken notes on it with a pencil. His hair was pale ginger, peppered with white, and he sported the kind of wide, thick moustache that was long out of fashion. His face split in a grin when he saw Jinty. 'Oh, it's you.'

'Desperate times,' Jinty declared. 'I know you're not open, but would you make an exception?'

Teddy checked the street, left, right and left again. The passers-by on Dyke Road appeared indifferent. 'Come in.' He ushered the women inside and locked the door behind them.

The place smelled of unwashed glasses and stale cigarette smoke, like the kitchen at Tongdean Avenue but on a more commercial scale. Further towards the bar, he indicated seats that were shielded from the door by a wooden screen so that, if anyone peered in, they wouldn't be able to see the women. There was a decided spring in Teddy's step as he took his place in front of the gantry.

Jinty slid on to the green leather banquette and removed her sunglasses.

'Well, ladies? What can I get you?' He sounded flirtatious.

'Gin and bitter lemon,' Jinty said promptly.

'Whisky for me, please,' Mirabelle added.

He turned to fetch the order.

'So,' Jinty made herself comfortable, taking off her sunglasses and the scarf. 'I still don't know why you came. I mean, Gerry's dead. Sure. But what's it to you?'

Mirabelle couldn't quite put her finger on it. 'I honestly don't know,' she admitted. 'I suppose I'm interested to know what he was like? Bad Luck Bone?'

Teddy's gaze dropped. He fussed with the glasses and then became fascinated by the top of the bar. He drew a rag from the sink and slid it back and forth over the surface.

'Bad Luck? He was a standard hood,' Jinty said, ever matter-of-fact.

'What did he do for you?'

'He hung around. He made it known there'd be him to reckon with. Not only him, you know. They're protection, if you see what I mean.'

'On top of police protection?' Mirabelle was trying to piece things together.

'The police money is so we don't get charged. None of my girls has ever been up in court. Me neither. Gerry and the boys see to the rest of the protection – it's just a different kind of thing. A guarantee.'

'Of what?'

'Well, so that nobody decides to use one of us as a punching bag or, if they do, they regret it. A guarantee that nobody decides to rob the house safe or knock me off when I'm on the way to the bank. You know, all that stuff.'

'Pimps, you mean.'

'Pimps are different. They get a slice of the action. They're in charge. Ernie was a pimp. Bad Luck and his boys take a standard fee. They're protection is all. I run the house. It's an improvement, don't you think?'

Mirabelle nodded, indicating she understood the niceties. 'Don't they ever? You know?'

'What?'

'Overstep the mark?'

'Yes. A few months ago, actually, Bad Luck turned up drunk and expected service.'

'Often?'

'Twice. I complained. You've got to hold your own. The house is an earner. They know that. We came to an arrangement.'

'So how did he end up dead, do you reckon?'

'Well, nothing to do with us, I'm sure. The guy had fingers in pies,' Jinty waggled her hands in Mirabelle's face. 'And he had a difficult personality. There's a lot going on in this town. I don't know what you're worried about him for. I mean, it's Father Grogan you knew, isn't it? Surely it's more important to figure out what happened to him, poor fella?'

'You never know what's important until it's too late,' Mirabelle said wistfully as Teddy delivered the drinks. Jinty sipped her gin.

'You heard about it, didn't you Ted?'

Teddy nodded. 'Talk of the bar last night. Course it was.'

Jinty turned back to Mirabelle. 'I showed you mine,' she said. 'Go on. Tell me yours. You know you want to.'

162

Mirabelle nodded slowly. She started to talk about the Sunday before. She ran over the afternoon she'd spent, watching the children's home and the church, Sister Taylor's unexpected arrival before Vespers and Father Grogan's demise. Teddy hovered behind the bar, polishing glasses and clearing the beer taps. He poured blackcurrant squash into a pint glass and sipped it intermittently, with no pretence other than that he was listening to Mirabelle's story. When Jinty finished her gin she motioned Teddy to bring another.

'Well,' she said when Mirabelle stopped speaking, 'that's far more intriguing than some hood buying the farm. The big issue is what on earth did Father Grogan go to the home for? It looks like it was that that killed him.'

'Do you think so?' Mirabelle eyed her second whisky as Teddy placed it in front of her. It was shortly after ten o'clock. It didn't feel too early, but it should have done.

'Absolutely,' Jinty continued. 'He can't have been going to see Sister Taylor. I mean, he'd spoken to her already. She'd brought him the problem, hadn't she?'

'Problem?'

'Sure. I mean, she was upset, you said. Something must have happened. She'd been at church that morning. Correct me if I'm wrong, but she'd been to church.'

'Yes.'

'And she was fine when you saw her straight afterwards?'

'Yes.'

'So we can assume that she got back to work. You left. Something came up. Whatever it was, she was upset about it, and she went to see Father Grogan for help or advice. The question is, what happened between lunchtime and Vespers to upset her? What was it that she thought he could help with? And then, what did he think he could do? He came down to the home the minute he was free. He came, I'd assume, to tackle this problem.'

'Maybe.'

'Definitely. The girls do it all the time – come to me with something that's gone wrong. So there are a few options. Do you think it was personal and a matter of her salvation?'

'Sister Taylor wasn't Catholic. And if it was personal, I'm sure she wouldn't have wanted to bring him to the home about it. She seems like an orderly kind of person, from what I know of her. Private.'

'So what else?'

'It sounds like she couldn't cope,' Teddy said sagely as he continued to rub a damp cloth over the surface of the long-clean bar. 'If you don't mind me cutting in. But there's something wrong with what you've described there.'

'What do you mean?' Mirabelle asked.

'Well, she was the sister, wasn't she? She was in charge of the nurses. The whole home, if it comes to that. The wife's cousin is a nursing sister. Those women run the place – ward, hospital, home, whatever it is. Usually the doctors go to them with problems, not the other way around.'

'So?'

'She must have been a capable woman – I've never known a sister who wasn't. So if she went to the priest, she was calling him in as an authority. She was upset. She needed his help. That's what it sounds like. And it must have been something big.'

'That's true,' Jinty agreed. 'If the problem was something medical, she'd have gone to a doctor, wouldn't she? I mean, if there was something procedural – the wrong medication or something like that – Father Grogan wouldn't have been much help. So it was a matter of people. Something between people. I mean, that's what priests sort out, isn't it? Deaths. Marital spats. Family feuds.'

'Emotions. Morals,' Teddy said sagely. 'Or mortal illness – something a doctor couldn't help with.'

Mirabelle brought the glass to her lips. 'There was no mention of a child more sick than usual – no suggestion of it,' she said. She'd assumed that what had brought the father to the home was Sister Taylor herself but, now she thought on it, Jinty and Teddy were right. 'They fought,' she reasoned it through. 'The other nurses were concerned for the children and the upset it might cause them. It seems as if, whatever it was, it was between the two of them.'

Jinty's lip pouted as she considered this. 'No. You've been told the two of them fought. They may have. Who's to say there wasn't more to it? I mean, nobody ever wants it to be their fault. When two of the girls have a spat they always say it was the other one getting aggressive. I have to sort out that stuff all the time. Look at little Rene in the kitchen this morning – I bet she doesn't think it was her fault that she came in and stuffed what she'd been up to in your face. And you don't think it was your fault for rising to it?'

Mirabelle blushed. 'I feel responsible, actually. I took a dislike to her.'

'Well, you're unusual to admit it.'

'But whatever it was, you're right. There's no evidence that Father Grogan had a fight with the sister. None at all.'

'Exactly. You don't know the sister's side of the story, or the father's, for that matter. And that's where the answer lies. Standing in the hallway just listening, my foot. If I were you, I'd find out more about those nurses. The other ones. I mean, they're the ones who won.'

'Won?'

'They're the ones who are still there. History is written by the winners. You must have heard that. There's more to that fight, Belle. You mark my words.'

Mirabelle ran over Jinty's logic. 'I spoke to one of them already. She definitely wasn't a murderer. I'd call her conscientious, if I had to choose a single word to describe her.'

Though, as Mirabelle said that, she thought back on Nurse Uma sitting on her sofa. Had she looked guilty, even as she said it wasn't her fault? Was there more to the tension between Uma and her lover? The way the doctor had tried to protect Uma?

Jinty motioned towards a jar stuffed with bags of peanuts next to the gantry. Teddy removed one and flung it over the bar. She caught it with admirable precision. It was a double act long in the making.

'Hookers know people,' she said, splitting the packet open and laying it on the table. 'Now you've had my take on it, you'll probably have the whole thing solved in an hour or two. You mark my words. Here. Have some breakfast.'

'I ate earlier,' Mirabelle said.

Jinty popped a handful of peanuts into her mouth and took a swig of the gin and bitter lemon. 'Well. Regardless. You need to speak to the other girls. Nurses, I mean.'

'You're right,' Mirabelle said as she reached for her handbag.

'What? Are you going already? Call that drinks? Not much of a session.'

Mirabelle nodded. 'Sorry,' she said. 'Apologise to Rene for me. It isn't her fault. Not really.'

Jinty nodded. 'Look, if you're still thinking you might fancy it, we're busy as can be and I can see a certain type of fella, you know, who'd fancy you rotten. Don't listen to Rene.'

Mirabelle put up her hand.

'All right. All right. All I'm going to say is that we've got a conference in. They're doing drinks at the Old Ship Hotel tomorrow afternoon. Four thirty. There's a private room on the first floor. If you fancy it.'

'The Old Ship?'

'Tomorrow. Down on the front. You know it?'

'I've been there for dinner.' The hairs on the back of

Mirabelle's neck began to prickle. It felt as if there was a creeping lack of morality everywhere. As if everything was somehow slightly dirty. She began to draw her purse from the interior of the bag.

'No you don't,' Jinty insisted, pointing as if she was directing traffic. 'I wouldn't hear of it. This one's on me.'

Chapter Eighteen

*There is nothing we receive with so much
reluctance as advice*

At Brill's Lane, Vesta did not mention the lateness of the hour when Mirabelle returned to her desk some time after eleven o'clock. Neither did she offer Mirabelle a cup of tea or pass her the newspaper or the copy of the *Picture Post*, which they had taken to sharing. Instead, she pointed at the large bouquet of flowers she had propped in a jug of water in the sink behind her. 'What have you been up to?' she asked, tapping her pencil on the side of the jug.

Mirabelle had completely forgotten about the bouquet. She scrambled in her jacket pocket and extracted the small envelope. Inside, the card said, 'I'll pick you up at 8. This time let's see if we can make it to dessert.'

A smile must have flickered across her lips.

'It's not like him,' Vesta said. 'Flowers. They smell lovely. Roses no less.'

'What?'

'McGregor. He's never sent flowers before.'

'Oh. It's not. I mean, it's the doctor.' She was aware she sounded giddy.

'They're nice,' Vesta said. 'He's got style, I'll give him that.'

Mirabelle turned the card over between her fingers. The flowers had arrived not more than half an hour after she'd left Chris Williams. He was a smooth operator. She wondered if he had an account at the florist and if he always sent a bouquet the morning after. Had he written the card himself or had he dictated it? She hadn't noted any hint of condescension when the delivery man spoke to her, but she had been taken up with other matters. If the doctor placed a regular order, did he always send the same thing? Or had he chosen these flowers especially for her? As the questions formed, she berated herself inwardly for even thinking that way. Suspicion was a habit – a corrosive one. Women who were happy didn't indulge in it.

'You'll be seeing him again then,' Vesta said casually.

'Dinner.'

'And where have you been?'

'I hurt my arm,' Mirabelle lied.

Vesta put down her pencil. 'How?'

'I bumped it. I went to the doctor.'

'The doctor? Your doctor, you mean.'

'Another doctor. A GP. You know, the NHS.'

Vesta lifted her pencil again. 'If you don't want to tell me, you don't have to,' she said.

The afternoon dragged. The office at Brill's Lane was hardly busy midweek, and Mirabelle, aware she might smell of hard spirits, sucked one peppermint after another as she worked methodically through the paperwork on her desk. The more she thought of it, the more what Jinty had said made sense. The nurses were unreliable witnesses. She needed to look into it.

Just before five o'clock, Vesta gathered her things. 'I'm going out with Bill tomorrow morning on his calls,' she said. 'The Hayward case. Mrs Hayward is in on a Thursday, remember?'

'Oh. Yes.'

'Mirabelle, you will try to have fun, won't you? Tonight?'

'Yes. Of course.'

'It's just you came in drunk. Late. In the morning. The peppermints,' she motioned.

'I'm not drunk,' Mirabelle objected.

Vesta ignored her. 'I'm not complaining, but if there's something going on . . . I know it must be rough with McGregor back on the scene. If you need help – I'd like to help you.'

'It's not him. It's not Alan.'

'I'd be surprised if he hadn't hit the bottle over you, you know. It's nothing to be ashamed of. You don't have to go out with this other guy just to make a point.'

'I'm not. Really, I'm not.'

'It's perfectly natural – having a fling on the rebound.'

Mirabelle cast her mind back to the night before and the electricity in the air over dinner. 'I think he might be more than a fling,' she said. 'It's just unexpected, that's all.'

Vesta gathered the bouquet out of the sink and wrapped it in newspaper. 'That's good,' she said, handing over the bundle. 'Well, here you are.'

'I'll lock up. You go and get Noel.'

The flat seemed almost abandoned when Mirabelle got back. She laid her key on the table and put the bouquet in the sink in the kitchen. She didn't have a vase. Inside the cupboards, most of the crockery was unused, still in the packets in which it had arrived. She gave up the search quickly and, instead, went to the window and stared at the vacant bench opposite the front door. Beyond it, a boy and a man stood at the shoreline, skimming stones. Three ladies walked past, their voices floating upwards but the words indistinct. Mirabelle glanced at the drinks tray but, heeding Vesta's concerns, she decided against having a dram to sharpen her nerve and walked past, scooping her keys off the table. This case was niggling at her. She couldn't seem to let it slide and just be happy. Automatically, she checked the clock on the mantelpiece, though it was still stopped. She didn't wind it. There was a notepad by the door. She scribbled *Change of plan. Meet me at the Old Ship. Around half eight.* Then she slammed the door behind her, stuck the note into the facing and took the stairs at a trot.

The gates of the cricket club were locked and chained when she arrived ten minutes later. She checked over her shoulder. In a residential area like this, it felt as if every window was a pair of eyes. Ahead, the panes of Sister Taylor's empty bedsit reflected the low, blinding sunlight of late afternoon. Mirabelle checked her watch. It was a warm evening and she'd have expected there to be members at the club practising at the nets, though perhaps it was still a little early. The lock was the work of less than a minute. Efficiently she unwound the chain and slipped through the gate. Inside, the pavilion lay in darkness, the nets hoisted, ready and waiting. Without hesitation, Mirabelle made for the back wall where three heavy iron rollers were stored, propped against the brickwork, ready to render the pitch flat enough for play.

Mirabelle hauled the smallest of these towards her. It was so heavy she needed to use her entire weight to get it to move. Slowly and with some effort she pushed the thick iron cylinder until it was stationed in the right place to afford her access to the back wall of the children's home. She propped the wooden handle against the bricks and, checking it was stable, climbed upwards. It was tricky in heels but the weight of the roller worked with her. Peering over the top, she could see the French doors to the downstairs ward had been closed. The children were inside, tea no doubt under way. As smoothly as she could, and with some effort, she hauled herself over the top and down the other side where, keeping to the fringes of the lawn, she crept towards the back of the house.

A quick peek through the glass doors confirmed that tea had been served on metal trays to Peter and his two companions in the ward. The other children would be in the dining hall, down in the basement. She'd have to be quick, she thought, as she bent to pick the lock. The three children watched her, looking up from the uninspiring plates before them, piled with boiled potatoes and pallid sausage. The lock picks grated and it took her a moment before she realised that the door had been left open. Inside, Peter grinned and waved her in.

'Wotcha, Mirabelle,' he said as she sheepishly turned the handle and slipped over the threshold. 'It's late for visitors.'

Mirabelle cast her eyes towards the door to the hallway, which was open.

'They'll be five minutes, I'd say.' The boy anticipated her correctly. 'They told you you couldn't come back, didn't they?'

'Yes.'

The little girl eyed her sausage and looked as if she might say something. Instead, she put down her fork and started to cough.

'Please don't turn me in,' Mirabelle said. 'I need your help.'

Peter smiled encouragingly. 'Well, you're the most interesting thing to happen in here today,' he said. 'Isn't that right?'

The girl looked uneasy. The third child – a boy – seemed almost a ghost. He was chewing silently, no more involved than if he was watching a play.

'What do you want?' Peter asked.

'I need you to tell me what happened the night Sister Taylor disappeared.'

'We didn't see a thing. It's lights out at seven.'

'I know you weren't actually there. But did you hear anything, Peter? Anything at all?'

'Well,' he said, a grin spreading over his face. 'That depends.'

'On what?'

'We could do with some decent grub,' the boy's tone was matter-of-fact. 'It's my birthday next week. I want a cake. For all of us. Everyone, I mean.'

Mirabelle nodded. 'All right,' she said. 'A cake. I'll have the bakery on Church Street send one down, shall I?'

Peter pushed a boiled potato to one side. She'd given in too quickly, she realised.

'And I'd like a jigsaw. A big one.'

'Well, why don't you let me buy you a surprise? Rather than making a specific order?'

Peter considered this. 'I don't always like surprises,' he concluded.

'You'll like this one, I promise. And the more you tell me about the other night, the bigger it'll be.'

The girl looked out of the window, pointedly turning away from the negotiations.

'And not just for you,' Mirabelle promised. 'For the other two as well.'

Peter paused. 'It's only fair. Though it'll be my birthday.'

'How old will you be?'

'Ten,' he said.

'That's a big birthday.'

'My brother got a bike when he was ten, but I can't ride one, can I?'

'I'll think of something special. I promise. What day is it?'

'Thursday.'

'Thursday it is then.'

The girl turned back. She nodded at Peter, who then cast his eyes at the other bed. The boy didn't move. It was almost as if he wasn't aware there had been a change in his routine.

'He never says anything,' Peter said sadly. 'No matter what happens.'

'Well, it's down to you two then, isn't it?' Mirabelle said.

Peter nodded. 'We didn't see what happened. The door was closed but there was a kerfuffle out there.'

'A kerfuffle?'

'In the hallway. People going back and forwards for ages. We were whispering, Laura and me. We thought one of the other kids might have died, but everyone was fine the next day.'

'Did you hear any shouting?'

'No. Some talking. Raised voices, perhaps. Not real shouting. More muffled, like when I locked my brother in the cupboard under the stairs at home. There were people running about. In and out the back. Up and down the stairs. Then, after ages, the bell rang.'

'The doorbell?'

'Yes.'

Mirabelle considered this. Nobody had rung the doorbell when she had been watching. Father Grogan had his own key.

'Are you sure?'

'Yes. The bell hardly ever goes at night so it was unusual.'

'Do you know who it was?'

'A man. We heard his voice, but not what he said.'

'Father Grogan had a key, Peter.'

'It wasn't the priest. I can tell the difference between an English mumble and an Irish one.'

'Are you sure?'

'Course I am.'

'And you didn't see a thing?'

'No. I was in here. How could I?'

Mirabelle considered. It was possible that somebody else had arrived at the home after Father Grogan left. But who or why they had come was more difficult to ascertain. The little girl started coughing again and Peter sat up straight. He motioned at Mirabelle. 'Quick,' he hissed.

On instinct alone, Mirabelle hit the linoleum floor and rolled under Peter's bed just in time. It was, she noted, spotless under there, the linoleum just as highly polished as the rest of the floor. The home was ostensibly very well run.

Nurse Frida's voice emanated from the doorway. Mirabelle squinted and made out the nurse's shoes, square on. Her ankles seemed somehow immoveable.

'Dear, dear,' the nurse said. 'I can tell you don't want pudding on the ward tonight.'

'Sorry, Nurse,' Peter said. 'We was talking.'

Nurse Frida paused; no doubt, Mirabelle thought, looking at the unresponsive boy in the end bed and the girl, now coughing furiously.

'If you and Laura want to chat, you can do so tomorrow. Eat up, then. Or there'll be no pudding. And it's jelly and Carnation tonight. You all like jelly, don't you?'

The children must have nodded.

'All right, then.'

The shoes disappeared.

Mirabelle crawled out and picked herself up. She brushed down her skirt. The children were now chewing too quickly to enjoy the food. Peter stuffed a piece of potato into his mouth and swallowed it without chewing.

'Father Sean had gone,' the little girl said between mouthfuls.

Mirabelle turned.

'Gone?'

'He'd left before the doorbell. And it must have been two men. There were hats on the hooks, you see.'

'I thought you didn't see anything? Peter said the door was closed.'

'I went to the lav.' The girl stuffed in another bite of sausage. 'And I saw two hats on the hooks. Brown ones. Sometimes the nurses have friends over.'

'Do they have friends over often?'

'Sometimes,' the girl said.

'Men?'

'Sometimes men. Sometimes ladies. It's up to them, isn't it?'

'And there were only men's hats on the rack that night?'

'Yes, miss.'

Father Grogan, Mirabelle recalled, wore a black hat consistent with his station.

'I'd like a dolly,' the girl continued. 'They left my dolly at home when they sent me away. I'm lonely without her.'

'I'll keep you company, Laura,' Peter said cheerfully.

Laura started coughing again. 'You're a boy,' she managed, between heaving for breath.

Mirabelle glanced at the doorway. There was hardly any time.

'Leave it with me,' she said. 'Thank you. You've been very helpful.'

Outside, she slipped along the side of the lawn, found a foothold and pulled herself back up over the wall. Two men, dressed in whites, looked up from their conversation in front of the nets as she landed on the grass at the other side.

'I say,' one said. 'Can I help you?'

'I left a cardigan,' Mirabelle managed. It had been a good enough excuse for Sister Taylor. 'I was here the other day, in the pavilion. I thought the gate would be locked so I climbed over the back to check.'

The man's gaze lighted on the back wall. 'I don't have the key to the pavilion,' he said. 'But if anything's been left, we have a lost property box. The caretaker will be able to help you tomorrow morning, madam. He's going to roll the field. He'll be here first thing. You can enter by the gate, you know.'

'Thank you,' Mirabelle said crisply. 'Wasted effort, then.'

'Yes, rather.'

The men stared as she retreated. She thanked her stars that the English hated poking their noses into other people's business.

'What an extraordinary thing,' she heard one say to the other as her heels clicked on to the paving stones and she turned up the street. Those poor kids, she thought. Next Thursday seemed a million miles off. It had been a long week already.

Chapter Nineteen

Undercover: to disguise identity to avoid detection

Mirabelle was up on Church Street by the time the sun set. She liked the edges of the day – the twilights and the sunrises. The world smelled different in those moments – something in the air changed. In summer it was a fresh smell and in winter it was salty. In the winter, on mornings when fog rolled in on the tide, she loved walking through it. There hadn't been any fog for months. She found an old bench beside the post office and settled down to wait. Then she ran over the children's story and placed these new facts in her timetable of events on the night of the murder – visitors arriving after she had left and nurses running up and down stairs, not simply listening as she'd been told. A bus passed and she checked her watch. It was still too early. Her stomach growled and she felt surprised. Mirabelle rarely felt hungry but the last few days she'd certainly had an appetite – and not only for whisky. Tonight she'd have the fish, she decided. Dover sole swimming in butter, with spinach.

She dragged her thoughts away from Dr Williams and the dining room at the Old Ship Hotel and instead tried to focus on the hats in the hallway. Father Grogan was on his way home, perhaps already dead, by the time the men had arrived. But where was Sister Taylor? Had she called the men to aid her escape or was she gone already? Laura had said the nurses had friends to visit. But why? Was there more to the sister than there had seemed? Or was she a victim in this, rather than a perpetrator? Either way, Nurse Uma, Nurse Frida and Nurse Berenice had all lied, not only to her, but to Robinson as well.

At two minutes past the hour, the bus approached and Mirabelle put out her hand to flag it down. She stationed herself to the rear of the carriage on the left and bought a ticket from the conductor, trying to make herself as small as possible in the seat. She was glad, again, that she'd chosen a dark dress and jacket today. She pulled her hat down as far as possible and comforted herself with the fact that people's eyes moved to the right, naturally. She should be at her least noticeable in the back seat in the left-hand corner.

As the bus drew up at the next stop she waited, holding her breath and, sure enough, she heard them getting on. The chatter of women as they took their seats, as they had before, halfway up on the right-hand side. She recognised Frida's voice first – out of breath from the rush to meet the bus's timetable.

'Little monkey,' she declared. 'It's his birthday next week and he'd sell his soul for a cake.'

'We should bake him a cake.' This was Uma.

'And then we'd be at it all the time, wouldn't we? Cakes for every one of them. I don't think so.' Frida was adamant.

'All the time.' This repetition was a third voice, echoing Nurse Frida's stout rebuff. Berenice. It was the first time Mirabelle had heard her speak.

The bus chugged away from the stop. Along the road, the dark windows of shops gave way to the electric light of pubs and restaurants and the neon of the cinema on the main street. From the upper deck, passengers disembarked for the dance hall. The conductor hummed a Vera Lynn song. 'Not that old stuff, darling,' a cheeky boy wearing a French navy suit winked at her. He drew deeply on a Capstan. 'You got to get with it, you know. Doris Day and all that.'

The woman's glare saw him off soundly at the next stop but she gave up humming.

'Well,' Mirabelle heard Frida say, 'another day, another dollar.'

'At least it was a quiet one,' Berenice replied.

Uma didn't join in; instead she looked out of the window, resting her forehead on the cool glass.

Then, just before Old Steine, Nurse Frida stood up. 'See you tomorrow,' she said.

The other two made a cheerful sound in reply. Mirabelle got to her feet. It would be difficult to walk past Uma without being spotted. These things were often about timing. She pulled her jacket around her frame and turned away slightly as the bus slowed. Outside the window, the street was teeming with people. Someone shouted. Another voice squealed. Uma looked at her feet and Mirabelle took her chance, walked smoothly down the aisle, and stepped on to the pavement. She wondered if she had got away with it. Her heart raced. She didn't dare raise her eyes to check if Uma was staring in her direction or, worse, following her.

The bus pulled away from the stop. Ahead, Frida cut past Brighton Pavilion, which was in darkness, and Mirabelle made to follow swiftly, glancing behind to check one more time. The bus was at the lights at Old Steine now, the exhaust chugging as it turned left. Uma and Berenice were still on board, both of them looking out of the window in the other direction. She'd got away with it.

At night the streets north of the town centre were quiet. The streetlights gave off an eerie glow like little clouds, lit from behind. A few local pubs were scattered around the Lanes but the rest of the buildings were shops, mostly. Nurse Frida crossed and crossed again, her cape swinging from side to side as she kept up a vigorous pace. She turned up one of the side streets and Mirabelle followed, keeping her distance. The houses were two up and two down – old brick terraces with outdoor toilets. Many people were abandoning them for the new flats out in the suburbs that had hot water systems and plumbed bathrooms. As a result whole terraces had fallen into disrepair. A fringe of trailing ivy grew from one roof into the gutter. The window frames flaked. On the upper floors, a broken window was patched with brown paper.

Nurse Frida drew a key from her pocket and let herself in at a front door about halfway up the left-hand side. Mirabelle watched. This terrace seemed fully occupied. It could be tricky. On streets like these, neighbours looked out for each other and the accommodation was cramped. She leaned against a wall a few doors down and sighed. She might as well check it out from the rear, she decided, but she knew already that there was no easy way in.

At the back, the small, square gardens formed a grid, the alleyway behind them strewn with debris and litter. The lights in the houses were on, right along the row. At one end of the alley, a little boy kicked a half-deflated football against a wall. Mirabelle crouched to speak to him.

'Do you know the lady who lives in that house?' she pointed. 'She's a nurse.'

'Yeah. Course I do. And her mum.'

'She lives with her mother?'

The boy bit his lip, as if he suddenly realised he had said something he shouldn't.

'I'm not a grass,' he said. 'I'm not peaching. Not me.'

Mirabelle slipped her hand into her purse and drew out a sixpence. The boy licked his lips. He did not take his eyes off the coin. 'I wonder if you might be a businessman?'

He smiled. He was about to say something. He had taken

a breath in order to do so, when a familiar figure wheeled around the corner, mostly in shade with the light behind him. Superintendent Alan McGregor crossed his arms. The boy's gaze flicked between the two adults.

'You're crazy, woman. I swear, you'll be the end of me,' McGregor said.

'What are you doing here?' Mirabelle tried not to let the ire sound in her voice.

'I might ask you the same. But I know what you're doing.'

'You do, do you?'

McGregor shooed the boy away. 'Go on,' he said. 'You'd better get going or you'll feel the back of my hand.'

The child looked on mournfully as Mirabelle put the sixpence back into her purse.

'Go on,' McGregor repeated, and drew back his arm as if he might strike.

The boy didn't wait to see if he meant it – he scooped up his football and took off down the lane.

'You didn't have to scare him.'

'At least I still scare somebody. What did I tell you about not getting involved?'

'I don't have to do what you tell me, Superintendent.'

'Actually, you do, Belle. I am an officer of the law.'

'I'm obviously on the right track then.'

'What makes you say that?'

'You're here.'

'I followed you, you ninny.'

'Followed me? Alan, that's outrageous.'

'You're the one being outrageous. One of my guys saw you climbing over the back wall of the children's home, for heaven's sake. He was in Sister Taylor's bedsit. I'm lucky he called it in. Have you been drinking?'

Mirabelle felt a twist of anger in her gut. The setting sun had made mirrors of the windows on that elevation. She had spotted neither the man nor the superintendent. He must have tailed her all the way along Church Street into town. McGregor's technique was good.

'You weren't on the bus, were you?' she checked.

'I was in a Maria. With a driver. Because I'm a police officer, not a madwoman.'

Mirabelle looked down. Her heels boasted a thin smear of dried mud that rose about half an inch. 'What was your man doing in the bedsit?' she said, at length.

'I'm not getting drawn into that. But I'll tell you what he wasn't doing. He wasn't following around an innocent nurse and planning to break in at the rear of her property.'

'I'm not so sure she's innocent. And how do you know I'd have broken in? I might not have. I hadn't decided.'

McGregor let out a sigh of frustration. 'Form,' he said. 'Let me take you home.'

Mirabelle cast a glance over her shoulder. He wasn't going to let her continue and she wasn't sure what she was going to do next anyway. Still, she wanted to engage him.

'Two men came to the home, Alan. After Father Grogan left. The nurses lied.'

'Two men?'

'The night Father Grogan died.'

'How do you know?'

'The children told me. That's why I climbed over the wall. To speak to them.'

'Really, Mirabelle. You're impossible. You can't go interrogating children. They make highly unreliable witnesses and they're minors.'

'Well, you should have asked them at least. Children aren't stupid and one or two of the kids in the home are really very bright. Peter is sharp as a tack.'

'Robinson already interrogated them. He interviewed everybody.'

Mirabelle waved a hand to dismiss the inspector. 'Robinson,' she said. 'You know better than that.'

'All right. What did these children say they saw?'

'Hats. Two hats. Brown. Men's. In the hallway. On the night in question. And they heard a good deal of coming and going too. The doorbell went late at night – after Grogan had left.'

'Thank you for the information, Miss Bevan. I'll look into it. Now.' He pointed to the top of the alleyway. Mirabelle stalked past him. He was a spoilsport, she thought. It wasn't fair.

McGregor accompanied her to the Maria which had cut its lights. He opened the door and she slipped into the back seat. 'Take Miss Bevan home,' he instructed the driver.

'You aren't coming?'

'No,' he grinned. 'Well, somebody better question that nurse, don't you think? Now that we're all here. And that person is me because I'm a police detective. Not you because you're a member of the public. You aren't to approach Nurse Frida, Mirabelle. You're a suspect. Do you understand? Give me your word.'

Mirabelle nodded curtly. 'All right,' she said.

The engine started. She sat forward in her seat. McGregor was enjoying this. He grinned from the kerb and tipped his hat. When the car turned the corner he had already disappeared back up the road. Mirabelle checked her watch.

'Constable,' she said, 'I'm going to dinner with a friend. Could you take me to the Old Ship Hotel?'

'Doctor Williams, is it, miss?' The man's tone was cheerful. Mirabelle crossed her ankles.

'Why do you say that?' She was aware her voice sounded clipped.

'We're not as stupid as you think we are, Miss Bevan. We know what's what. I'll drop you off, shall I?'

Mirabelle felt tears welling up. It was humiliating. McGregor. Williams. The way everybody knew. Worse was what was left unsaid. What they thought of her.

'No,' she said. 'Don't bother. Just take me home.'

The car glided westwards and, when it pulled up, the driver watched her walk up the path at the Lawns and open the front door with her key. Upstairs, the note she'd left on the door was gone. She didn't give the man in the car the satisfaction of switching on the lights so he would know she was safe inside. Instead, she stood like a shadow in the window. He waited for a minute or two, peered, squinted, and then started the engine, turning the car around and parking properly.

Mirabelle poured a full glass of whisky, hardly looking. She kicked off her shoes and wandered through to the bedroom. Outside the window, the autumn moon hung huge in the sky. She sipped the whisky but it didn't cover what she was feeling. A tear rolled down her cheek and she gulped back a sob. 'Bloody McGregor. Bloody Grogan. Bloody kids,' she whispered as she reached out and pulled the curtain across the glass, obscuring the wide night sky and the dark police car below. She drank the glass far too quickly. Then she lay back on the pillows. It didn't take long before she was fast asleep.

Chapter Twenty

A foul morn may turn to a fair day

The hangover was dreadful. She swung her legs over the side of the bed and tried to focus. She'd only had that glassful – a double perhaps. It couldn't have been more. Or did one glass constitute four measures? And on an empty stomach. The sound of voices wafted up from the street – laughter like the chatter of crows and the sound of an engine as a car passed. Then she realised the doorbell was ringing.

She got to her feet and stumbled across the drawing room and into the hallway. When she opened the door, Doctor Williams stood before her. He carried a copy of *The Times*, a paper bag which she could smell contained some kind of baked goods, a small bottle of milk and a flask.

'I made coffee,' he said. 'I realised you wouldn't have milk.'

Mirabelle leaned against the doorframe. He kissed her cheek and came inside, laying the shopping on the table. She followed him into the drawing room. Without fuss, he took off his hat and jacket and disappeared into the kitchen. A few seconds later he emerged with cups and saucers that Mirabelle only vaguely recognised. He must have found them in one of the unopened boxes.

'Doctor's orders,' he said, pouring the coffee. 'And it looks as if you could do with some aspirin. Do you have any?'

'In the kitchen,' she managed. 'The drawer.'

He fetched two and a glass of water, holding out the medicine and watching as she swallowed the little pills.

'I know what this looks like,' she said.

'I'm a doctor,' he replied with a grin. 'I've taken the Hippocratic oath. So I can't berate you for standing me up last night. Not until you're restored to health. I have to do what's best for you.'

He poured the coffee and positioned two chairs at the window. 'It's a nice day out there,' he said.

Mirabelle gave in. She sat down and sipped the coffee. It tasted good. A breeze slipped over the lip of the sill and brushed her skin. The movement of the sea was hypnotic. He sat next to her. She was suddenly aware that the air smelled sweet. For a minute or two the silence felt restorative, then she felt the need to speak.

'I'm sorry about last night,' she said. 'Something came up.'

Chris smiled. 'Was it bottle-shaped?'

Mirabelle put down her cup. 'It was McGregor. I was looking into something and he turned up. We had an argument. It wasn't much of an argument, really. I suppose I didn't take it well. Turns out, I'm a mess, and I seem to be losing all my manners. I'm sorry.'

Chris turned in his chair. 'You don't have to be perfect.' He offered her his hand. She took it. Then he raised her fingers to his lips. 'I would like to know what's going on, though. If the field is cleared for battle, I mean. If you're seeing McGregor that's your business. Your choice. Of course. But please, tell me.'

Mirabelle felt her face contort as she started to cry. It felt as if she was stretched in all directions. It would have been easier if Chris wasn't being so decent or if McGregor wasn't involved. If she could just get a hold on things. She sobbed, gulping in air as the doctor wrapped an arm around her shoulder and kissed her forehead. He smelled of laundered linen and antiseptic with a whiff of aftershave, then he ran his hand down her thigh and pulled her towards him and kissed her deeply. She felt herself slipping away but fought it, pushing him off. He put up his hands. 'All right,' he said.

'I don't know what's going on,' she managed to get out. 'It's as if the world is too slippery and I can't get a grip on anything. That's what it's like.'

He pulled a laundered handkerchief from his pocket. 'Start at the beginning. Go on. Tell me.'

Mirabelle blew her nose. 'I came to Brighton because of a man. After the war. He bought this flat for me.'

'Nice man.'

'I loved him. But he died of a heart attack. He never even came to live here.'

'And then there was the superintendent?'

'Alan was different but we rubbed along. I suppose, being a policeman, he had a lot on his plate. We had a lot in common – cases, you know.'

'I heard he took a bullet for you once.'

'That's true. He did. I thought he was one of the good guys but it turned out he was unfaithful.' She remembered Rene sitting in the kitchen at Tongdean Avenue the morning before and the body of the man Mirabelle had seen murdered – the man McGregor had done nothing to protect. The man had been a murderer himself, but still. 'I seem to be having some kind of crisis. It's not only the men. I don't want to make it all about that,' the words seem to stumble as they crossed her lips.

'I can see it's been difficult. You've had to manage on your own.'

Mirabelle shrugged. 'I have Vesta. I haven't been completely by myself.'

'Vesta?'

'My business partner. She had a baby last year. A gorgeous

little boy. It isn't that there aren't people around me. Usually I'm quite capable. We have our business, you see. We're doing all right there. I have some money that I inherited when my parents died. And now and then something comes up – a case. And usually that makes me feel good – you know, to do the right thing. But now, the world just seems grubby. I can't bear it. We fought, all of us, to make things right. And it hasn't helped. Not really. You fought, didn't you? Italy, you said.'

'I was in the Red Cross.'

'Not the army?'

'No. That's my dirty secret, I suppose.'

'You saluted the other day. When I first saw you.'

'I did.'

'You're a pacifist, then?'

'I said I was, but the truth is I'm not sure. I just didn't have the stomach for what was going on. The service seemed the easiest way to help. I had only just qualified. And afterwards . . . well, you get used to dead bodies, and going into the police was a sideways step. If I'm honest, I fell into it.'

Mirabelle nodded. She had never taken the easiest way, she realised. It wasn't that easier options hadn't presented themselves, but somehow they always required blinkers.

Chris stroked her hand. He toyed with her fingers. 'McGregor is bang out of order – he should stay away from you if it's over. How long have you been drinking?' he asked.

'Since I was eighteen. I used to drink gin and it. My mother drank that.' She suddenly remembered ice, clanking against a thick-cut glass and thinking that sound was sophisticated. It had been the summer, she recalled. Drinks had been served on the lawn, under the trees. The sunlight had cast shadows.

'I don't mean when was the first time you had a drink. I meant, when did it become the way that you coped?'

Mirabelle felt her cheeks burn. It was shaming.

189

'You can tell me. I'm a doctor.'

She laughed. 'You've gone out of your way to come here. It's kind of you but I'm not going to be the easiest way, Chris, if that's what you're looking for. I try to be good, but I'm not really. And I can't stay out of things.'

'Maybe I don't mind taking the long road – the scenic route. Perhaps it's time for a challenge. None of us is squeaky clean. Not a soul. You're nice to be around. And, for the record, you're allowed a drink or three.' He got up and poured more coffee. Then he fetched the paper bag. 'I bought fruit scones,' he said. 'I don't suppose you have jam?'

Mirabelle shook her head.

'Well, you need to eat something. Then I'll draw you a bath.'

Mirabelle felt herself relax. Her worries seemed suddenly nebulous. The scone was warm as she bit into it. The doctor smiled.

'I see people having a hard time all round, you know. The war's over and they want to forget but they can't – not everything. Not the good or the bad. Even people who came back and had a family to go to, or a career to pick up.'

'You didn't?'

'I'm on my own. I'd only just qualified when I went into the army. I had nothing to come back to.'

'You're a good man.'

The doctor looked down. 'There's no such thing, Miss Bevan. I'd like to be good. Tell you what: you're definitely a good-time girl. And more than that too. Come on, the doctor has diagnosed. Let's get you up and about, eh?'

After a bath she pulled on a summer dress and a pair of kitten heels. She scrambled to find a twill scarf that would match – a blue one. When she came back into the drawing room, he had cleared away the breakfast things and was sitting at the table with his hands clasped in front of him.

'You look nice.'

'I should go to work,' she said.

She was already late and the office would be unmanned. Vesta and Bill had the Hayward case to deal with.

'I'll give you a lift. But, before I do, I have something to tell you. I'm thinking of leaving Brighton.'

Mirabelle didn't admit it to herself but she felt her stomach twist. 'Where would you go?' she asked as smoothly as she could manage.

'Back to London. I finished my training in London. Guy's. They were the best days of my life in some ways. I thought you could come with me.'

'Me?'

'I know. It's quick. But I don't want to lose you, Mirabelle. I was hoping you'd be my partner in crime. I might have turned in my notice already if I hadn't met you. That's the truth.'

'London is only an hour away. I can come up for dinner. For weekends.'

'I'm thinking of specialising. There are various opportunities. They're short of doctors for this new NHS. There just aren't enough of us.'

'I see.'

Chris smiled. 'You're not the only one who feels in a mess sometimes, you know.'

'What's your mess?'

'Oh no. We're not going to cover that today. I'm the doctor, remember? And Mirabelle, you need to lay off the sauce for a bit. That's my medical advice. Easier said than done, I know. But maybe tone it down, eh?'

This morning that seemed possible. 'All right,' she said as she reached for her hat and a jacket.

'Have you got a busy day?' she asked, suddenly domestic.

Chris got to his feet. 'Well, yes. Sometimes I wonder if

what I do is actually helpful. I still have Bad Luck Bone on the slab and I am getting nowhere, poor chap.'

'Oh yes?'

'I can't figure out how he died.'

'Why not?'

'Degradation,' the doctor said. 'It destroys evidence. I'd be able to tell if he was strangled but, to put it bluntly, his eyes aren't there and his skin is compromised – he was in the water too long. I think strangulation is the most likely cause of death.'

'But you can't be sure?'

'Not this time. I've run some tests on his stomach contents, just in case. They'll come back on Monday. Come on. Ten thirty, eh? Not much of an early start.'

Outside, the front door banged behind them. The sun burned so brightly the sky seemed white with it. A beat bobby stood at the doctor's car. Mirabelle's gaze hardened.

'Morning,' Chris said cheerily.

The policeman tipped his hat. 'Miss Bevan.'

'Stop spying on me,' Mirabelle hissed.

The man looked confused.

'Get in, Mirabelle,' Chris said. 'I'd better get you to work.' As the car pulled up on East Street, he took her hand.

'Will you consider it? Coming to London?'

'It seems rushed.'

'It is, I guess. Needs must.'

'We'll see.'

'When a woman says that she means no, Mirabelle.'

'I don't mean no.'

His eyes narrowed.

'I don't,' she insisted. 'It's only that I have this,' she nodded in the direction of the office.

'An empire?'

'And I don't know you.'

'I think I know you. Well enough, anyway. Will you think about it?'

'All right.'

'I was going to take a rather nice flat in Mayfair.'

'Really?'

'I've been saving up. I can look after you.'

Mirabelle turned to say it wasn't about the flat or about money and she liked looking after herself, but as she did so, he pulled her towards him and kissed her again. She felt her knees weaken. It really was the most extraordinary thing. A policeman passed the car and nodded at the doctor as he sat back in his seat. A twinge of annoyance twisted in her gut but she decided not to say anything. As she disappeared through the doorway, the doctor started the engine; climbing the stairs, she could hear its roar as he drove to the bottom of the street and turned on to the front.

Upstairs, Mirabelle opened the office. For an hour she filed papers and took two payments that came in. The day felt more under control than it had. She thought it might be nice, when Chris moved up to London, to pack a bag at the weekend and join him for a few days. They could try it out, she thought. It would be good to be out of Brighton and not feel so consumed. Sometimes a place could become a trap. She hoped he'd accept that, as a start – a middle way. Then she thought about Bad Luck Bone, about whom nobody seemed to care – Jinty had been blithe about his death and in the Grapes it had only been gossip. She tried not to imagine what the doctor meant by the word 'degradation', but it brought too many memories back – bodies in the sea.

It was almost midday when Vesta and Bill arrived. They rolled through the office door on a wave of good cheer.

'We got him,' Vesta laughed. 'Paid in full. Hayward.' She swept her palms against each other, as if she was brushing the man right off.

'Cash?' Mirabelle couldn't believe it. A success – at last.

'It was a cheque, actually. But we stopped at the bank. His bank,' Bill said sagely as he patted Panther. 'Up on South Street. There shouldn't be any problems with it clearing. I had a word with the cashier.'

'What happened?'

Vesta took off her jacket. 'Well,' she started, 'we got there. It's a nice house. There was nothing to say they were in any financial trouble. Right enough, his wife was there. We made out as if we hadn't known. He was out, you see. But what was best, is she was there with her mother.'

Mirabelle let out a giggle. 'Mr Hayward's mother-in-law?'

'Yes. So we played it as if it was clerical error. Bill let slip he used to be a police officer and wasn't wholly clear that he isn't one any more. He said we were holding back prosecution because there had obviously been some awful mistake but that it needed to be cleared up quickly because it was in the system now. The mother was horrified. They phoned Hayward. He played along. He made out he was furious about the mistake but he told his wife to write a cheque immediately.'

'So what was he playing at before?'

'He just didn't want to pay up, I guess. And it puts us ahead on the month. The client will be delighted. I'll ring them once we've had a cuppa, shall I? Mrs Hayward was not forthcoming with tea and biscuits.'

Vesta put the kettle on to boil. Mirabelle sat at her desk. 'Mothers,' she said, vaguely.

'Nobody wants to look bad in front of their mother. Do they?' Vesta grinned. 'Hayward's lucky. My mother wouldn't have bought the line about a discrepancy. She'd have known and she'd have killed me.'

'Mothers,' Mirabelle repeated, and then got to her feet. 'Do you mind if I go out, Vesta? Just for a bit.'

'Not at all. What is it?'

'Only a loose end. Something I just realised,' Mirabelle said as she reached for her jacket and tucked her clutch bag under her arm.

'You no sooner come in these days than you go out again.'

'I'll tell you about it later,' Mirabelle promised.

As she made for the door she noticed Bill's shoes were scuffed. Odd – he was military trained like most men, and had years in the police force. Shiny shoes were a way of life for most like him. Still, he seemed cheery enough. Getting Hayward to pay up was a coup. Panther stared mournfully at her. 'I'll be back soon,' she said, and took the stairs smartly.

Chapter Twenty-One

*The best prophet of the
future is the past*

It was only a short walk to the Lanes but, when she got to the right street, Mirabelle couldn't remember which was Nurse Frida's house. The doors along the row were painted similar colours and the night before it had been dark. She pictured Nurse Frida walking ahead of her, but could only conclude that the correct house was one of three in the centre of the terrace. The houses all looked the same, with dark doors and chipped window frames, the glass panes obscured by lace curtains that in the bright sunshine seemed slightly grubby. The truth was that her head still felt muddled, despite the coffee, the aspirin and the scone.

She retreated down the street and looked around. Ahead, on the corner, the local pub had its door open. She started towards the gloomy interior. Inside, the floor was plain boards and there were no tables or chairs. Behind the bar a woman balanced on a set of steps and was polishing the face of a clock that was mounted over the gantry.

'Hello, dear,' she said as she looked Mirabelle up and down from on high. 'Can I help you?'

'I'm trying to find a friend's house. She's a nurse. She lives round here. I wondered if you knew her.'

'There's one or two nurses live locally, love.'

Mirabelle heard herself sigh. 'Could I have a drink?' she asked.

The woman climbed down. Her hair was arranged in a complicated series of folds that Mirabelle thought must have taken a long time and a whole packet of hairpins.

'No unaccompanied ladies allowed, dear. Sorry,' she said.

'But it's only the two of us here.'

'Oh, I don't serve any more. I'm just cleaning the place.'

Mirabelle put down her clutch bag on the bar. 'It seems very old-fashioned,' she said.

'I know what you mean. It didn't used to be that way. During the war, I served all the time. Alf was in the Home Guard and I looked after the bar. Unaccompanied ladies were welcome – we had all the ambulance girls. Don't know what we'd have done without them with so many fellas away.' She checked over her shoulder. 'I could do you a quick gin and bitter lemon, I suppose. As there's nobody else in.'

Mirabelle nodded. She'd intended to order an orange juice, but why not? Chris had said, after all, that she didn't have to stop drinking entirely. 'Thanks.'

The woman pulled a glass from beneath the bar and poured a generous measure of gin, emptying a small bottle of bitter lemon into it. Mirabelle sipped. The drink seemed to give her clarity.

'Your friend, then. The nurse. She got a name?' the woman asked.

'Frida.'

'Melanie Gill's girl?'

'You mean her mother? I heard she lived with her mother.'

'The father died at the beginning of the war. He was a common sort – and not in a good way.'

'Really?' Mirabelle encouraged the gossip. She took another sip.

The woman carefully folded the rag she'd been using to

clean the clock and leaned on the bar. 'He was in and out of trouble. In and out of work, too. All his life.'

'What did he do?'

'Labouring mostly. And God knows what on the side. He was the type for that too, I shouldn't be surprised. And he had a temper. He was older than her – Melanie, I mean. She was a nurse in her day as well.'

'I expect Frida takes after her mother, then?'

'I expect so.'

An elderly man entered behind Mirabelle and cleared his throat, clearly uncomfortable about walking in on two women.

'Afternoon Vera,' he said. 'A pint would be nice.'

'Right you are. Do you want another, love?' Vera offered Mirabelle, easily slipping into the role required. 'It's a hot enough day.'

Mirabelle looked at the glass in front of her. It was almost empty. 'Perhaps just one more,' she said. She wanted to keep the woman talking.

'Where's Alf, then?' the other customer enquired.

'He'll be here any second, I expect,' Vera said cheerily. She pulled the pint with some skill, Mirabelle noticed, the head settling into a perfect line. The man pushed a coin over the bar. 'I'll get that for the lady,' he said.

'Oh, there's no need.' Mirabelle's tone was insistent.

'It's all right, love,' the man said. 'I can buy a lady a drink, can't I? I'm not too old for that.'

'Two drinks,' said Vera.

The man grinned, revealing a gap in his teeth. 'Why not?' he said. 'A party.'

'I'm actually looking for a friend,' Mirabelle continued, but I can't remember the number of her house. It's only round the corner.

'Jimmy Gill's house,' Vera said.

'Number twelve,' the man said sagely. 'Though Jimmy's long dead now. One of the neighbourhood's first casualties, he was.'

'It's his daughter that I know.'

'Of course,' the man said, staring quite nakedly at Mirabelle. 'You'd be the same kind of age.'

Mirabelle hadn't considered it, but she supposed that was probably about right. The other nurses were younger, but Frida must be in her forties. The same as Sister Taylor.

'I met her through another friend. She's a nurse. Or rather, a sister. She lives on the other side of town. I don't suppose you've heard of her? Rita Taylor's her name.'

'There's one or two Taylors round here. It's a common enough name.'

'Any nurses you can think of?'

Vera and the old man shook their heads.

'You ask a lot of questions,' the man said and sipped his pint. 'I'll give you that.'

Mirabelle drank the gin and bitter lemon. 'Well,' she said, 'I'd best get going.'

Back out on the street, Mirabelle walked round to number twelve. She had every right, she told herself. She'd said to McGregor she wouldn't trouble Nurse Frida, but she hadn't said anything about her mother. She tidied herself as she knocked on the door. The woman who answered was old. Her hair was almost completely white and she wore a floral housecoat. Mirabelle thought it through – her mother, had she been alive, would have been in her late sixties by now. This woman was a decade older.

'Yes?' she said, so loudly that Mirabelle realised she must be deaf.

'Hello,' Mirabelle replied, raising her voice.

'Well, there's no need to shout,' the woman berated her. 'What do you want?'

'Are you Mrs Gill?' Mirabelle toned down her voice.

'Yes.'

'Superintendent McGregor sent me,' Mirabelle said smoothly. 'You know, the policeman who was here yesterday evening.'

'My daughter isn't in. She's at work at this time of day.'

'It was you he asked me to come and see, Mrs Gill. To check a few details.'

'I've nothing to do with it.'

'Nothing to do with what?'

'Frida's friend. The sister. I don't know anything about it.'

'Could I come in?'

The woman nodded. 'All right,' she said, peering around Mirabelle and down the street. 'It's probably best not to discuss things on the doorstep.'

Inside, a narrow hallway led on to an old-fashioned front room, which was comfortably furnished with three chairs around an unlaid, wrought-iron fireplace. The sun beat through the lace-fringed sash-and-case window, highlighting a universe of dust mites suspended in the air. Ahead, a whole wall was covered with photographs in wooden frames, some depicting images of people in Victorian dress. Several were of men in uniform, the photographs taken, Mirabelle imagined, before they left for war.

'How lovely,' she said. 'Are these family pictures?'

The old woman closed the door behind her. 'My brothers,' she said, vaguely. 'I had nine brothers, all older than me. They're gone now. What did you want to know?'

'The superintendent wondered if you'd met Sister Taylor? If you might know anything about her. I'm sure he explained last night that the sister has disappeared and we're following all avenues of inquiry. Anything you can remember, anything at all, might help.'

'I met her twice.' The old woman sat down and motioned

towards Mirabelle to do the same. A cross-stitched pillow cut into Mirabelle's back. It felt as if it was made of wire. 'I couldn't say I knew the sister. Not really,' Mrs Gill said.

'So you have no idea where she might be? Where she was from? Most people, you know, on the run, go somewhere familiar.'

'No, I don't know. I'm sorry.'

'How close were Sister Taylor and your daughter?'

'They worked together. That's all.'

'But you'd met her. Twice, you said?'

'In the street. Yes, twice. When I was with Frida. If you're out and about you bump into people, don't you?'

'Did Frida like Sister Taylor?'

'Nurses tend not to like the sister.'

'You were a nurse, weren't you?'

'Where did you hear that?'

'Perhaps I can just tell.'

The woman gave a tiny smile and wrinkled her nose. She pointed at a grainy black-and-white picture of a slim young woman in a pristine nurse's apron. 'The Great War,' she said. 'I started my training the day my brothers joined up. My sister and I went together. She's gone now too, of course.'

'And Frida followed you into the business.'

'It's a different thing these days. She has a cushy job over at that home. The pay's good and the children are easy. We had it rougher.'

'I imagine. Where were you?'

'We moved around. There were field hospitals in them days. The Serbs were good people. There was a lot of surgery. My mother looked after Frida.'

'Have you met the other nurses at the home? The younger girls?'

'They don't know they're born. That darkie and the little blonde one.'

'Uma and Berenice?'

'That's them. There's no surgery over there, see. It's all recuperation.'

'The place seems very well run.'

The old woman gave a half-shrug, as if she didn't like to heap praise, even on the establishment that employed her daughter. 'Well, Frida seems happy. They pay her well enough,' she managed.

'And working with children must be rewarding, I imagine,' Mirabelle kept fishing.

'Children. Yes.' The old lady's lips pursed.

'Don't you like Frida working with children, Mrs Gill?'

'Frida's all right. I'm sure she's a good nurse. She should be.'

Mirabelle leaned forward a little in her chair. 'But you have reservations.'

'She wasn't trained for children, that's all.'

'Specialist training, you mean?'

'During the war she worked in the women's ward. The other side of London.'

'What's that?'

'Oh, everyone thinks of wartime injuries. Battle injuries. Men, you know.'

'That was your training, wasn't it?'

'Baptism by fire, more like.' The old lady looked Mirabelle up and down. 'Well, you'd have never been to a field hospital. It's a baptism of fire being so close to the front. But Frida was posted to the women's ward out in the countryside. It was still military. Women don't go to the front line, of course, but they get injured too. Pilots. Munitions. Wrens. That kind of thing. They need to recuperate.'

'So, like you, Frida had a military training.'

'We were both army trained, yes,' she conceded.

Mirabelle sat back, shifting the uncomfortable pillow

to one side. Why was the old lady telling her this? 'It's fascinating,' she enthused. Mrs Gill almost smiled. 'So, do you think Frida oughtn't to be working with children, then?'

'I didn't say that. It's a good job. Pay and so forth.'

'Yes, you mentioned that.'

'But they didn't train her for it. After the war there was a scramble, you see. Most nurses went back to their families. There was a positive rash of weddings. On Frida's ward half the nurses married the doctors!'

Mirabelle thought of Uma and Ellen. That was how they had got together. That's what Ellen had said.

Mrs Gill continued. 'So that meant there weren't enough nurses after the war. I mean, the injuries slowed up, of course, but still, there were a lot of patients in the system. Frida got offered the job at the home – back here, where she'd started, in Brighton, with me. She had her pick, really. Her dad had died and her husband, well, we hadn't heard about him yet, but the news was in the post.'

'I'm sorry.'

The woman's eyes swam for a moment, as if she was focusing on something far off, in memory. 'Well,' she said. 'It just wasn't Frida's specialism, that's all. Children. If there's nothing else . . .'

Mirabelle got to her feet and the old woman saw her to the door. As it closed behind her, the street seemed particularly silent as she turned towards town. As she came down the hill there was a brisk breeze off the sea. The shady side of the street felt colder than before, cutting almost.

She ran through everything the old woman had said, wondering how difficult it might be to look after the children at the home. Most of them seemed on the mend. Still, it was obviously on the old lady's mind. Uma must have trained in India, she thought, but what about Berenice and Sister Taylor? What was their previous experience?

Back at the office, she clattered up the stairs. Vesta was at her desk.

'All right?' she asked, looking up as Mirabelle entered.

'Fine.' Mirabelle went to hang up her jacket.

When she turned round, Vesta was staring. 'You've had a drink, haven't you?'

'I did. I also spoke to the doctor about it. He says I'm fine, within limits.'

'What limits?'

'Well, a couple of gins in the afternoon.'

Vesta's palms lay flat on top of the paper she had been working on. Mirabelle couldn't help think that the ink was bound to come off on her skin. 'Without lunch, I suppose?' Vesta said.

'I had a late breakfast.'

The girl's eyes narrowed. 'I can't bear this,' she said. 'What on earth is going on? Mirabelle, you're sneaking out in the daytime like some kind of dipso.'

Mirabelle felt her hackles rise. 'Oh, for heaven's sake, Vesta. Stop it. Just because you've had Noel, doesn't mean the rest of us have to become members of the Mother's Institute.'

'What do you mean?'

'Time was, you'd have a drink with lunch.'

'You didn't have lunch, Mirabelle. I just asked you. If I can spot you've had a drink, our customers will be able to spot it too.'

'And what if I have? I'm not drunk.'

'You have drink taken.'

'That's a different thing, isn't it? I'm fine.'

'You're not fine. I know you too well to fall for that. It's been a rough week with Father Grogan dying and McGregor back on the scene. I can see.'

Mirabelle's temper flared. 'Don't start on about McGregor again. I think I'm beginning to hate him.'

'Does he think your drinking has got out of hand too?'

'My drinking has not got out of hand, Vesta.' Mirabelle felt tears stinging her eyes but she blinked them back, determined not to cry.

'Do you think I'd bring up something like that for fun?' Vesta crossed her arms.

Mirabelle didn't reply.

'Well?' Vesta pushed her.

'I think your life has changed so you think mine ought to as well.'

'You have changed, Mirabelle.'

'Maybe it's for the better.'

Vesta shook her head. Mirabelle relented slightly, the anger draining out of her.

'Look, I know it's been difficult the last few weeks. But I don't like all this criticism. I don't seem to fit in anywhere any more.'

She hated that she could feel a single tear trickling over her cheekbone.

'Well, drinking isn't going to help,' Vesta said smartly. 'Not being here for the business, it's crazy when we're doing so well . . .' The girl sounded frustrated.

Mirabelle reached for her coat and bag. 'I don't want to fight. I've enough to see to. I'll see you tomorrow.'

Vesta let out a sharp exhalation.

'It's my company,' Mirabelle turned on her. 'It's easy for you.'

'Easy?' Vesta puffed. 'With a baby to look after and all this?'

'You chose it. You didn't want to quit.'

'I don't want to. But Mirabelle, I miss you.'

She gasped. She bundled out of the door and down the stairs, almost running to get away. Back out on East Street she couldn't hold back the tears. She walked to Kingsway and crossed, taking the steps down to the pebbles. It was tricky to negotiate the bumpy surface even in kitten heels, but at least it gave her something to focus on. She sat on a vacant deckchair, only half checking for the man who took payment. Ahead, a wave washed in over the pebbles and was sucked back out again. Mirabelle scrambled in her bag for a handkerchief and blew her nose.

'You all right? Lovers' tiff, is it?' a voice said behind her. The man wore an apron and a peaked cap. 'It's tuppence, love,' he said. 'For the chair.'

Mirabelle hated having to pay to sit down, but she didn't want to argue any more. Reluctantly, she pulled a coin from her purse and handed it over. 'You got a front-row seat,' the man said cheerily. 'They found a body down here the other night. Just the other side of the pier.'

'I know,' Mirabelle muttered under her breath.

He walked away, stopping to talk to another fellow. She thought she heard him say something about her, something derogatory. 'That one down there, she's had a couple.' Some kind of snide joke.

Mirabelle pulled herself up so she was sitting tall. At school she'd taken classes in deportment. She peered round, intending to say something, but then she caught sight of a bobby up on the promenade. She didn't want to get involved in a fracas so she swung back round, hoping the man hadn't realised that she'd noticed what he had said. These days it seemed she wanted to shout at policemen and deckchair attendants and even Vesta.

It's not that bad, she told herself as she tried to calm down. *Lots of people have a far worse time than I do.* Father Grogan was dead and Rita Taylor was missing. She had responsibilities. She had better pull herself together.

Ahead, three teenagers were paddling in the surf, splashing and laughing. Further along, two old men were sipping bottles of beer and playing gin rummy, struggling to keep the cards in place when now and again there was a gust of wind. Above, the sky was crayon blue – as if a child had coloured it in. Mirabelle decided she'd sit for a while to gather her thoughts. Nobody was going to tell her what to do. Things would work out, she was sure of it. She'd get to the bottom of it all and then she'd feel better.

Chapter Twenty-Two

Do not be too moral. You may cheat yourself
out of much life

As the beach began to empty, Mirabelle gathered her thoughts. The afternoon was almost over. The sun was low on the horizon and a few streaks of cloud had formed. Vesta would have closed the office by now and rushed to pick up Noel and get back to her tidy family life. Mirabelle tottered up to the pavement and turned westwards. Jinty had said the party started at half past four, she recalled, and Mirabelle liked the idea of arriving slightly late. The doorman at the Old Ship Hotel recognised her as she approached. It should have been comforting, but today it made Mirabelle bristle. 'Good evening, madam,' he said as he opened the door and Mirabelle swept through.

The stairs were elegant; a shallow, carpeted sweep the colour of blood. Mirabelle felt herself becoming calmer as she made her way upwards and along the hallway, hung with gilded chandeliers and strings of crystal. A sign pointed the way to the 'salon'. It was easy to find – the sound of music drew her towards the rear of the building.

The room was busy – there must have been thirty people, most of them men wearing dark suits, clustered between the lush sofas and mahogany side tables. In the background a jazz record was playing on a gramophone – an instrumental tune that she didn't recognise. For a second Mirabelle stood at the door, and then she spotted Jinty in the heart of it. She was dressed in a figure-hugging, peach taffeta frock, regaling a group of three men with an anecdote they seemed to find amusing. 'Belle!' she squealed, and flung an arm around Mirabelle's shoulder as she approached, her ponytail bobbing. 'Here, have a glass of bubbly,' she said.

Mirabelle swept a glass off a tray but she didn't take a sip.

'This is Charlie,' Jinty introduced the men, 'and Michael and John. Gentlemen – Belle.'

The men nodded. One of them raised his glass in greeting, the others mumbled their hellos.

'The fellas were just telling me about their conference speeches today. About, what was it?'

'Statistics,' Charlie said.

'Yes. Statistics,' Jinty repeated. 'Fascinating. They're here for the whole weekend.'

'I'll drink to that,' Charlie said.

In no time Mirabelle was dancing with one of them though she had forgotten his name. When you stopped looking for differences, it was astonishing how similar these men were – short hair, neat silk ties, perhaps a pair of spectacles, and all married, of course. She felt a sense of freedom as the man twirled her, catching her by the waist and then twirling her again. The only people she knew here – Jinty and Rene and Tanya – wouldn't judge her for having a good time. On the sofa Rene was talking about going to the Midlands with a man she'd met – someone who wanted to take her away. Mirabelle raised her hands and let the man hold her close as the music slowed to a ballad. His skin smelled of shaving soap, she realised as he kissed her neck.

'I'm only popping in,' she said, laying her hand on his chest to keep him at a distance. 'I won't be staying.'

'You're not . . . one of the girls?'

'I'm only here for the party.'

The trays of half-filled champagne glasses disappeared at eight o'clock. Tanya had long gone upstairs with a tall man from Nottingham. Jinty was perched on a thin sofa with a man on either side. Mirabelle wondered what she had planned. Two bottles of brandy arrived on a tray and she found herself gravitating towards the little group.

'I'll be mother,' Jinty laughed as she poured.

There were, Mirabelle noted, about ten men left and four women – five if she included herself. She picked up a glass and took a sip. 'Well, I'd better be leaving,' she announced.

'Aww. Mirabelle,' Jinty got to her feet. 'Don't go. This is the fun part!'

Rene laughed. She looked nice tonight, if a little cheap, Mirabelle thought. She wore a red dress and the colour suited her blonde hair, which was curled in a tidy bun. The trouble was, these girls wore too much make-up. Mirabelle had always thought that. It gave them away.

'I'm meeting somebody for dinner,' she said.

'Your doctor? Oh, your doctor!' Jinty was exuberant. She gave an excited little clap. 'Well, that's all right then.'

Rene rounded, a glass of brandy in her hand. 'I thought you had it for Big Al,' she gushed.

Mirabelle clenched her teeth. 'Big Al?'

'You know. The super. Alan McGregor.'

'No. He's all yours.' Mirabelle managed to keep her tone light.

Rene giggled. She doubled over with laughter. 'What would I want him for? I only do it for the money, honey, and I'm very expensive, you know,' she said, and turned to the group of men to her left, none of whom seemed perturbed by this assertion; in fact, if anything, one or two appeared positively encouraged.

'But,' Mirabelle stumbled over the words, 'you and McGregor? He comes to see you at the house.'

'We don't do it in the house,' Rene laughed. 'We don't do it in the house,' she repeated for the benefit of the assembled men. 'Or only rarely. We do it in hotel rooms, mostly. Lovely hotel rooms, with hot water and nice linen. Like upstairs.' She winked.

Mirabelle felt the room swim. She put down her glass on a side table. The sound of it clicking on the wood echoed.

'Well,' said one of the men, 'maybe we ought to go upstairs and check it out. What do you say, ladies?'

One of them stepped back a little. He clearly wasn't game for the group nature of the suggestion. Jinty put her hand on his arm and whispered something into his ear. He nodded and checked his watch. It was an assignation.

'Well, why does the superintendent come to see you?' Mirabelle asked.

Rene winked again. It was a comedy wink for the benefit of the crowd. 'He knows my auntie. She asked him, you know, to keep an eye on me. He said he could get me a job doing something else.' She chortled. 'That's not going to cover my expenses, though, is it? A girl has a lot of expenses if she wants to look good.'

Mirabelle's stomach turned.

'But he came to see you at night, Rene. Ernie said that specifically. He came at night.'

'He's a policeman, isn't he? Policemen don't work regular hours. If it helps you any, he turns up in the afternoon sometimes too. I've got my own personal copper, gentlemen. So no getting out of line. In fact,' she hooted, 'form an orderly line, would you?'

Everyone laughed except Mirabelle.

'You mentioned your auntie?' she managed.

'My auntie Betty. She keeps house for the old git.'

'Miss Brownlee.' Mirabelle breathed out and found she couldn't breathe in again.

'That's her. She sends over boxes of biscuits, the dear. Butter shortbread and ginger thins. She loves baking. I prefer jewellery of course,' Rene couldn't help announcing.

'Right,' said the man who'd suggested decamping. He had clearly had enough of Rene's family tales. 'I've got a suite.' He fished a key out of his pocket. 'Come on. Upstairs, everybody.'

The man next to him scooped up the brandy bottles and Jinty got to her feet.

'Are you all right?' she asked Mirabelle.

Mirabelle managed to nod. Her mind was racing. 'I thought McGregor . . .'

'Well, he could if he wanted. What is it to you?'

'Nothing. Nothing.'

The party moved towards the door. The man Jinty had arranged to see privately held back. He sipped his brandy awkwardly and checked his watch once more.

'I don't suppose you'd like a spot of dinner, would you?'

Mirabelle shook her head. 'Thanks. I'm not hungry. Perhaps you should wait for Jinty in the bar. I bet she'll be quicker than you think.'

He nodded, compliant, took another sip of his drink and disappeared out of the door.

Alone, Mirabelle sank on to the sofa. The glass of the windows reflected the empty room, the open door back into the hallway a long black hole. Empty, thumb-marked glasses littered the furniture. The music stopped and the needle guttered. Then someone switched off the gramophone and she was aware that there was a figure beside her – a shadow.

'I don't want dinner,' Mirabelle repeated, waving him away.

The man crouched down, his blue eyes studying her face carefully. He reached out and wrapped his fingers around her wrist.

'I told you to lay off the sauce, Mirabelle,' he said.

'Oh God.' It was the most she could get out.

'How much did you have, sweetheart?'

'Gin at lunchtime.'

'One?'

'Two.'

'And here?'

'Some champagne and brandy.'

'Two of each?'

Mirabelle shrugged. 'I wasn't really counting. Perhaps only one of each, actually.'

Chris smiled. They both knew that two drinks wouldn't have left her in such a state. She was grateful that he didn't press the point. 'A couple of hours and you'll be right as rain.'

Mirabelle wished it was that simple.

'Dr,' she said, 'do you know anything at all about the missing woman?'

'Sister Taylor? They haven't brought her in, have they?'

Mirabelle shook her head. 'Not as far as I know. I was wondering about her medical experience. It came into my mind.'

Chris cocked his head sideways. 'I could ring round and ask,' he said. 'And maybe then you could manage a little soup. Soup is almost always a good idea for ladies who've had too many mixed drinks. Grape and grain, Mirabelle – that wasn't a good idea. Do we have a deal?'

'Deal,' Mirabelle nodded. But all she could think was that no matter how kind he was, she couldn't sleep with him, not now. She couldn't go off to Mayfair or anywhere else. Not till she'd apologised to McGregor and set the injustice she'd done the superintendent to rights. She felt her stomach heave.

'You're getting paler,' Chris diagnosed. 'Perhaps we should get you to the lavatory. Come along.'

Chapter Twenty-Three

The quarrels of lovers are the renewal of love

When Mirabelle woke up she was in a hotel room. The back of the door had an emergency notice that was headed, The Old Ship, with an engraved drawing of a schooner. Blearily, she sat up and looked around, peering through another door into the en-suite bathroom, but there was nobody else there. She patted the mattress next to her, but the bed was quite empty apart from a pillow that had been slipped under the sheet. She couldn't quite remember how she'd got here but she could guess. He really was an uncommonly decent sort of man, she thought – and he'd been helpful too, it came back to her. Sister Taylor, it had transpired, had a long history of working with children with respiratory complaints. That much she could remember.

Swinging her legs over the edge of the bed, she stumbled towards the bathroom and ran a sink of hot water to splash her face. Then she peered at herself in the mirror. She looked more fresh-faced than she felt. The bruises were almost completely gone. The sun beamed through the window, casting long shadows across the floor from the furniture. It seemed too high in the sky, she thought as she scrambled for her watch.

'Damn it,' she muttered, realising how late it was. McGregor wasn't the only person to whom she owed an apology. She got dressed quickly, smoothing her clothes, trying to make the outfit look fresh. Vesta would know, of course, that she'd worn that outfit yesterday.

There was no key in the room but she didn't intend to come back so Mirabelle left without locking the door, checking the surfaces quickly to make sure she hadn't left anything behind. At the end of the carpeted corridor she called the lift, and when the door pinged open Rene was inside.

'Morning,' the girl beamed.

Mirabelle stepped inside. 'Ground floor?'

'Yes please.'

Rene looked better than Mirabelle felt. In fact, she looked better than she had the night before. She was, Mirabelle thought, really quite a pretty thing without all her make-up. Prepared, the girl had brought clean clothes for the morning – a flat pair of pumps and a lemon cotton summer dress. Her hair was tied with a matching ribbon and she smelled faintly of a fresh, fruity scent – apples, perhaps. She might have been somebody's daughter in Brighton on holiday – here to enjoy a show and read a magazine sitting in the sunshine on the white pebbles.

'What have you been up to?' Rene quizzed Mirabelle, as she looked her up and down. 'Get a good offer, did you? Jinty will expect her cut, you know, if he was one of ours.'

'I bumped into a friend,' Mirabelle said.

Rene giggled. 'That's what it's all about. Best thing in life – bumping. I'm going to get a cup of tea and some breakfast downstairs. You can join me if you like. The blokes never mind if you put breakfast on their tab. They do sausages here – nice ones. I've had them before.'

'I'm late for work. It's almost eleven.'

Rene shrugged.

'I know your aunt,' Mirabelle said suddenly. 'She's a good woman.'

'Auntie Betty?'

'Yes.'

'She could do with some style tips from you, I'd say.' The girl's eyes lingered on Mirabelle's outfit. Mirabelle felt uncomfortable. 'I wouldn't have expected you two to be friends.'

'I bought her a silk scarf one Christmas but she doesn't seem to wear it.'

Rene giggled again as the lift door opened on to the main hallway. 'You can take a horse to water, isn't that what they say? I've tried to give her money a couple of times, but she won't take it. She shouldn't have to work at her age.'

'Perhaps she enjoys it. She is a very good cook.'

'Perhaps Superintendent McGregor likes keeping her in the kitchen. She's cheap, I expect, and she suits him.'

It was Mirabelle's turn to shrug. McGregor had promised Miss Brownlee's brother that he'd look after her while he served a term in jail. But that didn't mean he had to keep her employed. She suspected, though, that Miss Brownlee would not take willingly to retirement.

The hallway was busy. A stack of mismatched leather suitcases tottered beside the reception desk as a large party of tourists checked in. A maid was mopping the tiles at the door with her head down. Rene had excellent deportment, Mirabelle thought, as the girl strode across the hall in the direction of the dining room. Breakfast was probably over, but then the girl was used to getting what she wanted. She'd tip well.

'Goodbye, then. Have a nice day at the office,' Rene grinned.

Mirabelle felt she wanted to offer some advice or help or something – anything – but she couldn't think what to say.

'Goodbye,' she managed to get out, and then she turned and walked into the sunshine, the doorman tipping his hat as she passed. He didn't even smirk, Mirabelle thought, but that was probably the sign of a good hotel doorman – someone who knew your secrets and didn't judge you.

The sea air smelled warm again, as if it was still June – a throwback to the summer that was on its way out. Mirabelle turned left and walked the few blocks to East Street, turning out of the sunshine up the hill and through the shady office doorway. She climbed the stairs, pausing momentarily before opening the door. She'd just say it, she decided – throw herself on Vesta's good nature. Apologise. Explain. But as she pushed the door wide and stepped across the threshold, Vesta was not in the mood for listening. The girl was at her desk, dabbing her eyes with a handkerchief as tears streamed down her cheeks.

'Oh God,' she said. 'I thought you were a client and I just couldn't stop crying. Every time I think of it, I start again.'

'Vesta, what is it? What's wrong?'

Vesta sniffed. 'We didn't even notice.'

'What happened?'

'Julie died last night. Bill's wife. Someone rang to tell me first thing – one of Bill's neighbours. They said he wouldn't be in. Of course he won't be in. The poor woman's been ill, Mirabelle. She's been in and out of hospital for months and Bill didn't say a thing. Not a word.' The girl gulped down air as she tried to control herself but she kept sobbing. Her face crumpled. 'I thought he was being rude, you know, when he wouldn't come to our party the other weekend. I mean, that's what I assumed, because he was so obviously lying when he said he was busy. But he didn't tell anyone she was ill. Not a soul. That's what the neighbour said. The first thing anyone knew was the undertaker arriving this morning to make the arrangements. The neighbours knew she'd lost weight but they just thought – you know – it was the change of life or something. I mean, you'd hardly want to pry. That's what the man said. "You'd hardly want to pry." He called it unfortunate. Can you imagine? And all this time, Bill didn't say a word. Not a word. And he must have known she wasn't going to get better, Mirabelle. God.'

Mirabelle thought back on Bill's scuffed shoes, his poorly executed shave, how he'd stopped bringing a packed lunch, and the morning he had been late for work. 'We're not very good detectives,' she said quietly. 'Are we?'

This set Vesta off again. She let out a little howl. 'I mean, there he was with me, at the Haywards' house yesterday, chasing a stupid outstanding debt, and we went to the bank, and all along it was her last day alive and he was working. He shouldn't have even been here. If that was Charlie . . .' Vesta couldn't go on. She held the handkerchief up to her face and sobbed quietly. 'Poor Bill,' she managed at last.

Mirabelle sank into a chair. Vesta was right. She'd been the selfish one, caught up in her petty misapprehension about McGregor and flirting with Chris and on the trail of a ghost – Sister Taylor – when much closer to home there was someone really in need of her attention. It had felt as if she didn't have anybody, but she did – and it should have been down to her. Vesta didn't have the experience, but how could Mirabelle not have noticed? It was right under her nose.

'Do you know what it was? What she died of, I mean?'

'Cancer,' Vesta sniffed. 'It just ate her away.'

Mirabelle reached across the desk and squeezed Vesta's arm. 'I'm so sorry, Vesta. I've been absent, haven't I? I feel so stupid. And you were right to get angry with me yesterday. Quite right. I've been foolish and off the rails and I haven't been pulling my weight.'

She cast her eyes at Bill's desk with its empty chair. 'What was Bill's round supposed to be today?'

'Oh, that can wait, can't it?'

'Of course. We need to find out when the funeral will be and call round to offer our condolences.'

Vesta sniffed and nodded. 'It'll be next week, I suppose,' she said.

'Do you think you can forgive me?' Mirabelle asked.

Vesta nodded. 'Don't be silly,' she said.

'Thank you. I need to apologise to McGregor too, it seems. I've been a terrible fool.'

Vesta pulled out the phonebook. 'Their church is St Magnus, isn't it, Julie and Bill? I'll phone and ask about the funeral. Why don't you go and find McGregor? I mean, if there's one thing this sort of thing teaches you, it's that we shouldn't leave anything. Nothing at all. If you've something to say to McGregor, for heaven's sake, Mirabelle, go and say it.'

Mirabelle sat forwards in her chair. She looked momentarily at Bill's desk, the papers stacked tidily from the day before, when he hadn't known that it would be his wife's last day. Perhaps Vesta was right. 'All right,' she said. 'I'll do it now.'

Back outside, she walked up the shady side of the street, cutting through the cool air. It felt good on her skin. She thought of the day she'd met Julie, when she'd gone to Bill's house to offer him the job three years ago, maybe four. Mrs Turpin had always been there, in the background, encouraging her husband. In fact, she had literally always been in the background, it struck Mirabelle now. Baking in the kitchen, fixing Bill's shirts, quietly supportive. A wife.

At the desk at Bartholomew Square police station, Sergeant Belton nodded.

'Miss Bevan,' he said. 'How are you this morning?'

Mirabelle felt unsure how to reply. 'I'm looking for Superintendent McGregor,' she managed.

'The super isn't in, miss.'

Mirabelle sighed. 'Any idea when he might be back?'

Belton never gave anything away if he didn't want to. It would seem today he was not feeling generous. 'I couldn't say, miss.' She knew he had no reason to help her.

'Do you know where he's gone?'

'Police business,' he said implacably. Above his head the clock ticked.

'Did you hear about Bill Turpin's wife?'

Belton sucked his teeth. 'Terrible business. Bill's one of our own.'

'Vesta is checking when the funeral is. We had no idea, Sergeant. Bill never said a thing.'

'Well, he's a private sort of man. You wouldn't want to intrude, would you?'

That's what was wrong, Mirabelle realised. Nobody wanted to intrude. 'If you see McGregor, tell him I was looking for him,' she said.

Back outside, Mirabelle lingered. She leaned against the stone wall a moment in the shade, as if it might give her strength. Back down East Street, Vesta would be pulling herself together. Mirabelle raised her head and felt her eyes fill with tears. Ahead, the streets towards town were striped with sunshine and shade. She pulled her jacket around her shoulders and set off in the direction of McGregor's house. At least she'd get to see Betty Brownlee, she figured, and she probably owed her an apology too.

St James's Street was bustling. The shops were busy this morning and a queue outside the bakery signalled hot pies fresh out of the oven. Mirabelle cut down towards McGregor's guesthouse, thinking that she must eat something. It had been a while. She turned off the main road and hesitated outside, her heart beating faster. Then she opened the gate and rang the bell. Betty Brownlee looked quite regal when she answered – she was always ready for a new guest, Mirabelle realised. She looked older, close up, than she had in the street. Maybe Rene was right about the amount of work she took on.

'Hello,' said Mirabelle.

Betty's lips stretched without actually smiling. Her eyes hardened. 'Miss Bevan,' she managed.

'I saw your niece this morning,' Mirabelle said. 'She's most concerned about you working so hard.'

'She needn't worry about me.' Betty sounded as if she was spitting the words.

'Is the superintendent in?'

Betty wasn't accustomed to lying. She considered it, but knew she couldn't pull it off. 'He's upstairs,' she said. 'But he's busy.'

Mirabelle stepped over the threshold. 'Rene's misguided, that's all,' she said kindly. 'If it's any help, I think she's quite safe.'

'If I thought she wasn't safe I'd be up at that house myself . . .' Betty started, holding herself back from completing the sentence. 'She does it to vex her mother.'

Mirabelle smiled. That was unlikely. 'She does it because she wants the money, Betty. She says she enjoys it.'

'How could anyone enjoy it? All those men?'

'She'll come out the other side.' Mirabelle realised the words sounded like a promise. 'She'll appreciate your concern then.'

'It's her life, I suppose,' Betty sniffed to indicate that although it might be Rene's life, she wasn't happy about it. Then she stood back to let Mirabelle pass. 'He's upstairs,' she said. 'You know the way.'

It was strange being back in the house. It had been a long time. The hallway smelled of toast and, as Mirabelle walked upstairs to the first floor, there was the faintest tang of laundry soap. It was still familiar, as if Mirabelle had simply been on holiday for a while, and only now was coming home. A young couple emerged from one of the rooms – guests on holiday. 'Good morning,' they trilled, and disappeared noisily down the stairs, holding hands, and out of the front door. Mirabelle stood outside McGregor's room as if she was

221

a ghost of herself haunting all the times she'd visited there, all the times she'd stayed. She waited a moment, gathering her thoughts and realising it wasn't going to become easier. Then she knocked.

'Come.'

She turned the handle. Inside, McGregor was not alone. Two other officers were with him, the bed and chairs and table a sea of paper. Two crates of files were piled by the superintendent's chair. Three of the paintings had been taken off the wall and black and white photographs were pinned in their place. The young officer who had come to fetch Chris the other night sat on the bed, in a space that he had cleared, reading. Another was standing by the window, a file in his hand.

'Mirabelle,' McGregor said, springing to his feet from the chair he'd been ensconced in. She'd surprised him. He motioned to the other men. 'Could you give us a minute, lads? Maybe Miss Brownlee could sort you out some tea?'

McGregor closed the file he was reading and put it down as they left the room. Mirabelle listened to their footsteps receding down the stairs.

'You can't come here,' he said, his arms wide as he ushered her back towards the doorway.

'What's going on?'

'We needed some space to work on case files. It's too busy at Bartholomew Square. Are you all right?'

Mirabelle was unsure how to answer. 'It's all shifting sands,' she said vaguely. 'Bill's wife died last night.'

'Julie?'

'We didn't even know that she was ill. Vesta is devastated. I blame myself. I could see Bill wasn't his usual self. I should have looked into it.'

'Poor Bill. I heard the poor woman had cancer. I didn't know it had gone so far.'

Mirabelle nodded. 'Seems like you knew more than me. And about more than one thing, too. I met Rene last night. I mean, I realised about Rene last night. And I wanted to apologise. I assumed the worst of you, Alan. I thought because she was a young, pretty girl . . .'

McGregor's face split into a grin. 'You thought I was having an affair with a child. Yes. It did grate.'

'I'm sorry.'

McGregor touched her arm, pulling her towards him. 'There's nobody but you for me, Mirabelle Bevan. I don't think there ever will be. You know that, don't you?'

Mirabelle's eye was drawn to the boxes of files. Rene hadn't been the only reason she'd given up on her relationship with McGregor. There was the boy who'd been killed. What on earth was going on here, she wondered. 'I can't come back,' she said. 'I mean, there's what happened to Freddy.'

McGregor didn't react. She wondered for a moment, if he'd forgotten. He seemed to be thinking about something else.

'I can't bring him back. I let him down. That's true. Look, I admire you because you're upright,' he said. 'That's what I love about you. Well, one of the things.'

Mirabelle felt herself pull back. He made her sound like a monument.

'I only came to apologise,' she said. 'I told Brownlee that I thought she was working too hard.'

'She likes working hard.'

'You should have her take on another pair of hands, Alan. A woman of her age shouldn't be managing so much. It's a big house, what with all the guests.'

'Brownlee can do as she likes. I leave the running of the place to her entirely. If she wants help, there's money for it.'

'I think she should be encouraged to engage someone. For a woman like her, it's an admission she can't cope.'

223

'All right. I'll see what I can do.'

'I need to get back and find out about the funeral.'

As Mirabelle moved, McGregor caught her hand and pressed it to his lips. 'I wish you'd marry me,' he said. 'I wish you'd let it be easy.'

Mirabelle snatched her hand away. Outside she heard steps on the stairs. 'They're coming up,' she said.

'Think about it.' McGregor's gaze was steady. 'Please. There's so much grief everywhere. And we could be happy. We could buy a bigger place, down the coast. Brownlee would run it for us with an army of maids, if you like. I've missed you, Mirabelle. I miss you every day.'

'Why didn't you tell me about Rene? Why didn't you explain?'

'I am long past the stage of telling you what to think.'

Mirabelle looked at him as if from a distance. He was good looking enough, though it had never been McGregor's looks she'd particularly liked – more the thread of sadness that ran like a vein through him, and his ability to listen. His shy sense of humour and the fact that he knew her. She thought she'd known him.

'It's no good looking back all the time,' he said. 'We're not going that way, you know.' When he smiled she felt herself move, very slightly, towards him. Then she pulled herself together.

'I'd better go.'

For a moment he looked as if he might cry. Then there was a rap at the door. He reached past her to open it.

'Sorry, sir.'

'No. Quite right. We need to get on. There's work to do.'

He pulled it wider so that Mirabelle could leave.

'I'll see you at the funeral, then,' she said.

As she turned down the stairs, the door closed. She heard the mumble of the men's voices as they went back to work.

She put out her hand and grasped the bannister a moment, rocking on her feet, trying to steady herself. McGregor's proposal had thrown her. Downstairs the kitchen door opened and Brownlee emerged carrying a tray of tea things. She hung back, waiting for Mirabelle to come down the stairs.

'Thank you,' Mirabelle said.

'You can see yourself out,' Brownlee sniffed.

Mirabelle nodded. 'Of course.'

As she opened the front door, Brownlee disappeared upwards.

Outside Mirabelle turned left towards the front. A gull landed on the roof of McGregor's house and eyed her glassily. Two floors below, one of McGregor's men stood in the window, watching her progress down the pavement. McGregor had never been short of space at the station before, she thought, as she gave a small nod, acknowledging him before continuing on her way. It felt as if she'd turned her back on too much lately – Bill's predicament, Chris's kindness and now Alan's proposal. But there was so much to do.

She crossed on to the sunny side and wished she had her sunglasses with her. Inland, towards Kemptown, she could hear the church bells striking midday and she picked up her pace. Her mind wandered back to McGregor's bedroom – the room they'd shared for months that now seemed almost desecrated with those piles of papers. And then it struck her that she recognised one of the photographs on the wall. It was the car that had drawn up at Uma and Ellen's house and taken Uma away – or at least the same model. And there was a picture of a woman who also seemed familiar. Mirabelle tried to remember where she had seen her before, but drew a blank. She almost turned around and then dragged herself back to the matter in hand – Bill's bereavement was more important, of course it was. There were things she needed to put right, she scolded herself. There was so much to get on with. First things first.

Chapter Twenty-Four

We die only once and for such a long time

Once she had something to organise, Vesta's demeanour changed. By the time Mirabelle reappeared at the office, Vesta had put a note on the door that announced 'Due to Bereavement this office is closed this afternoon.' Vesta already had her jacket on. In front of her, two cardboard boxes sat on the desk.

'Food for Bill,' she explained. 'I had Charlie send over some things from the Grand. I'll order us a cab. We can't carry all that on the bus.'

It always seemed odd that the quiet suburban streets where people died still looked like quiet suburban streets. A crowd of children played a game of dice, clustered round a lamppost. Several front doors gaped open in the sunshine on to thin, dark, immaculately clean hallways. The sun didn't betray the bereavement that was under way privately behind the net curtains of one of the houses. You'd never have known. Mirabelle paid the driver as Vesta juggled the cardboard boxes.

'Ready?'

Vesta nodded.

A slim, pale woman with her hair tied in a brown cotton scarf answered the door when Mirabelle knocked. The resemblance to Julie was uncanny. Vesta gasped audibly.

'I'm her sister,' the woman said, her voice flat. 'I'm the older one.'

'We came to give our condolences,' Mirabelle replied, smoothly. 'It's a very close resemblance. Is Bill available?'

Inside, Bill sat in his armchair with Panther at his feet, as if they were both becalmed. A bottle of whisky and a bottle of brandy sat on the table, surrounded by a cluster of empty glasses on the white cotton tablecloth. Bill stumbled as Mirabelle came in, fumbling out of his chair, looking sheepish. Panther wagged his tail in greeting but didn't get up.

'You didn't have to . . .' he said, holding out his hand.

'Oh Bill. Of course we did. I wish you'd told us what was going on.'

'There was nothing anyone could have done. I didn't want you feeling sorry for me.'

'Forlorn hope now,' Vesta said with a smile, clutching Bill's fingers. 'Charlie sent this lot over. He said you liked rock buns and I think there's some pressed ham and some biscuits. He sends you his best.'

Bill gave a weak smile. 'He's a good man.'

Julie's sister took the boxes from Vesta and disappeared into the kitchen at the rear of the house. Mirabelle stared after her. Women were always there, organising everything, smoothing the way.

'She didn't want a fuss,' Bill said, as if he was apologising for his stoicism. 'I didn't want one either, I don't suppose.'

'Oh, Bill,' Vesta's eyes filled with tears, 'I'm so sorry. The priest at St Magnus said the funeral will be next week.'

Bill nodded. 'It's taken her mother by surprise,' he said.

'Julie's mother?'

'Poor old dear. She just lives around the corner. You don't expect your kids to go before you, even if they're ill. She knew it was coming but this morning she took to her bed. I'll be all right, you know. A bit scruffier than when Julie looked

228

after me. Not as well fed. It's Pat I feel for, and Debbie here,' he said as Julie's sister came back into the room.

'She'd had enough by the end, hadn't she, Bill?' Debbie said. 'There was nothing more they could do for her and the pain was terrible.'

'I can't believe you came with me yesterday and tracked down Hayward. And you could have been here. I'm sorry.'

'She wouldn't have had it. Julie insisted, you see. Business as usual. I was following orders.'

'You're not to come back to the office till you're ready – those are our orders.'

'That'll be tomorrow. I'm not hanging around here with all the neighbours coming round and everybody talking about her! No. I've got to do something to work up an appetite for that ham you brought.' Bill cracked an unconvincing smile.

'It's Friday today,' said Vesta, gently. 'We're closed tomorrow, Bill.'

'Of course. Yes. Of course.'

The back door opened and Debbie peered down the hallway. 'It's Mrs Close from number seven,' she whispered.

'Hello,' a voice called uncertainly.

'We're in here, love,' Bill shouted.

'People have been in and out all day. Julie helped everyone, you see.'

'She did,' the old lady announced as she came into the room. 'Oh Mr Turpin, she helped me with my laundry when I hurt my hip. I'm so sorry to see her go.'

'I wish she was still here, I mean for you to pay your last respects. They took her away, you see.' He sounded helpless.

'It's only Catholics who keep the body at home, Bill,' Debbie said. 'You know that.'

They all perched awkwardly on the three-piece suite. Debbie offered to make tea but nobody wanted any. Mrs Close said she'd help with Bill's housework. Bill stared forlornly at the grate in front of him and thanked her. Debbie said something about sorting through her sister's clothes but she didn't move.

'Was it busy today, then?' Bill asked. 'You know. At work this morning?'

Vesta shrugged. 'Not really,' she said. 'We can cover for a few days, I'm sure. Mirabelle saw the superintendent.'

'He sends his regards,' Mirabelle said. 'He was working from home.'

She thought about the picture of the Jaguar pinned to the bedroom wall.

'At home? That's unusual,' Bill said.

After twenty minutes of stilted small talk, they finally ran out of things to say. Vesta rolled her eyes at Mirabelle and the women took their leave. They decided to walk back into town, past the children who were now playing hopscotch on the paving stones, and on to the main road. It jarred that the world was behaving normally – it always seemed that way after something as devastating as a death, even one that wasn't a murder.

'He needs his routine,' Mirabelle said. 'We can't take that away from him.'

'Well, he'll have to wait.' Vesta cracked a plucky grin. 'I care about Bill, but I'm not opening on a Saturday. I don't understand it, Mirabelle. If Charlie died, I wouldn't be able to come in . . . I wouldn't be able to sit around chatting like that.'

Mirabelle had no doubt that was true. When Jack had died she hadn't been able to stand or speak or even think. That Bill was functioning to such a high degree was extraordinary, but then of course that's what he'd do – hold himself together.

'Everyone's different,' she said.

Vesta gave a little shrug. It always seemed to her the generation who made it through the war was made of tougher material than everybody else.

'They never had kids,' she said, sadly.

'No.'

'You wonder why that happens. Why some people do and some people don't. I didn't even want a baby – do you remember?'

'Yes,' Mirabelle smiled. 'You were insistent. You didn't want to tell anybody when you got pregnant.'

Vesta laughed. 'It seems strange now.'

A bus passed them, but there was no question of getting on. Vesta touched her hat lightly, checking her reflection in the window of a hardware shop.

'So, this case you're working on,' she said. 'With the sick kids . . .'

Mirabelle scrambled for the details. There seemed so much else going on. 'It's complicated,' she said. 'And not very nice.'

'Murder is never nice, is it?'

'You used to be interested in that kind of thing.'

'Tell me about it.'

'The nurses are covering up something. The night Father Grogan died, there were visitors to the home after he left and Sister Taylor disappeared. They lied, you see. They probably lied about the fight they had – Father Grogan shouting at Sister Taylor. It's likely they were all involved, but I haven't unravelled it yet.'

'And that other body? What about him?'

'Gerry Bone?'

'Yes. Has he anything to do with it?'

'I still don't know. He was most likely strangled and flung in the sea. I would say there wasn't a connection, but two bodies and a missing woman in as many days – we can't count it out.'

Vesta sighed, as if to ask, well, what have you been doing with your time?

'And you've looked into the nurses?'

'A little. I spoke to Nurse Frida's mother. And I visited Nurse Uma at home.'

'Anyone jumpy?'

Mirabelle thought for a moment. 'Not Frida. But Uma and her lover were. Uma got jumpy about her plants actually – she has the most extraordinary physic garden.'

'A lover?' And there was the old Vesta.

'A female doctor. They met in a clinic in India.'

'Oh, so that is the woman you asked me to check out – you know, for the cats?'

'Yes. In fact, she was jumpy in the home – sneaking cigarettes and goodness knows what else. She's unhappy about something – other than the death, I mean, and Sister Taylor's disappearance.'

'She's the weak link, then.'

Mirabelle wondered why she hadn't gone back to Uma. Vesta was right. 'I've been rather distracted,' she said. 'That's the thing. I can't seem to tie it all together.'

'You said woman,' Vesta said vaguely.

'What woman?'

'The woman doctor. The nurse's friend.'

Mirabelle wasn't sure what to say. 'Yes,' she managed.

'Lovers,' Vesta said. 'Gosh. I've never heard of that. Well, Uma is the weak link, then.'

Mirabelle wondered why she hadn't gone back to the nurse. Vesta was right. 'The nurse got picked up by a man. He drove her off. The doctor wasn't pleased.'

'Well, she wouldn't be.'

'Not that, Vesta. Picked up in a car. Uma was going to work for him, I think. She was in her uniform.'

'A man in a car needing a nurse and not a doctor?'

'Yes.'

'What kind of man?'

'He looked like a hood. He had a thin moustache and, well, frankly, a bad suit. He drove a Jaguar.'

'Did you get the registration number. What model was it?'

Mirabelle looked forlorn. 'I don't know,' she said. 'You're much better at that kind of thing. It was blue. I suppose we could check with a garage, if there was one sold down here.'

'If you want a Jaguar you have to buy it in London.'

They crossed the road. Mirabelle breathed in the rush of sea air. 'We're lucky to be alive, aren't we? I mean, that's what it comes down to. Poor Julie Turpin, sick all that time and we never knew. Father Grogan poisoned out of the blue. Every day we're just lucky to be here.'

Vesta nodded. 'Yes,' she said. 'It's a duty. At least, that's what my mum would call it.'

'A duty?'

'To be happy. To make the best of things.'

Mirabelle paused. She'd never thought of happiness as a duty. It cast a new light on things. If she was choosing between McGregor and Dr Williams, thinking of it that way made it an easier choice.

Two ice-cream vans parked at the bottom of Old Steine played music out of time with each other. The women turned into the maze of streets, away from the shrill noise on the hot air. A group of small boys, wearing shorts of various lengths, leaned against a lamppost.

'I can help if you like,' Vesta offered. 'With your case, I mean.'

Mirabelle smiled. 'Really? Would you?'

'Well, for a start, someone needs to look into the clinic where these two women met, don't you think? In India.'

Vesta had always been good at getting to the bottom of things. 'Good idea,' Mirabelle said.

'And I suppose it might be a good idea if I went over to the children's home. There was a little black girl you mentioned?'

233

'Oh Vesta, she'd love that. It'd be wonderful if you could check on Lali.'

'It's going to mean you minding the office for a change,' said Vesta. 'Finishing up everything for us to start again on Monday.'

Mirabelle smiled. 'Maybe it's about time.'

Inside, Mirabelle left the 'Closed' notice in place. She opened the office window to air the room. The sound of a passing car snaked up from the street below. Bill's desk was tidy already, but she carefully put Vesta's papers in a pile and then pushed the girl's chair into place. She washed a single dirty teacup and laid it out to dry and smoothed the newspaper without reading it. Then Mirabelle leaned against her own desk and surveyed her kingdom.

Perhaps McGuigan and McGuigan had had its day, she thought. Maybe she'd go to London with Chris Williams after all – to live in his flat in Mayfair. She could walk in Hyde Park every morning and go shopping – the buzz of the big city sounded rather attractive. They'd look back at Brighton as the place they met – with its wide blue skies and the crowds on the beach. London was, after all, where she'd come from. After all these years, it seemed suddenly possible to go back there and make a home. To get away from Brighton and its piles of dead bodies, its grubby affairs – the mess of the place. Not that the big city was in any way tidy, she smiled. But still. She remembered what someone had once said about Brighton – that when London turned upside down, the loose change fell out of its pockets and landed at the south coast. Brighton felt like that these days – grubby, fluffy change with scraps of old paper. The thing was, it had never seemed possible to leave Jack before.

Mirabelle picked up the telephone and called the city morgue. The number rang half a dozen times.

'Brighton Morgue, can I help you?'

'Could I speak to Dr Chris Williams? It's Mirabelle Bevan here.'

'Hold, please.'

The telephone clicked and whirred and the doctor picked up.

'Hello.'

'I think I owe you dinner,' she said, surprised at her flirtatious tone – how light she sounded.

Chris was duly encouraged. 'Great! Tonight?'

'Do you think we might ever get to finish a meal at the Old Ship?'

'You mean finish it properly?'

She didn't answer that. 'Busy day?'

'Always. I issued Bone's death certificate.'

'Strangulation?'

'Well, it wouldn't be an unexpected end for a man in his position and I can't find anything else. I thought you'd want to know.'

'I've been considering your offer. About London.'

'Good. I'll see you at eight, then. Shall I pick you up?'

'No. I'll see you there.'

The phone clicked. She could almost feel herself blush at how forward she'd been but there was no point in playing games. No sooner had she replaced the receiver than the phone rang. Mirabelle picked it up with a wry expression on her face.

'Can't you wait?' she teased him. 'It's only a few hours.'

'Can't I wait for what?' It was Vesta's voice.

'Nothing. Sorry.'

'Mirabelle, you had best come down here. That Indian nurse of yours . . .'

'She's hardly mine, Vesta.'

'She's just tried to kill herself.'

Chapter Twenty-Five

Blood spilt cries out for more

Mirabelle paid the cab driver and didn't wait for her change. As the cab drove off, she strode up the steps of the children's home and rang the doorbell. Vesta answered immediately.

'They won't let me see her,' she said, pulling back into the shady hallway and sitting down on one of the mismatched chairs that ran down the side. 'But they haven't asked me to leave. I said I'd just wait.' Mirabelle closed the front door behind her. The hallway was silent and the air felt heavy. The door to the sunny downstairs ward was closed and so was the door to the rear of the house, where the office was situated. The only light came from a small window halfway up the stairs, the fanlight over the front door and a single, yellowing bulb of curiously low wattage that hung from a pendant fitting above them.

'What happened exactly?'

'Well, Lali is going home tomorrow. When I turned up, I think they thought I'd come to pick her up early. You know, because there are only three black women in the whole of England and we're all related.' Vesta rolled her eyes. 'I explained I'd just come to visit – to check the kid was OK. I didn't mention you, of course. I said I was a friend of the family. She's a sweet little thing – bright too. Can you imagine sending away your daughter like that? I mean, the child is sick and you just put them on a train?'

Mirabelle licked her lips. 'I expect they sent an ambulance. That would make more sense, wouldn't it?'

'Still. On her own.'

'In the care of the medical profession.'

'Suicidal nurses,' Vesta objected. 'And the sister just went missing. This is hardly a happy place. I wonder how much the parents of the children know.' It was clear that if and when Noel got sick, he would not be leaving Vesta's sight. Not even in surgery. 'Anyway, they said of course I could visit. They took me into the back garden but there was a kerfuffle back inside – screaming and the like. I ran in to see what was going on. Which brings me to the Indian nurse.'

'Uma, you mean.'

'Yes. As far as I can understand it, she took something from the medicine cabinet – an overdose, I expect. They found her on the floor in the office at the back. All hell broke loose and the other nurses grabbed her and made her sick. They took her upstairs to one of the wards. That's when I took the chance to call you from the office.'

'Did they call the police? Afterwards, I mean.'

Vesta shook her head. 'Not that I saw, and nobody's turned up. Not a doctor. Not a policeman. Nobody.' The girl raised her eyes towards the top of the stairs. 'They said to wait here. I offered to go back into the garden and play with the kids, but the older nurse wouldn't have it. "We're dealing with an emergency," she said. "Staff only. We'll come and get you when things are settled," she said. "If you want to wait." So I did.'

'I see,' said Mirabelle. 'Well, fair enough. You hold the fort, then.'

'But . . .' Vesta got to her feet.

Mirabelle put her fingers to her lips. 'They don't know I'm here. Leave this to me – I'll have a snoop and see what I can

237

find. You just cover if you have to.' She motioned for Vesta to sit down, which she did, albeit unwillingly.

Gingerly, Mirabelle climbed the stairs, her heels echoing on the linoleum as she rose higher. She moved on to her tiptoes and made it to the top silently. The upper hallway was smaller than the reception area on the ground floor and it was lighter too. Several doors opened off the upstairs landing and another, thinner, set of wooden stairs jutted upwards at an angle to what must at one time have been servants' quarters. An equally awkward and thin set of stairs ran down the back of the house, where a passageway had been knocked through to the adjoining property. Carrying somebody up the stairs or along the passage would be tricky – the opening was not much more than two or three feet wide and the stairs turned at a sharp angle. No, Mirabelle reasoned, having got Nurse Uma up here, if there were beds on this floor, they'd choose one of those.

She opened the first door on to an empty dormitory that was tidy but smelled of damp washing. Then she tried the next door, which revealed a similar room, though this time appreciably warmer, with the window open and the sun streaming in. To the rear of the hall there was another door marked 'Toilet', which left only one option – a final doorway. Mirabelle rapped on it and waited.

'Yes,' said a woman's voice. She sounded uncertain. Then the handle turned and Nurse Berenice's face appeared. At the sight of Mirabelle, her eyes sank to the floor. She appeared to be alone – the other nurses must have left down the back stairs.

'I thought you weren't supposed to come here again,' Berenice said. 'Frida forbade you.'

'It's rather awkward circumstances today – unique, you might say. Dr Simpson sent me to see how Uma is.' Mirabelle kept her voice businesslike and brisk. Berenice seemed to accept this.

'We got her to evacuate,' the nurse said. 'That is, we got her to be sick. She's sleeping now. I thought Ellen must be on the ward, at the royal. I suppose they rang her.' She pulled back the door to allow Mirabelle to pass.

This must be the smallest dormitory, Mirabelle realised. It looked out on to the back garden, where the children were running around with all the energy of balls on a pinball machine. The remaining two nurses were with them. Frida was playing catch with a circle of small boys.

'Thank goodness somebody is looking after the children,' Mirabelle said, nodding towards the window.

'They were outside. They probably hardly noticed,' Berenice said. 'They're playing all right now anyway. If there's one thing I've learned, children are extraordinarily resilient.'

One little girl had braved the swing and had pushed herself so high, it looked as if she could make a decent attempt to jump through the first-floor window. Now and then there was a shout, partially muffled by the half-drawn curtains.

'It's difficult to believe how ill some of them are,' Mirabelle said as she turned her attention back into the room. Along the back wall, there were three single hospital beds. Uma was so thin that it almost looked as if she was a dark puddle that had melted on to the pillow and slipped beneath the bedclothes.

'Do you know what she took?'

Berenice gave a half-shrug. 'The cabinet toppled. Everything is broken and muddled on the floor. We're just lucky she didn't grab the belladonna or something like that – something more instantaneous. That's all.'

'Do you know why she did it?'

The nurse grasped a small gold cross that sat at the nape of her neck on a thin chain. 'How would I know?' she said. 'She didn't confide in me.'

'Was there a note?'

'Nothing.'

'That's very unusual. Berenice. Do you know what happened to Sister Taylor?'

'I told the police everything.'

'You didn't tell me.'

'Well, Frida said not to.'

'Not to tell me?'

'It's none of your business, is it? I don't know. All these bodies. One after the other.' She stared forlornly at the figure of Uma, who didn't move. 'Father Grogan, God bless his soul, and poor Mr Bone.'

Mirabelle laid her hand on the bedsheet. There had been no indication before that Gerry Bone was known to the women in the convalescent home. This was new.

'He was a nice man, wasn't he?' she said, smoothly, without registering her surprise. 'I was most upset when I heard he'd drowned.'

'You just can't tell what's going to happen next,' Berenice said, inexplicably.

'It must be terribly difficult for you. I'll bet Father Grogan was an awful loss.'

Berenice nodded sadly. Mirabelle thought of the brown felt hats that the little girl had seen hung up in the hall and the fact that Bad Luck Bone had pushed his luck with the women up at Tongdean Avenue.

'Did you know Mr Bone well? Better than the other men, that is?'

'Not better, no. But he was always pleasant enough to me.'

'Why did he come here, Berenice?'

The nurse looked suddenly panicked. 'You'll have to go,' she said. 'Frida won't like it, no matter that Dr Ellen sent you. She's going to be all right,' she motioned towards Uma, who gave a little sigh. 'She needs to sleep it off, is all. I'll sit with her.'

Mirabelle's gaze wandered across the bedside table. A small brown glass bottle was perched in a kidney-shaped dish. They had sedated the poor woman.

'Well, I'd best get going,' she said.

Berenice looked relieved.

'Do you need anything sent up? When I go back down, I mean?'

'No. Nothing.'

Mirabelle closed the door quietly behind her. She slipped back down the stairs, stopping and pulling back just where they turned, so she couldn't be seen. Below, in the hallway, Vesta was speaking to somebody.

'I'm sure we can count on your discretion, Mrs Lewis. For the sake of the family,' the voice was saying.

'But she'll need help. Support,' Vesta objected.

Mirabelle peered over the edge. Nurse Frida had arrived in from the garden and was guiding Vesta towards the front door.

'Help and support is what we do here. We're nurses,' Frida pointed out. 'It's really the best place for her.'

Vesta spotted Mirabelle over the nurse's shoulder. 'Couldn't I say goodbye to Lali? Just for a moment? You could come with me, if you like. It means I can say to her mother that I know she's all right – after what happened, you see.'

Frida sighed but she relented. 'You'll need to be quick,' she said. 'It's almost time for juice and biscuits.' Turning, she led Vesta through the downstairs ward.

Mirabelle tiptoed the rest of the way down the stairs and let herself out of the front door, crossing the road to take up her usual position in front of the rose bush. Vesta appeared at the top of the steps not much more than a minute later. Nurse Frida must have rushed Vesta and Lali's goodbye. She had hardly crossed the threshold when the door snapped shut behind her.

Vesta looked smug as she crossed the road. 'That is, without doubt, the worst den of snakes I ever walked into. And that's saying something.'

'Bone had been there,' Mirabelle said. 'In the home.'

'Bone? The man who washed up on the beach? Why?'

'I don't know. But he was a gangster and hardly appropriate company for sick children and nurses. The nurse upstairs treated it as normal – I'd say he'd been there more than once.'

'Perhaps you ought to tell the superintendent?'

Mirabelle bit her lip.

'Mirabelle, do you think this place is some kind of ghastly cover operation? They could be running drugs out of the place. Or the white slave trade. Or patching up mobsters who get into fights. Or anything.'

A giggle escaped Mirabelle's lips. 'Slave trade,' she repeated. 'I don't think so.'

'Well, who is there to look after these children properly? Who?' Vesta put her hands on her hips, as if she wanted, herself, to get on with the job.

It occurred to Mirabelle that this was, of course, what Father Grogan had been trying to do.

'It seems above board. They're doing good work. At least some of the time. I'm sure of it. I asked Lali if she was punished or abused in some way, but she seemed bemused at the idea.'

Vesta checked her watch. It was three o'clock.

'Are you sure about Father Grogan? Are you sure he wasn't involved in something shady? Whatever it is they're up to?'

'I'm not sure of anything,' Mirabelle admitted. It seemed to her suddenly that she had been wandering about in a daze. 'But, given what's happened, I think we should go and see the doctor, Uma's lover, don't you?'

The bus arrived in good time up on the main road and the women climbed aboard. Mirabelle paid the fares and

Vesta took the tickets as the conductor punched them. The women gazed out of the window as the bus drove eastwards. Passing through town, there was already a queue outside the cinema – people leaving work early on a sunny day, maybe one of the last sunny days of the year. Everyone kept saying it couldn't last for ever. Then the bus turned north, leaving the sun behind it.

At the hospital, two nurses came down from the top deck and got off ahead of Vesta and Mirabelle. They stubbed out their cigarettes on the paving stones and trotted up the steps. The Royal was busy – there must be a change of shifts and, of course, there were visiting hours at this time of day, Mirabelle remembered.

Vesta led Mirabelle smartly through the front door and up the main staircase in the direction of the maternity unit. On a Friday afternoon, visiting would be especially crowded, Mirabelle thought. It seemed odd to be back for the first time after the freezing December evening when she'd rushed to make sure Vesta was OK, and had met Noel for the first time. Today the ward was awash with babies and bunches of flowers as proud new fathers and grandparents flocked to the beds. Laughter was interspersed with the sound of one baby crying, and when that baby stopped, another started, as if they were part of some kind of tag team.

Vesta motioned to her friend, Marlene, who was at the nurses' station with her sleeves rolled up, changing a nappy.

'What are you doing here?' Marlene mouthed. She looked annoyed.

'We're in search of a doctor,' Vesta said. 'A female one.'

'Dr Ellen Simpson,' Mirabelle cut in. 'Do you know the ward?'

'She works with the elderly downstairs. I'd try Seven or Eight if I were you. Why?'

'Her lover tried to kill herself this afternoon.'

'The Indian girl? No.'

'You know about them?'

'Everyone knows about them,' Marlene warmed to the subject. 'Lesbians,' she said sagely, under her breath, as she fixed the nappy in place with a pink enamel safety pin and kept one eye trained over Vesta's shoulder, to make sure nobody was close enough to hear what she was saying.

Mirabelle sighed. Marlene lifted the baby and surveyed her work. 'Go on,' she said, 'if Sister catches you here for no reason . . .'

'Thanks,' Vesta grinned.

Back downstairs, the elderly wards were more sedate and, although visiting was under way, you'd hardly know it. The smell of talcum powder disappeared and instead there was a bitter tang on the stale air – a mixture of urine and bleach and paper-thin skin. A single visitor perched uncomfortably beside one of the beds. A nurse was serving tea on Ward Seven, dispensing Rich Tea biscuits with every cup. 'Excuse me,' Mirabelle enquired, 'I'm looking for Dr Simpson.'

'She'll be in her office at the end of the hallway on the right.' The nurse trotted out.

'Thank you.'

Mirabelle was silently glad that Julie had died at home – dying here would be doubly depressing. She thought of the Turpins' tidy house and the sound of children playing in the street as Julie slipped away. Vesta nodded at Mirabelle, motioning her to knock on the doctor's door.

At her desk, Ellen Simpson looked up and took a moment, it seemed, to recognise Mirabelle. When she did, she got to her feet, as if she might slam the door again. Mirabelle and Vesta slipped inside too quickly.

'What on earth are you doing here?' the doctor snapped. She glared at Vesta.

'This is my business partner, Vesta Lewis. We've come about Uma. Today, at the children's home, she took an overdose. We thought you'd want to know.'

'What?'

'She's all right. The nurses made her sick and now they have sedated her in one of the dormitories. Nurse Berenice is sitting with her. But I thought they might not have told you and, well, you ought to know. Vesta happened to be visiting, you see.'

Doctors, Mirabelle thought, were invariably calm, practical people. Ellen hesitated for only a second. 'Thank you,' she said as she pulled off her white coat and left it on her chair. 'I had better go.' She scrambled behind her desk for her handbag, which was more a kind of satchel, and then picked up a leather doctor's case as well. 'Do you know what she ingested?'

Vesta cut in, 'I was there, but all I know was that they were some kind of white pills she found in the office. There were pills everywhere, actually.'

'When did she take them?'

'It must have been about an hour and a half ago. Around then.'

They followed the doctor into the hallway towards the front door.

'Did you know Mr Bone, Doctor?' Mirabelle tried.

'Mr Bone?'

'Gerry Bone. The man whose body was found on the front?'

'No. Of course I didn't know him.'

'He'd been to the children's home, you see. Who is the man in the blue Jaguar? The man who came to pick up Uma the other day.'

'Look, I need to get going. All that isn't important now.'

'All what?'

The doctor banged through the front door and took the steps outside at a lick. There was a short rank of taxis on the other side of the road and she headed for them with some determination.

'Thanks for coming to tell me,' she said, as the driver at the head of the queue sprang out and opened the door for her.

'Just a name, that's all we want,' Vesta pressed.

'A name?'

'Any of the men involved. It would help such a lot.'

'Help whom?'

'Maybe Uma.'

The driver closed the door. Mirabelle knocked on the window and the doctor rolled it down unwillingly. There were tears in her eyes now – the shock had hit.

'Do you know why Father Grogan died?' Mirabelle asked.

'He was poisoned.'

'Yes. But why?'

The engine started. The driver turned to ask the destination. The doctor trotted out the address with a sniff.

'We didn't have anything to do with the priest dying. Not me. Not Uma,' she said. 'Please, leave us alone. We'll have to leave now, don't you see?'

As the taxi pulled out into the road, Mirabelle and Vesta could only watch it recede down the sunny street.

'She knows all about it,' said Vesta. 'Doesn't she?'

'Of course she knows. They all do,' Mirabelle replied. 'It's just getting it out of them. We need names – someone who knows the people.'

'Or the car,' Vesta said decisively. 'Blue is an unusual colour. Most Jags are black or British racing green.'

'Well, yes, there's that. But I don't even have the number plate.'

Vesta crossed her arms. She took a deep breath, as if she

was making a decision. 'Well, we can try. I have an idea – there's a garage.'

'You said it was in London.'

'The Jaguar garage is in London. That's different.'

Mirabelle smiled. Vesta, once she got going, never gave up. It was nice to have her back. Mirabelle felt suddenly incredibly grateful.

'Come on,' Vesta said. 'We can get a bus. It'll give us time to think and it's cheaper.'

Chapter Twenty-Six

Judge a man by his questions rather than his answers

Vesta was always at home around vehicles. She'd spent eighteen months working at Halley Insurance, down the hall from McGuigan & McGuigan, before she took up with Mirabelle. She claimed these were the most boring months of her working life, but she'd retained a knowledge and interest in cars that was quite out of Mirabelle's reach.

The women caught a bus down Eastern Road back towards town, but only for a couple of stops. Vesta rang the bell and the driver came to a halt. 'Come on,' she said, hopping back on to the hot paving stones. The two women walked back up the hill a little way, the sea breeze at their backs, until they reached a garage, painted white with a sign that said 'Kemptown Motors'. It was, Mirabelle noted, conveniently placed – close to town. The paint was flaking, and there was a single petrol pump to one side. Several cars were parked at the entrance, including two Black Marias that Mirabelle knew must be old police cars.

'Hello,' Vesta called to no avail.

An acrid whiff of rotting rubbish hung on the air, alongside a heady undertone of petrol.

'This place looks pretty down at heel,' Mirabelle said.

Vesta checked her watch. 'Those are the best garages. Good mechanics don't bother to, you know, maintain anything other than engines. Hello,' she called again, into the interior of the garage from the door. Her voice echoed. A pigeon landed on the skylight and then flew off. There was no reply.

'Do you think they might have finished early?' Mirabelle ventured.

'And left the pump unlocked and the door open? No.'

Then a voice shouted Vesta's name from outside. The women spun round in the direction of the street to see a small man in greasy overalls on the edge of the pavement opposite. A lit cigarette dangled from his lips.

'Vesta!' he shouted again, and he crossed without properly checking for traffic, his arms held wide. 'Hello, girl. Haven't seen you in a while,' he said, his cigarette still in place as he clasped his fingers around Vesta's arm, and excitedly gave it a squeeze.

'I changed jobs, Mike.'

'Did you now? Who's this?' He held out a grease-smeared hand towards Mirabelle.

'Mirabelle Bevan,' she said, shaking it as enthusiastically as she could. Mike smelled of engine oil.

At least, Mirabelle thought, it was better than the smell on the air.

'We're looking for a car,' Vesta said. 'Details. Just on the off-chance. I was hoping you might be able to help.'

From the other side of the road a bell chimed as another man walked out of the doorway. 'Mike,' he shouted over the road. 'You want the rest of this?' He held up a small plate with a half-eaten roll on it.

'Yeah. Go on then,' Mike smiled. 'And the tea.'

The man disappeared inside again, past a hand-painted sign that said 'Café Here'. He emerged with a mug and carefully crossed the road, where he deposited it on the hood of one of the parked cars.

'Thanks, Johnny. I got all excited spotting Vesta here. She's one of my best customers. Well, the source of them.'

'Best garage in town,' Vesta insisted with a grin. 'Where else would I send my clients?'

'Exactly.' Mike removed the cigarette, stubbed it out, picked up the roll and bit into it. He chewed unenthusiastically. 'Eggs ain't up to much when they've gone cold,' he said. 'And there's that smell too.'

'Want me to make you another?' the other man offered. He sniffed. 'It's not so bad today, is it? The other week, whooph! I just about fainted when I came over.'

Mike shook his head. He took a long slurp out of the mug and patted his stomach. 'I've had enough. It's put me off, so it has. So, Vesta, what have you been up to, then?'

'I went to work in debt collection. McGuigan & McGuigan Debt Recovery,' she announced proudly, presenting Mike with a business card from her handbag.

Mike sucked air through his teeth as he examined it. 'Tricky business, that. You'll need all your skills.'

'And some new ones,' Vesta winked.

Mike laughed. He reached into his pocket, pulled out a packet of Capstan cigarettes and lit one, placing it in his mouth. Mirabelle looked at the petrol pump with dubiety. Faded but clearly in place there was a No Smoking symbol.

'Don't mind that, love. You light up if you want to,' Mike said cheerily.

'I'm fine,' said Mirabelle. 'Thank you.'

The man from the café cleared the crockery. He poured the rest of the tea into the gutter. 'See you tomorrow,' he said, and crossed back over the road, disappearing back into the café with a tinkle of the bell.

'Well, I suppose that explains it. I thought you were dead or something. I thought you'd got married.'

'Oh, I did get married,' Vesta grinned. 'Sorry. I should have said.'

'I suppose you're a married lady too?' The mechanic eyed Mirabelle.

'No. Not at all.'

He raised an eyebrow. 'Do you want to be?' A thick, hacking, phlegmy cough emanated – the sound of him laughing at his own joke.

'I had a baby – a little boy,' Vesta changed the subject.

'Well now. Congratulations. And now you need a car, is that it? Come to cash in on all those customers you sent me? I've got a sweet little Triumph in the back. I can fix it up and it'll run like a dream, you'll see.'

'No. I have a bicycle, actually. Can you see me on a bike? No! But I love it. The thing is, Mike, we came because we're looking for the owner of a car. A Jaguar, actually. A blue one. I wondered if you knew the vehicle. A blue Jaguar is quite unusual and, if they knew their onions, they'd get you to service it, rather than sending it up to London every time, wouldn't they?'

Mike looked left and right down the street. He pulled back his shoulders. 'A dark blue Jaguar, you mean?' he checked. 'Navy.'

'Yes,' said Mirabelle. 'Driven by a man with a moustache.'

'Been in an accident, has it?'

'No. Nothing like that,' Vesta assured him.

'Does the driver owe somebody money?'

'Not on our books. Mike, do you know who he is?'

Mike motioned the women to come inside the garage. Mirabelle looked up and down the street. There was hardly anyone to be seen. Inside, Mike drew deeply on his cigarette, clutching it between forefinger and thumb. He did this three times.

'Are you in some kind of trouble, Vesta?'

Vesta laughed. 'Not that I know of.'

Mike stared at her, as if he was reading her face. 'Well,' he said. 'I'd keep away from that guy, if I were you.'

'Is that so? Why?'

'They're not nice people. That's all.'

'You've fixed the car, though?'

'Yes. You don't turn those guys away.'

'What guys?'

'Down from London,' Mike said mysteriously. 'Not on holiday neither. Just down from London, if you see what I mean. I can't imagine why you'd even want to know who that guy is. My advice is to keep away from him.'

Mirabelle laid her hand on Vesta's arm.

'Thanks,' she said. 'Well, I guess we'd best be going. I don't suppose you've any idea where we might find these men?'

Mike shifted. 'Don't go looking for them, miss. That's my advice.'

'You don't have an address?'

Mike shook his head. 'No,' he said, 'I don't. And if I did I'd think twice about giving it to you. It's good to see you, Vesta. Shame it's taken so long.' A small piece of ash floated to the ground from the end of his cigarette.

'Thanks,' Vesta said. 'It's good to see you too.'

Back out on the street, the women turned towards the sea. The breeze offered relief from the heat. The smell quickly disappeared and the fresh air seemed sweet by comparison. It struck Mirabelle as strange how quickly they had got used to it.

'Well,' said Vesta, 'that wasn't like Mike. Not the way I remember him. He's always been such a cheery chappie.'

'The mob will do that to the cheeriest,' Mirabelle said.

'The mob?' Vesta hoisted her handbag further up her forearm.

Mirabelle thought for a moment. 'Poor Sister Taylor,' she said. 'What I don't understand is what are they doing at a

children's home in the first place? Or ferrying nurses around?'
Mirabelle took her sunglasses out of her bag and put them on.
'I'm not sure yet but there's more than that question. There's
something bigger. And you know, I'm interested – what is the
operation that McGregor is working on? He had a picture of
that car. And a woman too. So, what exactly is he on to?'

Chapter Twenty-Seven

The hardest victory is over yourself

Much as she wanted to return to the children's home, Mirabelle couldn't stand up the doctor two nights in a row, and it was getting late. Vesta disappeared in the direction of Mrs Treadwell's house and Mirabelle walked right along the front, watching so many clouds form ahead of her that, for the first time in weeks, the evening sun disappeared behind them, leaving the promenade looking gloomy.

As she slipped into her flat to get changed, the cogs in her mind clicked one way and another. It wasn't news that there were organised gangs of criminals in Brighton – she'd come up against more than one before. Nor was it news that there was an easy accommodation between the police force and some of the gangsters – tentacles of connection that, among other things, kept Jinty and the girls out of jail. Only the year before, McGregor had been banned from taking action against an illegal gambling operation. Gangs down from London made it their business to be well connected and to smooth over their operations as much as they could. What the world didn't see, the world didn't comment on, and in exchange for good odds, or women, or black-market goods, or simply for the greater good, the police were prepared to turn a blind eye. Nobody liked a petty official who enforced the law without discretion. In frustration, McGregor had ended up sanctioning the vigilante action that fell into place when the law didn't abide by itself. That's how poor Freddy had ended up dead.

Mirabelle applied a slick layer of lipstick in the mirror and thought about Tongdean Avenue, where the women were probably already at work for the evening. She knew there weren't easy answers to every question. She'd accommodated more than one tricky dilemma during the war. Jack had always talked about the greater good, not as an empty phrase but as the best he could do – a practical solution. 'The one hundred per cent easy decisions are taken much further down the line,' he always said. 'By the time things get to us, we're lucky if we're talking seventy/thirty. Morally, I mean.'

They'd do something bad to avoid something worse. Of course they would. They'd send someone to die, knowing that there was an advantage to be had from it, though she reminded herself, she wasn't in Whitehall now, with the weight of the Establishment behind her and the world at war. Freddy had died because the police couldn't touch him and he'd killed another man whose friends weren't prepared to let that slide. She didn't entirely blame them, but McGregor should have stepped in – he should have done something. Mirabelle watched the reflection of the clouds darkening in the mirror as she changed. She wondered where she might have put her umbrella. She hadn't needed it for weeks.

As she searched in the coat cupboard, she thought that it was difficult to let go – and not only of Jack, but also of that sense of purpose. The sense that a 51/49 decision was worth it. The life she'd built in Brighton. When she thought about it, watching Uma disappear into the back of the navy Jaguar did not feel as if it was for the greater good. Mirabelle remembered the nurse's head, as she'd seen it in profile, bowed just a little, and Ellen Simpson, standing in the doorway watching her go. Poor Uma – sometime between that day and now, she had tipped over the 50/50 and it hadn't seemed worth it to her any more. Vesta was worried about the children at the home and, in fairness, Mirabelle had been too, right at the beginning when she'd first met Lali. But the men's interest was in the nurses, it seemed. It was the nurses who were under pressure and therefore in danger – not the kids.

As Mirabelle came out of her garden gate, a beat bobby was biding his time at the lamppost.

'Good evening, Miss Bevan,' he said.

Mirabelle bit her tongue. 'Good evening,' she managed, and smartly turned left, swinging her brolly and striding out for the Old Ship. She wondered if the man reported directly to McGregor.

There was a chill on the air. She'd worn the wrong jacket, she realised. Now the summer had turned, it almost felt like a relief. As she got closer to town she passed a girl clasping her boyfriend's jacket around her frame while he, in his shirtsleeves, smoked a cigarette beside her. 'Come on, Claire, pick it up, love,' he complained. 'It's going to rain.' A boy at a newsstand had only three copies left of the evening edition. 'Bumper Summer for Brighton Weddings,' the stand said. People had been coming to the coast to tie the knot because of the Indian summer. 'Wedding, madam?' he gestured in her direction. She inclined her head.

Turning off the pavement, Mirabelle swept past the doorman. She cast only the most peremptory glance at the red carpet on the staircase and instead turned into the dining room. 'Miss Bevan,' the waiter greeted her. He was a slim young man and seemed very eager. 'The doctor booked your usual table and a suite, I believe. Would you like me to put your jacket in the room for you?'

Mirabelle felt the corners of her mouth twitch. 'Yes please,' she smiled, as if she had known. The boy took her things and pulled out the chair at the window table.

'I'll have a martini, please. As dry as you like.'

Distracted by the prospect of staying the night, she daydreamed for a moment about Mayfair. She wondered if the flat that Chris had in mind had a view of the park. It would be strange waking up without the gentle motion of the sea within sight. All summer Mirabelle had slept with the windows open, the sound of the water on the pebbles bringing her slowly to consciousness most mornings.

The martini arrived. Mirabelle sipped. It was icy and delicious. Another two tables were seated – both couples, now studying the menu avidly. She checked her watch.

The shadows next to the table shifted a little. 'Are you on your own?' The woman's voice was familiar. Mirabelle turned in her chair. Jinty wore another taffeta cocktail dress – this time tailored in black. Her eyes were as sparkling as the diamond studs in her ears.

'I'm waiting for my doctor. Would you like a drink?'

Jinty slipped into Chris's seat. Outside, the light was fading from the sky. The streetlights had come on along the front and the strings of bulbs on the pier glistened against the darkness. A spit of rain appeared on the window.

'I'll have one of those,' Jinty motioned at the waiter, gesturing towards Mirabelle's martini with a sweep of her elegantly manicured nails. 'Well, this is cosy,' she said. Mirabelle breathed in the cloud of oriental perfume that wafted across the table.

'I don't suppose you're familiar with a chap in a blue Jaguar?' she asked.

Jinty smiled. 'You're really on the case, aren't you?'

'Mobster?'

'I suppose.'

'Friend of Gerry Bone's?'

'Mmm. Really, Mirabelle, I don't know why you're always banging on about the most awful people. Do you like your men rough? It's a fascination, isn't it? A fetish? You can tell me if it is, you know.'

This time the waiter brought a small dish of salted crackers, which he laid between the women before discreetly disappearing.

'Are you meeting anybody special?' Mirabelle enquired.

'They're always special,' Jinty said smoothly as she lifted her glass. 'That conference is still on. They're here for days. Did you sort out those nurses?'

'Oh. Liars every one. You were right.'

The women clicked the rims of their cocktails. 'I'm not surprised,' said Jinty. 'It's the earnest professions you need to look out for – the ones who think they're doing good. People think we're dodgy – the loose women, that is. But in my experience, we're the ones who are up front about what we do. I suppose that might go for debt collectors as well, if you want it to.'

'Oh no. I play my cards as close to my chest as a nun.' Mirabelle's eyes twinkled.

'I bet you do.'

Mirabelle leaned in. 'Jinty,' she asked, 'I have to ask – do you know why he died? Gerry Bone, I mean?'

'Not really.'

'What do you mean, not really?'

'We're not all in it together, if that's what you're thinking. It's not a club. I'm like you, Belle. I'm watching from the outside – closer maybe, but I work with them, that's all.' Mirabelle was about to object but then she remembered Julie Turpin's death. People didn't discuss things with the people around them.

'I can guess what's going on,' Jinty continued. 'I can surmise from comments or what people do. That's all.' She sipped her drink. 'So I don't know. Not really.'

'What do you surmise, then?'

Jinty put down her glass and laid her hands flat on the white tablecloth. 'About Gerry? He didn't follow orders. He was lazy by nature. I mean, turning up like he did at the house those times – he did that because he thought it would be easy. Not that it worked. I've heard a bit here and a bit there – Gerry was the kind of guy who took shortcuts. Thinking about it, maybe he wasn't too bright. Mobsters aren't all Neanderthals, you know. I mean, the guys in charge are smart and they're dedicated to what they do – to getting it right.' She raised a finger and tapped the side of her head. 'Bone pissed them off. I reckon he took one shortcut too many.'

'So someone strangled him and flung him into the sea?'

'Probably one of his mates, or someone he knew, at any rate. An inside job.'

'And you trust these people?' Mirabelle let a long breath out through her mouth. 'Jinty, I worry for you.'

'I don't trust anybody. But I couldn't run my business without these guys unless we went back to the old days of having a pimp. It's my body, Belle. Mine. And this way nobody gets to tell me what to do with it.'

Mirabelle was about to take issue with this, when the door to the restaurant swung open. She was, she realised, acutely aware of who came in because she was waiting for Chris. The man who burst through the doors, however, wasn't Chris Williams. He was short and overweight and was pulling on a thick cigar as if his life depended on it. Jinty smiled at him and the waiter moved towards the table. Mirabelle thought it must be awful not being able to choose your customers.

'Get your coat, Jinty, gal,' the man said in a low voice. 'Now.'

Jinty languidly looked at her watch. 'I've got a customer in less than ten minutes, Tony,' she said. 'I can't just go off.'

Mirabelle felt relieved for the girl – hopefully her customer would be more attractive. Tony puffed on his cigar again and leaned towards her, putting one hand on the table. 'Now look,' he said, 'I don't want a scene. We're pulling out. They sent me to get you.'

'I'm working,' Jinty insisted.

'Sir,' the young waiter tried to intervene. Tony raised his eyes in the boy's direction and his expression stopped the interruption dead, as ineffective as a sparrow tweeting instructions to a bull. 'Fetch me a brandy,' Tony said. 'A double.'

He looked around, his gaze lighting on a vacant chair that he pulled over to Mirabelle's table and, taking off his hat, he sat down.

'This is my friend, Belle,' Jinty said.

'Charmed,' Tony growled, without looking in Mirabelle's direction.

Jinty giggled. 'You're the worst,' she said.

Tony smiled, revealing a lower set of teeth that were crusted in yellow. 'Maybe that's why they sent me. It's not a request.'

'Well, I don't take orders from you guys. I have a customer waiting and we have an arrangement. You're out of order.'

The waiter placed Tony's glass in front of him and hovered momentarily. Tony reached into his pocket and pulled out some coins, which he thrust into the boy's hand. The waiter disappeared again as Tony lifted the glass to his nose and took a sniff. Mirabelle tried not to laugh. It seemed impossible, amid the fug of cigar smoke, that he'd be able to smell anything.

'Armagnac,' he said. 'Reminds me of France.' He swilled the dark liquor around the glass, held it up to the light, and then downed the double in two steady gulps. 'I've got the car waiting,' he said, lifting a key from his pocket. 'I don't want to have to drag you out of here by the hair.'

'You wouldn't.'

'Try me.'

'All right,' Jinty finished her martini. She pushed back her chair.

'Look,' said Mirabelle, 'you don't have to . . .'

But Jinty raised a single finger.

'If you want me to come, you're going to have to make me,' she said, grasping the knife at Chris's place setting. 'You're strong all right. I suppose it depends on how quickly the police arrive. Because they'll call them. And I'll hang on to anything I can. As long as I can. I'll stab you with this and I'll scream the fucking place down. Go on.'

Tony considered this.

'The police will get you,' he snarled, 'if you don't come. You know that.'

'We pay the rozzers separately, remember? Your little world's falling apart, Tony. Not mine; and if you guys quit town, I'll just need someone new for protection. That's how it looks to me.'

Mirabelle noticed the man's leg tensing as if he was about to attack. She decided she would grab the bottle of wine from the neighbouring table and hit him with it if he went for Jinty. She was about to spring into action, when he got to his feet and stepped back from the table.

'You little bitch. We'd have seen you started fresh,' he growled, and then he turned and put on his hat as he walked out.

Jinty slipped her seat back towards the table. Her jaw was set. She checked over her shoulder. The other diners hadn't noticed or, if they had, they were ignoring what had happened. The girl wrapped her fingers around her empty glass.

'I suppose I owe you an explanation,' she said.

Mirabelle didn't move. She felt shocked.

'Well, it's Birmingham,' Jinty said. 'If you must know, they're shipping out to Birmingham. They've sold it to Rene

261

of course. She thinks it sounds marvellous. Not me. The minute she gets there she'll have a pimp again – that's what they're after. Easy income.'

'What do you mean?' Mirabelle realised her hand was shaking too much to be able to pick up her martini.

'They're pulling out – the mob boys you were asking about. Apparently the game's up.'

'What game?'

Jinty groaned. 'God, you're dense sometimes,' she snapped as she pulled her clutch bag towards her. 'Bad Luck Bone's Lazy Bastard Blues. That game. They'll all end up hanged. The game's up. So they're leaving town for the time being – hoping it'll blow over, I guess. Nobody wants to get hanged, do they?'

'That's an occupational hazard, isn't it? For men like that?'

'Not without a body it isn't.'

'But Bone's body turned up,' Mirabelle objected.

Jinty reached over and drank the rest of Mirabelle's martini. 'Jesus, Mirabelle! Mobsters don't count. You don't know anything, do you? When those guys kill each other, it's a message as much as anything else. They wanted Bone's body to be found. They knew the police would never figure out who did it – not exactly – so no one could face charges. But they wanted the body to turn up because they wanted everyone to hear about it. You think another guy will cut corners on disposal again? They said the police surgeon couldn't even establish cause of death, poor Gerry was so, so . . .'

'Degraded,' said Mirabelle.

'Yes.'

'What do you mean disposal? You said "cut corners on disposal",' Mirabelle pressed.

Jinty pushed away the glass and got to her feet. 'I have a client in five minutes,' she said. 'I'm going to the powder room.'

Chapter Twenty-Eight

Distrust any enterprise that requires new clothes

As Jinty swept out of the dining room, Mirabelle peered out of the window. She couldn't make out which of the passing vehicles was Tony's car, so she strained to see if Chris's car might have rounded the corner at the bottom of Old Steine. She didn't feel like eating, she realised. Not any more. When she checked her watch she calculated that the doctor was late by more than half an hour, which didn't seem like him; though she admitted, she didn't know him very well. She told herself it would be fine and steadied her hands. The woman at the next table laughed – a tinkling sound that cut through her mood. Something was afoot tonight. Maybe, when Chris got here, he'd be able to tell her exactly what it was.

Then she saw him – just an outline in the middle distance, washed yellow by the streetlights. The squat figure of Tony and another, taller man, walking back towards the hotel with a sense of purpose. They had parked on the other side of the road. Tony was still puffing his cigar and the other man had something in his hand. Mirabelle thought it might be a coiled piece of rope, but it was difficult to tell from so far away. Tony raised his arm, pointing at the window of the dining room. Mirabelle pulled back from the glass, her heart racing. The waiter hovered.

'They're coming back,' she said, keeping her voice low. 'Call the police.' The boy didn't move. 'Now!' she snapped and, without thinking any further, she took off, through the restaurant door, past reception, and towards the ladies' toilets to the rear of the building. She burst through the door so violently that it smacked into the wall behind. Inside, there was a plush suite – a powder room had been installed, lined with mirrors in gold leaf, rococo frames. A row of glass vases held – alternately – flowers, cotton wool and tiny wrapped lemon boiled sweets. The room next door contained the lavatories. Her heels sank into thick, pale carpet. 'Jinty!' she called. 'Are you in here?'

'Mmmm.'

The girl was in one of the cubicles behind a thick mahogany door. Mirabelle swept through. 'He's coming back. Tony's coming back,' she said.

'Oh, hell.' Jinty's voice seemed to echo off the tiles.

'Come on.' Mirabelle checked over her shoulder. 'You've got to get out of here. He's with another man.'

The sound of the lavatory flushing preceded the lock being drawn back. Jinty emerged, straightening her dress.

'There's no time for that,' Mirabelle snapped.

'It's nothing to do with you.'

'You introduced me, thanks very much. He knows I know you. Do you think he's going to be reasonable with either of us?'

Jinty sighed. 'Sorry,' she said. 'That was stupid of me. Where are they?'

'I saw them coming towards the front door. They don't know you're in here but they'll figure it out. There's only so many places to look for a woman in an hotel and the waiter will tell them you walked out alone. I expect he's worse than useless.'

'Well, if they're going to snatch me, they have to get past

264

the doorman, at least. He's ex-forces. You just need to hide, that's all. I meant what I said. I'll scream the place to a halt. They'll hear me in Hastings.'

Mirabelle was impressed with the girl's fighting spirit, though being up for a fight didn't mean you'd necessarily win it. 'I think it would be best if it didn't go that far,' she said. 'He's the kind of man who'd want to hurt you, isn't he?'

'Oh, Tony's a pussy cat. Lots of those mob guys are pussy cats, you know, once you get them in the sack.' She sounded woozy. Mirabelle peered into her eyes. The pupils were extraordinarily open.

'Jinty, what did you just take in there?'

'What do you mean?' Jinty laughed.

'That's not the booze talking. What else have you taken?'

'It's just a little sharpener, that's all. For the action, you know. To relax me.'

'You have to sober up now.' Mirabelle put her hand on Jinty's arm. 'Look, these men mean business. There isn't time for bravado, and relaxed is the worst thing you can be. If they take you, how do you think you're going to get away? You're not thinking straight. Not being afraid isn't brave, it's foolish in this situation. Your life is at stake.'

Jinty squinted slightly. 'Oh. Oh no,' she said, panic rising in her tone.

Mirabelle scanned the lavatory's back wall for some kind of exit, but there was only an air vent high up and it was no more than six inches square.

Jinty crossed her arms. The tension was palpable, her mind evidently not clear, but, Mirabelle hoped, clearing. In the other room, the door opened suddenly and both women jumped as two young girls burst in, giggling and prodding each other. 'Your daddy said so,' one taunted the other. 'And don't think I won't tell him.' They fell on the glass jar with the sweets and then skipped happily into the back room and disappeared into two of the cubicles, slamming and locking the doors with extraordinary synchronisation.

'There must be back stairs,' Jinty hissed. 'I can just hail a cab and go home. They're leaving, after all. I'll just take myself out of the way.'

Mirabelle's gaze was hard. 'You can't go home. That's the first place they'll look. Look, you need to disappear, Jinty. You'll probably need to disappear for a while – a few days, anyway. And don't take a taxi if you don't want to be followed. Never.'

'But . . .' Jinty began to object again, but Mirabelle ignored her, instead pushing open the last cubicle in the row. There was a small window halfway up the wall. She smiled. Then she put down the toilet seat and climbed on to it, feeling for the catch on the casement. A stream of cool air flowed in, along with the smell of the damp seaside. 'It opens to the rear,' she reasoned out loud. 'It's a laneway at the back, I think. Come along. We can get out this way.'

'But . . .' Jinty repeated, her eyes on the doorway. 'They work for me.'

Mirabelle climbed down and squared up in front of the girl with her hands on Jinty's elbows. 'These men want to take you with them. To Birmingham,' she smiled. 'Now, you don't fancy that, do you?'

'But I'm the customer. They're just contracted, that's all.'

'You want to whip out your contract with Tony, do you? Or ring your lawyer? Or just have an argument? You have to trust me here. You're not compos mentis.'

Jinty's breath was uneven. She was clearly having difficulty processing what was going on.

'You took them on because they didn't play by the rules, right? Well, surprise! They don't play by the rules. This game of yours isn't easy-come-easy-go. It's not a savings scheme to get you out to a nice village and the Women's Institute. It's money, don't you see? And power. I need you to trust me. If I'm wrong, you'll lose a couple of nights' earnings. If I'm right, we're saving your life.'

Jinty was about to say something when, as coordinated as when the girls had gone in, the toilets flushed in unison and two doors opened. The girls slunk out, visibly more subdued, avoiding the women's eyes. Neither so much as glanced at the wash hand-basins.

'Come on,' said Mirabelle. 'They will have checked the restaurant now. It won't take them long. We need to get out of here.'

Jinty seemed to accept this. She climbed on to the toilet and Mirabelle jimmied her up and through the window. It was awkward but Jinty made it. There was a crash on the other side. Mirabelle jumped on to the toilet and peered through the hole. Jinty had landed on some old boxes and knocked over a rubbish bin – perhaps, Mirabelle considered, it was best the girl was a little bit relaxed. She'd have landed more safely. Mirabelle followed. She pulled herself through, making a more graceful descent, finding her footing, tiptoe, on a bin. She closed the window behind her.

'Now what?' Jinty sounded cross. 'My client will be down by now.'

'Forget your client. Forget going back to Tongdean Avenue. They are going to clear you out and all of your girls.'

'I should warn the others.' At least, Mirabelle thought, the gravity of the situation was sinking in.

'Jinty, it's too late. We can try – but once you're safe, OK? You look far too identifiable. We need to get you some new clothes. Secondly, we need to find you somewhere to hole up. To hide.'

'You've done this before?'

'Not exactly. But I know how. Come on.'

At the end of the laneway, Mirabelle peered round the

corner. There was no sign of Tony or his friend, just a Friday-night street in the September rain. A woman held her coat over her head to protect her hair as she ran up the other side of the pavement.

'This way,' Mirabelle pulled Jinty by the arm.

Halfway up the street, Mirabelle cut into a pub, still pulling Jinty behind her. It was warm inside and the flood of conversation hit them in a babble. There were several couples sitting at dark wooden tables, nursing their drinks over cigarettes. More people crowded around the bar. Mirabelle hovered next to a lively group. One of the girls smiled her way.

'Out for the night?' Mirabelle started the conversation.

Jinty kept her eyes on the door, as if she was only now figuring out there was a danger she might have been followed.

'Yes,' the girl said cheerfully. 'You?'

Mirabelle leaned in. 'We're actually on the run and we could use a bit of a hand. My friend here is avoiding her boyfriend. He turned nasty on her.'

'Oh dear,' the girl said. 'A bad lot, is he?'

'We got away from the other pub,' Mirabelle confided. 'I was wondering if you could help us?'

'Me?'

'Yes. Do you like Jinty's dress?'

The girl smiled. 'It's lovely. Very smart.'

'Fancy swapping? And the shoes.'

Jinty stared at Mirabelle, clearly furious. The dress was worth a lot of money. It was the kind of thing you'd only get in a London boutique and she'd picked up the heels at Selfridges. Mirabelle brooked no argument. The girl looked down at her own dress – plain cotton with a repeat pattern of hollyhocks. She'd probably made it herself. 'All right,' she said. 'I've always fancied being a bit of a glamour puss.'

They retreated to the lavatories.

'Take off the jewellery,' Mirabelle hissed at Jinty, who began to fumble with her earrings as the girl slipped out of her cotton dress. Jinty sighed as it appeared over the top of the closed toilet door and her cheap blue pumps appeared below. 'Go on!' Mirabelle's tone was insistent. Jinty undid her zip and slipped off the black taffeta, swapping her outfit. The girl emerged, glowing. She inspected herself in the mirror, her gaze falling to the black heels. It was a considerable transformation.

'I look a smasher!' she said. 'Thanks a bunch.'

'He won't spot my friend so easily now.'

'I suppose not. Well, thanks again,' she said, and bounced out of the room.

Jinty studied herself in the mirror. She turned to the side, which clearly from her expression did not improve the effect.

'Put down your hair,' Mirabelle instructed.

'I don't wear my hair down.'

'Exactly. And rub off that lipstick.'

Jinty complied. She glared at her reflection. 'I look like a Lucy from Hangleton,' she said.

'That's good. Now, we need to find somewhere for you to lie low. Somewhere you haven't stayed before.'

'Well, that's most decent hotels counted out.'

Mirabelle smiled. 'I suppose it is.'

They cut back through the pub and out on to the street, walking in silence in the direction of Old Steine and crossing the road. The passing cars made a swishing sound on the wet tarmac as they cut up St James's Street. The shops were closed, their windows dark. Only the pubs shone light on to the reflective surface of the pavement. Mirabelle wondered if the cold would sober up her friend, who was walking with her head bowed, staring at the pavement. They came to a halt at the top of Superintendent McGregor's street. Mirabelle reached into her handbag and brought out a five-pound note. Jinty took it.

'Don't pick the nicest one,' she pointed out his house. 'Pick one of the other B&Bs. Book in as Lucy Hangleton, maybe. Take a room and stay in it – don't go out.'

'Lucy Hangleton?' Jinty let out an unexpected giggle.

'It's a good name, as a matter of fact – it sounds ordinary. I'll come and find you in a few days once the coast is clear. I promise. And I'll ring your house, just in case. I'll try to tell the others. I'll leave a warning with Doris – they won't take her, will they? Don't you worry.'

Jinty's eyes filled with tears. 'I guess I need guys to keep my guys in line to keep my guys in line,' she said. She hugged Mirabelle.

'Will it take long to wear off?' Mirabelle asked.

Jinty shook her head. 'A couple of hours usually. It just numbs me a bit. Thanks,' she said. 'You're a pal. I'll pay you back.'

Mirabelle gave a half-shrug. 'You understand what's going on, don't you?'

'Yeah. They're on the run. They'll be gone. You're probably right – it's best to get out of the way.'

Mirabelle didn't like to say, but she'd realised there was more than that. It was best not to elaborate. The most important thing was to get Jinty out of sight.

'Bad Luck Bone . . .' she started.

'Well, I'll cover myself twofold from now on. This is a lesson, Belle. Jesus – some lesson.'

'No. I mean, you walked away when I asked before. But do you know what Gerry Bone did with the bodies – the ones he didn't dispose of properly?'

'What?'

'What you said in the restaurant at the hotel. You suggested there were other bodies and you said his job was disposal. It's not a surprise exactly – only, I wondered, what did he do with them?'

270

Jinty took this in. 'They're supposed to get rid of them on the Downs. You can bury almost anything up there. There's acres of space – people have been using it for ever. But I don't know what Bone did with the ones he didn't take up there. Except they were in town. That's what I surmised, anyway.'

'Was it many bodies, do you think?'

Jinty shrugged. 'I don't know. I shouldn't think so. It's harder to kill people than you think and mostly not necessary. Mind you, I wouldn't have thought they'd have come for me like they have. Killing people is the last resort, isn't it?'

Mirabelle wasn't so sure. Jinty shuddered.

'Go on,' she said. 'It's cold in the evenings now. Stay inside.'

The girl set off down the street. Mirabelle watched as she passed McGregor's house and then turned up the path of a bed-and-breakfast place three doors down. The 'Vacancies' sign swayed in the wind as she rang the bell. The door opened, Jinty walked inside and the door closed.

Mirabelle lingered. The rain pinched at her skin. She rubbed her arms. The summer jacket wouldn't have been much help, she told herself, thinking of the suite at the Old Ship. Of dinner. It was too late for all that now. The lights in McGregor's room on the first floor were out. The curtains hadn't been drawn. Once Jinty was out of sight, Mirabelle opened the garden gate and rang the bell. Betty Brownlee came to the door, the hallway lit warm yellow behind her.

'Oh,' she said. 'It's you. Well, he isn't here.'

'I know,' Mirabelle said. 'I came about Rene.'

An expression of uncertainty flickered across Miss Brownlee's face. It was the first time Mirabelle had ever seen her look anything other than already decided.

'You have to ring the house at Tongdean Avenue,' Mirabelle said. 'There's been trouble tonight. If you can get hold of Rene, tell her to tell her friends that Jinty's left town already

271

and they should do the same. Don't bring them here. Do you understand?'

'I wouldn't let those women over the door,' Brownlee spat.

'They're in real danger, Miss Brownlee. Please. Do you have the number? Can you do it now?'

Brownlee hesitated. Behind her the sound of laughter emanated from the dining room.

'It's more important than McGregor's guests. I wouldn't be asking if it wasn't.'

The old woman nodded curtly. 'Well then,' she said.

The door closed. Mirabelle turned back down the pathway. Then she remembered something – a newspaper report that came into her mind as if she had been searching for it for hours and she had simply turned to the right page. It was the name of the woman whose picture had been on the wall of McGregor's bedroom, right beside the navy Jaguar.

'Mary Needle,' she said out loud. Mirabelle had read about the case in the *Argus* and the story had made the London *Times* too. Mary had gone missing on a trip from the capital right at the start of the heatwave. It must have been early in May. Mirabelle hadn't taken an interest. It seemed odd to her now, but then she had been numbed for months, or, at least, that's what it had felt like. Now she was alive again. She tried to remember. The police staged a search but there wasn't a single trace of the woman. Several investigative reporters had got involved, trying to figure out her movements, but then they discovered that Mary wasn't just any woman down from London – she was a prostitute. 'Lola,' Mirabelle whispered. That had been her working name. The press had discarded the story after that. What was McGregor doing with a picture of Mary Needle? she wondered, looking over her shoulder up at the dark window above. What had she missed?

Chapter Twenty-Nine

Courage is knowing what to fear

Back at Old Steine, Mirabelle continued to walk away from town. She had made a plan, such as it was, and was determined to see it through. On the streets opposite, she noticed several Black Marias going back and forth in the direction of the police station at Bartholomew Square. None of them was running their flashing lights. She squinted to see who might be inside but couldn't make out any faces, and she wondered if they were coming from Wellington Road police station and, if they were, what was McGregor up to? She'd find out, she told herself, but first she had something to check. Jinty and her friends weren't the only women in danger this evening – not by a long chalk. Further up, she managed to flag down a taxi.

'Busy night?' she asked the driver as she slipped into the back seat.

'No, miss. Not really.'

'Noticed anything much? I saw there were quite a few police cars out.'

The man regarded her in the rear-view mirror. 'I expect we'll read about it tomorrow in the *Argus*,' he said. Silently she cursed her luck – a careless-talk-costs-lives type. Then she checked out of the back window, just in case. It felt as if Tony was only over her shoulder. The night was hooded in menace and she knew they'd had a close call, but the street was quiet for this time of the evening and there was no sign of trouble.

'Going home?' the driver asked.

'Yes,' she said. 'West Drive, please.'

He dropped her at number seventeen and she didn't tip him. As he drove off, Mirabelle made for the front door and rang the bell. There was no reply. She stepped back, hesitating a moment. The windows were in darkness – at the front of the place anyway. Decisively, she nipped down the alleyway and found the same foothold in the bricks she had used to hoist herself up only a few nights before. Then she peered over the top of the gate. The house was dark to the rear this time, and the side gate was as securely bolted as ever.

'Damn,' she murmured under her breath.

As she squinted into the darkness, however, she realised that the garden had changed. Some of the plants were missing. It was difficult to tell because the moon was obscured by cloud, but it looked as if somebody had harvested certain areas – the little greenhouse was practically empty. Mirabelle stepped down on to the paving stones and retraced her steps to the front of the house, considering her options. She decided she didn't have many. The curtains were still drawn in the front room, so methodically she checked the catches. Sure enough, one of them was undone, and the window pulled open smoothly. As she slipped over the sill and on to the carpet, she suddenly wondered why there hadn't been a spate of cat burglaries in Brighton over the summer – the papers were headlining the boom in weddings, but the hot weather probably had other effects too. Everyone's windows had been open – or at least unlocked – all over town. It was too easy.

The house was silent. She crept into the hallway, cursing the sound of her footsteps and considering switching on the light. The place felt abandoned. 'Hello,' she called. There was no reply, so she snapped on the tall lamp beside the hall table. A jacket lay strewn on a chair. The vestibule door had been left open. Mirabelle sighed. She started to check the house room by room to see if there was any sign of a struggle. Uma might not have put up a fight, she thought, but if Tony or any of his friends had arrived, Ellen would have.

The room at the back of the house was tidy, the books still piled on the side table and the overgrown, lush plants in their pots. In the kitchen there was a faint smell of cumin seeds but nothing out of place. There was no sign of the cat. Perhaps they had managed to take the cat with them, she thought – that and the plants from outside. It was an odd set of priorities, but it suggested at least a measured departure rather than a kidnapping. She was about to go up to the bedrooms and try to figure out if the women had had time to pack, when the doorbell sounded.

The noise cut shrilly into the silence like a jangling alarm. Mirabelle's stomach turned over. She regretted turning on the light, suddenly acutely aware that she was alone and nobody knew where she was. Trying to keep her breathing regular, she grabbed a sturdy, carved wooden ornament from the hall table, in case she needed to defend herself. Then she crept up to the door and, from the side, peered through the thick, twisted glass. She let out a sigh of relief. The image was indistinct but it was a woman. Mirabelle put down her weapon and opened the door.

The visitor was wearing a dark brown suit made of cheap material. On her feet, a pair of scuffed sandals matched the outfit and a brittle-looking straw hat topped it off. Even in the half-light it was clear the woman had been crying.

'You've got to help me, doctor,' she said, twisting a white cotton handkerchief clumsily between her fingers.

'Oh. I'm not . . .' Mirabelle's voice trailed as the woman pushed past her into the hallway, shoulders heaving.

'Please,' she gasped. 'I'm desperate.'

'What is it?'

'We've got six already and I can't even manage that.'

Mirabelle glanced at the thin gold band around the fourth finger of the woman's hand.

'They don't do that here, surely. Not at home.' The words slipped from her lips as she remembered the last few days in snippets – the blood on the side of the lavatory in the children's home, the clouds of clary sage and pennyroyal in the back garden, Frida's mother's insistence that her daughter had worked the 'woman's ward' and not with children, and then, Nurse Uma disappearing into the back of the blue Jaguar, unwilling but doing her duty – a duty she couldn't bear.

The woman began to beg. 'I'll go anywhere, doctor,' she said. 'I have money.' She thrust her hand into her bag and pulled out two crumpled five-pound notes – a fortune for someone like her, someone whose clothes were so cheap and worn. 'I can get more.'

'Sundays,' Mirabelle realised. 'At the children's convalescent home.'

Suddenly it made sense. Sister Taylor's distress and Father Grogan's fury. The nurses had been giving women abortions. The mob had got involved – they'd have their own uses for that kind of procedure. She wondered what Jinty did about taking care of herself. Girls like Jinty. Girls like Mary Needle, she realised, making the connection.

'Thank you,' she said to the woman, touching her arm lightly.

'But where do I go, doctor? Where?'

'I'm sorry for your trouble,' Mirabelle said. 'But they're not here any more. They went away.'

The woman gasped, clearly horrified. 'You're not the doctor then?'

'No.'

'Oh God. Are you with the police?'

'No.'

Mirabelle tried to sound reassuring but, having merely conjured up the idea of police involvement, the woman panicked. She clutched her handbag to her chest and began to back away. Mirabelle wished Vesta was here – she was much better at dealing with people who were upset.

'Look,' said Mirabelle, 'perhaps . . .'

'Don't worry. I'm sorry to have troubled you,' the woman gulped, and disappeared back through the front door.

Mirabelle sank on to the chair in the hallway. She'd been such a fool. So naïve. It wasn't as if she didn't know such things went on. The woman's face seemed imprinted on her mind's eye and she couldn't think straight. She got to her feet and stumbled back into the fresh air. Outside she checked left and right but the woman was gone – Mirabelle couldn't even say in which direction she'd gone. At least now it began to hang together. The nurses offered their services on a Sunday – the day Father Grogan didn't come to the home, when the children were out all morning at church. But Sister Taylor hadn't known. When she found out she fetched the father. The nurses couldn't risk being uncovered. They called in the mob – the men with the brown hats for whom they were probably working, at least some of the time. Father Grogan was poisoned and who knew what had happened to poor Sister Taylor? It was, she supposed, possible the sister was still alive. Mirabelle banged the front door of Uma's house closed and turned towards town.

She knew she had been lucky – both Jack and McGregor had been the kind of men who took precautions. But there were plenty of women in the service who had been caught short – shotgun weddings or rushed adoptions – right through the war. Women disappearing for months on a 'rest cure' or 'compassionate leave'. One girl Mirabelle knew had slipped on a ring, moved away, and just pretended that her husband had been killed in the fighting. She wanted to keep the child. Why not? There were so many more important things during wartime – the truth was she'd never given more than a passing thought to the absences. They were just another set of casualties. Why, if those women had been able to take the train to Brighton and get help – real, medical help – it would have been perfect. She remembered reading somewhere about hot baths, horse riding, raspberry-leaf tea with strong spirits – that's how you got rid of it. But she knew that wasn't the only way. She hoped the woman who had come to Uma's front door didn't harm herself, because that was the alternative. Mirabelle felt her whole body tighten. The back room in the children's home and that bed with the tiling behind it made sense now. However awful, it seemed so much more civilised than the half-blind, haphazard, desperate panic of trying to get rid of what had happened.

Closer to the front, the breeze off the sea was chill. Mirabelle shivered. Somewhere far off there was the sound of church bells – half past the hour – nine, or was it ten?

So, she thought, if the mob were leaving town tonight – rats off a sinking ship as McGregor closed in, they would try to take as much as they could with them. They'd failed with Jinty. Betty Brownlee would try to warn Rene and the others. Mirabelle just hoped Uma and Ellen had got away. Poor Uma – it had been too much for her. And that made sense now too. Mirabelle remembered her fierce assertion about wanting to help people. That's what she had been doing, of course, and Father Grogan had died for it. 'Disposal,' Mirabelle whispered under her breath. Of course. What did you do with the body of a prostitute, or just some poor woman like the one at the door? What did you do when it went wrong?

Striding out, she realised how far she'd come. Passing

Lali's bench, dripping in the rain, she kept walking. It was strange; there hadn't been a single beat bobby all the way along the front – not for over a mile. She cut up towards the home. Her clothes were drenched now but she ignored the discomfort, instead slipping her lock picks out of her handbag and smoothly opening the gate at the cricket ground. There would be no policeman tonight at Sister Taylor's bedsit to oversee her. There were no policemen anywhere because there were bigger fish to fry – all hands on deck.

Across the cricket pitch, the roller was where she'd left it next to the wall and she slipped over the top easily – it was always easier when you'd done it before. The lights at the back of the home were out and the curtains drawn upstairs. Mirabelle switched on her torch. The beam seemed fragile. The batteries must be fading. She hurried towards the compost heap on the other side of the lawn. This was what Uma had been doing, she realised – disposing of the detritus. The girl's anger at the cats was proof of a sort, though she couldn't take that to McGregor. She looked around for something to dig with.

Frida's mother had assumed Mirabelle hadn't seen a field hospital when they had spoken. That wasn't true. It had only been for a few hours, but it had been awful. She remembered feeling guilty that she was glad to get away. Some people were superstitious about white and red together after the war. They said it reminded them of blood on bandages. To Mirabelle, it was blood in soil that was more horrifying – the smell of it. Limbs left behind. As she poked at the compost heap she smelled it again – the stench of human decay. The thin light from her torch seemed blue but she could just about make out thick clots of blood and something else. Something more terrible and unidentifiable and sad. She put her hand over her mouth and tried not to sob. The torch faded to a thin yellow trickle.

It was distress that stopped her seeing Frida approach. The first she knew was a hand on her arm, clamped insistently in place. A trickle of cold rain slid down Mirabelle's back. Her hair was soaking.

'What are you doing here?' the nurse said as she pulled Mirabelle away.

Mirabelle turned. She snatched her arm free of Frida's solid grip. 'I know what you've been up to. What's been going on.'

'Well, that's a shame,' said Frida, 'I wondered if you'd be on our side.'

'Murdering people?'

'It's not murder. The women are desperate, most of them.'

'I mean Father Grogan.'

'There was nothing for it. The priest wouldn't agree to just taking the money again. We couldn't pay him off.'

'Money?'

'Oh yes. He'd had five hundred pounds only a couple of months before. It practically cleaned us out – we were trying to do the right thing, you see. He and Rita Taylor had found out. We promised both of them we'd stop, but of course we couldn't. They weren't supposed to find out and then Rita copped it – a smear of blood in the toilet and she knew.'

The roof, thought Mirabelle. The church roof. The father must have been beside himself making that decision. She remembered the phrase he'd written in his notebook. *Crooked logs make straight fires.* Yes, and taking money, explained why he had come to deal with the matter himself, rather than just contacting the police. It explained why Sister Taylor had gone to him. They had made some kind of pact and they thought they could sort it out themselves.

'Father Grogan spoke German.'

Frida sounded surprised. 'A little. He had taken confession in a prisoner-of-war camp during the war. How did you know about that?'

Mirabelle ignored the question. 'What about Mary Needle?'

The nurse's head cocked to the side. 'You're well informed. Poor girl. It was a haemorrhage. There was nothing any of us could do.'

'If there'd been a doctor present . . .'

The nurse paused, almost smiling. Her lips moved outwards and her eyes took on a knowing expression. 'Ah, you don't know *that*, then. Not so clever, after all. Our little Uma is a doctor. Trained in India. She took the Hippocratic oath and everything.'

'And you?'

'Nurses don't take the Hippocratic oath. We take the Nightingale pledge – to stay pure. To help. The doctor's promise – that's the bloody problem.'

'What do you mean?'

Frida sighed. 'They promise not to give abortive care. But it's nonsense. Abortive care is exactly what the patients need. If they don't get it, they just get rid of the baby themselves and that's a bloody mess. If you're looking for dead bodies that's a good place to start. At the start we did it just for the locals. Some pennyroyal and mugwort and the babies bled away easy. The women were desperate, you know. Then Uma started taking later-stage pregnancies. D and C. It's a small procedure. Uma and her girlfriend had a clinic in India. They'd been doing the same but they got caught. Nobody anywhere in the damn world wants women to be allowed to take the decision of whether they do or don't want a child. Me – I'd been working up north in a women's hospital during the war. We helped girls out if they needed it. Anyway, when they were found out in India, Uma took responsibility for what had been going on. Ellen kept her doctor's qualification but Uma was struck off. She and Ellen got away – she'd have gone to jail otherwise. Uma became a nurse – she did

281

a qualification here, you see, under Ellen's name. I don't suppose a woman like you would understand.' Frida tugged Mirabelle's arm, pulling her towards the back door of the home.

'But it's dangerous,' Mirabelle held her ground. 'It's a dangerous thing to do.'

Frida rounded. Even in the dark, Mirabelle could see her eyes flash. 'Yes it is. Just like childbirth is dangerous. Look, these women deserved better. It's all right for people like you – women with education! Women brought up properly. Fancy clothes and nice manners. But everyone deserves a choice, and we give it to our patients – whether they come from Patcham or Rottingdean or wherever. Whether they're on their first child or their tenth. Whether they're married or not. Whether they wanted it or whether they were raped. And it was all fine until the men got involved. They heard about us and started bringing down women from London. The poor things hardly knew what was happening. They'd arrive exhausted or drugged up or just being told it was an away day. A jolly! Can you imagine? Some of them were OK with it, but for those who weren't, there was nothing we could do. They had us. They could turn us all in – and that would mean jail for me and Uma and Berenice. So we decided we'd do their damn jobs, we'd take the money, and we'd use it to get what we wanted.'

'You did it for money?'

'Not for us. Money to help the kids. To help local women. To educate them. You'd think it hadn't been going on since the beginning of time. Lots of women come to us and they know hardly anything. These are married women. They've got kids. But they don't know what they can and can't do. It's medieval.'

'And if it went wrong, Gerry Bone got rid of the body.'

'Yes.' Frida sounded furious. She tugged Mirabelle's arm,

but whether on instinct or by training, Mirabelle broke away. The advice was always to get off as quickly as you could – Jinty had taken it and so would she. She dropped the torch and set off, making for the back wall where she began to scramble up the brickwork. Frida followed, trying to pull her down. Mirabelle kicked, her heel catching the nurse's cheek, slashing the skin. Frida let out a cry. She grabbed Mirabelle's calf and pulled hard and Mirabelle fell on to the lawn on top of the nurse. Her leg ached. There would be a bruise, she thought, but she turned immediately and tried once more to climb over the wall. 'They're leaving town – the men are leaving town,' she gasped. 'Don't you know? The police are on to them. There's no need for this.'

Frida gripped the skirt of Mirabelle's dress. The material ripped as Mirabelle pulled away and managed to pull herself over the top, finding her feet on the grass roller on the other side. She turned back. Blood was dripping down the nurse's cheek.

'It's time to stop, Frida,' she said. 'The men are going. They're probably gone by now. But the police are on to something with Mary Needle. I think Uma and Ellen have left.'

Frida put her hand to the wound.

'Fuck you,' she said, 'with your fancy clothes. You never have to worry about anything.'

Mirabelle stared over the wall, taken aback. Frida, she realised, was trapped. She'd lost her husband, she'd been bullied into something she didn't want to do, and she couldn't leave because of her mother. If the police tracked her down, she'd be here. 'I'll speak to the superintendent,' Mirabelle said. 'I know him.'

'Fancy friends too.'

'If he knows, I'll urge clemency. And, for the record, I do know what it is to worry.'

283

With that, Mirabelle climbed down on to the cricket pitch and hurried towards the gate. It seemed odd, when she glanced over her shoulder, that Frida hadn't followed.

284

Chapter Thirty

A crime is a matter of law

It was almost eleven by the time Mirabelle got to Bartholomew Square. The station was always open twenty-four hours a day, but at this time of night there were usually only a couple of sullen men charged with being drunk and disorderly in the system, even on a Friday. By ten the front desk generally had a sleepy, seaside air, no more than mild misdemeanours being expected – a couple of drunken brawls. Tonight every light in the place was on, there were four Marias parked outside and the reception area was buzzing. Sergeant Belton stood behind the desk like a conductor poised before his audience.

'Good evening Miss Bevan,' he said, more kindly than she might have expected. 'Are you all right?'

Mirabelle looked down at the long rip in her skirt. Now she was in the light she could see her hands were dirty and that a smear of compost ran up her leg, which, more importantly, was aching where she had fallen and sported a long, blood-flecked graze. She reeled a little but remained upright. A small puddle of water was gathering at her feet.

'I'll be fine, thank you,' she said.

A gale of laughter emanated from the back office. Belton closed the door.

'Well?' he said. 'Can I help you?'

'I need to speak to Superintendent McGregor.'

The sergeant had one of those faces that seldom showed any expression and now was no different. 'The superintendent is busy,' he said.

'It's personal,' Mirabelle lied, thinking on her feet. Belton was often difficult but she had to find a way in. There was no way forward, she thought, without some help from McGregor – she didn't want to report what had been going on to anybody else, but he needed to know what she knew, if he didn't already. She gave a weak smile. 'As you can see I have got into a spot of bother. Actually, I feel a little shaky.'

She tried to look vulnerable. Belton thought for a moment, then he bought it.

'Would you like me to get one of the WPCs to help you clean up?' he offered.

'Yes please,' she said. 'That would be very kind.'

'I'll fetch you a towel.'

Mirabelle didn't know the officer Belton finally managed to track down ten minutes later. She was a tidy, faun-haired woman with freckles, a toothy grin and a small first-aid kit. She led Mirabelle to the female toilet, which had only been installed a couple of years before, carved out of two storage cupboards when it became apparent that the first WPCs at the station required their own amenities. The room was tucked behind reception and it was tiny. There wasn't enough space for two people, but the two of them got in somehow, rammed between the sink and the toilet bowl. The WPC's wide flannel skirt seemed to fold itself round the rim. Having dried herself as much as she could, Mirabelle wrapped her hair in the towel. At least it stopped it dripping.

'Busy night,' she said as she turned on the hot tap and a trickle of tepid water flowed half-heartedly into the sink.

'They told me not to tell you anything,' the WPC said, 'so there's no point trying.'

'You sound as if you're from London.'

'Yes. I've been seconded.'

'For the operation, you mean?'

The woman sighed. Mirabelle kept going.

'What's your name?'

The officer hesitated, but then relented. There was no harm in that. 'WPC Bunch,' she said.

'Mirabelle Bevan. I'd shake your hand, but . . .' Mirabelle began to soap her hands. The water ran brown as she washed them. There were smears of grit on her forearms so she tackled those as well. It warmed her up. The room had a strange smell of bleach and some kind of cheap perfume.

'I have iodine,' said WPC Bunch, putting down the toilet seat and opening the first-aid kit.

'Any arnica cream? I had a bash,' Mirabelle said. 'That's the worst thing. It aches.'

'I'll have a look. What happened to you exactly?'

'Nothing. I fell, climbing over a wall, that's all.'

'A wall?' the policewoman repeated, her eyes falling to Mirabelle's heels, which had survived the escapade in more pristine condition than she had. 'Here is the arnica.'

Mirabelle took the tube and squeezed a dot of the white cream on to her finger. 'Excuse me,' she said, and raised her skirt so she could smear it on to her skin, which had already started to discolour. She bruised easily – always had. Her skin was covered in goosebumps. 'It's going to be autumn soon and we'll be back to stockings before we know it,' she said cheerfully. 'Don't you have a first name?'

'It's Jessica,' said the officer, and sucked in a breath through her teeth. 'Maybe we should take you to the police doctor,' she said and then stopped. 'Oh.'

'Dr Williams?'

'Actually, my mistake. He's . . . not on tonight.'

Mirabelle remembered he'd been half an hour late for dinner, if he'd turned up at all in the end. It seemed longer than three hours ago. 'They'll have got him back in, surely?' she said. 'McGregor has a serious operation under way. They'll need a doctor.'

'Well, there aren't any bodies.' Jessica stopped herself short again.

'That's a relief.' Mirabelle ignored the woman's indiscretion. She put out her leg and Jessica dabbed iodine where it had been scraped by the bricks.

'Sore?' she asked.

'A little bit.' Actually, it was a lot, but better than having an infection, Mirabelle told herself. 'I don't suppose there is a needle and thread in there,' she nodded at the first-aid kit. 'My skirt, you see.' She illustrated the point by pulling open the rip.

'I could go and see if I can find one.'

'Thanks.'

As the WPC left, Mirabelle turned off the tap. She didn't look too bad, she told herself, checking in the mirror, and now she might have three minutes if she was lucky. She just had to find him. She opened the door and peered down the corridor. There was nothing to see – the sound of typing seemed to fill the offices to her left. Mirabelle knew this station – she'd been here many times. The holding cells were downstairs and the interview rooms were further along on this level. Quickly she decided she didn't have time to make it to the cells and, besides, she knew there was a locked grate at the end of the corridor so the interview rooms were the better bet. There was no time to waste. She stepped on to the linoleum and began to make her way along the hallway. Her hip still ached. It was worse when she walked on tiptoes but she persevered and turned the corner. The rooms had frosted-glass doors along here – a new addition. She stopped at the first doorway and listened but couldn't make anything out, though inside there was the hushed sound of men's

288

voices, and through the glass she could make out two men on one side of a table and another two on the other. It was difficult to see which were the policemen and which were the interviewees. Next door she had more luck. The interviewee was shouting.

'Damn you! What the hell have you been doing? Spying on me.'

Lower, McGregor's tone was insistent. She couldn't make out what he was saying but Mirabelle recognised his voice. She leaned in. Whatever the superintendent said, he infuriated the other man, who got to his feet. She jumped back against the wall as the interviewee lurched towards the glass-panelled door. It was odd, she thought, that McGregor hadn't stood up more quickly to stop him. The handle turned and the door opened.

'Sir.' McGregor followed Chief Constable Ridge into the hallway. The men were so involved in their argument that they didn't even notice her standing as far back as she could, out of their way. McGregor's face was pink with fury. He caught the superior officer by the arm. 'I'll arrest you if I have to,' he spat. 'You don't want that.'

At the end of the corridor, Sergeant Belton appeared with another officer, whom Mirabelle vaguely recognised. She couldn't quite remember the name.

'Green!' McGregor gestured. 'Talk some sense into the chief.'

Ah yes, she thought. Green was from Scotland Yard. He'd been involved in a case she'd got caught up with four years before – a friend of Vesta's had been arrested and taken up to London. Green was one of Scotland Yard's best officers. In some circles he was considered practically psychic, but all those years ago he hadn't been able to save Lindon Claremont from being killed in his cell. That's odd, she found herself wondering: what was Superintendent Green doing here?

Whatever it was, he produced a pair of handcuffs.

'You wouldn't dare,' Ridge sneered.

'Now sir,' Sergeant Belton cut in, his gaze moving between the chief and Mirabelle – he was, she noted, the only one who realised she was there. 'You'd best not make us arrest you, sir. That can't be for the best. Not for anyone. As I understand it there is a deal to be done.'

'Cut them all loose, you mean? My men. Your fellow officers?'

'Exactly that. I, for one, am sick of bent coppers. With respect, times are changing.'

Ridge's face flushed. 'How dare you? We keep the peace. We keep the peace more effectively in Brighton than you'd have dreamt of as a constable. I'm right, Belton, aren't I? Cooperation works well for everyone – the public included.'

'It's got out of hand, sir.'

'So you thought that rather than arresting the criminals, you'd arrest your friends?' Ridge rounded on McGregor. 'You think you're so superior, bringing in Scotland Yard. Playing for the big time, are you? And all over some whore who got herself pregnant, Superintendent. You think that's worth bringing down good men? Good men with long service?'

McGregor cut in. 'You have some choices, sir, that's all. Do you want to go down with the others, or will you sanction an inquiry and manage the revelations? If you come on board, it's Brighton Constabulary sanctioning itself. Otherwise—'

'It's down to us,' Green cut in, 'and the Yard will bring High Court prosecutions against everyone – you included. There are no more backhanders, Ridge; it's only about how you want it to go. It's in all our interests to manage the way the force is presented. But we can do it the other way, if you won't play ball.'

'And me?'

'It doesn't touch you, sir. You retire. That's the deal.'

'They said I'd get a knighthood one day.'

Green's eyes fell to the floor. 'I can't see it, sir, if I'm being honest,' he said. 'But you won't go to jail. We're working to the Home Secretary himself on this one.'

'And he sanctioned this? Police officers over criminals?'

'If we arrest the offenders, sir, they'd testify against our officers, wouldn't they?' Green pointed out. 'We'd rather manage it as an internal matter. That's the instructions – the Home Secretary's view. Sort out the good guys first and we can pick up the bad guys in time, once the collusion is done with.'

The chief constable seemed to sink a little.

'Well, then,' said Belton. 'Why don't you go back into number three and work out the details, sir?'

Ridge didn't like it but he seemed to accept Belton's suggestion. Green followed him back into the interview room, his eyes locked on the back of Ridge's head. As McGregor turned to join them he saw her. His gaze hardened. 'Mirabelle,' he said.

'You want me to wait, do you? While you chat to your lady friend?' Ridge spat from the doorway.

'No, sir. Of course not.' McGregor sounded contrite.

The three of them marched back into the interview room. When the door closed, McGregor's eyes were still on her. Jessica Bunch appeared at the head of the corridor. 'I found some black,' she said, 'it's all we've got.' She held up a needle and a spool of thread.

'WPC Bunch. Could you bring Miss Bevan this way?' Sergeant Belton barked.

'Yes, Sarge.' Bunch looked confused.

The three of them walked into the back office, where two officers were huddled over cups of tea. 'Out,' said Belton.

The men scrambled to their feet and disappeared through the door.

'WPC Bunch, you are singularly ineffective. I give you one job to do and you let Miss Bevan go further into the station on her own. What did I tell you?' He waited.

'It's not Jessica's fault,' said Mirabelle.

Belton hissed. 'What did I say to you, Bunch?'

'That she's a slippery customer, sir. Into the lavatory and out again – that's all.'

'And in the meantime, she persuaded you to take up embroidery, did she?'

'There was a rip in her skirt, sir.'

'It was supposed to be a wash and a brush-up, Bunch. Not a dress fitting.'

'Look,' Mirabelle started. 'Blame me—'

Belton cut in. 'That's enough, Miss Bevan. This is a serious business. I hope for the sake of the public good that you will have the grace not to repeat what you've heard here tonight. I hope I can have your word on that.'

Mirabelle nodded. 'But it'll come out, won't it?'

'There will be an inquiry. That's the aim. It'll be announced imminently. Formally. Without the need for busybodies or gossip. Do you understand me?'

'And all these police officers are down from London . . .'

'To help us enforce the action against the Brighton officers who have been in league with the criminal element. You should be proud of the superintendent – he's struck a blow against corruption this evening.'

'I thought McGregor was investigating the death of Mary Needle.'

'It's a complicated situation, miss. It's bigger than just one case. I should clap you in the cells, but I have no more room. So you're on your own recognisance. Can I trust you?'

Mirabelle paused. Then she nodded.

'Shall I see if I can find somebody to drive you home?'

Mirabelle shook her head.

'Right,' said Belton. 'Well, if you don't mind?'

'I'm sorry,' she said to the WPC. 'I didn't mean to get you into trouble. I just had to see McGregor about something. I didn't realise.'

The sergeant opened the door and Mirabelle swept back into reception and out on to the street, only half glancing at WPC Bunch, whose head had dropped so that she seemed to be examining her regulation flat black shoes in some detail.

The night air felt cool on Mirabelle's skin. It had stopped raining. The moon was obscured by clouds. She leaned against the wall of the police station. Somewhere, far off, three drunk men were singing a Frank Sinatra number. They stumbled over both the words and the melody. She struggled to take in this new information. Ridge was an icon of the Brighton Police force but even he, it seemed, had been on the take.

Slowly, Mirabelle turned towards North Street and began to walk in the direction of home. It was too much to take in, almost – the nurses, Jinty, the mob leaving town in disarray. It would be good to sleep. She wondered if Brighton would feel different tomorrow – less grubby somehow, with no corrupt police officers and the gangsters they'd colluded with gone. On Church Street she stopped and sat on the wall outside Father Grogan's church. The coldness seeped through her skirt and numbed the pain in her hip. Behind her, Sandor's grave was lit by a streetlight and Jack's plot was in darkness. Soon Father Grogan would be joining Sandor in the ground. Would his murder remain unsolved, she wondered. Would Sister Taylor's disappearance be resolved? And what about Mary Needle? McGregor had used her death to justify his intervention to Scotland Yard, she realised. He must have. She could see him pointing out that this was where it had gone too far – the line that shouldn't have been crossed, whatever Ridge thought about the poor woman's death.

Were there more than these three, she wondered. She wished she'd paid more attention to the photographs on McGregor's wall that afternoon. There had been a lot of them – twenty, perhaps, at an estimate. Were those that weren't cars, pictures of murdered people? The superintendent had done a good thing. There was no doubt about that. She thought of the death she'd been holding against McGregor – Freddy Fox, the year before. This would put paid to vigilantes. The police wouldn't be able to sweep murderers wholesale under the table any more – Freddy Fox, Tony and Gerry Bone. Wearily, she got to her feet again, and with only a fleeting backwards glance at the graves, she crossed the road and turned down towards the front.

Chapter Thirty-One

Every man is guilty of all the good he did not do

There was nothing to make Mirabelle suspicious at the front door. All along the terrace, the long windows were dark. Waves broke on the shore as usual and the front was completely deserted as Mirabelle disappeared inside the tall white Georgian building. The wind was bracing – autumn had arrived all at once. She climbed the stairs to the first floor, the still air inside some kind of comfort. It wasn't until she reached her flat that she realised her door had been tampered with. She scrambled in her bag and then regretted dropping her torch on the lawn at the children's home. It was difficult to see in the dark but someone had definitely been here. The door wasn't closed properly.

Had Tony found out where she lived? It was unlikely, but tonight, even if it was only a burglar, she'd be bottom of the list for police attention. After what had happened at the station, there was no point even calling – Belton would be on the desk.

Mirabelle took a moment to steel herself. She made a plan, such as it was, drew up her strength and then, her pulse racing, she burst through the door, grabbing a paperweight from the small table in the hallway so she would be able to defend herself. She snapped on the light in the drawing room, taking stock of the place. Had she left that glass, she wondered? She couldn't remember. There was a dent in the sofa, but she might have sat there herself. The flat remained bound in silence. Moving on, she checked the kitchen, which was empty, and then walked towards the bedroom door, freezing as she heard movement inside. Grasping the paperweight, she kicked the door open and, adrenalin pumping, flung herself at the figure beside her bed.

'Jesus!' He spun around, trying to hold her off, but she was in full flow and brought down the paperweight on his temple with a smack. He was bigger than she was, and stronger. As he turned she pulled back her arm once more to strike a second blow, but then she saw his face in the light from the drawing room.

'Oh no! I'm sorry!' Mirabelle managed to get out.

Chris Williams staggered backwards and, tripping over a sheet that was trailing off the edge of the bed, he landed on the floor. At once, Mirabelle dropped her weapon, which hit the carpet with a thump. Then she reached out to help him.

'It's all right. I must have given you a fright,' he said. He put his hand up to his face as he scrabbled to his feet. 'You've got a good swing there. That hurt!'

'What are you doing here, Chris?'

'I wanted to see you.' He sank down on to the mattress with his hand at his temple. 'We were supposed to have dinner but things got in the way. I came here but you weren't in. It must be after midnight now,' he looked at his watch. 'I was tired. I fell asleep. I hope you don't mind.'

'You broke in?'

'I'm sorry. It was a rotten night outside. Will you forgive me?'

A rotten night was understating it. Mirabelle found her throat had tightened. Tears streamed down her cheeks. She gasped. It had been a night of disappointment, horror and revelation. She still hadn't worked it all out but she knew she was glad to see him. Sandor, Jack and Father Grogan couldn't comfort her, but Chris was here. Alive.

'But your car?' she said. 'I didn't see it outside.'

'I didn't want anyone to know.'

He reached out to hold her as she sank down beside him on the bed.

'I'm sorry I didn't turn up for dinner,' he said. 'Looks like we're fated not to eat together.' His arms were something to rely on, she thought. They felt that way. She leaned into him.

'That doesn't matter,' she said. 'I thought they'd have you on duty, what with the . . . operation.'

He kissed her hair. 'So you know then? What's been going on at the station.'

'I think I do. There's been quite a lot to take in.'

'I'll bet. I'm sorry, Mirabelle. I wanted to avoid it all. I knew it was wrong, of course.'

Mirabelle pulled back.

'Oh,' she said. 'What do you mean?'

Chris sighed. 'Oh God. I'm so sorry. There's no nice way to present it. I'm just going to tell you.'

'Your best bedside manner?'

He didn't smile. 'The thing is that I took money like the rest of them. I mean everyone was taking money and I took it too.'

'Not everyone.' Mirabelle pulled herself free from his grip.

'No. I suppose not. But it felt like everyone. And you know, it kind of worked. I mean, crime was down.'

'Not Father Grogan's murder. Not Mary Needle or Sister Taylor or God knows who else,' she babbled, her voice rising.

He put up his hand. 'I know. I know. I've been an idiot. I didn't realise – I didn't make the connections. I'm a doctor, not a detective. The thing is that it all seemed so normal. I mean, you fix up some chap and they just give you an envelope. You attend a crime scene because, you know, there's a body, and they slip you twenty quid and tell you what to say because they're not taking it any further. And then when I copped what I'd done . . . I mean, I was part of it and it was completely wrong and I was an idiot.'

'So you thought you'd just run away to London?'

'It's not far enough away now,' he said sadly. 'Is it?'

'Did they come to arrest you?'

'I don't know. I left the mews. I came here. I wanted to see you.'

That was why he'd broken in. He could hardly wait in full view, on the street in the rain. That was why he had hidden his car.

In the gloom, Mirabelle made out a case next to her wardrobe. It didn't belong to her.

'You're on the run, Chris.'

'You make it sound lame.'

'At the least.'

'Why don't we have a drink, eh?' His voice sounded bluff.

'I don't want a drink,' she said.

He didn't reply, just got up and walked through to the drawing room. The light was still on and she watched him pour a Scotch and then down it. He reached towards the window and twitched the curtain so he could peer outside – the action of a wanted man.

'I'd be gone by now, if it wasn't for you,' he said. 'I'd have gone a week ago. I'm only the doctor. It might have been OK if I had just got out of here.'

'Don't let me detain you. For heaven's sake.' Mirabelle kicked off her shoes. Her leg ached and she felt exhausted. 'There's no point in dragging up everything. Why don't you let yourself out? Run off, wherever you're going. There were far worse men than you involved, I'm sure. You're not a detective, like you said. You were just on the team.'

She lay down on the bed. The blankets were soft and the window was still open only a sliver. The cold air felt refreshing now. He walked back into the bedroom and stood over her, a dark outline with the halo of the electric light behind him. 'Don't you want to know where I'll be?'

'If I don't know, I can't tell, can I?'

'I hoped you might come too.'

'I can't.'

'Because I'm bent? Because I took the money?'

'Because I don't know you, really. Tonight I met a woman who needed a doctor she could trust. She was pregnant.'

Chris stared at his shoes.

'You knew that's what was going on at the children's home, didn't you? Those women were in trouble, Chris. Those women were performing abortions for the mob on prostitutes who were being pressed into it. Father Grogan died because of it. And people were just taking envelopes of money. You were taking envelopes of money.'

'What women?'

'The nurses at the home.'

He considered this. Mirabelle realised that he might not know as much as she assumed. Taking an envelope and asking no questions encouraged a person to ignore a lot, she imagined – and not make the connections.

'My own view is that abortions should be available,' he said. 'I've always thought that. But, ironic as it sounds, I wouldn't break the law.'

'I think they should be available too,' she replied, remembering the look on the woman's face as she had barged into Uma's hallway earlier that evening. 'But not under duress.'

'Of course not. Look, I'm sure a million awful things have happened.'

'And that's all right, is it? Gangsters and coppers in league?'

'No. Of course not. It wasn't only the envelopes, you know.'

'What do you mean?'

'I patched them up if there was a problem they couldn't take to a GP. A knife wound. A gunshot. Well, there was only a gunshot once.'

'They paid you extra?'

'Yes. It piled up, as a matter of fact.'

'And that's how you were going to finance a flat in Mayfair?'

Chris nodded. 'It made the post-mortem on Bone difficult. It's always more difficult when it's a patient.'

'Do you know what he did? Gerry Bone? Specifically?'

'No.'

'He got rid of the bodies. He messed it up. That's why they killed him.'

Chris sat on the edge of the bed. 'You've worked it all out.'

Mirabelle shrugged. 'Probably not all of it. I can't take it in, quite.'

He moved to one side, so he could see her in the light, and then he leaned in, attentive. 'Are you hurt?' he asked, noticing the state of her.

'I'm fine. A WPC helped me. She put iodine on the grazes and arnica cream on the bruises.'

'What happened?'

'I was assaulted by one of the nurses. I scraped my leg on a wall. I don't know how they are going to clear everything up. I mean, do you arrest a woman like that? If you prosecute half the police force, it seems you have to let the people involved in the criminal activity get away with it. Otherwise, they grass you up. That, as I understand it, is the reasoning.'

He took her hand. 'I don't deserve you.'

'No. You don't.'

'You have to believe me, I would never, ever do anything like this again.'

300

She laughed. The sound made her forget how tired she was. She did not pull back her hand.

'Is there anything I can do to make it up to you?' he asked.

'I don't think so.'

He pulled her fingers to his lips and kissed them. Then he bit the flesh below her thumb. 'Let me put you to bed,' he said, stroking her forearm. 'Let me look after you at least.'

She didn't reply, but she didn't stop him as he began to unbutton her blouse. He slipped it off, expertly, and dropped it on the floor. Then he unzipped her skirt, leaning in and kissing her. He was a very good kisser, gentle and yet insistent. 'You'll sleep soon,' he murmured. 'Sleep is what you need.'

Then he kissed her again. She knew she should stop him, but that involved a decision.

'It's wrong,' she said weakly. But it felt like a relief.

'Let me love you, Belle. You need love, don't you?' His lips brushed her neck, feathering kisses on her skin so that she tingled. Then he slipped the damp skirt over her hips and down her legs, and laid it on the bedside chair. 'You are beautiful,' he whispered. 'Perfect, even.'

She decided not to reply. If she replied she'd have to reject him, and just now he was her best chance of some kind of escape, if only for an hour or two. She pulled him towards her. He slipped one hand underneath her body and loosened his tie with the other and then she lost all sense of time, moving with him wordlessly until there was skin on skin and they were beyond words, anyway. Afterwards they wound their bodies around each other and slipped seamlessly into sleep.

When she woke she was alone. The suitcase was gone. She turned over, pulling a pillow from the stack beside her and hugging it. Outside it was raining. She could hear it pelting down, hammering on the window. Along the side of the curtain a thin line of grey light confirmed the summer's demise. It seemed impossible that a week ago she was setting out on a sunny day for a barbecue at Vesta's house; Father Grogan was alive, Sister Taylor was in charge of the convalescent home, and she hadn't even met Chris Williams. She didn't think about where Uma and Ellen had gone, or the doctor for that matter. She didn't think about Bad Luck Bone or McGregor pinning pictures of Mary Needle to his bedroom wall. Right now she just wanted to feel warm and safe and comfortable. She ignored the fact that her leg stung as she turned over, the flesh still tender. She didn't even look at the bedside clock. Instead she closed her eyes and went back to sleep.

Chapter Thirty-Two

Wisdom: to make good decisions

When Mirabelle woke it was the middle of the afternoon. She sat on the edge of the bed and stared, disbelieving, at the empty flat. Then she closed her bedroom window to stop raindrops dripping inside the sill and, reaching for her robe, she walked barefoot into the drawing room, opening the curtain on to a drizzly scene of light fog and grey skies. The beach was deserted save for one forlorn dog walker, hugging her coat around her body against the wind as the dog, a collie, bounded ahead, clearly enjoying itself despite the squalls. Leaning against the frame, Mirabelle could hardly even make out the pier in the distance.

She walked into the kitchen and put on the kettle to boil, searching out camp coffee and dried milk in the cupboard. The long weekend stretched ahead. She stared through the open doorway into the hall at the telephone, and wondered who on earth she might call. McGregor would be working still. It seemed unlikely he would have had any sleep. Vesta was ensconced with her family. The revelations of the night before bounced around her head – the home, the nurses, Jinty, Bad Luck Bone and Chris Williams. The mobsters, she thought, were probably gone by now, but best to wait a day or two and check in with McGregor. She'd retrieve Jinty once she was sure it was safe.

Taking her coffee with her, she rummaged through the cupboard for winter clothes – a brown cashmere sweater, a tweed skirt and a pair of boots – and then she decided to walk into town. Puddles strewed the pavement all the way along the front. The rows of tall Georgian windows seemed half asleep – shutters half closed, and only an occasional electric light bringing colour to the windowpanes. Closer to the pier there were a few children at the shoreline, dressed in wellington boots and mackintoshes, running away as waves bubbled between the white pebbles. She squinted but couldn't see any faces from the home; anyone she recognised.

At Old Steine she turned back out of town again in the other direction. Rain dripped from the last of the summer leaves on the trees that lined the main street. A bus cut through a puddle, spraying the pavement in a frenzied shower. On instinct, Mirabelle realised where she was going. She stood at the bus stop for only a minute or two before the service came.

On board the air was steamy. She bought a ticket and sat next to a woman who was clutching her handbag so tightly it might have been a child. Behind, two schoolboys were sharing an illicit cigarette until the conductor took it away, throwing it out of the door on to the road. Mirabelle counted the stops – the windows were dripping with condensation and it was impossible to see how far they had come. After four stops, she hopped off and walked the final couple of rain-glossed streets to Bill Turpin's house, only realising at the door that perhaps she should have brought something as a gift. Bill wouldn't want flowers, she thought. All Bill wanted was his wife back.

She rapped the door knocker and waited. Debbie opened it.

'Miss Bevan,' she said, standing back to let Mirabelle into the hallway.

The house seemed half dead itself. It smelled of abandoned cups of cold tea. It was unlikely Bill had eaten, Mirabelle thought. Julie had been the cook. Then, out of the front room, Panther trotted towards Mirabelle and nudged her knees. She patted him.

'I came to visit Bill,' she said. 'I thought I'd see if he needed anything.'

'He went to the pub.' Debbie's expression was disapproving. 'I don't know which one. He said he might walk over to Kemptown. He's got mates there from his police days. I thought I'd wait in case anybody came,' she said. 'I've been sorting out Julie's things.'

'He left the dog?' It wasn't like him.

'I think he's forgetful. If you ask me, he's in shock.'

She led Mirabelle into the front room. On the table, Julie's clothes were folded in two neat piles and on top there was a wooden-backed hairbrush, a felt hat and a packet of talcum powder. A small scatter of dress jewellery sprayed outwards, like a pile of spilled sugar lumps. An empty cardboard box sat on a chair.

'It doesn't come to much,' Debbie said with a shrug. 'I'm not sure what to do with it all. I suppose the Salvation Army might want it. Cuppa? Please. Sit down.'

'I'm fine for tea, thank you.' Panther sat on Mirabelle's feet and nuzzled her leg. Mirabelle pushed the dog away, but he would not relent, and licked her graze with some enthusiasm.

'It's tough on you as well,' Mirabelle said. 'Losing a sister.'

'Do you have a sister, Miss Bevan?'

Mirabelle shook her head. 'I'm an only child.'

'I was lucky to have her,' Debbie said. 'She was a wonderful woman. And they were happy, you know. They had known each other since we were all kids. They used to go courting down the town. My father caught them once, snogging on the beach. Julie was fifteen but she knew her mind. He gave her such a hiding. I don't think she ever forgot it. But Bill was everything to Julie. He saved up for this place for three years and then they got hitched.'

'They were lucky, then.' The words had come out of Mirabelle's mouth before she had even thought about them.

Debbie began to cry. She pulled a crumpled blue handkerchief from her sleeve. 'I don't want to be here, you know. All her things. Her house. But he won't sort it out, and somebody's got to.'

Mirabelle stood up. 'Please,' she said, 'don't let me keep you. You've done more than enough for today. It's still so fresh – the bereavement, I mean.'

Debbie sniffed. Her eyes fell to the dog.

'I can take Panther, if you like,' Mirabelle offered. 'I'll look after him for the weekend. Get him out of the way.'

'My husband isn't keen on dogs,' Debbie said.

Mirabelle looked around. Her gaze lighted on Panther's leash, hanging in the hallway beside the front door. She fetched it. Panther sprang up, tail waving like some kind of navy signal from ship to ship.

'Come on,' Mirabelle said kindly. She'd never looked after the dog – not since the first day when a grateful client had given her Panther as a puppy. Bill had been so delighted, it had always fallen to him. 'Poor Panther was supposed to be mine, you know. Will you let Bill know? And I'll see him on Monday, though he doesn't have to come in, of course. Only if he's ready.'

Debbie nodded. 'Thanks,' she said.

She didn't want to take Panther on the bus. He was too excited that he was outside, so the two of them set off smartly down the main road back towards town. Mirabelle stopped at the grocer's and bought a packet of dog biscuits to see him through the weekend, and Panther became even more excited than he had been about her fetching the lead. She fed him one on the pavement. Bill, she knew, would not approve. He was a stickler for routine with animals, but she judged Panther had been bereaved too.

It felt comforting to have the dog with her – she didn't consider him much in the normal run of things, but today she liked the way he nuzzled her leg when she stopped to look into the shop windows. It had been a troublesome few days.

Back at the front, the pier seemed deserted. The shops that opened full day on a Saturday were now closing. The weather had clearly shocked people into inaction, though the pubs seemed busy, the sound of chattering voices spilling on to the street on a hoppy tide of damp cigarette smoke as they passed. At the front, Mirabelle let Panther off the lead on the pebbles and he ran off to splash in the surf. She waited for him, lingering beside the huge supports that held up the pier and watched as he bounded in and out of the waves. Nearby, the deckchair attendant was securing a tarpaulin over a stack of chairs. He touched the rim of his hat in greeting.

'Afternoon, miss.'

'No one's sitting out today,' Mirabelle commented.

'Doesn't look likely. You never know, though. That's the great British weather – comes and goes, doesn't it? There's always tomorrow.'

Mirabelle leaned against the rack of chairs. 'And he was here,' she said vaguely.

'What's that?'

'I was thinking about that body. You mentioned it the other day when I rented a chair. He was a bad man, the chap who washed up. At least, that's what I've heard.'

'He was one to stay away from, all right.' The attendant pulled a pack of cigarettes out of his apron and offered it to her. Mirabelle shook her head. The man lit one for himself, pinching the end between his thumb and middle finger and sucking on it hard. The smoke was exactly the same colour as the clouds.

'I bet you see everything along here,' she said.

'I saw him all right. He was an early bird. There aren't many people, down on the beach in the mornings. There's vagrants now and then, and some dog walkers, of course. But he was a regular.'

'When he was alive, you mean?'

The man nodded.

'Did he hire a deckchair?'

'I reckon he liked it along here first thing is all. It's peaceful when the sun comes up. Just the gulls overhead. And me, of course. He never stopped or made conversation or anything. He marched like he was going somewhere. Most people wandering along the pebbles take their time, but he was practically a sergeant major. Mostly I made out like I never saw him, to be honest. You're right – he was a bad one.'

Mirabelle thought about Jinty's description of Bad Luck Bone. He was fat, she'd said, and lazy. What the deckchair attendant said didn't square with Bone being up with larks, or even the gulls, marching along the pebbles. The man pulled in another deep draw from his cigarette.

'You're a good-looking woman, when you ain't crying,' he said.

Mirabelle bit her tongue and ignored the comment. Sodden from the surf, Panther circled back towards her. The man bent down to pet him.

'I didn't know you had a dog, neither. They're talking about banning them from the beach but I think it would be a crying shame.'

'Where exactly did you see the man who died? Was it near here?'

'Under the pier.' He gestured vaguely. 'That's the direction he always came from. Ironic that's where he wound up, really.

He'd come out from under the pier and then straight up the steps, quick as you like. You get them sometimes. Them as can't sleep.'

'Thanks.'

She raised a hand as she walked away. There was no harm in having a look, she told herself, as she wandered between the uprights with Panther following in her wake, distracted by the detritus on the pebbles. There was more litter under the pier, though out of the wind the air felt warmer. Someone had lost a scarf, which half wound around one of the pillars and was studded with cigarette butts.

Mirabelle breathed in the brine and iodine that lingered under the walkway, the structure framed by barnacles and straggling fronds of seaweed. Someone had carved their initials into the paintwork. TW loves DRB. Down here, it felt as if the pier itself was pushing down on her – an ominous, heavy weight from above. From below you couldn't see the candyfloss signs, the striped canopies and the rows of electric lights. A blast of carousel music snaked downwards, sounding further away than it was. Panther found a piece of wood that had been washed up and cheerfully picked it up in his mouth and padded behind her.

At the end of the stones, she realised that she had seen the wooden doors before but never thought about them. The beach stretched off to the right and left, miles in both directions. Standing here, the doors seemed to be at the centre of something – an apex. Mirabelle felt the sting of suspicion. There were three entrances built into the head of the pier, right under the road. Each was painted in faded red paint. All of them were locked. Behind Mirabelle, the deckchair attendant had disappeared, finished for the afternoon. She checked left and right but there was nobody to see what she was up to, so she took out her lock picks and decided to start on the door furthest to the right.

The first door opened on to a spiral staircase which, she realised, connected to the pier itself. There was an office somewhere. Perhaps it had something to do with that. She closed the door, locked it again and moved on. The middle door opened into a large storage cupboard, containing casks of cleaning fluid, netting and coiled rope. She eyed a dusty shelf where two large torches were stowed and decided to take one of them. She checked it worked properly, sliding the switch on and off twice. Then she moved on. The third door opened on to a concrete chamber with a further door on the other side. Panther put down his piece of wood and barked in its direction. He looked hopefully up at her, his brown eyes trusting.

'In for a penny, eh?' Mirabelle said. 'Come on then.'

She switched on the torch and closed the outside door behind them so she could work without being disturbed. Panther jumped up, excited, and she batted him away. The lock on the interior door was tricky – heavy and multi-levered, it took her a couple of minutes before she finally felt the mechanism turn. 'Well, boy,' she said. 'Are you ready, then?' The door creaked as she opened it on to a dark passageway and the smell hit her straight away – so rancid that she felt her gullet tighten as if it were locking. It wasn't chemical exactly. It didn't smell of one thing – more a mulchy, stomach-turning richness. She wondered if it might engulf her. As she stood up, Panther came to heel, and together they stepped into the long chamber, which disappeared out of the torch's reach. Panther seemed markedly more enthusiastic than Mirabelle felt. She must be underneath the road now, she thought, right at the bottom of Old Steine.

The corridor ended at a metal ladder, drilled into the concrete floor and descending into a void. She wondered if this was some kind of huge air-raid shelter. She hadn't visited Brighton until after the war was over, but there must have been public shelters – somewhere to go if you were on the pier when the sirens sounded. What had people done? The torch's beam disappeared into the darkness as if it had been swallowed. She peered over the edge, unable to make out the bottom of the ladder. With resolve, Mirabelle picked up the dog and managed to attach the torch to the waist of her skirt. Panther's tongue, hot and wet, licked her cheek as she began to climb down, counting eighteen rungs. At the bottom it was wet beneath her feet and the smell was stronger. Ahead there was a brick-lined chamber, she realised, that opened in four directions, as if it was the apex of a maze. She thought about going back to the surface and getting in touch with somebody. She wasn't sure she should tackle this alone. But then, who would come and help, how would she explain what was on her mind and, she told herself, what else did she have to do this weekend? The police were busy enough as it was.

Smartly, she snapped the lead on to Panther's collar.

'All right, boy,' she said, more to comfort herself than him as she popped him back on to the ground.

In situations like this it was important to be logical. She decided to start from the right and investigate each of the openings in turn. It was like exploring a cave when she was a child, although here the walls weren't stone but a bewildering spiral of pale bricks that made distance difficult to judge. As she set off down the first opening, the passage branched, left and right, and the ground became wetter. Panther barked again and the noise reverberated. Ahead there was the sound of running water. Mirabelle followed it into a wide, circular opening. It was like joining a river. She shone the torch downwards and realised that it wasn't a river at all; she was standing in a sewer – rather a grand one. She remembered reading somewhere that, during the war, resistance fighters had lived in the labyrinthine sewers beneath some of Europe's major cities, but she'd never thought about where Brighton's waste disappeared to.

She gagged. The mud-brown tide swept past her feet and disappeared under a wall. Ahead it was like a highway, the groove in the ground tear-shaped, so that it carried the water along. The ceiling was higher than she'd have imagined. You could live down here, she told herself, reluctantly. Perhaps. If she remembered correctly, the resistance fighters had survived for years. She was, she realised, already getting used to the smell.

Panther shared none of Mirabelle's foreboding and dragged her forward with the lead taut, his instinct as a tracking dog kicking in. Mirabelle smiled. It was hardly the ideal Saturday afternoon, but if Bad Luck Bone had the key to this place, she could see how it could be useful. Bad Luck Bone had been a disposal man, after all. Those were the words Jinty had used, and she reasoned bodies left here would degrade quickly in the dampness and they needn't block the main run of sewage – the rivulets of the underground maze were wide. In fact, she decided, the sewage would help get rid of the evidence. She wondered suddenly what Chris would make of her theory – he was the one who would know the likely state of the remains. But he was gone. If she was right, there'd be another police doctor to help, she told herself, trying not to think of him.

She wondered how far the sewers stretched? She'd been walking all afternoon above ground but she seemed to have lost track of herself quickly down here without a familiar landmark. She looked over her shoulder, but there was no sign of the pier, where she'd started. She wondered how long she had been walking? Was she even at the limits of Georgian Brighton yet, where the Victorian houses began to take over? She visualised the streets that ran from the bottom of the pier, but she couldn't comprehend the scale of them in comparison to the path of the sewer.

The torch lighting the way ahead of her, she slowed, still moving forward and entering another star-shaped chamber with more tributaries running in all directions. She pulled Panther to a halt and spun round. This was a spider's web. There was no saying the individual tunnels even corresponded to the streets above. She turned again and realised with a stab of concern that she couldn't remember which tunnel she had entered by.

'Oh dear,' she said under her breath, as she tried to remember a story about Minotaurs and lost maidens that lingered on the fringes of her memory. It was too late for skeins of thread, anyway. She put a hand on Panther's head and patted him gently.

The main thing was not to panic. That was always the best advice. However, it was easier said than done. The walls and entrances looked startlingly similar to each other, the pattern of the bricks was mesmerising and she had no proper light, only the torch's beam. Mirabelle crouched. 'Come on, boy,' she said to Panther, keeping her tone light. 'Which way is home?'

Panther nuzzled her shoulder and tried to pull her in the direction they were already going, but she knew it definitely wasn't that way. She stumbled as she pulled him to heel and the bottom of her skirt dipped into the sludge. 'Right,' she said. 'Right.' The material felt damp and heavy as it rubbed against her skin.

Panther barked once more and kept trying to pull her onwards. 'I suppose,' Mirabelle said out loud as she figured it out, 'there must be manholes.' She'd seen them on the streets, but now she couldn't remember where. It was odd, she thought, how disorienting it was below ground. She knew Brighton's streets well, but not in total darkness, without the advantage of being able to see the distance from the pier or the Pavilion or the sweep of Old Steine. Reluctantly, she decided to let the little dog have his way. As she followed him she cast the torchlight upwards on to the concave ceiling above, which ran in a disconcertingly smooth arch.

It took a few minutes, but the excitement she felt when she spotted the circle of metal above her head was worth it. The bricks leading upwards were staged to create a built-in ladder. These sewers must have been constructed a century before, but whoever designed them had been clever.

Panther began to whine because she had pulled him to a halt. Mirabelle picked up the little dog smartly, his filthy paws scrabbling against her cashmere sweater. She wondered if she would ever get the smell out. Panther was bucking furiously now. He kept barking and squirming so it was impossible to hold him in place and keep the torch steady. Mirabelle put the animal back on the ground and he tried to set off once more, further along the same tunnel. Dogs, of course, loved strong smells.

'No,' she tugged his collar. 'Heel.'

Then Panther executed an operation she wouldn't have thought possible. He slipped his lead and, in a matter of seconds, disappeared on his own into the darkness. Mirabelle hesitated. She checked, fleetingly, upwards. If there was one manhole, there'd be another, she told herself, and she imagined Bill's face on Monday morning if she had to tell him that Panther was lost underneath the city, missing in action. She couldn't let that happen. She cursed the offer she'd made to take the dog over the weekend. Bill made looking after him seem easy.

'Panther,' she called, crossly. Somewhere ahead, the dog barked. The acoustics underground were strange. He sounded miles away, as if his bark had been carried towards her on the wind in a wide-open space. 'Panther,' she called again, and began to follow him into the darkness.

Chapter Thirty-Three

Essential are: something to do,
something to love and something to hope for

Bill was considered an expert on the training of animals but, Mirabelle decided, some hours later, he had done no job at all on Panther. She kept catching sight of the dog ahead, splashing delightedly through the filthy detritus as he ran towards her, but she couldn't quite catch him. She gave up calling his name. He would not come to heel. Slowly, she lost hope she'd ever catch up in the darkness, but then she'd hear him bark and push herself to follow the sound, and now and then she was rewarded with a glimpse of him, disappearing joyfully down one tributary and on to another main artery of the system, where he would bark encouragingly again. There must be miles of these passageways, she realised, reaching the very fringes of town. Miles and miles of them.

She was tired, hungry and cold when she caught up at last, lunging in the half-darkness and dropping the torch as she managed to grasp hold of his collar. He barked as if trying to shout her down. 'No,' she said firmly, picking up the torch. She no longer even considered what she must look like, or made any attempt to keep clean, as she reattached the leash and made sure the collar was tight enough to hold the dog in place. When she stood up the darkness crowded in. The bulb faltered. The torch must have got wet. 'Oh no,' she said, her voice breaking in desperation as the light guttered.

She switched it on and off but the sewer remained in darkness, so she shook it and tried again. 'Panther,' she complained. 'This is your fault.' The dog was still trying to pull her onwards and she stumbled after him in the dark. Then she had an idea. She reached out to feel the wall, keeping her hand on the bricks as they moved onwards. Perhaps she would feel a ladder. Eventually there would have to be one.

Several years ago, Mirabelle had rescued Superintendent McGregor and Vesta from an underground cellar. It had taken a while for Vesta to recover. She said she had lost all sense of time. Mirabelle understood that better now. She felt exhausted. It must be getting late. She tried not to think about the articles she'd read about archaeological investigations in Egypt. Howard Carter discovering Tutankhamun's tomb. Damsels bricked up as a form of punishment.

Getting hold of herself, she pulled Panther to heel and fed him a biscuit from her pocket; then she bit into one of the biscuits herself, patting the dog's coat as she made herself chew and swallow it. At last, she wound the leash around her wrist and sank on to the ground. The wider tributaries had a walkway running down the side. The ground was damp beneath her but Panther snuggled into her body and Mirabelle felt the dog's hot tongue licking her hand. Things would look better, she hoped, once she had rested.

When she woke, Panther was breathing deeply next to her, out for the count. She sat up and checked her grip on the leash and then tried the torch once more, but it still wasn't working. Determined not to give up, she decided to take it apart and slowly, by touch, she placed the components one by one, on her lap. The batteries were icy and slightly damp. She dried them on the lining of her jacket and reassembled the component parts. The torch flickered momentarily and then cut out again. Mirabelle shook it. She tried once more but it remained dead, so she twisted off the head and, once more, removed the batteries. This time she blew sharply up the barrel to try to dry it out, and slowly reassembled it, fumbling over the barrel. It still didn't work. Panther stirred and gave a little sigh. Mirabelle rested her head on the brickwork and waited. Her leg ached from where she had fallen earlier. At length, the dog stirred. 'Hello there.' Mirabelle stroked his coat. 'We've got to get out of here.' She sounded, she realised, more optimistic than she felt.

She got to her feet and tried to decide on a direction. She turned on the torch again. This time the light flashed, cut out and then shone once more. Mirabelle found she was laughing. The light didn't make all that much difference, she realised. There was nothing to see. A river of sewage. A tunnel with no identifying features. But it made her feel better. Panther pulled on the leash. 'Steady,' she said, but she allowed him to lead. He was refreshed by his rest and bounded ahead. Mirabelle tried to keep up. He strained, wanting to lead her into another side tunnel. 'No,' she said firmly, pulling him back. 'We should keep to the main tributaries.' The ladders, she reasoned, were more likely to be placed on the larger sewers.

Panther was insistent, however. Mirabelle flashed the torch ahead down the cut-off, and what she saw stopped her in her tracks. On the left-hand side of the tunnel there was something caught in the filthy stream – a small piece of material. Clothing perhaps. She followed Panther, who sniffed it appreciatively and picked it up in his mouth. Mirabelle held out her hand and Panther delivered. It was only then she realised it was a nurse's cap, just like the one that Nurse Frida wore. When she turned it over, the word 'Taylor' was sewn inside on a piece of muslin, almost obscured by the filth it had been sitting in.

Mirabelle flashed the torchlight further down the tributary. 'Rita,' she called. 'Sister Taylor. Are you there?' There was no reply. She hadn't really expected one. She put the cap into her pocket and tried not to think how gruesome it was.

'Go on,' she said encouragingly to Panther, who continued ahead. The smaller tunnel connected to another and then another. The dog could be leading her round in circles, for all she knew, but Mirabelle stumbled on, the torch cutting in and out like some kind of fairground ride.

It was in the moment when it flashed brightest that Mirabelle saw the body. A wave of sadness washed over her as the light flickered; the only sound was the sewage guttering as it flowed across her feet. Sister Taylor had been dumped alongside the remains of another two or three people, all of them so decomposed it was difficult to tell. Rita Taylor was only distinctive because of her dark blue uniform, which was flecked with detritus from the stream of sewage and an inky smear of what, Mirabelle realised, was blood. Chris Williams would be able to tell what exactly had happened, but it looked as if her flesh was decomposing more quickly than her clothes. Mirabelle peered. The bodies were, she thought, all women, but she might be wrong. She'd have to describe this to someone, eventually. When they got out. If they got out.

Panther wagged his tail enthusiastically. The smell must be dreadful, Mirabelle thought, but she couldn't sense it. Still, she bent over and vomited into the passing flow. Bad Luck Bone had dumped them here. Poor Sister Taylor. Mirabelle knew she couldn't do anything – carrying the bodies was out of the question. There was no way to mark the spot. But she knew they were here now. She tried not to notice the creeping sense of horror that was overtaking her. This was a responsibility.

'Come on, boy,' she said. 'We have to get out of here.'

Not much further on, the torch faltered again. This time

the onslaught of darkness didn't even break her stride; she just kept one hand on the brickwork and stumbled on. It might have been a mile. It might have been less or more, but when she felt bricks protruding from the wall, her heart sang. Her fingers fumbled above and below and, sure enough, they formed a ladder, just as before. Directly above, a pinprick of light twinkled through a tiny hole in the metal disc, like a star in a far-off constellation. Mirabelle scrambled to pick up Panther and secure the torch in her waistband, then she felt her way up the frets one by one. Halfway there, the torch dropped with a clatter, but she left it. At the top she tucked the dog under one arm and held him tightly as she pushed hard against the manhole. It wouldn't budge. She tottered momentarily, trying to find her feet, and gave it another try, but the metal was too heavy.

'Help,' she called. 'Help.' She banged her fist against it so hard her knuckles began to bleed.

Then suddenly, Panther squirmed, Mirabelle swayed, almost losing her footing, and the dog slipped out of her grasp, dropping back into the darkness of the sewer.

'Panther!' Mirabelle called as she scrambled down the indented bricks to reach him. He was whining. 'I'm sorry,' she said, feeling his body, checking him over by touch. As she put her hand on his back leg, he pulled away sharply.

Mirabelle scrambled for the lead and then, slowly, she felt her way around the rancid pool, searching for the torch. It was lodged at the side of the sewer, soaked. She picked it up and felt liquid seeping out of it. There was no hope of it working now. Still, she wound the lead around one of the frets to stop Panther slinking off, and climbed up again, this time using the torch to hammer on the metal. At least it was useful for something. An age passed. Her arm cramped. She began to cry. She stopped. She started again. She screamed. Then she climbed down. Above, a car rumbled over the manhole. She let out a cry of frustration and rubbed her arm as she pulled Panther on to her lap. 'I'm sorry,' she said.

The noise came hours later. It was easy to imagine it had taken days, but the tiny pinprick of light had turned to darkness only once. It's Sunday, she thought. And then she heard it. Someone whistling. It sounded as if it was underwater, but it was distinctive – 'Love Letters in the Sand', just as if Pat Boone himself was up there. She scrambled up the frets and resumed banging with the torch. 'Help! Down here! I'm in the sewer!' The whistling came marginally closer and then it faltered. A voice called nervously. 'Hello.' A man's voice.

'Help,' she screamed. 'Help.' She couldn't remember ever feeling so desperate. She pushed upwards but the metal still wouldn't budge, so instead she hit it so hard she thought the torch might shatter. Then, miraculously, it shifted on its own. A wedge of light cut into the darkness from above and a man's face peered down, his body behind at a strange angle, in policeman's uniform. He put his arm over his mouth and nose. 'Blimey,' he said.

A fine mist of drizzle descended as Mirabelle emerged. The light on the street seemed blinding, though the sky was clouded over. She narrowed her eyes. A smile spread involuntarily across her face and she felt unaccountably grateful. 'My dog is injured. He's still down there. I dropped him when I was trying to get out.' She babbled. She reeled. The look on the officer's face betrayed his disgust but she didn't care. As she looked down at herself, covered in effluent, she began to laugh. The light rain wasn't strong enough to wash it off. She'd need to be hosed off and soaked in a light solution of bleach, she thought. Was that even possible? Then, from below, Panther barked and gave a little growl.

'I'll get him,' Mirabelle said, and climbed back into the hole.

Panther, she realised, as she looked at him in the light, was in no better state than herself. As she climbed back on to the street, the officer had leaned over and was being sick into the gutter. Mirabelle hauled herself on to the pavement, patting Panther's head. He whimpered a little and then started to lap at one of the puddles. Mirabelle thought that she was thirsty too. Drinking from a puddle seemed the least stomach-turning thing she had done in the last day, but she held herself back.

'I want to speak to Superintendent McGregor. There are bodies down there. Dead people.' She looked around. The street was familiar now her eyes had adjusted to the light. It wasn't that far from the front. She could have sworn she'd walked miles. 'Where is this?' she asked.

'You're at the bottom of Kemptown, miss,' the officer said.

'Yes of course,' Mirabelle replied. She was just round the corner from the garage – Vesta's friend. She remembered the smell of the place – petrol and the whiff of something else they'd thought at the time smelled disgusting. She laughed again. It felt as if she'd never be able to smell anything again.

'Are you all right?' the policeman asked.

'I'm fine,' she said. 'It's the dog that's hurt. I expect we'll need the services of a vet.'

Chapter Thirty-Four

Beauty is everywhere a welcome guest

The sight of them caused quite a stir as Mirabelle, Panther and the policeman rounded the corner. A few women closed their front doors but the police officer knocked them up and insisted they fetch buckets of water. He opened his police box and fetched a wooden fruit case so Mirabelle could sit down on the edge of the pavement. Someone balanced a large umbrella next to her but the rain was almost off.

'I know one of the victims,' Mirabelle said. 'She was a nurse. A sister.'

The constable put up his hand to halt her. 'We can't put you in a Maria. Not like that,' he said.

'But . . .'

'Ah, thank you madam.' The officer spoke over Mirabelle's head as one woman threw a bucket of water over Panther. It hardly disturbed the sewage clinging to his coat, although a little ran off into the gutter, at least.

'Poor little thing,' she said. 'Don't worry. We'll get you clean again.'

'His leg is injured, actually,' Mirabelle cut in.

The constable disappeared back inside the box and the sound emerged of him speaking on the telephone, calling the incident in. A few doors down Mirabelle heard one housewife say to another, 'It's hardly sanitary, is it?'

The policeman leaned out. 'Name?' he asked.

'Mirabelle Bevan. These bodies are connected to the death of Gerry Bone, Sister Rita Taylor and Father Grogan,' she said. She scrambled in her pocket and took out Sister Taylor's cap. 'Here. This is evidence.'

The woman with the bucket peered at the cap. 'You'll never get those stains out,' she said. 'I could make you a cup of tea. How about that?'

'Mirabelle Bevan,' the policeman said, enunciating each syllable. 'Oh yes? Missing person, eh?'

'I'm not a missing person,' Mirabelle objected.

'Well, you were reported missing, miss.'

Two more women arrived with buckets and both doused Panther. One of them had brought a piece of bone. She laid it on the pavement and Panther began to gnaw at it.

'There,' she said, proudly. 'I thought you'd like that.'

Things seem to be happening in the wrong order, Mirabelle thought. Everyone was focused on getting the dog clean, but there were bodies down there, right under their feet. A crime had been committed. More than one.

In the first-floor windows, several lace curtains twitched. A young girl emerged from further down the street with an old flannel robe over her arm. 'My mum says you might want to use this. Them clothes will have to go out, she says.'

The women with the buckets huddled. 'Seems a shame,' one of them chipped in, 'but Margaret's right.'

Mirabelle stood up. 'I found bodies,' she said again. 'Underneath the street. This street, or at least very close to it. Four or five of them. This is all very well, but that's what we ought to be thinking of.' One of the bucket women put her arm around the young girl's shoulder. 'She's hardly twelve yet,' she hissed in Mirabelle's direction. 'You don't want to scare her, do you?'

Mirabelle felt like stamping her foot. The policeman

emerged from the box. 'They're sending a van,' he said. 'As I thought, a Maria is out of the question.'

One of the women gingerly touched Mirabelle's boot and got hold of the zip. She pulled it down. 'There,' she said. 'You won't be wanting these things, Tommy, will you? They ain't evidence, are they?'

The policeman wrinkled his nose. 'And where would we keep them, even if they was? Not in my box, I can tell you that. I can't see as we'll need to keep them.'

Mirabelle stepped out of the boot and removed the other one. She undid the zip on her skirt. The women all looked at the policeman. 'All right,' he said, 'you can go in there,' he motioned towards the box. 'Lean over, love,' someone said, and when Mirabelle did she emptied cold water over her head. Mirabelle struggled momentarily to catch her breath. She licked her lips and then realised several of the women were wincing – heaven knows what she had just ingested. Ignoring them, she limped inside the box, removed her filthy clothes and changed into the dressing gown. A film of sewage lingered on the surface of her skin. When she came out, somebody handed her a jam jar full of hot, sweet tea and someone else had removed the umbrella. It looked as if the sun might come out.

'Ain't you got a cup, Ivy?' someone asked.

Ivy didn't reply. She wasn't using her best china on a madwoman covered in excrement. 'That can go out afterwards,' she said, nodding at the jam jar.

Mirabelle sipped. Her stomach felt warm and a glow circulated around her body as the tea had its effect. 'That's better, eh?' Ivy smiled. 'Tea's antiseptic, isn't it?'

A few minutes later, the police van pulled up with a very young constable at the wheel. From beside him a man with a leather doctor's case sprang on to the pavement. He was old with rheumy brown eyes and he had a limp.

'Oh dear,' he said to the officer at the police box. 'You weren't joking.'

'The dog has hurt his leg,' Mirabelle said, pointing at Panther. 'I'm fine. Are you Dr Williams's replacement?'

The doctor locked eyes with the policeman. 'Yes.'

'Down from London?'

He nodded. 'How well do you know Dr Williams?'

'He was my doctor,' Mirabelle said. 'I don't have a GP.'

'Ah, that was my next question.'

The man crouched next to Panther and gingerly touched the dog's hind leg. 'Well boy,' he said kindly. Panther growled and then whimpered. The doctor took a splint from his case and began to bandage it. 'He'll need to go to a vet, but this will help. How on earth did you get down there?'

'I broke in. Under the pier. I suspected that Gerry Bone had been using the place and I wanted to investigate.'

The policeman took out his notepad and started to scribble. 'Broke in,' he mumbled as his pencil crossed the paper.

'I was right,' Mirabelle said, keeping her eye on him to make sure he kept taking notes. 'As I said, there are bodies.'

From around the corner she heard the sound of a bell approaching as a Maria pulled up round the corner and McGregor got out. To his credit, McGregor's face registered little surprise when he laid eyes on her. The superintendent was good like that – he just accepted what was in front of him.

'There are bodies,' Mirabelle repeated and gestured towards the road. 'In the sewer.'

'All right. That's enough,' McGregor said. 'Show's over.'

The assembled women hesitated for a moment and then began to make their way back inside. 'We were only trying to help,' one of them mumbled. The doctor got to his feet.

'Is Miss Bevan all right, doc?' McGregor asked.

'Seems so. You need to get clean, Miss Bevan, and then I'd

like to administer a tetanus shot, but you may well have an infection that arises. We'll need to keep an eye on you for the next few days.' He turned towards McGregor. 'She says she doesn't have a GP.'

'No.' McGregor's tone was vague. He nodded in the direction of the car and the doctor got back inside. 'That's all, Constable,' McGregor said. 'You can lock up your box and be about your rounds. Turn in a report at the end of your shift, eh?'

The constable looked doubtful. He lingered a moment but didn't challenge McGregor's instructions, and within seconds he banged the door closed, locked it and lumbered away. The Maria pulled off with the doctor, and the young constable lifted Panther into the back of the van and then climbed into the driver's seat to wait.

'Do you know where Chris Williams went?' McGregor asked.

Mirabelle shook her head. 'He said London was too close but that's all.'

'I've been worried sick about you.'

'What do you mean?'

'I thought you'd gone with him – Williams, I mean.'

'Sometimes you don't seem to know me very well. Why would I run away with a handsome, talented young doctor when I could be lost, knee-deep in raw sewage with an injured dog?'

A shadow of a smile played on McGregor's face. 'Well,' he said, 'I know what a good-time girl you are. It's true.'

Mirabelle squirmed. She reassured herself she looked better than she had before she took off her clothes, but probably worse than when he'd seen her as she came to in Father Grogan's bathroom.

'The doctor's right, I need to get cleaned up,' she said.

McGregor looked around. Shadows lingered behind lace

326

curtains but the windows were all closed. 'You thought I'd let it be,' he said, keeping his voice low. 'Didn't you?'

'Let it be?'

'Last year. Freddy Fox's death. Everything that was going on.'

Mirabelle half shrugged. McGregor was right – she hadn't forgiven him or forgotten, whatever Freddy had done: what had been meted out wasn't justice. 'I want you to know I didn't let it go. I want you to know that the last four days we've nicked every bent copper on the Brighton force who could be nicked.'

She stared at him blankly. Alan McGregor didn't do anything by halves.

'I want this to make up for it. As much as it can, Mirabelle. I couldn't do much last year – it takes time. But I've changed the force so it won't happen again. Do you see?'

She touched his arm. 'I misjudged you horribly, didn't I? First Rene and now this . . .' she said. 'You're a good man, but you look as if you haven't slept.'

'I look better than you do, if you don't mind me saying so.' There was no measure in denying it. 'We've been in every newspaper across the country,' McGregor continued. 'It's a national scandal but we're done. The Brighton force will be straight from now on.'

'And you're not interested in dead women? Not as interested as you are in bent coppers, anyway.'

'I'm interested all right. I'll send a team down this afternoon.'

'Rita Taylor's there.' Mirabelle handed over the nurse's cap.

'Thanks. I guess you don't let things pass, either.'

McGregor put his arm out to guide her towards the van but Mirabelle hesitated.

'You said four days,' she said.

'Yes.'

'But you made the arrests on Saturday night.'

McGregor nodded. 'It was the night they least expected it. Belton's still processing the last of the poor buggers. It's gone well in the main. Chris Williams is missing in action – a couple of other guys too. Ridge is furious – well, you saw – but I did what I intended. We won't make the charges stick with everyone, but none of those guys will work on the force again. Two men have put in to emigrate to Australia.'

'Four days from Saturday is Tuesday.'

McGregor looked after the car that had left, clearly worried he'd let the doctor depart too soon.

'Was I down there all that time?' Mirabelle continued. 'Two full days, that would be.'

'Vesta reported you missing on Monday when you didn't turn up for work and there was no sign of you at home. She's been worried sick. I had somebody nip up to let them know. Bill Turpin has been out with a dog whistle on the beach – he reckoned if he could turn up Panther, he'd turn up you as well. Or your body. We've been worried sick.'

Mirabelle began to walk towards the van. She had trouble keeping steady. 'I didn't mean to worry anybody,' she said under her breath.

McGregor held the door for her. 'I can only imagine that you've been worrying people since birth,' he said.

'I'll go and see them now.'

McGregor caught hold of her hand. 'They'll be at Julie Turpin's funeral.' He checked the watch on his other wrist. 'I was about to leave when the call came in.'

'I should go.'

McGregor looked her up and down. 'I think you're off games, Miss Bevan. You can't turn up like that, can you? You know that you can worry me as much and as often as you like. I'm just glad you're all right.'

Mirabelle sat down on the bench in the back of the van.

McGregor climbed up and pulled the door behind them. He banged the side, the engine started, and he took a seat next to her. 'The city's never been so safe,' he said. 'No bent coppers left and all the criminals have scarpered. It's a whole new Brighton.'

Chapter Thirty-Five

Justice in the extreme is often unjust

Belton arranged a hot bath at the public pool. The cubicles were generous and you could hire a towel and buy a tiny bar of soap for sixpence. WPC Bunch sat on a stool outside the wooden door as Mirabelle worked her way through three bars and refilled the water several times. She wondered if the bottle of peach bubble bath in her own bathroom would help. For the first while, the smell seemed to be getting worse, not better. Further along, someone abandoned their cubicle, complaining loudly. 'It's the hot water, love,' she heard the attendant explain, 'the poor woman was trapped in a sewer. It's all got to come off her.' Then the door slammed, and further along a window high in the wall creaked as somebody opened it.

Gradually Mirabelle felt the air clearing and the water ran clean. She stepped out of the bath and towelled herself dry. A whiff of carbolic hit her like a curiosity.

'Jessica,' she called. 'I think my sense of smell is returning.'

WPC Bunch made a sound that indicated she had heard but wasn't sure what to reply.

'Do you know if they found the bodies yet?' Mirabelle called over.

'I can't go and check. I'm not allowed to leave you, Miss Bevan,' Bunch declared. After the spool-of-thread incident,

Mirabelle could hardly blame her for not doing anything extra.

'I'm coming out,' she said. She opened the door with the towel wrapped around her. 'I don't have any clothes to put on.'

'They'll organise something, I'm sure.' Bunch got to her feet to escort Mirabelle through to the women's changing room, where a smiling female doctor applied a tetanus injection into her buttocks and dispensed a vitamin tablet and another cup of tea. 'The super will want to see you,' she said. 'After they're done. He'll need to take a full statement. But for now you can go home.'

'I don't have anything to wear,' Mirabelle repeated.

'Oh. Yes. Of course.'

The doctor disappeared for a minute and came back with a grey woollen blanket and a worn pair of wooden-soled sandals. 'They don't have anything else,' she said apologetically. 'They want the sandals back.' Mirabelle pulled the blanket around her. 'It's fine,' she said. 'It's not far.'

WPC Bunch drove Mirabelle home along Western Road as the sky was beginning to darken. The chimney smell of fires lighting in the twilight enriched the coming darkness.

'Were you scared?' Bunch asked as the lights on New Church Road turned green.

'Not really. I was too busy trying to figure out how to get out,' Mirabelle said. 'I fell asleep twice.'

'Down there?'

'At the side. During the war, resistance fighters lived in the sewers.'

'I knew the Jews got out through the sewers. In Warsaw,' Bunch replied. 'I didn't know anybody lived down there.'

'What did you do during the war, Jessica?'

'I'd only just left school at the end. I was a secretary,' Bunch said. 'APC.'

'I did secretarial work as well.'

On the front, Bunch pulled up the car at the door. She'd clearly been comprehensively briefed.

'I'll be all right,' Mirabelle insisted.

'Sergeant Belton said to see you inside, miss.'

Bunch silently followed her upstairs. Her still gaze took in the flat, the cornice catching the last of the light from outside. She closed the front door behind them with a click. Mirabelle switched on a lamp.

'Drink?'

'Not on duty, miss.'

Mirabelle sank on to the sofa. 'Me neither.' She didn't want Bunch to leave, she realised. She didn't want to be alone. The policewoman seemed to sense it. She hovered beside the table. 'Is there anybody I could call for you?'

'I wouldn't like to trouble them.'

'A neighbour perhaps?'

Downstairs, the flat was almost permanently empty. Upstairs, a man had moved in. Mirabelle had seen him twice on the stairs, both of them studiously not mentioning the tragedy that had happened to the last occupant and the fire that had ripped through the building as a result.

'No. There's nobody.' She glanced through to the bedroom, remembering Chris Williams and what they'd done there.

Then Mirabelle jumped as a brisk knock sounded on the door. She wondered if it might be McGregor but, when Bunch opened it, Vesta and Charlie stood in the frame. Charlie clutched Noel in his arms, wrapped in a soft blue blanket. The baby was sleeping. Vesta held a pile of brown paper parcels.

'I thought you'd be hungry,' she said.

Mirabelle felt tears prick her eyes. Charlie disappeared into the kitchen to fetch plates. Vesta dumped the chips on the table and put her arm around Mirabelle.

'You gave us quite a fright.'

Mirabelle began to sob gently.

'Well, I'd better be going.' Bunch hovered momentarily and then disappeared out of the door.

'They're calling it Dead Man's City down there,' Vesta said. 'You must have been terrified.'

Mirabelle blew her nose on a handkerchief.

'That blanket looks terrible on you. Grey isn't your colour,' Vesta grinned as she disappeared into Mirabelle's bedroom and emerged with her robe. Mirabelle pulled it around her and Charlie set the table, tucking Noel neatly into place on one of the armchairs. He got to his knees in front of the fireplace and began to pile wood into the grate, twisting newspaper spills into the gaps and lighting them. I'm a crooked log, she thought. Just like in Father Grogan's notebook.

'You want me to fix that?' Charlie asked, indicating the stopped clock on the mantel.

Mirabelle nodded. 'Thanks,' she said. 'I've been meaning to wind it for ages.'

They ate with their fingers, Mirabelle's appetite returned only as the food hit her stomach. Panther was recovering, Vesta said. Bill had taken him for a swim in the sea. He swore by the saltwater as a cure. 'I think looking after Panther is helping him, you know.'

'I'll see him tomorrow. I'm sorry I missed the funeral.'

'Don't come in tomorrow, Mirabelle. Sleep,' Vesta said, licking her fingers.

Afterwards, Vesta folded the paper carefully and tipped it on to the fire. The flames curled around the edges, engulfing it. Charlie slapped his stomach and turned his attention to the clock.

'I can't imagine not wanting . . . you know – a baby,' Vesta said, glancing at Noel. 'All those women.'

'Not everybody is in the same position as you.'

333

'Even if I was on my own,' Vesta said.

'You weren't happy to start with when Noel came along.' Mirabelle glanced at Charlie, who was winding the mechanism furiously.

'I just can't imagine making that decision. I mean, living with that decision. Afterwards.'

The clock began to tick loudly. Charlie closed the back. 'I reckon it's a lady's choice,' he said. 'They should be able to make that call.'

'And you'd have said that even if I had . . . you know, when I was pregnant with Noel?'

'Baby, I wouldn't have been happy, but when did I ever tell you what to do?'

When the Lewises had left, Mirabelle sat staring at the charcoal-grey ocean beyond the glass. It felt as if the world had changed. She had unravelled a knot and now the threads of it had simply disappeared. Gone, like the summer. She wondered if the sewer ran under her house and if she and Panther had passed beneath it. She'd notice the manhole covers now, she thought. She'd make a point of it.

Epilogue

We will burn that bridge when we come to it

Mirabelle could tell it was windy outside because of the waves. They broke on the shore in a particularly energetic fashion, the grey surface of the sea whipped up like churning butter. She lay in bed, making a list of things she needed to do, and then she opened the wardrobe and sat in front of it, staring at her clothes. It took her half an hour just to get dressed. Checking herself over in the mirror, she slammed the front door behind her and headed towards Church Street. At the bakery she ordered a cake to be delivered to the children's home the following day and a tray of sausage rolls.

'And the inscription?' the assistant asked.

'Happy Birthday, Peter,' Mirabelle said. 'Could you deliver it in the morning?'

'Yes, miss.'

'With the compliments of Mirabelle Bevan.'

When she reached Western Road she clattered upstairs to the bookings office for the variety. Inside, the wall was covered with black-and-white photographs of acts she'd seen at the Hippodrome and the Royal Pavilion. A bored-looking woman with long red nails slid a sharpened pencil between her fingers as if it was a weapon.

'Tomorrow?' the girl said in reply to Mirabelle's enquiry. She slid the pencil down the bookings in the diary.

'In the afternoon,' Mirabelle insisted. 'I would like a magician and somebody to sing. It's a children's party.'

'I don't know. It's short notice.'

Mirabelle drew out her purse. 'I'm sure you can help me.'

Slowly, the girl smiled.

Five minutes later and a full ten pounds lighter in the wallet, Mirabelle continued to the front, where she collected her summer jacket and umbrella from the desk at the Old Ship.

'Sign here, Mrs Williams,' the clerk said, turning around the Lost Property book and offering Mirabelle his fountain pen. She decided not to argue. As she signed, she realised the man was staring at her and wondered if it was because he knew she was no more Mrs Williams than the Queen herself, or if he'd heard about her escapade in the sewers. He was far too discreet to say which one was on his mind, though not discreet enough to hide his curiosity.

Back outside she turned towards Kemptown, ignoring the headlines on the newspaper stand about the dead women whose bodies she'd found and the disarray of the Brighton Force as Chief Constable Ridge announced the upcoming inquiry. Across Old Steine and up St James's Street, she turned off to the right, slipping past McGregor's house and up the path of the B&B where Jinty had booked in.

'I'm looking for Miss Lucy Hangleton,' she said when the door opened.

'Gone,' the woman declared and crossed her arms.

'Do you know where she went?'

'I know she left in the night on Sunday without paying her bill,' the woman said. 'Like a thief.'

Mirabelle's forehead creased with concern. 'Was she alone? I mean, did she have any visitors?'

'Not that I know of. She seemed so quiet. Little cow,' the landlady added. 'Forgive my French. I knew there was something funny – a girl like that with no luggage, arriving at night. She didn't leave her room either. I wouldn't take her again, let me tell you that.'

The woman closed the door.

Mirabelle walked back down the pathway. She loitered on the pavement, waited a moment, and then took the decision to rap on McGregor's door. Brownlee appeared.

'Oh,' she said. 'It's you.'

This, Mirabelle thought, was an improvement. At least it constituted some kind of greeting.

'I wanted to check you'd found Rene.'

Brownlee shook her head. 'Gone,' she said. 'And all the girls with her. Mr McGregor went up to that house and it was cleared out. Even the maid.'

'And Rene's friend – did you know Jinty?'

'I didn't socialise with them, Miss Bevan. Mr McGregor has put out feelers. He'll find Rene.'

'I'm sure,' Mirabelle said. McGregor, it turned out, was steelier than she'd reckoned.

'Well. He's not in,' Miss Brownlee snapped, as if she could read Mirabelle's mind.

On St James's Street she bought a bunch of dahlias and then she walked up to the churchyard at St Magnus. Julie's grave was marked with a wooden cross, the earth newly turned over. Mirabelle laid the dahlias on top of it and hovered for a moment. She couldn't pray. She'd been like that for years now. Still, it marked her respect at least.

Afterwards, she walked back to the front. The wind still whipped off the ocean, catching her breath as she continued, taking the stairs on to the pebble beach. She raised her hand to hail the deckchair attendant, handing over a coin without even being asked.

'You sure? It's breezy today.'

Mirabelle nodded. 'Over there,' she pointed halfway down the beach. 'I want to keep away from the pier.'

He cast her a glance but didn't show any sign of bringing up what had happened as he set off to put the deckchair in place. Mirabelle pulled her coat around her shoulders. Above, a couple kissed, leaning against the rail. The wind caught the man's hat and it flew off, over the pebbles and into the water. The attendant wandered back up the beach as Mirabelle sat down. The front was quieter than it had been for weeks – only a dog walker and a tramp passing in over an hour. At midday the clouds parted, revealing a patch of vivid blue sky. Mirabelle smiled, feeling the sun on her face. When McGregor approached, she didn't notice him at first.

'Enjoying the weather?'

'I'm recuperating,' she replied.

'Quite right. You should be good to yourself. I spoke to Mary Needle's mother this morning. She said to thank you.'

'And the others?'

'We're working on it. We'll identify them.' He paused. 'Mirabelle, I meant what I said. What I asked you, the other day. About us.'

Mirabelle stared at him. The wind was whipping the edges of his mackintosh and his cheeks were slightly flush. He seemed tall from where she was sitting – taller than usual – bigger than she'd thought he was. He'd changed things – set them right, or tried to. He wasn't the monster she'd decided he was – the man she'd been avoiding for the last year. She felt a twist of guilt about Chris Williams.

'Things have changed me,' she said. 'These last few days, in fact, I've felt differently about everything – I've made mistakes, I know I have. Perhaps the way forward isn't as clear as I thought.'

'It's not too unclear, I hope.'

'I don't want to investigate any more, Alan.'

McGregor laughed. 'Well, good. Maybe you could leave things to me?'

338

'And I want to be honest. I was seeing him. Chris Williams, I mean. Romantically.'

'I know. I've never been the jealous type. You've had a tough time, Mirabelle, and arguing about that kind of thing won't help either of us. He's gone and, well, I've done things too, haven't I? Can you forgive me for what happened to Freddy Fox?'

Mirabelle considered. Slowly she nodded. 'I'd rather it hadn't happened that way,' she said.

'Me too.' He reached out and squeezed her hand. 'I suppose what we've both learned is that you can only do your best.'

He was right.

Above, the sun showed for a moment and he took his hand back. She still hadn't answered his question.

'Do you know where Jinty went?' she asked, changing the subject.

McGregor shifted. He didn't like to push her – Mirabelle had been through a lot. She needed time. 'As far as I can tell, she disappeared on Saturday night – last seen at the Old Ship having a drink with you, by all reports. Later I must take a statement from you about it – all of it.'

'She booked into a bed and breakfast that night but she absconded on Sunday night.'

'Do you know where she might have gone?'

'Maybe you should check the railway station? She was wearing a summer dress. I can give you a description.'

He nodded. 'Come in to Bartholomew Square and we'll get all the details.'

'Tomorrow?'

'That's fine. If you'll have dinner with me tonight, that is.' He couldn't quite leave it alone but she smiled. Perhaps she didn't want him to.

High above, a gull was gliding on the breeze. She could swear the bird was enjoying itself. 'Anywhere but the Old Ship,' she said.

'I'll pick you up at eight.' He bent to kiss her on the cheek. 'You make a difference,' he said. 'You have made a difference. You know that, don't you? That's all any of us want, Mirabelle.'

She felt like crying. 'I'll see you later,' she said. He turned up the beach.

Perhaps things would seem less grubby now. Perhaps they could set things straight. She settled in the deckchair and watched McGregor as he picked his way back to the promenade. As he turned, she raised her hand and he raised his, then he disappeared up East Street.

AUTHOR NOTE

The quotations and misquotations used to open each chapter are taken from the following sources:

All things are only transitory: Goethe. How paramount the future is when one is surrounded by children: Charles Darwin. Nature does nothing in vain: Aristotle. Memory is the art of attention: Samuel Johnson. Alibi: a form of defence wherein the accused attempts to prove that he was in another place at the time an offence was committed. Excellence is a habit: Aristotle. A good marksman may miss: traditional. The life of the dead is in the memory of the living: Cicero. Reason is not what decides love: Molière. Knowledge is true opinion: Plato. The lonely wear a mask: Joseph Conrad. Justice is moderation regulated by wisdom: Aristotle. Live your beliefs and you can turn the world around: Henry David Thoreau. Admiration and love are like being intoxicated with champagne: Boswell. Grief is the garden of compassion: Rumi. Between men and women there is no friendship possible: Oscar Wilde. The gods are too fond of a joke: Aristotle. It is never too late to give up our prejudices: Henry David Thoreau. There is nothing we receive with so much reluctance as advice: Joseph Addison. Undercover: to disguise identity to avoid detection. A foul morn may turn to a fair day: traditional. The best prophet of the future is the past: Byron. Do not be too moral. You may cheat your self out of much life: Henry David Thoreau. The quarrels of lovers are the renewal of love: Jean Racine. We die only once and for such a long time: Molière. Blood spilt cries out for more: Aeschylus. Judge a man by his questions rather than his answers: Voltaire. The hardest victory is over yourself: Aristotle. Distrust any enterprise that requires new clothes: Henry David Thoreau. Courage is knowing what to fear: Plato. A crime is a matter of law. Every man is guilty of all the good he did not do: Voltaire. Wisdom: to make good decisions. Essential are: something to do, something to love and something to hope for: Joseph Addison. Beauty is everywhere a welcome guest: Goethe. Justice in the extreme is often unjust: Jean Racine. We will burn that bridge when we come to it: Goethe.

Acknowledgements

Thanks always to Jenny Brown, my brilliant agent. To my editors, Krystyna Green, Amanda Keats and Penny Isaac, for your eagle eyes. And lastly to my own Big Al and to Molly, for meaning the world.